Darius set his wineglass down and stood. "Let me help you."

"No." Ariel sat up all the way and reached for the crutches. "I can't haul you back to civilization and have you carry me from place to place. Imagine how that would look."

He studied her for a long moment, as if he were imagining that. "We'd attract attention."

"That we would." She picked up the crutches, put them into position and somehow got to her feet.

Darius hadn't moved. His gaze met hers and this time, the sadness was gone. She got a sense of deep loneliness and strength.

He cupped her face. His touch was gentle. He ran his thumb over her lips. She opened them just a little. She wanted him to kiss her. She'd never wanted anyone to kiss her like this before—so much that her entire being felt the longing.

He leaned toward her, sliding his hand to her shoulder and bracing her. Then his mouth brushed hers. It felt as if he were going to move away, but she caught his lips. They parted and the kiss deepened . . .

Books by Kristine Grayson

UTTERLY CHARMING

THOROUGHLY KISSED

COMPLETELY SMITTEN

Published by Zebra Books

4 — 4

COMPLETELY SMITTEN

KRISTINE GRAYSON

ZEBRA BOOKS
KENSINGTON PUBLISHING CORP.
http://www.kensingtonbooks.com

For my niece, Priscilla Wolfe, with much love

Acknowledgments

Many thanks to John Scognamiglio for all his work on these books and to Merrilee Heifetz for believing in them. I owe a great debt of gratitude to the Malibu Brain Trust for that discussion on historical philanderers (you guys are so brilliant!). Thanks also to my husband for dragging me into the Idaho wilderness where I learned two things: how very beautiful and primitive some parts of the United States are, and how much I love civilization.

The Sentence
(2,700 Years Ago)

One

"Cupid is stupid." Darius stabbed his javelin into the ground and crossed his arms.

The sky was an unbelievable shade of blue and the grass was emerald. In the distance, Mount Olympus disappeared into the clouds. To his left, a silver pool with a golden waterfall released spray that haloed in the sun.

He was covered with sweat from his practice session. He spent most of the day with the javelin. The day before, he had concentrated on his discus throw. In a few weeks' time, he had to defend his position as the first winner of the Olympic Pentathlon, and he was not about to give up his title.

The Fates stood before him. They wore white gowns that were held in place by a gold brooch on the right shoulder. Their sandals were also made of gold.

"Cupid?" Clotho asked. A large replica of a spool of thread held her blond hair in place.

"Whom are you calling Cupid?" Lachesis asked. Her red

hair had been divided into sections, which Darius took to be representative of Lots. Her supposed duty as a Fate was the Dispenser of Lots, the one of the three who theoretically assigned each living person a destiny.

"Eros." Darius answered the question with more than a little annoyance.

"Eros?" Atropos asked. A golden set of shears held up her long black hair in an elaborate style. "No one calls Eros Cupid."

"The Romans do."

"Those pretenders who give so much credence to Romulus and Remus?" Clotho asked.

"Those pretenders are going to be important," Darius said. "Just you watch. I think they're power-hungry, greedy, and more than a little vicious. I bet in a couple hundred years, everyone will have heard of Rome."

"You're not here to wager on anything," Lachesis said. "You are here to answer our questions."

He knew that. He had known that the moment they had whisked him away from his practice session near Athens. He had no idea where he was now. He had been about to throw his javelin and then, one blink later, he was standing next to this pool.

Darius knew the pool was magical. Water could turn silver in the moonlight and golden in the sunlight, but it was never both at once.

"Ask away," he said. "But get me back before the sun goes down. I have a lot of work left to do."

"Throwing that stick?" Atropos asked.

"It's not a stick," he said. "It's a javelin."

"We know," Clotho said. "But you are not a warrior. You are a gamester."

"We do not approve of games," Lachesis said.

"I've heard you don't approve of much." Darius was getting tired of this. And he was getting cold. The air here had a chill and his sweat hadn't dried yet. Although it should have. Were they doing this deliberately to torture him?

"Really?" Atropos asked. "Who told you this?"

Darius shrugged. "People talk, you know."

"About us?" Clotho asked.

"About everything." He didn't want the Fates to know he had checked up on them. He figured they weren't much of a threat to him, but it was always good to know your potential enemy.

"You listen to gossip." Lachesis frowned. "Is this where you get your information about Eros?"

"What information?" Darius said. "All I did was tell you he's stupid."

"You dare malign the God of Love?" Atropos asked.

"He's no more the God of Love than I am." This conversation was going nowhere. Darius wished he had a tunic, but he didn't want to spell one while in the Fates' presence. That would show them he was uncomfortable, and he didn't want to be at a disadvantage. "Eros is a little spoiler who likes playing with people's lives. Just because he's decided to use his considerable magic to bring couples together doesn't mean that I have to respect it."

The Fates raised their chins in unison. They did most things in unison. They were the ruling tribunal of the magical, the court of last resort. They had the power to punish those who misused their magic, and their sentences were feared throughout the known world.

Feared by everyone except Darius. He'd done a little research on the Fates. He'd found out that they were students of the Powers That Be—interns, to be more precise, practicing their newly acquired knowledge on those below them.

If the Fates misused that knowledge, they'd be demoted, returned to the ranks of the average mage. There was no guarantee that they'd move into the exalted ranks of the Powers That Be anyway. There hadn't been a vacancy in that august body since Earth was covered with primordial ooze.

"Did you or did you not induce the mortal known as Homer to write of Eros . . ."

Then Clotho paused and a piece of parchment appeared in her hand. A moment later, parchment appeared in the hands of Lachesis and Atropos.

They read in unison:

> *Evil his heart, but honey-sweet his tongue.*
> *No truth in him, the rogue. He is cruel in his play.*
> *Small are his hands, yet his arrows fly far as death.*
> *Tiny his shaft, but it carries heaven high.*
> *Touch not his treacherous gifts, they are dipped*
> *in fire.*

Darius frowned. "That wasn't Homer. I told Homer to ignore the bastard."

"Eros is not a bastard," Lachesis said.

"His mother is one of the Powers That Be." As Atropos said that, all three Fates bowed their heads and spread out their hands in a reflexive movement.

"She would be quite angry to hear you speak like this." Clotho cringed just a little, as if she were afraid of Aphrodite.

Darius ignored them. They seemed to prattle a lot. "It was another poet whose name escapes me. They're all alike, thinking—well, thinking too much, for one thing. And they never exercise. Whoever said writers were touched by the gods were wrong. Writers are ignorant, easily manipulated, arrogant—"

"Did you or did you not force those words to be written?" Lachesis asked.

"Well, I didn't force them," Darius said. "It was more like a suggestion."

"While you were pretending to be this mortal poet's muse?" Atropos asked.

"I wasn't pretending. I was his inspiration. I've inspired a dozen poets. They sing of my athletic prowess. They—"

"Eros is very angry about the phrasing in this so-called work of art," Clotho said.

"Particularly the 'tiny his shaft' part," Lachesis said.

"It was all we could do to prevent him from showing us how inaccurate that was." Atropos grimaced, as if the memory were distasteful.

"You brought me here because of a poem?" He'd heard that the Fates were capricious, but he had no idea how capricious.

"Of course not," Clotho said. "There are other complaints."

Darius resisted the urge to roll his eyes. He was certain there were other complaints. The battle between him and Cupid or Eros or whatever the little troublemaker wanted to be called had been going on for the last ten years.

It had started when Darius was fifteen. He had been walking through the agora in the center of town. He wasn't shopping, although he had bought himself a few too many glasses of wine at some of the market's booths, but he was still steady on his feet.

Out of the corner of his eye, he saw some movement. A slender man wearing a loincloth was pointing an arrow at him. Darius hadn't come into his magical powers yet, but he was the fastest man in Athens. He managed to snatch the arrow away from the man before the man had a chance to release it from his bow.

At that moment, Darius realized the man he was dealing with had wings—dirty little stumpy wings—and he was very angry.

He wasn't used to being thwarted when he was shooting his arrows of love. Darius had misunderstood the reference at first, and when he finally did understand it (after much shouting), he grew even angrier.

Darius believed that Cupid—as he started calling the little bastard almost immediately (having learned that the barbarian name irritated the golden-haired cherub)—should have recognized another mage, even if the mage was six years away from gaining his powers.

Cupid, on the other hand, said his power over love extended beyond mortals to mages, an argument which irritated Darius to this day. Mortals, in Darius's opinion, were useless creatures with the lifespan of gnats, certainly not comparable to the magical immortals who could live for thousands of years.

When Cupid pointed out that Darius took that attitude because he hadn't lived as long as most mortals and didn't know what magic was, the damage had been done. Darius decided the two of them were enemies for life.

"What other complaints?" Darius asked, as if he didn't know all the things he had done to the winged troublemaker.

"You tipped his arrows with lead," Lachesis said.

"So?" Darius said.

"Couples who were supposed to fall in love hated each other on first sight," Atropos said.

"So?" Darius asked. "Why should it matter? If emotions are that easy to trifle with, maybe they should be banished."

"You have disturbed the cosmic order," Clotho said.

"You're telling me that little idiot's arrows are part of the cosmic order?" Darius shook his head. "What purpose would that serve?"

"I grant you," Lachesis said, "it is a crude device and our predecessors—"

The Fates looked at each other and shuddered slightly.

"—could have been more subtle," Atropos finished.

"But they had a master plan," Clotho said.

"They believed that love is the essence of all existence," Lachesis said.

"We still believe that," Atropos said.

"It is the basis of our prophecies," Clotho said.

"What prophecies?" Darius asked, then mentally kicked himself. He really wanted to get back to practice. He needed to finesse his javelin technique and he was here, talking with these glorified secretaries. He planned to win his second Olympic competition like he had won his first—without magical intervention of any kind. That meant he had to be in tip-top physical condition. A missed day was a missed opportunity.

"No one has told you of the prophecies?" Lachesis frowned and looked at the others.

"You are in charge of destinies," Atropos whispered to Lachesis.

"Assigning them, not explaining them," Clotho said.

"I know that." Lachesis sounded annoyed.

"So what is Darius's?" Atropos said.

"I don't remember if you ever shared it with us," Clotho said.

Darius was getting annoyed. How disorganized were these women?

Lachesis patted her tunic as if she were searching for something. Then she snapped her fingers, and another piece of parchment appeared.

"He must have a heart before it can break," she said.

"What in Hades does that mean?" Darius asked. "I have a heart. I can feel it beating every time I run."

"A heart does more than beat," Atropos said.

"Most hearts," Clotho said softly to her companions. "Remember, we are speaking of Darius here."

"Ah, yes," Lachesis said. "The man who destroyed several perfect love matches all for the sake of a grudge."

"The man who tried to kill the God of Love," Atropos said.

"That twerp is not the God of Love!" Darius said.

"That is correct," Clotho said. "Eros is not the God of Love, but he is the closest thing to it that we have at the moment."

"At least until he serves out his sentence," Lachesis said.

"By my calculations," Atropos said, "he still has seventy-five arrows left in his quiver."

Clotho sighed. "That's too many. It will take him another three hundred years to go through them."

"It was not our sentence," Lachesis said. "Our predecessors believed this would work."

Atropos nodded. "It was fine when mortals were primitive, but if a boy like this one can see through the cherub with the arrow routine—''

"I am not a mortal!" Darius said.

"We know that," Clotho said. "But it really doesn't matter. You shouldn't have been able to see what he was doing."

"We are not here to discuss Eros," Lachesis said. "We're here to discuss his complaints."

"They're more than complaints," Atropos said. "Some are quite serious."

"Particularly the last," Clotho said.

"If you mean the hot wax thing," Darius said, "I can explain."

"You do not need to explain," Lachesis said. "You interfered with the greatest love of all time. The redemptive love."

Darius rolled his eyes. He hadn't done much. Cupid had fallen for a beautiful, smart, and cold woman named Psyche and made her promise not to look at him. Stupid promise, which of course she couldn't keep. So one night, Darius talked her into looking at Cupid in his sleep, and then Darius made hot wax from her candle drip on his shoulder.

Cupid, like the baby he was, ran home to Mommy, and Psyche, to Darius's surprise, cried like the world had ended.

"They weren't suited," Darius said. "She's as cold as winter in the mountains and he doesn't have the brains of a newborn lamb."

"You are too young to know this," Atropos said, "but one of the things we do is create myth."

"He is heart and she is soul. They must be united before any relationship can last," Clotho said. "By separating them, you doomed all lovers to impermanence and heartache."

Darius shook his head. "I don't have that much control."

"No, you do not," Lachesis said.

"Eros has returned to Psyche. But the damage was done. It is now extremely difficult for soul mates to unite," said Atropos.

"Love at first sight is no longer enough," said Clotho.

"The winged arrow becomes only the first step," said Lachesis.

The afternoon was waning. Darius shifted on his feet, anxious to leave. "What does this have to do with me?"

"You," Atropos said, "must be punished for meddling in things that only the Powers That Be should touch."

At the mention of the Powers That Be, the Fates again bowed their heads and moved their hands.

"Punished? How can I be punished for something I didn't know was wrong?"

"Ignorance of the law is no excuse," said Clotho.

"He wasn't ignorant," Lachesis said. "He thought it amusing to meddle with Psyche's psyche."

"He does not know what damage he inflicts," Atropos said.

"Hey," he said. "I'm standing right in front of you."

"In the terms of an immortal's existence, you are less than an infant," Clotho said.

"But even infants must have their hands slapped to learn the limits of their behavior," Lachesis said.

"So," Atropos said, "we sentence you thusly—"

"Thusly?" Darius asked. "Who talks like that?"

Clotho crossed her arms and glowered at him. "We do when we are about to make a pronouncement about someone's fate."

"Listen closely, Darius," Lachesis said. "We are about to take control of your future."

"Sure you are," he said, grinning at them. "As if you have that kind of power. You're just glorified secretaries."

All three women rose to five times their normal height. They towered over him, making him feel quite small indeed. Since he was a tall man, feeling small made him uncomfortable, but he tried not to show it.

"Who is your mentor, Darius?" Atropos asked.

"Bacchus," he said.

"That drunkard?" Clotho frowned at her companions. "I

thought we decided he would never again mentor a young mage.''

"We did," Lachesis said. "But Darius's assignment had already been grandfathered in."

"What did Bacchus teach you?" Atropos asked.

"Besides how to drink wine without paying for it yourself," Clotho said.

"He did a week's worth of work with me, showed me how to use my powers, told me that I had enough discipline since I was an athlete, and then sent me on my way."

"He what?" Lachesis grew even taller.

"He said I should come back when I was twenty-five. By then I would know what kind of troubles I faced and we'd deal with them."

"Have you gone back?" Atropos asked.

Darius shook his head. "I was thinking of going after the Olympics. But I've been busy."

"He's been unsupervised," Clotho said.

"He is young," Lachesis said.

"He does not know the law," Atropos said.

"And he's standing before you," Darius said. "Can we include me in this conversation?"

"Still, he has no discipline," Clotho said.

"He has no respect for traditions," Lachesis said.

"He has done more than any other to destroy loving relationships," Atropos said.

"Probably because he has not had one himself," Clotho said.

"Hey!" Darius said. "I have family."

"Loving family?" Lachesis asked.

Darius frowned. He hadn't seen his family since he was ten. That was when he had been sent to Athens to apprentice to an older mage. That mage had been Bacchus, who had left him on his own until he came into his powers, then gave the lessons that he had just described to the Fates.

"He cannot answer," Atropos said. "He does not know."

Clotho sighed and shrank to her normal size. "Standard judgments might be inappropriate here."

Lachesis shrank too. "I did like the idea of tying him to a tree and shooting him with arrows for a thousand years."

Atropos smiled. It was not a nice smile, especially at three times normal size. "And having him pluck the arrows out before the shots could be fired again."

"Such a punishment will only push him farther into darkness," Clotho said. "Right now, his actions can be attributed to ignorance and a need for attention."

Darius didn't say anything. For the first time since he'd been spelled to this place, he was worried. He hadn't thought they could do much to him, but this talk of thousand-year punishments was beginning to upset him.

"No one has taught him appropriate behavior," Lachesis said.

"Perhaps we should tie Bacchus to a tree." Atropos finally shrank to her normal size.

"I think all we need to do with him is deny him wine for the next millennium," Clotho said. "That will be punishment enough."

"But what of Darius?" Lachesis asked.

"He needs to learn the true nature of love," Atropos said.

All three Fates stared at him. The hair on the back of Darius's neck rose. "I'll learn. I promise. You can teach me anything."

The women smiled in unison. It was a very unsettling look.

"Don't worry," Clotho said. "When we're through with you, you'll know more about love than anyone else in the world."

"Why does that sound like a threat?" Darius asked.

Lachesis put her hands on his shoulders. "Because," she said gently, "it is."

The Aging, Annoying God of Love

(Last Year)

Two

Ariel Summers should have heeded the warnings. Every portent had shown that this trip was going to be strange.

She wasn't superstitious, not really. Sure, she had her rituals before every race just like other athletes she had met. Some athletes kissed their religious medals; others carried a lucky rabbit's foot; still others recited a little mantra or prayer.

Ariel laid out her transition equipment in a very special way—shoes first, then bike, then shirt—and she always put on her swimming cap exactly fifteen minutes before the swimming portion of the race started, no matter how hot it was. She painted on her own numbers, starting with the right leg, and never let anyone else pin her singlet to her shirt.

Rituals were important because they told her body that it was about to participate in a triathlon, and it helped her mental preparedness. It had nothing to do with superstition. She really didn't believe that because she forgot to put on her cap at the right time on the day of the Ironman Canada, she had been doomed. It had only been coincidence that she had torn her rotator cuff. It had nothing to do with failing to follow her rituals.

Nothing at all.

But she couldn't help feeling a little odd about this hike into Idaho's River of No Return Wilderness Area. First of all, there was the name: the River of No Return. Part of her worried that it was prophetic.

Then there was that incident with the park ranger as she headed onto the trail. Usually trailheads in areas this remote were unguarded. A hiker signed in and then was left on her own. The little sign-in box was miles from anything or anyone. Often there wasn't even a Port-A-Potty nearby, just a rickety wood outhouse that could barely stand and lacked toilet paper.

But three days ago, when she started her hike, a man stood right next to the sign-in box. He looked like the cartoon character Dudley DoRight (not like Brendan Fraser, who played him—quite admirably—in the movie)—oversized chin, small piggy eyes, and exceptionally muscular chest. He wasn't wearing a Canadian Mounted Police Uniform since it would have been out of place in Idaho, but his brown rangers' uniform had a similar effect, right down to the narrow pants, which he had tucked into his boots.

"Where're you going, miss?" he'd asked in a booming cartoon character voice, and she'd nearly aborted the trip right there.

After all, it had been clear where she was going. She was already in the mountains. Ahead of her was a narrow trail that led through the tall pine trees toward the river. The trail only ran in one direction, and since she had just arrived at the trailhead, it would be logical that she was going into the wilderness.

"I'm, um, going on a hike," she said.

"You should have a companion." He had frowned at her, and if he had volunteered to accompany her, she would have ended the trip right then and there. The whole point of this hike was to do it alone, to test her own strength and stamina, and to reflect on her future.

She didn't need an oversized cartoon hero baby-sitting her in case she encountered a crazed squirrel.

"I decided to go this one alone," she said.

"In that case, sign here." He gave her a big grin and patted the paper attached to the box. She gave him a reluctant look, then filled out one of the sheets and shoved it through the little hole, just like she was supposed to do.

When she was done, she frowned at him. "I've never encountered a ranger at the trailhead before."

"Just waiting for a friend, ma'am," he had said, and for an odd moment, she was afraid he'd give her a salute. But instead, he nodded at her and wished her well.

And so she started down the trail, feeling disconcerted, as if time had gone out of sync.

The feeling really hadn't left her. It was the morning of her third day and she was almost halfway through the trip. This night would be spent at a hot springs often used by rafters. She had thought it would be a good idea to stop at public sites a few times along the way, to see people, just in case she did run into trouble.

She hadn't so far. The weather was lovely—cool in the evenings, warm during the day. The sun was out all the time, but it was thin at this altitude, and it wasn't as hot as she had expected, considering she was making the trip in July.

Her backpack—in which she carried everything she needed—was comfortable, and the wilderness area was lovelier than she had been prepared for.

For the last two days, the trail had run above the river. Two thousand feet below, the river's waters frothed over rocks and down waterfalls. Rafters went by, the guides looking serious and the rafters themselves screaming or laughing and having a good time. They almost never looked up and saw her, and she was grateful.

Ariel always did best alone. She had learned that after

her parents died. Before that, she had been a coddled only child, touched by fairy dust, as her mother used to say. The world had seemed safe and easy.

Then, three days after her twelfth birthday, her parents' car had been hit by a truck that had crossed the median, and there had been nothing left—of the car, of her parents, of her life.

Ariel had gone to live with her unmarried aunt in Monterey Bay. By the age of thirteen, she had made no friends. She had come home one afternoon to hear her aunt talking to Social Services.

"She's such a strange child," her aunt had said. "Never speaks, just watches television. I don't even think she's cried. I have no idea what to do with her."

"Are you able to care for her?"

"Well enough, I suppose," her aunt said. "After all, she should stay with family, although God knows I never wanted children."

That was all Ariel heard. She dropped her books, banged out the back door, and ran as far from the house as she could get. Midway through her mad dash, she realized that running felt good. It made her feel like a strong human being—one who could survive on her own.

From that moment on, Ariel became determined to be the strongest girl in her class. She could out-run, out-jump, out-ride, and out-swim all the girls and most of the boys. Her aunt hated the athletics, saying they weren't feminine, but Ariel loved them and refused to give them up.

Which was why she was here, on this mountainside, all alone. Every time she hit a setback, she spent some time by herself, proving her own strength. This hike would allow her to focus on her future. She had some important choices to make.

The rotator cuff injury was too severe. Her doctors had ruled out any more competitive swimming. They might have allowed her to participate in a sprint tri, but she wasn't good at the short length. Her strength was the Ironman—a

2.5-mile swim, followed by a 100-mile bike ride, and ending with a 26.2-mile run—all done within a single day.

She loved the challenge of it, pushing her body to extremes. That was why she was here.

Walking through the primitive area of Idaho alone was an extreme.

And it was strange. That morning, it had gotten even stranger. As dawn's thin light was just filtering through the evergreen branches, she had crawled out of her tent to pee. Dew glistened silver on the grass, and overhead she could hear birds chirping.

She had tiptoed across the cold ground toward the two rocks she had designated the night before as her bathroom site, when she saw a man pointing a bow and arrow at her.

He was short, bathed in gold, and he had little wings on his back. Gold curls rimmed the bottom of his skull like a skirt, but he was bald on top. Wrinkles covered his face, and it looked as if his nose had been flattened by a steamroller. He had a scar on his shoulder, and in his mouth he clenched a half-smoked cigar.

"For this," he said, "I come out of retirement. Like I still owe the Fates something. I was drunk that night I told the *Enquirer* everything. It wasn't like I blew too many secrets. A single one-time punishment, they said. Jeez. What kind of trick will they pull next time they need a marksman, I ask you?"

He grimaced at Ariel.

"Why am I asking you? You, who are so uneducated as to have no clue who I am. You, who fail to realize you are in the presence of greatness."

Then he released the arrow.

That snapped her out of her reverie. She ran for the trees, her breath coming hard, her body working without warm-up. She moved faster than she ever had—she was not a sprinter—and finally she found an outcropping of rock that protected her.

When she looked back, the little man was still there,

cursing. The arrow was stuck in the ground. He bent over and grabbed the shaft, tugging at it.

"Like those three harpies will ever know," he was mumbling. "As if I wanted to help him in the first place. Why they assumed we'd become friends, I have no idea."

He pulled, and the arrow finally came loose. He looked at it and frowned. Then he broke the arrow over his knee. Wisps of smoke, in the shape of red hearts, floated out of the arrow's center, and then faded as if they never were.

"Good enough," he said, and shoved the broken pieces of arrow back in his quiver. Then, in a blinding flash of white light, he disappeared.

Ariel rubbed her eyes. She was crouched on the damp ground, behind the rock cropping, breathing hard. Dawn's light still filtered through the evergreen boughs, and dew still covered the grass—except in the places where her footsteps had disturbed it. Footsteps that made it look like she had been running.

But there was no little man with a cigar and wings, and there was no broken arrow that created smoky red hearts. She must have been asleep and dreaming.

Sleep-running.

That was a new one, and a bit disturbing too, especially since most of her campsites from now on would be near the river. What if she sleep-ran into the water—or over the edge of a cliff?

That was the thought that had been worrying her all day. She really wasn't thinking about competitive swimming or torn rotator cuffs. She was wondering if the stress of the last few months had damaged her mind.

Twigs, leaves, and broken branches covered the dirt path. Even though the hiking trail had been open for a month, no one had bothered to clear the winter debris. A sign, posted at the fork, warned of slides and unstable rocks, but Ariel didn't plan to dislodge any of them.

She was smart enough to keep an eye on her surroundings at all times. People died every year in Idaho's River of No

Return Wilderness Area. She didn't plan on being one of them.

She planned to come out of this trip refreshed, her confidence in her body's abilities renewed. The rotator cuff injury had shaken her, and the loss of the Ironman—particularly when she'd been favored to win Hawaii this year—was especially hard.

Some of the other tri-geeks, people she'd known since she started running tris in high school, told her to swim through the pain. But she had done some research on her own. If she did, she might lose the use of her arm altogether. She planned on living another seven decades, and she felt that the use of her arm was more important than being in some record book as the winner of the Hawaii Ironman.

Even if it did come with endorsements and great publicity. She hadn't been doing triathlons for the money anyway. She had been doing it for the challenge.

Hiking was a challenge. It was just a different kind of challenge, one that she hadn't tried before.

Physical activity had always been her escape in the past. She saw no reason why it wouldn't work now.

Darius sat on a hillside, feeling grumpy. He had no reason to feel grumpy. The day was beautiful—the sky a clear blue, the sun shining down through the pine trees. The air smelled fresh and clear, summer in the mountains. In the distance he could hear the roar of the river, and it wasn't even accompanied by the screams of rafters.

The hiking trail was empty. He hadn't seen anyone all day except, of course, Cupid.

Cupid had shown up at Darius's front doorstep shortly after dawn, looking angry, disgruntled, and generally out of sorts. Darius's greeting hadn't helped.

"They still making you wear diapers?" Darius said as he peered through the screen door.

"Fine way to greet a man you haven't seen in five hundred

years." Cupid's voice rasped from too many cigars. The butt of his last one stuck to his lower lip and moved when he talked.

"Hello, Cupid," Darius had said. "I thought you gave up the arrows and wings around the birth of Christ."

"I thought so too. Damned Fates decided I needed a refresher course. They slapped the wings on me last night. I think they're just drunk with power."

"They have been holding the same job for a very long time."

"Too long, if you ask me." Cupid shuddered. "You know it's cold up here at this time of the day. May I come in?"

Darius looked at Cupid's wings. "If you don't shed."

Cupid snapped his fingers, but the wings didn't disappear. He sighed. "Guess I haven't finished my little task. Or is there a mandatory time limit on form-altering spells?"

"I have no idea," Darius said as he held the screen door open.

Cupid stepped inside. "I'd heard that the Fates made you four feet tall with a long white beard and a hideous mug."

Darius started. He hadn't realized any of the magical knew about that part of his sentence. They knew about the other part, of course. He was a laughingstock because it had been nearly three thousand years and he still hadn't put a hundred soul mates together.

He'd just finished the ninety-ninth couple a few months before and he had come to his Idaho house as a getaway. The Fates granted him two weeks every year—taken either in whole or in part whenever he chose—when he got to look like himself. For the last few years, he'd been taking a week in solitude, up here.

"But you look just like you always did," Cupid was saying. "How'd you keep from losing your hair?"

Darius didn't answer that question. Instead, he asked, "Where'd you hear that I got slapped with a different body?"

Cupid shrugged. "Bacchus, maybe. Or whatshisname, later called himself Rasputin—crap. The brain's going."

"So are the wings," Darius said, looking pointedly at the feathers covering his hardwood floor.

"They'll be gone by the end of the day, I'm sure," Cupid said. "And none too soon. They itch."

He sat on Darius's overstuffed couch and put his feet on the coffee table Darius had made out of a tree stump.

Darius debated whether or not to offer him food. The sooner he got Cupid out of the house, the sooner he'd be alone again. "To what do I owe this visit?"

"Old times," Cupid said, pulling the ancient wool blanket Darius had on the couch over his torso. "Do you know there're not a lot of folks who can remember Ancient Greece anymore?"

"You just mentioned Bacchus."

"The last time I saw him was Spain four hundred years ago. He did something to really piss off the Fates and disappeared into deep storage around then."

"What about Pan?"

"Went legit about ten years ago. Does concerts in the style of Yanni. Makes a mint, and doesn't like talking to the riff-raff."

"Hermes?"

Cupid rolled his eyes. "I don't talk to Hermes anymore."

"You never willingly talked to me either," Darius said. "I interfered with your sentence from the Fates, or so you said."

"So they said. Seems to me that's why you've been playing matchmaker for most of your life." Cupid leaned back on the couch, then exclaimed with pain as he crushed his wings. "Still not used to the damn things. Listen, offer me breakfast, and then I'll get out of your way. I'm too damn tired to whisk myself back to Monte Carlo."

"What're you doing in Monte Carlo?" Darius asked.

"Running a casino." Cupid took the cigar out of his mouth. "Don't look so surprised. Casinos are safe. They're one of the few places in the world where young lovers are scarce."

"What does Psyche think about this?"

"Psyche?" Cupid grinned. "She loves the games, man. It was her idea to open the place. She's a lot more adventurous than she looks."

He leaned back and closed his eyes. Within thirty seconds, he was snoring. Darius sighed and stood. He and Cupid had reached a sort of peace five hundred years ago. Of course, it had come at a price. Cupid had spent most of that last visit laughing at Darius for failing to complete his sentence. Cupid seemed pleased that Darius was still paying for the things that had happened two millennia ago.

Darius still didn't like the little creep. Breakfast was all he was willing to do. He made pancakes and sausages and poured some of his homemade syrup into a pitcher.

When he finally served the food, Cupid was too busy stuffing his face to talk. He'd made Darius get up three times to bring him more syrup and then, when they'd finished eating, Cupid had disappeared without a real good-bye.

But he'd never been good on manners. It was one of the many things that Darius still disliked about him. The other was the stench of cigars that he couldn't seem to get out of the house.

Darius had come to his favorite reflecting spot just so that he could get some fresh air. He still didn't see the point in Cupid's visit. They hadn't talked about old times. They hadn't talked about much at all. Darius got a sense that Cupid had remembered why their mutual dislike was . . . well, mutual.

A twig snapped, pulling Darius out of his reverie. He sighed and hoped this hiker wasn't in trouble. The last few were so relieved at seeing a house, they stopped just for conversation. After this morning's visitor, the last thing Darius wanted was conversation.

Then a woman emerged from the trees. She was too thin. He could see the bones in her arm even from this distance.

But it wasn't a thinness caused by excessive dieting or illness. This was an athlete's thinness, the kind that came from pushing a body to its very limit. A kind he both recognized and respected. The body he wore at the moment—his original body—had that kind of thinness.

He had always found that look extremely attractive.

With a shrug of her shoulders, she adjusted her backpack. It looked heavy—at least fifty pounds—and she carried it as if it weighed only five. Within easy access she had rope, a knife, a flashlight, and a bottle of water. She was prepared.

She wore her auburn hair pulled back from her face. Darius strained to see her features but couldn't make them out clearly.

She moved with an athlete's grace, with a confidence that very few people ever attained.

He inched closer to the tree, peering around it so that he could see her better. She walked with her head up, taking in the beauty of her surroundings. He looked too, trying to see this familiar vista through her eyes: the jagged mountain peaks, the bright summer sunshine, the ribbon of water running through the valley below.

She was conquering this place, hiking through it alone, making it her own. He, on the other hand, came here to hide. He used an airstrip that had existed since the 1930s, and he had never hiked in, not once, in the more than one hundred years he'd owned the house, hidden in the woods above him.

She had just passed beneath him when he heard a snap and then a rustle. He stiffened, hoping the sound didn't portend what he thought it did.

He looked down, saw tiny rocks sliding toward her. She saw them too, and tried to step backward, but it was too late.

The path disintegrated beneath her and suddenly she was falling toward the raging river, a thousand feet below.

Three

The path crumbled beneath her hiking boots. Ariel jumped backward, but not quickly enough. Her weight made the path disintegrate faster. She reached for the stable part of the mountain, but her hands couldn't find purchase.

She suddenly found herself on her back, sliding down the cliff toward the water. She couldn't grab anything. Her pack was between her and the ground.

Using all her strength, she rolled over and grabbed her knife from her belt. The rock-strewn ground cut into her bare skin, abrading it. She stabbed at the dirt, trying to slow her slide so that she could grab a tree branch or a root or anything that would keep her from sliding the thousand feet into the river.

The strain pulled at her barely healed shoulder. She could feel the rocks scraping her skin, but she couldn't seem to hold on to anything. She was sliding faster and faster and she couldn't stop.

And the worst part of it was, no one was here to see her

fall, to help her, to record her death. She would plunge into the river and she might never wash up again.

No one would ever know what had happened to her.

She struggled harder, her fingers raw and bleeding. Her knife was finally slowing her fall. She could feel the movement ease, her body remaining stationary while the dirt slid beneath her. All she needed to do was dig herself in somehow and she would be all right.

Carefully she shoved her toes into the ground, then stuck the fingers of her free hand in as well. She found herself hoping to see the crazed arrow guy. She'd pay him to haul her off this mountainside. She'd even explain to him how to do it, since she doubted that anyone who ran around the woods while wearing diapers thought of carrying rope.

The mountain seemed steady. The little landslide had ended and she hadn't slid any farther. She breathed a deep sigh of relief.

Then her blade snapped and the fall started all over again, faster this time. Suddenly she was in free fall, no longer touching the ground at all.

This was it then. She was going to die, alone, unnoticed on this mountainside.

The portents had been right after all. This trip was a strange one—and it was going to end in her death, the strangest journey of all.

Darius hurried out of the trees, running toward the path. The woman was sliding on her back like an overturned turtle. She wouldn't be able to do anything from that position.

Then, to his surprise, she righted herself and pulled out her knife all in the same elegant movement. She dug the blade into the ground, trying to slow herself.

She didn't seem panicked at all.

It had been years since he'd seen an ordinary mortal who was so calm in the face of death. The last one had been Napoleon, and he hadn't been calm, he'd been crazy.

Darius stopped just shy of the place where the slide began and watched her fall. She was slowing down—the blade was working—and he knew then that she would be all right.

He stayed above her, though. She might need his assistance getting back up the mountainside. Normal, humanlike assistance, with rope and a lot of effort. No magic at all.

She stopped sliding near the edge of an embankment. The mountainside turned into a cliff face not a hundred yards from her feet. She dug her fingers and toes into the dirt and sighed with relief. Darius started the spell for the rope, hurrying toward her as he did so.

With a crack, the knife blade snapped, and she was sliding again, faster than before. He ran toward her, but he was too late. She slipped over the edge of the cliff and vanished.

She didn't even scream.

He knew what that edge looked like. It was a sheer drop to the river. No one would survive that fall.

Not without help, anyway.

Darius raised his arms and cast a spell, one he hadn't used in a thousand or more years. He made it as specific as possible. He was creating a ledge, one that would break her fall, so it had to appear below her.

He only hoped he got to her in time. If the ledge was too far down, he'd kill her, and nothing he could do would bring her back. Not even the Fates would let him revive her.

The air crackled with lightning and thunder as the magical power left him. Then he heard a thud. He started down the slope, but more ground loosened, and he nearly lost his footing. So he murmured another spell and floated over the edge.

The ledge had formed about thirty feet below him. She was sprawled on it, face down, her body twisted at an unnatural angle. He floated toward her, terrified that she was dead.

He landed on the ledge and crouched over her. She was breathing, but she had been badly injured. Blood trickled out of her nose, and she made a strange whistling when she breathed.

It had been so long since he had used magic for anything other than parlor tricks and transportation that he had forgotten almost everything he'd learned. He wasn't supposed to heal injuries or sickness from natural causes, but he might be able to slide this one by on a technicality.

He had created the ledge, so the injuries couldn't be natural. They were his fault. At least, that was what he would tell the Fates when they decided to punish him all over again.

Darius closed his eyes and tilted his head back. The river roared beneath him and he thought he heard the scream of a rafter. A warm breeze caressed his face. He forced himself to blot all that out, trying to remember the exact words of the healing spells he'd learned from a midwife in King Arthur's court.

After a moment, the words came to him. He clenched his left fist and extended his right hand over the woman's back. She was still breathing, but her breathing was shallow. Then he recited the words of the spell. Light appeared through his fingers and illuminated her skin through her clothes. He saw blood spilled inside her stomach disappear, broken ribs knit, a punctured lung mend.

He moved his hand, repeating the spell over her head, and then again over her arms and her twisted legs. He was careful, though, to make sure it was only internal injuries that got healed. External ones had to remain. She would remember the fall and think it suspicious if she didn't have scrapes and bruises.

When he was done, he felt dizzy. He sat down and put his face in his hands. He had forgotten how draining using real magic was.

But he wasn't done. He had to make the ledge disappear before the seasoned rafters noticed it and realized it was new, and then he had to get the woman to a place of safety.

He scooped her up in his arms. She was lighter than he expected. He could feel her muscles beneath her skin. She moaned as he picked her up. Her eyes fluttered and then opened.

They were a rich green, almost an emerald color, and they were natural, not contacts at all. The color enhanced her ivory skin and her auburn hair. He found himself staring at her as if he had never seen a woman before.

"My pack," she whispered.

Her pack? It must have broken off after she started to fall the second time. He didn't see it anywhere.

"It's got everything . . ." Her voice trailed off, but he could still see the concern in her eyes. She wouldn't rest until he told her what happened to it, and if she didn't rest, he wouldn't be able to get her off this ledge.

"It's fine," he lied. "I'll get it after we get you taken care of."

She smiled and mouthed "Thank you" before closing her eyes. Her body went limp as she lost consciousness again.

He cradled her to him, feeling her warmth against him, then recited a levitation spell. They rose up the cliff face.

A yellow raft made its way down the river, and one of the guides stared up at him. The guide tapped someone beside him and pointed. At that moment, they hit white water, and the guide nearly toppled out of the raft.

Darius reached the edge of the cliff and landed on a safe area away from the slide. That guide would remember what he saw, but he wouldn't be able to prove anything.

Still, Darius felt careless. One of the many rules of the magical was to avoid calling attention to himself and his spells. He should have used a location spell. Obviously, he wasn't thinking as clearly as he would like. That irritated him. But the proximity of this woman, the nearness of her death, and the fact that he had used more magic in this one afternoon than he had used in the past hundred years was clouding his judgment.

He would have to be careful from now on.

He raised his hand, balanced the woman against his hip, and used the spell now. Their surroundings vanished. For a brief half second, they existed in darkness, and then they appeared in the guest room of his house.

The guest room was big, with a comfortable bed made out of logs. Log furniture sat in the corners, and a desk he'd owned since the mid-seventeenth century sat beneath one of the windows. The main window opened into the forest. The green rug that covered the floor had grown threadbare, but it would do.

At least the room didn't smell of mothballs. He'd had the window open during most of his stay.

With a nod of his head, he used a slight spell to change the sheets. He couldn't remember having a guest sleep over since Ernest Hemingway stayed here more than eighty years before. For all Darius knew, the sheets hadn't been changed since then. It was probably less a reflection on his housekeeping skills than it was on his need for privacy. He hadn't allowed anyone to stay in this house for a very long time.

It seemed odd to him that this woman was here now, right after his visit from Cupid.

Darius stiffened. Cupid hadn't used those silly arrows on him, had he? Darius would have noticed.

Or would he?

Was that little creep finally getting his revenge?

The woman moaned again, and Darius focused on her instead. He laid her on the bed. Her hair had spilled out of its ponytail and cascaded across the pillow, accentuating the pallor of her face. She still looked as if she were in pain, but that could be simply the aftereffects of the fall. Her forearms were scraped raw and she had a large bruise on her right cheek.

He went into the bathroom and got his medical kit. From it, he removed some wet disinfectant pads and some bandages.

Then he went back into the guest room and cleaned off her scrapes.

She tossed her head from side to side. It appeared that what he was doing hurt her, but not enough to wake her up.

After he got the wounds cleaned, he bandaged them, then covered her with a blanket. He was staggering with exhaustion now—the magic use having taken its toll—but he still had several things left to do.

He went outside and reversed his ledge spell. From the river below, he heard shouts, followed by a curse, and then laughter. Apparently more rafters had been going by, but only one saw the ledge disappear. Darius smiled. That person would talk about his rafting hallucination for a long time to come.

Darius walked to the good part of the trail before doing his last spell. He watched the river, saw several rafts float by, and waited until he didn't see them anymore. Then he raised his arms and did a summons spell.

At first, he thought it didn't work. Then a water-soaked backpack emerged from the river. The pack was torn and pouring water from its side. It rose the thousand feet, then dropped in front of him, landing with a soggy thud.

He wasn't sure how he was going to explain this one to her. She was all right, but her pack had gotten wet? It had somehow fallen into the river and he had managed to fish it out, despite the steep canyon walls and the dangerous currents? Maybe he would tell her that a rafter had thrown it the thousand feet from the river below. Surely she would believe that.

He smiled. He was exhausted. He was getting punchy. Any more magic use would take the last of his reserves. That was what happened when a man didn't stay in shape. If his best friend Aethelstan were here, he would be able to do all these spells and not lose a bit of energy.

Darius had become lazy over the centuries, and he hadn't even realized it. All of the parlor tricks he had done to impress recalcitrant lovers had taken very little of his magical energy.

Then, in his mind's eye, he saw her bruised face, heard her soft voice, filled with despair.

My pack. It's got everything . . .

He knew what it was like to lose everything in a single moment. It was a sensation he never forgot, no matter that thousands of years had passed in the interim.

Slowly, he raised his tired arms to cast one more spell.

Heaven smelled like spaghetti.

Ariel kept her eyes closed. She lay on the softest surface she had ever been on in her life. A light, smooth blanket covered her, and her head was cushioned as if it were on air.

Everything was so clear. She remembered sliding over the edge and then falling, unfettered, toward the river and the rocks below. She had died on a beautiful day, in one of the most beautiful parts of the world. If a woman had to go out, she might as well go out spectacularly.

She didn't remember hitting—someone had been merciful there—and then an angel had come for her. Only it wasn't one of the golden cherubs from the murals in her childhood church. This angel was even better.

He had curly golden hair and eyes so blue that they couldn't have existed on Earth. His nose was perfect, his lips thin, his face filled with concern. It was almost as if someone had plucked the image of the perfect man from her mind and then let him cradle her as she made the transition from life to afterlife.

He was what a grown-up Cupid should look like, not like that wizened little man she'd seen in the woods. Wouldn't it be funny if the Greek myths were the true version of the afterlife, not the Christian versions she'd learned in her parents' church or that hokey white-light stuff she'd seen on countless TV shows?

But if the Greek myths were true, shouldn't she be on a river right now, trying to find fare to pay the scary guy who was supposed to ferry her to Hades? And if she was dead in the Christian universe, the one that she had been raised in, shouldn't she be standing at the Pearly Gates, talking to St. Peter so that he could decide whether or not she was supposed to go up or down?

She had seen white light, but that was sunlight glinting off her angel's curls. She would swear to it. She thought, as she half-opened her eyes, she had seen eagles flying above him in the beautiful blue sky. A pair of eagles, obviously in love . . .

She smiled, stretched—and immediately whimpered. Every muscle in her body ached. If she were in heaven, then someone had screwed up. She *hurt*.

Ariel opened her eyes. She was in a bedroom, with windows that had a view of a forest. Sunlight dappled across a thin green carpet. An end table covered with very old books sat across from her, and beneath the window an antique desk rested, a quill pen and an inkwell on its edge. The bed itself appeared to be made of logs, cut and polished but otherwise left in their natural form. Other furniture in the room seemed to be made of logs as well.

This was not heaven, although it did smell of spaghetti. She was in someone's bedroom, and she was still in the Idaho wilderness.

She frowned, wondering how much of what she remembered was real and how much a dream. She had fallen off the edge of that cliff—she knew that much. She would never forget the way time slowed down, the way she could feel every second, the strange calmness she felt when she knew she was going to die.

She had thought she was alone, and she accepted that. No one would witness her fall. Even if she managed to survive it, no one would save her. She had been on her own.

As she hit the open air, she had thought that she'd better enjoy the view because it would be her last.

But she obviously hadn't been alone. Someone had seen her fall and had rescued her. But how? She had been on a sheer cliff, and she knew she wasn't going to hit anything. She had looked down in those slow-motion seconds and seen nothing between her and the river.

It was a spectacular sight—frightening and beautiful at the same time. Part of her had felt like Wile E. Coyote—as if she wouldn't fall until she realized she was in trouble.

But she had fallen, and somehow she had come out alive.

Ariel pushed herself into a sitting position and let out another cry of pain. Her back muscles hurt. Her shoulder was so sore, she wondered if she had damaged the rotator cuff again. Even the muscles in her arms and fingers ached, probably from trying to grab hold of the ground.

She'd thought she had too, and then her knife blade had snapped. Snapped and sent her falling to her death.

Maybe heaven was like they portrayed it in the movies—a place that was somewhat familiar. Hence the guest room and the lovely smell of spaghetti sauce.

But that didn't explain the pain. Only living bodies felt pain. And it wasn't just her muscles that hurt; the skin on her arms and chest burned.

She looked at the sore places on her arms. Someone had bandaged them. Then she pulled her shirt back and saw a raw scrape that ran from her breastbone to her navel. She wondered if the entire front of her body looked like that, then realized it probably did.

She had ridden down the mountainside on her stomach. Of course she would be scraped.

Obviously the person who had saved her hadn't known about this. She would have to tend to it herself.

She sat all the way up, letting the pain shiver through her. Slowly she eased her legs off the side of the bed. They throbbed too, and her knees burned. More scrapes, she assumed. More scrapes and pulled muscles.

Then she slid off the bed and her left leg buckled beneath her. She crumpled to the ground and sat there for a moment, pain so pure and fine coursing through her that it took her breath away.

She eased her leg out from beneath her and then looked at it. Something was wrong. If her leg wouldn't support her weight, then some bone was probably broken.

She ran her hands along her thigh, over her knee, and down her shin. The skin was scraped and raw over the knee and part of the thigh—whoever had bandaged her arm hadn't found these wounds either—but it was her ankle that caught her attention. It was puffy, red, and three times its normal size.

Broken.

Ariel gritted her teeth and straightened her leg. This was just one of life's new challenges. She was very lucky. She wasn't dead. She had to remember that.

Using her elbows, she levered herself up, careful to keep her foot from touching the ground. She stood one-legged, searching for something that would act as a cane and seeing nothing.

So she had to hop out of the room. She sounded like an elephant, thudding her way forward. She hoped the floor was sturdy enough to take all this jumping. Otherwise, she might need to be rescued again.

The room next to hers was a bathroom, long and narrow, with a window that had a view of a private garden. The bathroom dated the house to the 1970s at the very least, even though the furnishings were modern—porcelain and chrome.

A medical kit sat beside the sink, apparently the same kit her rescuer had used to bandage her arms. She found a clean washcloth on the shelf above the sink. Then she sat on the edge of the bathtub, extended her leg so that she wouldn't bump her ankle, and proceeded to clean up her wounds.

Vivaldi played softly on Dar's battery-operated boom box. The boom box was on the counter, beside the sink, so that he could listen whenever he cooked—which was often up here. Back home in Portland, he acted like he had never made a meal in his life. Cooking was Aethelstan's province—Aethelstan Blackstone, who had been Dar's friend for more than a thousand years.

Most people in the country knew Aethelstan as Alex Blackstone, the famous chef. His restaurant, Quixotic, was a destination for most upscale tourists when they hit town. He also had his own line of gourmet food products, recipe books, and cooking accessories.

Ostensibly, Darius worked in the restaurant, managing its advertising and its work force. He didn't need the money. He was richer than Aethelstan, richer than almost anyone he knew. And why wouldn't he be? If a person lived nearly three thousand years and hadn't learned how to earn and save money, then he was a fool—at least in Darius's opinion.

He worked at the restaurant because he liked Aethelstan's companionship and it gave him a cover for the work he had to do to fill out his sentence. While he was in Portland, he'd put two couples together: Aethelstan and his wife Nora, and Aethelstan's former fiancée, Emma Lost, and her husband, Michael Found.

Darius stirred his spaghetti sauce. The sauce required a lot of attention, particularly since he hadn't cooked it at this house in perhaps fifty years.

No electrical power wires ran to the house. There weren't power poles this deep in the wilderness. Most of the electricity ran on two large generators that he kept fueled in the garage. Some of the rest of the power came from the solar units he had added to the house in the 1980s.

And sometimes, when he ran out of fuel for the generator or when he simply had to watch a video or go out of his mind, he conjured up some electrical power all on his own.

Right now, though, he was cooking on the Franklin stove that he had installed in the house in the 'teens. He considered that quite a sacrifice, because he had to build a fire in the stove to make the burners work, and the stove heated the kitchen unbearably. But this particular sauce had been his specialty since the mid-nineteenth century, and he had to make it.

He wanted his guest to experience the best of everything while she was here.

He wasn't sure where that impulse came from—perhaps he was lonelier than he thought—or maybe he felt sorry for her. But he doubted it. He was attracted to her courage. He had never seen someone think so quickly or act with such competence. She was amazing. She was clearly an athlete, and a very smart person.

Darius sighed. He hadn't been attracted to a woman like this in centuries—maybe ever. Especially a woman he hadn't spoken to. He couldn't ever remember being attracted before a conversation started.

It was still too early in the evening to open any windows to catch the cool mountain breezes. He had taken off his shirt in preparation, but it didn't feel like enough. The kitchen was hot and stuffy, although the smell of garlic and oregano and the tomato-based sauce was divine.

Then the music thudded. Darius frowned. Vivaldi never thudded, not even when played by a particularly bad orchestra—and the recording he had was certainly thud-proof. He turned, wondering if the sound had come from the guest room.

He shut off the Vivaldi and listened for a moment but didn't hear anything else. Finally he turned the Vivaldi back on and continued to stir the sauce.

Then he heard the thud again. It was followed by another, and another. He shut off the Vivaldi and listened to the thudding. It was irregular, and it definitely hadn't come from outside.

Which meant his visitor was awake. Although he had no clue what was causing her to thud.

He hurried down the hallway. The door to the guest room was open, and the covers were thrown back on the bed. He peered inside the room but didn't see her.

Instead, he saw a movement out of the corner of his eye. She sat on his bathtub, her left leg extended, her shirt unbuttoned.

She wasn't wearing a bra. Her breasts were perfectly shaped ski jumps. Stunning, except for the long red scrapes running down the front.

She hadn't seen him.

He looked away, silently cursing himself for not thinking that she'd be scraped under her clothing. If he'd thought of that, he would have had to repair the scrapes, or at least bandage them, which would require cleaning out the wounds, which would allow him to run a cloth along that upturned skin, down to the nipple . . .

A trickle of sweat ran down his forehead. He was hotter than he'd thought he was. Damn that stove. Its effects even reached back here.

He backed away, considering himself fortunate that she hadn't seen him. He moved silently, going back into the living room. He grabbed his shirt, wiped off his hot face, and slipped on the shirt. Then he started whistling the Vivaldi as he made his way down the hall.

Something clanged against the porcelain tub, followed by a soft female curse. He walked more slowly, giving her time to cover herself up—although part of him wondered why he was doing that. He would never have done so in the past. But then, he wouldn't have cooked his special sauce for just anyone either. He would have radioed for a plane and gotten the offending tourist off his property as quickly as possible.

He looked into the bedroom as if he hadn't known she was gone. Then he looked in the bathroom.

She was still sitting on the edge of the tub, but she had covered herself. She clutched the washcloth in one hand. The medical kit had fallen into the tub.

He hadn't realized how very beautiful she was. In repose, she had been merely lovely, her angular features almost mismatched. But with light in her eyes and animation in her face, she became the most beautiful woman he had ever seen—and he'd seen some world-famous beauties, from Helen of Troy to Emma Lost.

He attempted nonchalance. He leaned against the door frame and crossed his arms. Then he smiled.

"Hello," he said, and waited for her response.

Four

Ariel clutched the damp washcloth in her right hand. She was unable to move, unable to speak. Her dream angel stood before her.

His voice was as stunning as he was. Deep, rich, warm. He had a bit of an accent, one that she couldn't place except by elimination. It wasn't Southern or Midwestern. It had a clipped edge, but it wasn't British or Australian, maybe not even European. It seemed almost uniquely its own.

She hadn't imagined him. He had carried her from the cliff face. He had brought her here, to his house, and bandaged the wounds on her arms. He had put her in his bed and covered her with his blanket.

He had held her close, just like she had dreamed.

He was staring at her, waiting for some kind of response to his greeting.

"Hi," she said, feeling like a complete idiot. He had saved her life and she couldn't say anything other than "hi"? He probably thought her as dumb as she felt.

"How're you feeling?"

She shrugged. "Pretty good, considering."

That was dumb too. She should have told him about the ankle, about the muscles and scrapes.

His skin glistened. He looked completely robust, the picture of health. "I didn't realize how badly scraped your legs were."

"I'm scraped all over," she said, and flushed.

He averted his gaze, as if she were sitting in front of him naked. "I only saw your arms."

Was that an apology? "I figured that out from the bandages."

She set the washcloth on the side of the tub. She wasn't going to work on her scrapes, not while the handsomest man she'd ever seen was standing right in front of her.

"What happened?" she asked. "I mean, after I slid off the cliff."

His gaze met hers again, and something passed through his eyes. She got the oddest sense that he was about to lie to her.

"You landed on a ledge."

That wasn't what she had expected him to say, and yet it felt right. She remembered lying on stone when she first saw him, remembered the eagles flying overhead.

"How far down?"

"Thirty feet or so."

"Wow." Falls like that killed people all the time. "I really must be tough."

He turned his head quizzically. "What?"

She grinned. "People always said I was superhuman. I guess this proves it."

He grinned back. It added an impish charm to his face. "I guess so."

A strange euphoria was building inside her. Maybe it was finally becoming clear to her deep down that she had survived the impossible.

"No one'll believe I came out of a thirty-foot fall with

scrapes and a broken ankle. Absolutely no one. You didn't, by chance, make a video?''

"What?'' The grin had left his face.

"A video,'' she said. "To show my friends, maybe sell to those late-night real-life video shows—'Amazing Disasters' or something like that.''

He stepped into the room. "What happened to your ankle?''

She tilted her leg toward him. "I think I broke it.''

He stared at her ankle as if it had betrayed him. "I thought I went all the way down your leg.''

"What?'' she asked.

He blinked at her, as if hearing her for the first time, and said, "I didn't know you'd broken your ankle.''

"Me either,'' she said, "until I tried to get out of bed and landed flat on my butt.''

"That shouldn't have happened.'' He took a step closer to her.

"That's what I said. Well, what I thought. I think I probably said nothing intelligible . . .''

She let her voice trail off as he knelt before her and held his hands over her swollen ankle. He flattened one hand and reached toward her injury with the other.

The last thing she wanted to do was have anyone touch her swollen skin. She slid her leg back.

He clenched his hand into a fist. "I'm sorry.''

She shook her head. "No. I'm just skittish. It hurts.''

"I'm sure it does.'' He continued to stare at her ankle, as if he hadn't seen anything like it before. "I had no idea. I'm really sorry.''

Almost as if it were his fault. She smiled. Good-looking and kind. How lucky could a girl get? "It's okay, really. I mean, it's not okay. It hurts, but it's not your fault. After all, what could you have done? You're not a doctor, are you?''

He bit his lower lip, and she had that sensation again. It felt like he was preparing to lie to her. "No.''

And yet the word had a ring of truth. How odd. She thought he was lying and telling the truth at the same time. And she didn't really care. She was so attracted to him that she could scarcely believe they were in the same room together.

She had never had a reaction like this to anyone. Perhaps she was still in shock.

"It's just ..." He paused, as if he were choosing his words carefully. "If I had known that you were hurt this badly, I'd have radioed for an airplane."

She sighed. She didn't want to think about the plane and what it meant to her trip. Not yet. "You said that ledge was thirty feet down. How did you get me back up?"

He glanced at her. "You don't remember? You were talking to me."

She grinned. "I don't think I was myself. I thought we were flying."

He studied her for a moment. Then he swallowed and glanced at her ankle again. "I guess that makes sense. I used a pulley system to lever you up."

She frowned. "I remember you carrying me."

"I did." He rocked back on his heels and then stood up. "Once I got you off the ledge, I carried you to the house. You seemed okay except for the scrapes. How do you feel?"

"Sore," she said. "But otherwise pretty healthy. I mean, a broken ankle is a problem, but it's not like I punctured a lung or something."

He looked away again. Her comment had disturbed him somehow, yet she couldn't figure out how. What was going on up here? Did he have something to do with her fall? Had he booby-trapped the trail or something?

But that didn't make sense. She knew that the mountains slid all the time. Nothing set them off; the slides just happened. The books she'd read preparing for this trip had warned her. People who'd made the hike had warned her. Even the signs on the trail had warned her.

Besides, she had seen the small bits of rock move even

before the trail slid out from underneath her. He had had nothing to do with it.

So why was he acting so guilty?

He ran a hand through his curls. They fell back into place perfectly. "It's getting dark. I can radio for help, but they can't land a plane here at night. I have an airstrip. I suppose I could ask for a helicopter, if they're willing to send one in. I'd tell them you were injured. That might bring them faster."

She was shaking her head even before he finished speaking. A plane was going to be expensive enough. She had researched that before hiking into the wilderness area and had opted not to hire one to get her in or out just because of the cost. A helicopter, sent to rescue her at night, would be even more expensive. And Idaho, like other western states, made people who put rescuers at unnecessary risk pay for their rescues.

Better to wait for the morning.

"I don't mean to put you out," she said. "If you don't mind helping me one last time, we could pitch my tent near your airstrip and you wouldn't have to see me again."

He raised his head. Those blue eyes met hers and she felt a jolt of electricity shoot through her. "You don't need to do that."

She shrugged. "I was planning to camp the entire time I was here. I wouldn't mind."

"But your ankle—"

"That's why I would need your help," she said. "After we get the tent up, though, I'd be fine on my own."

And then she remembered. She hadn't seen her pack since she woke up.

Her expression must have changed because he frowned.

"My pack," she said. "Did you manage to lever it off the ledge as well?"

His frown eased. This time he seemed pleased with himself. "Your pack is in my living room. It seems no worse for wear."

She let out a small sigh. She had spent more money than she had spent on her first racing bike to outfit that pack. Even though she wasn't going to finish this hike, she didn't want to lose all the equipment—the lightweight pots and pans, the dehydrated food, the tiny fold-down tent and air mattress. She had even splurged and gotten herself a Palm Pilot so that she could read at night. All of it had been in that pack.

"Great," she said. "If you don't mind, I'll finish cleaning up and then we can set up the tent."

"No."

The word seemed a bit harsh. "No?"

He shook his head. "You don't have to leave. I've got the extra bed and I've made dinner. I'd feel terrible if you were outside, injured like you are. I think you need someone to keep an eye on you."

For some reason that phrase made her bristle. She'd never needed anyone in her life. Ever. "I'm fine."

He raised his eyebrows and looked at her ankle. "You're not fine, and we're still not sure about the extent of your injuries. The last thing I want is for the plane to arrive and find you in even worse shape than you are now."

She bowed her head. Even that movement hurt. It was amazing that nothing else seemed to be broken. She didn't feel weak either, which would happen with internal injuries. And she hadn't peed blood. But he was right: It was better to have someone around, just in case.

"Whatever you're making does smell heavenly," she said.

He smiled. It was a relaxed, joyful smile, and it transformed his face. If she had thought he was as handsome as a man could be before, she had been wrong. He was even more handsome now.

"I'll get you something for that ankle," he said. "I think we should try to splint it and then ice it."

His hand extended again, and then he clenched it into a fist. She wondered what that movement meant.

She bit her lower lip. He was right, of course. She had helped splint a tri-geek's leg at her early races—the small ones without any backing or medical facilities. The splint always prevented the injury from getting worse, but putting it on was extremely unpleasant for the injured.

"I think I have something," he said, before she could respond. Then he hurried into the hallway.

"Um—" she started to call after him, then stopped herself. She didn't even know his name. He had risked his own life rappelling down a cliff face to save her, and she hadn't even asked him who he was. Maybe she was hurt worse than she realized.

A light flashed in the hallway, almost as if a flashbulb had gone off. Then he returned, carrying bandages and small pieces of wood. "This should work."

It certainly looked like it would. She stared at all of it, wrapped in his long fingers.

"Are you a doctor?" she asked again.

"No," he said as he knelt beside her leg. "I just play one on TV."

Her eyebrows rose. She never watched those doctor shows. That would explain everything: his looks, the house, the need for privacy.

He glanced over his shoulder. "It was a joke."

"Oh," she said. "It's just that you're—"

She stopped before she embarrassed herself by saying he was gorgeous enough to be an actor.

"I'm . . . ?"

She shrugged. "Familiar somehow."

"You were sort of conscious when I brought you up here."

"That must be it then," she said. But it wasn't. It didn't explain that sense of duality she'd felt from the moment he entered the bathroom, the way he seemed to say one thing—convincingly—when she thought he was going to say another.

They were staring at each other again. She felt like an awkward schoolgirl.

"I'm sorry," she said. "You've done all this for me and I never even asked your name."

He smiled, his gaze not leaving her face. "My name is Darius."

And then the smile faded, just a bit, as if he had surprised himself.

"That's unusual," she said. "I don't think I've ever heard the name before."

"It's Greek." And with that, his smile fled completely, as if his words had chased it off his face.

She nodded. "I'm pleased to meet you, Darius."

"Dar," he said.

She raised an eyebrow. "What?"

"Dar. Call me Dar. It's less of a mouthful."

"Dar." She tested it. The shortened version suited him better. The fact that he had an unusual name fit him. He seemed like an unusual man. "I'm Ariel."

"You don't seem ethereal to me," he said.

Had he misheard her? "What?"

"Your name," he said. "It's Hebrew for ethereal."

"Actually," she said, "my aunt had a dictionary with name meanings in the back. That said my name was Hebrew for divine feline."

"Divine feline." He grinned. "You like that better?"

"I've always hated it. I don't even like cats."

His grin faded. "You don't?"

She shook her head. "Why? Is there one here?"

"No," he said, "but there should be."

She frowned. "What do you mean?"

"Never mind." He laid out the bandages and the pieces of wood. "I think you should trust me on this one. The name means ethereal, not divine feline."

It took all her strength not to pull her leg away from him. "And you're sure of this because . . . ?"

"Because names are a hobby of mine."

"So what does Darius mean?" she asked.

"It means incredibly stupid and arrogant."

She laughed. "Surely no parent would name anyone that knowing the meaning."

"Who says they knew?" He looked up. "I have a hunch sitting on the side of the tub while we do this is a bad idea."

She looked behind her. The medical kit sat in the middle of the porcelain like a portent of things to come. She didn't want to fall for a second time that day, third if she counted the way she crumpled out of the log bed.

With a sigh, she raised herself on her hands and was going to lever herself off the tub edge when he said, "No."

She froze.

"Let me." He came over to her and braced her leg as he eased her down. Even that hurt. She couldn't imagine how it would have felt to do it on her own.

Still, his arms were as strong as she had remembered, his embrace as wonderful as it had been in her dreams. Her face was only inches from his, and for a moment, she thought he was going to kiss her.

Then he set her on the tiled floor and moved his face away as if she had burned him.

"All right," he said with false heartiness. "This should only take a moment."

He set up the wood around her ankle. A piece brushed her skin, sending rivers of pain up her leg. She gasped, and he gave her another guilty look.

"This would probably be easier if you closed your eyes," he said.

She shook her head. "I've been injured before. I can watch."

"Yeah, but you might anticipate my movements and flinch. I'm sure real doctors are used to that, but I'm not. So let's just see how quickly we can get this done, all right?"

She usually didn't trust anyone so readily. But he had already seen her unconscious and he hadn't done anything untoward. He hadn't even known she had scrapes under her blouse.

"All right." She closed her eyes and leaned against the tub, listening to him move in the small enclosed space. The bandages rustled, the wood shifted, and he cursed once, softly. Then she didn't hear anything at all.

She didn't feel anything either. The room was eerily silent. In the distance, she thought she heard violins. How strange was that? Violins in the wilderness?

Then she felt a pressure on her leg, some pain that magnified and receded before settling down to a dull throb.

"There," he said. "You can open your eyes."

Her leg was beautifully splinted. His work had been so delicate that she hadn't even felt his touch.

"You've got a gift," she said.

He smiled. "Yes, and I only ply it on female hikers."

They stared at each other for another moment, then he eased himself off his knees.

"I, um, should get you some ice," he said.

She nodded.

"And maybe move you off the bathroom floor."

"Find me a cane," she said, "and I'll move all by myself."

"I think I might be able to do better than that," he said, and hurried out of the room.

Again, she saw flashing lights. She pressed the back of her hand to her eyes, wondering what was causing that, and hoping it was nothing too serious.

He was back a moment later with ice packs and a pair of crutches.

"Crutches?" she said. "Are you sure you're not a doctor?"

He smiled. "I'm sure."

"Then why—?"

"I'm a klutz," he said.

But she didn't believe it. He was too graceful for that.

He moved like a professional athlete. He was built like one too, all muscle and sinew.

Maybe that was why she recognized him. Maybe he played for some pro team somewhere and she'd seen him on television. Or maybe she had run with him in the handful of charity races she'd run last year.

"Let me help you," he said, bending down to pick her up.

"No, I've got to learn to do this myself." Without waiting for his response, she levered herself onto the tub. She didn't want to become too dependent on his help.

On anyone's help.

Other people's help usually disappeared when she needed it most.

He handed her the crutches, then put his hand on her back to lever her upward. She didn't protest this time, but she would in the future. This was something she was going to have to get used to.

He was still holding the ice. "We forgot this."

"I guess I'll have to find a place to put my feet up," she said.

"The couch," he said. "It has a lot of pillows and it's close to the kitchen."

"All right," she said. "Lead on, McDuff."

"I never was McDuff," he muttered. "I was always too short."

"What?"

"Nothing," he said. "Inside joke. I'm probably the only one left who remembers it."

She frowned at him, but he didn't explain. And somehow she knew better than to ask him again.

Five

Darius dropped the noodles in the boiling water. The kitchen was still too hot, but he didn't dare take off his shirt this time. Ariel was seated on his living room sofa, pillows against her back and under her injured leg. He'd wrapped the ice around it to bring down the swelling and found a few Advil to reduce the pain. But he didn't dare help her any more.

Too much would be suspicious, especially now that she was awake.

He had to be careful too. He felt guilty about missing that ankle. He had moved his hands over her legs to heal them, but he knew he had stopped short of the feet. He probably just missed the ankle.

"This is a nice place," she said.

"Thanks."

"I read in one of the books about the Wilderness Area that they don't allow people to live up here."

"They grandfathered a lot of us in."

"Really?" She frowned at him. "You don't look old enough to be grandfathered in."

He had forgotten how he looked. He made himself shrug. "What I meant is that they don't tear down existing buildings. They just don't let anyone build new ones."

"Oh." She leaned back against the pillow.

He needed to change the direction of the conversation. "Want anything to drink?"

"What've you got?"

Anything she wanted, but he couldn't tell her that. "Some pop, wine, beer—you name it, it's probably here. But the refrigerator runs on a generator, so I really don't want to hold the door open while considering."

"One generator?" she asked. "Doesn't a refrigerator use a lot of power for that?"

Caught. He had put in the regular refrigerator because he hated to be without one—refrigerators were one of the best things about modern civilization, he thought—and he maintained it with his own magic, without thinking much about it.

"There's more than one generator," he said.

But she didn't seem to be paying much attention. She was tapping a forefinger against her lips. "I'd love a glass of wine. Do you think that would be a problem?"

"Why would it be a problem?" he asked. "All I had to give you was Advil. Wine would probably be good for you. This place has a great wine cellar. Just tell me what kind you want and I probably have it."

She smiled. "I'm not a connoisseur. I just like it. So bring me something red, heavy, and cheap."

"Sorry, no can do, ma'am," he said. "We don't have cheap around here."

But he didn't have to leave the kitchen to get her wine. He already had a nice cabernet breathing on the counter. Or he did the moment she said "red."

He poured them both a glass, then carried hers through the archway into the living room. He'd never appreciated the openness of the design of this place as much as he did right now. He wasn't used to having company, so he had forgotten what it was like to entertain a welcome guest.

He didn't think of Cupid that morning as a welcome guest.

Darius bent down to hand Ariel her glass and as he did, she looked up at him. A jolt went through him. In the depths of her emerald green eyes he saw something he didn't want to see.

Ariel had a soul mate.

"Son of a bitch," he said. The Fates had given him the ability to see whenever someone had a soul mate by looking directly in that person's eyes. He hadn't been looking before. He really hadn't been looking now, but he had seen it.

He didn't know who her soul mate was. He just knew she had one.

And that changed everything.

She blinked and leaned away from him. He got the sense she would have stepped away if she could. "What?" she asked.

He had to cover, and fast. "Don't you smell that? I think dinner is burning."

She smiled and took her wineglass from him. "I'm sure it's fine. Sauce usually only burns on the bottom."

It sounded as if she were speaking from experience. He hurried toward the kitchen as if he really thought something were burning, even though leaving her side was the last thing he wanted to do.

He wanted to make certain what he had seen in her eyes was true.

She had a soul mate. And he was required to find that soul mate.

It was the last thing he wanted to do.

Ariel ate with gusto. She hadn't realized how much she missed food made from fresh ingredients. Dehydrated meal packs took care of her hunger, but they weren't satisfying like this meal was.

She had never had spaghetti sauce this good. The tomatoes tasted fresh. The sauce had a number of vegetables in it which she wasn't used to, and it also had some kind of spice that she didn't recognize.

Darius had served her food to her on a lap tray, complete with a rose in a bud vase on one corner. When he had set the tray before her, he had smiled.

"Such service," she had said to cover her nervousness.

"I normally make my guests do everything," he had said, "but since you can't stand, I thought I'd change my policies just this once."

She had laughed and then lit into the food. He probably thought her some kind of pig, the way she was eating. But it all tasted so fine. He'd even made fresh garlic bread. She couldn't complain that the stove heated the building so much—not when it enabled the food to be this good.

He had a lap tray too. He sat across from her in an overstuffed chair that looked as if it had seen better days. The upholstery sagged, and one of the sides looked as if it had been scratched by a cat, even though there was no cat in evidence.

In fact, he had said he didn't have one—although he had also said that he needed one, a comment she had found strange at the time.

He had his feet up on the coffee table and seemed completely relaxed. Not at all like a man who had rappelled up the side of a cliff with a limp body in his arms and then had proceeded to cook a delicious dinner on a wood-burning stove.

"How long have you been hiking?" he asked.

She swallowed, feeling self-conscious. Did he think she was eating a lot because she hadn't eaten in weeks? "Five days."

"Five days?" he asked. "All alone?"

She nodded.

"Most hikers who come through here have a companion."

"You can't think about things if you have a companion."

"Ah," he said, taking a sip of wine. "A vision quest?"

She shook her head. "Just a chance to be alone after a hard year."

She didn't want to tell him about the rotator cuff and the choices she was going to make. After what had happened today, that just might be too much. He probably felt sorry for her already.

"Boyfriend doesn't mind?" he asked.

Normally, that wasn't a question she liked to answer. Letting strange men know she was unattached often led to unpleasantness. But he wasn't a strange man. She felt as if she had known him for a long time.

Still, she took another bite of that excellent garlic bread before she said, "There is no boyfriend."

"No boyfriend?" He seemed both shocked and dismayed, as if it were important to him that she have someone in her life.

"No boyfriend, no husband, no pet iguana. My friends and family know I'm here." That was a bit of a stretch. One friend knew she had left, but no one else did. She didn't want to be talked out of this. "But there's no significant other to keep the home fires burning while I'm away."

In fact, there were no home fires either. She had given up her apartment for the summer and placed everything she owned in storage. She had planned that when she thought she'd be in Hawaii, training, and she saw no need to change it.

She needed a new place, and she hadn't found it yet.

"I'd think, then, you'd want to take a trip with someone," he said.

She shook her head. "There are just times in your life when you want to be alone, you know?"

"I do." He swirled the wine in his glass. Her comment seemed to make him sad.

"I'm sorry," she said. "I'm intruding on your privacy."

He raised his head. "I never said that."

"You didn't have to." She leaned over and grabbed the wine bottle off the coffee table, somehow avoiding spilling her tray in the process. Every one of her muscles screamed in agony at the movement, but she ignored them. Muscle pain was something she was used to. "A person doesn't live this far away from civilization because he likes company."

He watched her pour the wine into her glass and made no move to help. She appreciated that. It meant he wasn't overprotective. She had been a little worried about that after he put the splint on her leg.

"I don't live up here," he said.

"Oh? This is awfully well appointed for a rental." She finished pouring, then offered him the bottle.

He took it and poured some wine into his glass before putting the bottle back on the table. "I come up here a couple of times a year. I like the isolation on a short-term basis, but living here would drive me crazy."

"Winters," she said. "Snow, mountains, and no escape."

He nodded. "No movies either."

"I don't know," she said. "You could get a satellite dish."

"I could," he said, "but I think a DVD player would be more useful."

"You have a Blockbuster in this neighborhood?"

He laughed. "I could bring a year's supply of DVDs with me, and leave only when I run out."

"There's a measure of a person's time. He must emerge from his sojourn in the wilderness when he has seen *The Matrix* fifteen hundred times."

He frowned at her. "*The Matrix?* I was thinking of *Treasure of the Sierra Madre.*"

"Yeah," she said, "something light and happy to help you through your solitude."

He set his tray on the floor but kept the wineglass. "All right, what do you think I should be stranded with?"

"All the films of Chaplin," she said.

"Are they even on DVD?"

"They should be."

"With director's commentary."

"No." She shook her head. "They're silent films. You don't want to ruin that with narrative. You'll get written notes in a file you can open on the side."

"Touché," he said.

She smiled, then picked up her tray. She was going to lean over and set it on the floor, but he was too quick for her. He got up and took it from her.

He looked in her eyes again. That same deep look he had given her before, as if he saw into her very soul.

Whatever was there seemed to upset him.

"You sure," he asked, his face just inches from hers, "that there's no one special in your life?"

His voice was very soft. She could hear the threads of sorrow in it.

"I'm sure," she said.

"No one you admire from afar? No great long-lost love?"

She laughed, feeling a bit uncomfortable. At the same time, it felt right that he should ask these questions. As if he needed to know.

As if she needed to tell him.

"No," she said. "I've dated, but there's never been anyone serious."

His gaze went to her lips, and for a brief moment, she thought he was going to kiss her. Then he moved back to his chair.

"Sorry," he said. "I'm usually not this serious."

"It's all right." She plucked her wineglass off the tray beside her. The glass had become a lifeline.

"No," he said. "It's inappropriate. I guess I keep thinking there's someone out there who had a weird vibe this afternoon and is now worried about you. Silly, huh?"

She shrugged. "Probably a natural reaction to what we went through today."

"Not my natural reaction," he said. "My reaction to something like this is to joke about it inappropriately."

"I don't believe that." She swirled her wine just as she had seen him do. The wine had a marvelous red color and a smoothness she wasn't used to. She had a hunch it was very expensive.

"Oh, it's true," he said. "If there's an offensive comment to be made, I usually find it."

"You haven't been offensive to me."

"I guess you caught me at a bad moment."

She sipped the wine. "Or maybe a good moment."

"If that were possible." He leaned back in his chair. "Lenny Bruce fired me. He said my jokes were too tame."

"You're not old enough to write for Lenny Bruce," she said.

He raised his eyebrows at her. "You know about Lenny Bruce?"

"I've seen his routines."

"Not live," he said. "You're not old enough."

"Or lucky enough," she said. "He was good."

"And funny."

"And raunchy." She grinned. "*And* he wrote his own material."

He grinned in return. "Caught me."

"If you're going to impress me with your raw wit, you have to do better than that."

His grin faded. He looked down at his glass. Something she said had changed his mood.

"Mostly," he said, "I just offend people. I figure if I can piss them off, they're not worth my time."

"Really?" she asked. "I always thought that if a person was smart enough, he could piss anyone off."

He raised his head and gave her a measuring look. "Why? Is that a hobby of yours too?"

She shook her head. "I'm one of those Milquetoast people who works hard at keeping everyone calm."

"I don't think a Milquetoast person would have been

hiking alone, let alone have enough presence of mind to roll over and catch herself with a knife blade.''

He had seen that. They hadn't talked much about her fall. She was still unclear about what exactly had happened.

"Not that the knife blade worked," she said.

"It worked long enough for me to be able to help," he said and bit his lip.

She leaned back on the pillows. Something about this entire topic made him nervous and she wasn't sure what it was. "Was that when you saw me?"

He nodded. "I heard something odd, then saw you digging that knife in. I'm not even sure I would have known you were there if you hadn't done that."

She ran her thumb along the glass's warm side. If he hadn't known she was there, she would have died on that ledge. Even if she had regained consciousness, she had no idea how she would have climbed back up. She didn't have mountain climbing tools, and then there was the small matter of the broken ankle.

"I owe you everything," she said softly.

"No," he said, "you don't."

He sounded almost panicked by her words, as if he didn't want anyone to be in his debt. Still, she had to ask. "What can I do to repay you?"

He stood, went to the window, and pulled it open. The cool evening air poured in, making her realize just how stuffy the house had been. Then he came back to his chair and sat on the arm.

She got that strange sense of duality again, as if he were going to tell the absolute truth and lie to her at the same time.

"I'm not used to visitors," he said. "The last person who slept in that guest room was Hemingway."

At first she thought he was joking, but he seemed too serious for that.

"Really?" she asked. "Which one? Mariel?"

He smiled. The look on his face was fond. "No. Ernest."

"You're kidding, right? You weren't even born when he died."

Darius started, as if he were coming out of a dream. For a moment, his expression was sheer surprise; then he picked up his wineglass. He didn't drink, though.

"I didn't say it was recent," he said. "He was here in the Twenties. He used this as a hunting shack."

"So you bought it from his family?"

Darius shook his head. "This has been in my family for more than a hundred years."

She had no idea the place was that old. There'd clearly been a lot of renovation. "Wow. How did your people find this place?"

"Accident," he said. "It was a mining shack. I—um, I think this was squatter country. I don't think anyone paid for the land."

"Well, someone paid for the house."

"Oh, yeah," he said. "I did a lot of the renovations."

"But no electricity, huh?" She couldn't comprehend living in a house with no electricity. Camping without it was one thing—she didn't expect to flick a switch and have lights. But living here without the benefit of power seemed strange to her.

He slid into the chair. He was now sitting with his back against one arm and his legs draped over the other. It looked like a teenager's posture—or an athlete's.

"No lines come up this far. There weren't phones either, until some idiot invented cellular technology. Now you can't get away from anything."

"Sure you can," she said. "You just have to choose not to bring a phone with you. Besides, they told me cell phones don't work up here."

"They don't," he said. "You need a satellite phone. And no, I don't have one. I'm a bit of a Luddite."

"So I've noticed," she said. "I haven't seen a stove like that outside of a museum."

"I have two generators, but I prefer not to use power for things that I can do myself."

She nodded. "I guess that's why I like camping. I feel as if I'm getting back to nature, even though I know I'm not."

"Yeah," he said. "Back in those natural days, no one had aluminum pans."

"Or lightweight tents."

"Or water filters."

"Or dehydrated food."

"Well, I'm sure they were all sad about that."

She smiled. "Is that one of those biting comments I've heard so much about?"

"That wasn't biting. That didn't even qualify as sarcastic. If anything, it was mildly amusing."

She stretched and leaned back on her pillows. "This is a great place. If I had a haven like this, I'd never leave it."

"Don't you like civilization?"

"Most of the time it's all right. But I think it takes away our opportunities to test our limits."

He slid around so that he sat properly in the chair. "Actually, I think civilization gives people the opportunity to test their limits. Otherwise, they'd simply be struggling to survive. Life has improved a lot over the last few thousand years."

"There wasn't civilization three thousand years ago?" she asked.

"Of course there was," he said. "I just meant—"

"I know what you meant." She smiled sleepily. She could banter with him all night, but the day's events were beginning to take their toll on her. "I just wonder sometimes if we forget why we're here."

He bent over, resting his elbows on his knees and turning the wineglass around in his fingers. "Do you think people should always do what they're supposed to do?"

"What do you mean?" she asked.

He shook his head. "Too much wine. Now I'm not only

serious but maudlin. You don't need that tonight. You need to laugh."

"Actually," she said, "I need to go lie down. My brain wants to keep going, but my body has had enough for one day."

"Found its limit, huh?" Darius asked with a smile.

"Oh, I suppose I could push it farther, but I've never had the chance to sleep in Hemingway's bed before." Then she blushed. She usually didn't say things like that. What had gotten into her?

Darius set down his wineglass and stood. "Let me help you."

"No." She sat up all the way and reached for the crutches. "I can't haul you back to civilization and have you carry me from place to place. Imagine how that would look."

He studied her for a long moment, as if he were imagining that. "We'd attract attention."

"That we would." She picked up the crutches, got them into position, and somehow got to her feet. She had no idea how people who weren't athletic did this. It was hard enough for her.

Darius hadn't moved. His gaze met hers, and this time the sadness was gone. She got a sense of deep loneliness and strength.

He cupped her face. His touch was gentle. He ran his thumb over her lips. She opened them just a little. She wanted him to kiss her. She'd never wanted anyone to kiss her like this before—so much that her entire being felt the longing.

He leaned toward her, sliding his hand to her shoulder and bracing her. Then his mouth brushed hers. It felt as if he were going to move away, but she caught his lips. They parted and the kiss deepened. He took a step closer to her, putting one hand on her back to help her keep her balance.

Then he pulled her against him.

She almost dropped the crutches. The kiss took something from her, and made her feel as if she'd found something as well. She was no longer just her—she was part of a them, part of something greater than herself.

She let go of her right crutch and slipped her hand in his golden hair, feeling the softness of his curls. The crutch fell sideways, knocking against his chair before clattering to the floor.

His hands slid down her back, pressing her against him. His body felt marvelous against hers. For the first time, she was kissing a man who was the right height, who didn't have to reach up or bend down to kiss her. They fit together.

And then, suddenly, he let her go.

She staggered on her one good foot, losing her balance, but before she could fall, he had caught her again.

"Sorry," he said, and it felt like he was apologizing for more than knocking her off balance. "I'm so sorry."

"I'm not," she said.

He held her until she was steady and then he reached for the crutch. She wanted to ask him to join her in Hemingway's bed, but somehow that no longer felt appropriate.

The mood had changed, and she wasn't sure why.

He handed her the crutch, keeping a distance between them.

"Good night, Ariel," he said.

She nodded once. Perhaps it wasn't as incredible for him as it had been for her. She had never felt a kiss like that. But he was a handsome man, practiced, desirable. Maybe the kiss was nothing special to him.

She gave him what she hoped was a cheerful smile. "See you in the morning, Dar."

He didn't answer her. But she felt him watch her as she made her slow and painful way down the hall toward Hemingway's large—and empty—bed.

As soon as he was sure she had made it safely to her room, Darius picked up the wine bottle and took it outside. What was wrong with him? He knew better than to mess with someone else's soul mate. He'd learned that lesson in King Arthur's Court, when he thought no one would care about a blond stranger's fling with Guinevere. Well, Arthur had cared, and he'd mistakenly blamed his good friend Lancelot. And nothing Darius could do when he reverted to his short form and his then-identity as Merlin could change Arthur's belief.

So much for Camelot. History hadn't remembered the blond stranger, taking Arthur's version as truth, but Darius did.

He never made that mistake—at least not in that same way—again.

Darius sat down on the porch steps, extending his long legs to the pine-covered path. The air was cool and still smelled of warm pitch. In the distance, he could hear the roar of the river, and not too far away, an owl hooted.

Darius took a swig from the wine bottle. Some of the cabernet dripped down his chin, and he wiped it off with the back of his hand.

He had been honest with her and he had no idea why. He told her his real name—something the magical never did, something not even his best friend Aethelstan (who'd met him 1500 years into the sentence) even knew. Darius had told her that he spent time alone here to think about things, and he'd told her about Hemingway.

In fact, he'd had to cover for himself because he kept blurting so many different things. He'd almost told her about that last, stupid argument he'd had with Lenny Bruce.

She had to leave first thing or he wouldn't be able to lie to her any longer. And he had to lie to her, or at least mislead her, if he was going to act as her matchmaker when he returned to his short form.

His attraction to Ariel was wrong, and he probably had Cupid to thank for it. Cupid, who might have done something to Darius while Darius had his back turned. Cupid probably wanted to humiliate Dar, as if his sentence wasn't punishment enough.

Or maybe Cupid wanted to make sure that the sentence continued, that Darius never successfully united the hundredth couple.

That was probably it. Darius had assumed that Cupid had changed in the past 3000 years, just like Darius had. The old Cupid would have wanted Dar's humiliation to continue. Cupid had even mentioned it, sounding disappointed that he didn't find Darius looking short, squat, and ugly.

Darius took a swig from the wine bottle. It was still half full, but it wouldn't be for much longer.

If Ariel was supposed to be part of his hundredth couple, he'd find her soul mate. He'd even make sure she lived happily ever after, even though that wasn't part of what his task as matchmaker was.

This deep attraction he had to her wasn't real. It was a spell, designed to divert him. He knew better than anyone how real spells could feel.

And how much they could hurt.

Six

Ariel awoke to the sound of someone clearing his throat, and not in the polite way that folks had when they were trying to get a person's attention, but in that obnoxious way they had when they were trying to clear phlegm.

She opened her eyes, saw the log beams run across the ceiling, and smelled the crisp air of the mountains. She hadn't dreamed the day before. She was here, injured, in Darius's house.

And he had kissed her.

The throat-clearer—and it couldn't be Darius, because this didn't sound like him—continued for another moment, then stopped abruptly. There was a faint curse—and this time, she could have sworn that was Darius—followed by whistling.

The tune was familiar, and almost as annoying as the throat-clearing. It was "Whistle While You Work."

After one verse, the whistling ended, and more throat-clearing followed. Then a nasal male voice said, "Testing,

one, two, three.'' She heard a deep sigh followed by a faint
"Dammit," and the whine of a radio.

The voice started to recite call letters.

She sat up and wiped the sleep from her eyes. If anything,
she was even more sore than she had been the day before.
That made sense. Muscle aches got worse the second day,
peaked on the third, and then started to recede.

She should have been used to aches by now—although
these were excessive.

"Variance to Emerald Aviation," the nasal voice said.
"Come in, Emerald."

Outside, the birds chirruped. Rose-tinted sunlight fell
across the antique desk. Ariel glanced at the clock beside
the bed. It wasn't even 7 A.M. yet.

A crackle of static with a voice buried in it made its
way to her. She frowned. What was this? Who was this? It
certainly wasn't Darius.

"Have an injured hiker at Variance," the voice said.
"Need a plane today."

She felt her heart sink. She wanted to stay longer.
Although Darius had been worried about getting her out
quickly. He was afraid that she might have internal injuries—at least, that was the impression she got.

He'd been somewhat worried. Ariel put her fingers to her
lips. A man didn't kiss a woman like that when he was
completely worried.

"If I were a doctor, then that'd be a different matter."
The nasal voice sounded belligerent. "But I'm not."

Static.

"What do you expect, me to grow wings and fly her out
of here?"

Ariel smiled. Maybe she wouldn't fly out of here today
after all. Maybe she would be able to stay a little longer.

More static followed. She could barely make out another
voice raised in agitation. She wondered where the radio was
and why she could hear it so clearly.

"No, buddy. I think you're the one who misunderstands.

Once I've notified you, she becomes your responsibility, not mine . . ."

Ariel eased her legs over the side of the bed. She wondered why Darius wasn't making the radio call. Maybe it wasn't his radio. Maybe that was a friend he'd contacted, which was why the radio sounded so close.

". . . she's clearly an experienced hiker. Which means she knows about search and rescue. Well, you don't have to do the search, but the rescue is important . . ."

She grabbed her crutches and tucked them under her arms, easing herself off the bed. Her injured ankle felt like a large, puffy, painful basketball. She was grateful for the splint, which made the effort of holding her leg off the floor easier.

". . . don't really care about your schedule. The sooner you get here the better . . ."

Ariel made it to the bathroom. She couldn't take a shower—not with the splint—but she wanted to dress her scrapes and to clean up as best she could. Even though she had cleaned up some yesterday, she still probably smelled like she'd spent the last few days in the wilderness which, of course, she had.

And she wanted Darius to get close to her again.

In the bathroom, she couldn't hear the strange voice. The more she woke up, the odder the voice seemed to her. The throat clearing, the whistling, and then the radio seemed strange.

Somehow she hadn't expected to find other people so close by, but it made sense. Even when people sought isolation, they achieved it. Human beings clustered. Besides, the regulations governing this part of the primitive area might have been different from other parts. Neighbors might have been closer than she realized.

But she didn't realize people could travel with their radios. Showed how much she knew these days.

By the time she had gotten out of the bathroom and changed into clean clothes (and they seemed even cleaner than they had when she was hiking—as if they'd been freshly laundered and replaced in her pack), the voice had stopped speaking.

The birds were even louder, suggesting that the man had moved away from them. The house smelled of coffee and fresh baked bread. Ariel's stomach rumbled.

Apparently being injured did wonders for her appetite. Either that or she'd really have to rethink this dehydrated food the next time she decided to take a hike.

She made her way down the hall, her heart beating in anticipation. She'd dreamed of Darius all night, of the feel of his body against hers, the way his lips had brushed hers so gently. Her cheeks grew warm.

When she stepped out of the hallway, she was surprised to find the living area empty. The kitchen was still hot from that immense stove, and the front door stood open, the screen keeping the bugs at bay.

The table, made from varnished pine, had a single place setting. The chair was pulled back slightly, revealing a footstool covered with pillows just beneath the table. There were plates of food near the single chair: muffins, a loaf of bread, and a steaming plate of scrambled eggs. A pitcher of orange juice sat next to a pot of coffee. A single red rose sat in a clear vase near the juice glass.

Ariel made her way to the table. As she got closer, she realized what she had taken for a paper napkin was actually a folded piece of paper with her name written on it in flowing script.

She picked up the paper, jabbing herself in the ribs with the crutches as she did so. Using her thumb and forefinger, she opened the note with one hand and read.

Dearest Ariel,

 I'm afraid I was called away this morning on some personal business and I won't be able to see you off. I've contacted a plane for you. It'll arrive before nine. The pilot will help you board. I told him to come into the house so that you wouldn't have to wait near the runway.

In the meantime, enjoy breakfast.

I'm sorry that we missed each other but I'm glad we met.

I shall never forget you—

                                                        Dar

Ariel stared at the letter for a long time, her breath caught in her throat.

He was gone. He had left her here, alone. Someone else had called for the plane. Someone else would help her board. Someone else would make sure her ankle got tended.

She would never see Darius again.

I shall never forget you was a dismissal. He really and truly was gone.

Ariel sank into the chair and propped up her injured foot. She set the crutches aside and stared at the table before her. This was not a meal a man made when he was trying to get rid of someone. This meal took a lot of time and energy. It was a meal meant to impress.

And where did he get the single rose? She had seen no bushes about. Besides, roses didn't do well at this elevation, at least not in the dryness of an Idaho summer.

If only she had gotten up earlier. She would have come out here and talked to him while he was cooking.

She would have found out what the personal business was.

How did he even find out about it? Just the night before, he had said he didn't have a phone.

Maybe Nasal Voice had been using Darius's radio. Maybe Darius had sent the friend here to help him out.

She grabbed her crutches. Hungry as she was, she wasn't going to leave here without seeing Darius one last time. Or at least finding out where he had gone.

She did a cursory search of the main level of the house. She found another room beside hers, set up with reading

lamps and big comfortable chairs. Books were piled everywhere, along with CDs, record albums, and forty-fives. A
tiny shelf system with a five-disk changer sat on top of a
console stereo from the 1950s. Beside that was an ancient
hand-crank record player that looked as if it were still being
used.

The room had no obvious plug-ins, yet all this equipment
seemed to be here for someone's enjoyment. She thought
that odd.

A door beside this room led up a flight of stairs. The
house was old enough, then, to have doors that cut off
entire sections to preserve heat. Or maybe that remained a
convention in this part of Idaho since there was no power
up here. No sense heating an entire house when one section
would do.

At first, she had no idea how to get up the stairs. Then
she realized she could do it. She would just have to be
careful. First, she'd try it with her crutches, and if that didn't
work, she would sit on the steps and pull herself up with
her arms.

She smiled. That would certainly impress Darius.

As if she expected him to be upstairs. If he was up there,
he was hiding from her—and after finding that note, she
knew he wasn't. He was somewhere else. But she might
be able to tell where he'd gone from something he'd left
upstairs.

At least, that was what she told herself. Truth be told,
she wanted to see where he slept, to know more about him.

She made her way up the stairs carefully. It was harder
than she thought, mostly because the crutches got in her
way. When she reached the landing, she tossed them up the
remaining stairs, and then, holding the banister, hopped to
the second floor.

The second floor was smaller than the first. In fact, the
ceiling slanted on the north and south sides, obviously following the roof lines.

There was a large room directly across from the stairs, and another large room at the end of a short hallway. Two smaller doors led to under-the-eaves storage, filled with more junk than she had ever seen.

Darius wasn't up here at all.

She couldn't even tell which room was his. Both had beds in them, and both beds were made. There were no suitcases or anything out of place. Everything was hung in closets. The bedside tables all had books with bookmarks in them.

The second story smelled faintly of mothballs mixed with the scent of freshly baked bread. She went to the windows and looked out.

The runway was visible from here. It was long and flat, a scar on the land. Behind it was a huge garage with cars inside that looked as old as the hand-crank record player.

Otherwise the entire house was surrounded by trees.

She saw no sign of Darius. None at all.

For a long time, she stood at the window, staring at the runway. She couldn't go outside looking for him. She had no idea where he'd gone or how he'd gotten there. She could negotiate stairs with a broken ankle, but not the uneven trail or the cliffside.

Maybe he'd change his mind. Maybe the circumstances would change and he'd be able to come back.

Maybe the pilot wouldn't be able to pick her up.

Her stomach growled.

Ariel sighed and made her careful way down the stairs. When she reached the living area, she stopped.

The eggs were still steaming.

How in the world had he managed that?

Darius sat on the hillside where he had been when he first saw Ariel. He probably should have popped himself to Boise or New Delhi, somewhere very far away, so that he wouldn't be tempted to see her again.

But he hadn't. He couldn't. He didn't want to be far in case something else went wrong.

He'd been awake all night thinking about her, about the soft auburn of her hair, the way her cheeks dimpled when she laughed.

About the evidence of a soul mate he'd seen in her lovely green eyes.

He wished he were younger, a mage who hadn't learned his lessons yet, or one who had no scruples. He would have taken her for himself then, the Fates be damned.

But he knew the price of such an action. The world would be a different place if Camelot hadn't shattered under the strains of his actions.

Love, he'd learned slowly and painfully, was something to be respected at all times.

He wrapped his arms around his legs, hugging his knees to his chest. The plane had to come soon.

If it didn't, he'd go back to her and never leave.

No matter what the cost.

The eggs were hot, but the stove had cooled down considerably. There were no dirty dishes in the sink, no evidence of anyone else's presence in the house at all.

The hair had risen on the back of Ariel's neck. She was really and truly unnerved now. The egg platter sat on the tabletop with nothing beneath it to keep the eggs warm.

Maybe she was still asleep and dreaming. Maybe this entire house was a dream—and she was lying on that ledge, delirious.

She grabbed a muffin and stared at the eggs as if they were her enemy. There were too many mysteries here this morning: the man with the nasal voice, Darius's disappearance, and now the eggs. Not to mention that in her thorough search of the house, she'd found no evidence of a radio.

She took a bite of the muffin. It was blueberry, light and

fluffy, not too sweet, yet somehow perfect. The best muffin she'd ever tasted.

Ariel frowned at it. Muffins weren't supposed to be this good. Just like eggs weren't supposed to stay warm for an hour, and handsome men weren't supposed to disappear.

She finished the muffin and helped herself to another, avoiding the scary, steaming eggs. Then she heard the buzz of a plane's engine, growing closer.

Her ride was here.

She set down the second muffin and went to the porch. The air still held the night's coolness. Dew dampened the furniture. A brick path wound its way down into the trees. It must have been very hard for Darius to carry her up here. The extra weight, the unevenness of the bricks, must have made him lose his footing more than once.

Yet he'd managed it, and he hadn't seemed the worse for wear.

The plane's buzz grew louder. She only had a few minutes left.

"Dar!" she shouted. "Dar!"

If he were nearby and heard the plane, then heard her yell, he might come back, just long enough to say good-bye. That was all she wanted, really. A chance to thank him.

A chance to see him one last time.

Her voice echoed down the mountainside, making her feel alone for the first time on this trip. The buzz had become a roar, and she could see the plane overhead.

One final chance.

"Dar! I'm going to have to leave! Please come up and say good-bye!"

A single-engine plane, battered and old, circled overhead, as if searching for the runway. That didn't give her much confidence.

She held her breath, looking all around, at the morning shadows under the trees, the path, the runway to her left. No Darius.

But she'd give him a minute. Maybe he was running toward her even now.

Good-bye wouldn't hurt. One word. Simple, eloquent.

Darius hugged his legs to his chest even harder, making sure his fingers were laced so they couldn't create a spell.

He'd magic the entire problem away—the ankle, the pain—hell, he'd even magic her memory of the entire event away, later, when they were all done. Who would know?

Besides him.

He let out a loud sigh. He wasn't that kind of man anymore. He hadn't been for centuries.

If he did that, he'd loathe himself forever.

Dar!

She wanted to see him. He wanted to see her. So simple. Except for the pilot, who had only met Darius's alter ego, Andrew Vari, and who would wonder where Vari was—especially since Vari had radioed in for the plane.

That had been hard. Darius had to fake the voice that came with the other body—his short, squat, punishment body—and that had been more difficult than he'd imagined. He almost had to spell himself for that too.

The plane's engine was so loud now, he wouldn't be able to hear Ariel even if she were still shouting for him.

What if she were in trouble? What if she needed help? Maybe he should go to her, to make sure she was all right this one last time.

The plane's engine shut off.

If there were any problems, the pilot could handle them now. Ariel was no longer Darius's responsibility. And, if he managed to avoid her in the future, helping her find her soul mate wouldn't be his responsibility either.

In just a few moments, he would have his life back. He would be able to spend the rest of his time alone, just like he had planned.

Just like he wanted.

Like he always wanted.

Even now, when he thought he wanted something else.

The pilot was a tall, rangy man in his mid-fifties, his face tanned and lined from too much time in the sun. He wore a red flannel shirt over a black T-shirt, tucked into a tight pair of blue jeans.

"I'm Duke Milligan. You must be the injured girl, huh?"

Ariel bit her lower lip. She wasn't sure which comment she was trying to prevent from emerging—the fact that she didn't believe anyone, no matter how macho, could be named Duke, or the fact that she hadn't been a girl for a number of years.

"I'm Ariel Summers," she said, keeping her voice level.

He nodded, as if he had already known that. "Vari said I was to help you out."

Vari must have been the man who had used the radio.

"My stuff is inside," she said. Then she frowned. "But could you help me with something else first?"

Duke Milligan glanced at a scratched analog watch. "I'm already off schedule."

"It's just that the man who found me isn't here, and I wanted to say good-bye—"

"Miss, I'm sorry, but I've got some paying customers arriving in fifteen minutes, and I'm going to have to explain to them already about being late. Once the heat of the day starts, flying over these mountains gets a bit dicey, and I—"

"It'll just take a minute." She indicated her foot. "I can't look for him myself. Would you just walk around the house, maybe, see if you see him?"

He let out a small sound, a cross between a sigh and a Bronx cheer. "If we go as soon as I get back."

"I promise," she said.

He shook his head slightly, then went around the side of the house, walking with great speed and determination.

He wouldn't find Darius. Ariel knew that. If Darius had been nearby, he would have come when she yelled his name. But she wanted to make sure. The entire morning had unsettled her, and she wanted to have one final chance at finding him.

She made her way back into the house. She had to pack yesterday's clothes in her backpack. As she passed the table, she grabbed the note and placed it in the pocket of her shirt.

When she reached the guest bedroom, she stopped and stared at the antique desk. She had a sudden, very clear sense that the note she held had been written on it, using some of the old paper and the inkwell.

But that didn't make sense. She was a light sleeper. She would have woken up.

"Hey!" Duke yelled from the front door. "Ain't nobody here but us chickens."

"How original," she muttered.

The screen door banged. She still stared at the desk. Duke joined her. "This your stuff?"

"Yeah." She hadn't put the clothes in it, but he was already unzipping the pack, shoving the clothes inside.

"Can you walk to the plane?" he asked. "Or do I gotta carry you?"

The idea of being carried instantly lost its appeal.

"No," she said. "I'll be fine."

"Then let's go," he said.

"I can't move all that fast."

He slung her backpack over one shoulder as if it weighed less than a pound. "Do your best."

And then he disappeared down the hall.

She went to the desk, pulled the chair back, and grabbed a piece of vellum. Putting her crutches aside, she sat down in the very seat that Darius had used while she slept and slid the inkwell toward her.

The pen had been meticulously cleaned. She uncapped the inkwell and dabbed the pen in it, and then wrote:

Dar—
Thank you for everything.

She paused. There was so much more to say—*You kiss like a dream; you look like a dream; I've never met a man like you; call me when you return to civilization*—but she wrote none of it. It all sounded too high school, and she was feeling much older than a high-school girl right now.

Finally, she scrawled:

I hope we meet again soon.

Ariel

Outside, she heard Duke bellow. She tapped the end of the pen against her lips.

If only she had a phone number to give him, some way of contacting her. But her furniture was in storage and she no longer had an apartment. She had let her cell phone account lapse, and she didn't know where she was going to end up.

Duke yelled again.

She sighed, capped the inkwell, and wiped off the pen. Then she put the note on the bed.

"Hey!" Duke had come back inside. He was standing in the doorway, looking cross. "I thought you were coming outside."

"I was," she said. "I just remembered I hadn't thanked him."

"Done now?" Duke asked.

She doubted she would be done with this one for a long time. But she nodded anyway and let herself be led back to civilization.

Darius waited until he could no longer hear the drone of the plane's engines before straightening his legs. He waited until the sun had moved across the horizon before standing up. He waited until the shadows were so long he could barely see before returning to the house.

It still felt empty.

Although he caught a trace of her scent, still lingering in the air.

He clapped his hands, commanding "Lights" as he did so. He wasn't willing to monkey with generators tonight. He would make things as easy as possible.

All the lights in the building sprang on. The eggs still steamed on the table, and he cursed silently. He had spelled them to stay hot and fresh, but apparently the spell had gone slightly off—making them stay the way they had been when he set them there.

He hoped she hadn't noticed that.

A half-eaten muffin sat on the plate, and an orange juice glass lined with pulp sat beside it. Otherwise, all the food he had made so meticulously during his long sleepless night had gone uneaten.

The rose still rested in its vase, wilted and looking defeated.

But his note was gone.

He had wanted to say so much more. But he couldn't. And now she was gone. Unreachable, unless he went into McCall on his own, checked the hospital, and found out where she was going to spend the night.

Instead, he sank into the chair she had used just that morning and touched the half-eaten muffin. She was gone.

A quick snap of the fingers would bring her back. She'd be surprised, but he'd explain it. All of it. The magic, everything.

A quick snap of the fingers.

So simple even Cupid could do it.

Cupid.

Darius clenched his fingers. This had all been planned. A test from the Fates, along with a small warning, to see if he had really learned his lesson. Would Darius put himself and his own interests first, or would he remember all that he had learned?

He remembered. He would always remember.

And no matter what it cost, no matter how it felt, he would do the right thing.

Seven

The plane dipped and rose over invisible bumps in the air. Its battered metal frame rattled, and the engine sounded louder on the inside than it had on the outside.

The fact that the entire thing smelled of a combination of diesel fuel and gasoline did not encourage Ariel. The fumes were so strong, she was afraid that if she lit a match the entire plane would burst into flames.

She had mentioned the smell when she first climbed into the plane, but Duke had professed himself unworried. He sat beside her now, a toothpick in the side of his mouth like a poor cigarette substitute. He flew the plane as if he were driving a car—one hand on the steering mechanism and the wrist of his other hand resting on some sort of joystick.

Ariel didn't know a lot about planes, but she would have felt a lot better if Duke were paying more attention. The mountaintops seemed uncomfortably close—at one point it seemed like she could reach out and touch them—and she kept having visions of the small plane crashes she'd seen in movies—the one from the Patsy Cline biopic *Sweet Dreams* came horribly to mind—where the plane slammed into the side of the mountain and burst into flame.

Somehow she had the feeling that dying like that wouldn't be as mercifully short as everyone said it was. She thought time would slow down, maybe even freeze, and she would know exactly—

"Um." The word came out of her mouth even before she knew it.

Duke didn't glance at her, like she would have preferred. He looked at her. "What?"

Keep your eyes front and center. Keep your hands on the controls. Fly the damn plane!

"Um, how long have you been flying up here?" It was the only thing she could think of to say that didn't sound totally offensive.

He grinned and finally looked out the windshield like he was supposed to. "Seems like most of my life. I just love these mountains. Flying 'em can be real dangerous. You gotta know what you're doing."

Was he baiting her? Maybe she had turned a particularly awful shade of green, or perhaps the way she was threading her hands in her lap gave her away.

"They must seem very familiar to you," she said, gritting her teeth. *So familiar that you don't care if you hit one.*

His grin grew wider. "I could fly this with my eyes closed."

"Please don't," she said, and this time her voice actually shook.

He looked at her again. "Am I making you nervous, little lady?"

There, he did it again: offended her while asking her a question. Was he deliberately rubbing her the wrong way, or did he treat every woman like this?

Well, she could be macho she-woman of the mountains or she could be honest. Honest probably wouldn't get his respect, but then, she was never going to see him again.

"A little," she said.

"A tough cookie like you?" he asked without a trace of irony. "Vari told me you saved yourself from going down the side of a cliff by using a hunting knife."

Almost saved herself, but who was going to quibble? "I prefer hiking to flying," she said, deciding to be vulnerable, hoping that would make Duke change his habits, at least for this trip.

"You'd be surprised how many of my passengers say that."

Oh, no, I wouldn't. She just smiled and looked out the grimy window to her right and then started. The tops of some pine trees looked suspiciously close to the bottom of the plane.

He must have noticed her expression (why didn't he keep facing forward, dammit?) and said, "The way that the air currents get around the peaks, sometimes it's better to skim."

That was it. She'd had enough of this conversation. She swallowed hard and wished she hadn't agreed to get on this plane. If anything, the fumes had gotten heavier and the interior of the cabin too warm.

"Um," she said again, mostly to control her thoughts. If she thought about something else, she might make it through this joy ride. "Have you flown to Dar's place before?"

"Where?" Duke bit hard on his toothpick, breaking it. He pulled it out of his teeth, gave it a dissatisfied look, and tossed it on the floor.

She looked down. It was messier than the floor of her car, which was saying something.

She looked back up immediately, saw a sheer cliffside ahead of her, and turned her head toward the right side of the plane. Not that that helped much—those treetops were still too close.

"Dar's place, you know. Where you picked me up."

"Variance?"

"What?" This time she looked at him, thinking maybe

he was using some important plane-flying jargon and she had to do something.

"Variance. That's where I picked you up."

"The region has a name?"

He shook his head, reached into the breast pocket of his shirt, and removed another toothpick. He rolled it around in his fingers as if he were smoothing the tobacco in a self-made cigarette. "Not the region. The house. It's called Variance."

"Oh," she said. "How come?"

"Because it's Vari's."

She frowned. This conversation was as confusing as the plane ride. "Dar's last name is Vari?"

"What's Dar?"

Why hadn't she learned his last name? How had she overlooked that? And why hadn't she realized it until now?

"Not what," she said. "Who. Dar is a who."

Now it sounded like she was quoting Dr. Seuss. *Ariel Hears a Who.* Who's on First. Who is? Who. It was an easy segue into Abbott and Costello.

She shook her head. Maybe she was going crazy.

The plane rose above the cliffside at the very last moment. She pretended not to notice.

"Dar is a who," Duke repeated. "Oh. You mean a person."

"Yes," Ariel said.

"The guy you were looking for?"

"Yes. He's the one who lives in the house."

"You mean Andrew Vari."

She didn't like how this conversation was going. "He said his name was Darius."

Duke shrugged and put the toothpick in his mouth. "Guy's weird enough to say anything."

"He didn't strike me as weird," Ariel said.

Duke turned toward her very slowly, his eyes wide with obvious disbelief. "He didn't?"

"No. He was very kind. He cooked me dinner—"

"Yeah, he always brings too many provisions."

"—and he carried me off that cliff—"

"Andrew Vari?"

"Well, he said his name was Darius."

"The guy in the house."

"Yes, the guy in the house." Maybe it wasn't a coincidence that she thought of Abbott and Costello. Apparently she had just landed in one of their routines.

"Short little guy, maybe five feet in high heels, carried *you* into his house."

"What short little guy?" she asked.

"Andrew Vari."

"Look out!"

He turned his attention back to flying in time to pull up and clear the top of a lone pine tree on a mountain peak. His face paled and beads of sweat formed on his forehead.

She wasn't exactly calm. She was gripping the ripped plastic of the co-pilot's seat so hard that she had probably ripped it some more. Maybe that was how it got ripped in the first place.

She certainly didn't blame it. Anyone in their right mind had to be ripped to get into this plane.

When he leveled it and there didn't appear to be any more peaks ahead, he said, "You're telling me Andrew Vari carried you to his house."

"I'm telling you the man who owns the house, who called himself Darius, carried me to the house."

"This Darius, he looks like one of the seven dwarves come to life, right?"

This time it was her turn to give Duke an amazed look. "He looks like a Greek god."

"Whatever floats your boat," Duke said, making an expression of distaste.

"No," Ariel said very carefully. "I meant he looks like a Greek god. He's tall, blond, and probably the most handsome man I've ever seen."

Duke frowned. "Tall?"

"Tall."

"How tall?"

She shrugged. "Taller than you."

The mountains were leveling out. Ariel thought she could see a valley in the distance.

"That can't be Andrew Vari," Duke said.

"I'm getting that impression."

"But it's strange." Duke was finally keeping his eyes on the scene before him. "I mean, I flew Vari up there, and he didn't say anything about a guest."

"Dar was very comfortable in the house. He knew where everything was and he knew its history."

"Hmm." Duke shifted in his seat. "You think Vari's in trouble?"

"From Dar?" Ariel's voice raised slightly. "He saved my life. Why would he do anything harmful to someone else?"

"I dunno." Duke's frown grew deeper. "But I would have known if he was going to bring anyone in."

"Why?" Ariel asked. "Because they had to fly?"

"Well, yeah." Duke glanced at her.

She raised her eyebrows at him deliberately, and he gave her a sheepish grin.

"Okay," Duke said. "So he could have walked in."

"Hiked in."

"That too."

There was a valley. The land was flat; the mountains were in the distance. Tiny buildings dotted the ground and a ribbon of highway flowed through the center. Ariel was never so glad to see anything in her life. She would be getting out of this plane soon.

"I'll just ask him about it when I see him again," Duke was saying.

"Who?" Ariel asked. Her heart rose in expectation. Maybe she could see Darius one last time.

"Vari."

"You're going to see him?"

Duke nodded. "Next Wednesday. Gotta pick him up, seven A.M. If I'm late, he don't pay for the flight. It's been our agreement forever, before me even."

"Before you? I thought you've flown this route for years."

"Yeah," Duke said. "Vari's been around forever. He had that same bet with the guy who flew the route before me. Guess someone was late once, and it really torked Vari off. I guess he's not a guy you've ever seen mad."

"I take it you've never seen him mad."

Duke shook his head. "Don't want to either. He's unpleasant enough when he's nice."

"No wonder you didn't think he rescued me," Ariel said.

The plane eased toward the highway. The buildings were getting larger, the ground was getting closer, and she still didn't see anything resembling a runway.

"I didn't think he rescued you because he's too short to carry you. It'd be like being rescued by an eight-year-old."

"He's that short?"

"Lady, he's the shortest adult I've ever seen."

It looked as if the plane was heading toward a flat, square building. Ariel gripped the side of the seat even harder, her fingers finding the stuffing. This plane ride was never going to end.

"When we land," Duke said, "Evelyn's gonna drive you to the hospital."

"That's not necessary," Ariel said.

Duke let out a barking laugh. "What do you think you're gonna do, catch a cab?"

She hadn't given it any thought. "I don't know. I thought—"

"No sense wasting an ambulance ride on you. You're okay enough. Even though Vari wanted you checked out. He was real insistent about that." Duke frowned at her. "You sure you didn't see him?"

"I'm sure." Ariel was the only one looking at the windshield now. The building was too close. It was made of some kind of corrugated metal and painted gray. The roof was flat and huge. Did he plan to land on the roof?

"Because he was awful insistent about what happened to you. And . . ." Duke paused. He probably meant it for dramatic effect, but it was just annoying. ". . . he's paying for this flight."

"What?" That got Ariel's attention. It even made her look away from the windshield.

"Hang on a sec."

Duke said that last casually, but Ariel was convinced he had just realized they were going to hit the building. He spit out the toothpick and leaned forward as if he were nearsighted and had forgotten his glasses.

The engines roared even louder and the plane continued to head toward the roof.

At the very last moment, the plane cleared the roof and a runway appeared. Apparently the building had hidden it from view.

Ariel let out a sigh of relief. Duke brought the plane down on the runway too fast. The plane bounced, rose in the air again, then sank to the ground, the squeal of brakes so loud that Ariel's ears hurt.

She could smell burning rubber, and she knew if she looked behind them, she would probably see smoke, tire marks, and maybe sparks.

Oh, good. Sparks. That was just what they needed, given the fuel fumes inside the cabin.

Duke brought the plane to a complete stop. Ariel's fingers were permanently embedded in the passenger seat. She'd need to get them surgically removed.

A fiftyish woman with straight gray hair made her way to the side of the plane. She slid a tiny stepladder to the door and then pulled it open.

"You Ariel?" she asked.

Ariel nodded.

The woman held out her hand. "Evelyn. I got a car waiting. Let's get you to the hospital."

Ariel tried to protest, but it had no effect. Within minutes, she'd been bundled out of the plane and into the tiniest car she'd ever seen.

She managed to say good-bye to Duke and to thank him, but in the confusion, she wasn't able to ask him any more questions. And she wanted to know why he thought this Andrew Vari was paying for her plane flight, not Darius.

She wanted a lot of answers, and she hadn't gotten them. In fact, the flight left her with more questions than she'd had before.

Darius couldn't take the silence anymore. One night without her—after only one night with her—and he was going out of his mind, questioning his decisions, worrying that he had made the wrong choice.

Being alone in the wilderness had lost its appeal. He needed some reassurance, but he wasn't going to get it here.

Not that he had anyone to confide in. All these years, all this time, and he hadn't talked to anyone about his sentence, his predicament. No one at all.

In the middle of the night, he had thought he might just see the Fates, challenge them, find out why they had sent Cupid to him, why they were still testing him, but in the clear light of morning, he decided that was a bad idea. What if he angered them all over again? Then they might add extra time on to his sentence. He couldn't have that.

He thought of going to see Cupid, to find out what the little bugger had done this time. That idea seemed even better than visiting the Fates—until he really examined it. What if Cupid had done nothing, had really come to see an old friend just as he had said? Or what if he had just come to mess with Dar's mind?

If Darius visited him, then Cupid would know he had won.

Visiting Cupid would have to be his last resort.

But by morning, Darius was pacing. He had to do something. He couldn't stay here, alone with his thoughts, his worries. If he remained here much longer, he would probably lose control. He'd go to the hospital and see if he could find out what happened to Ariel. And then all his resolve would be for nothing.

He took a long walk and whistled all the music he could remember from *Camelot,* but even that shameful episode in his past wasn't helping his resolve.

No. He had to do something else—and quickly.

After a moment's consideration, he finally had a good idea. He had to remind himself what he was working for. Besides himself, of course. If he were only thinking of himself, he would go see Ariel. He would have no choice.

Instead, he snapped his fingers and found himself sitting on a concrete bench on a university campus. Behind him was a square Greek revival building, across the street was some odd concoction of styles, all of which meshed into what was obviously a student union, and across from him was a concrete library that looked like it doubled as a bomb shelter.

The air was hot and humid, and sweat trickled down his back. Not too far from him, children played in a shallow fountain. Students, wearing as little as possible, lay on the grass, reading books and talking softly to each other.

Darius frowned. He'd wanted to see the last couple he'd united—Michael and Emma Found—but he'd thought he was going to their home. His magic had to be malfunctioning. He didn't see them anywhere.

Then he heard Emma's laugh, loud and feminine at the same time. She was standing a few yards from him, her long black hair wrapped around the top of her head. She wore a sundress that revealed most of her back, and she was barefoot. Around her wrist, she'd wrapped a leash.

Darius followed its length and saw a fat and sassy black cat at the end of it, studiously eating a piece of grass.

Michael Found stood beside Emma. He was dressed as

casually as she was, and laughing just as hard. They'd been married now for almost a year, and they seemed happy.

Then Emma turned sideways, and Darius gasped. She was pregnant. He hadn't been sure that was possible, with the way that magic worked and her strange life. But she was— and for her, that was a dream come true.

He almost stood up so that he could congratulate her. But she wouldn't recognize him. None of his old friends knew what he really looked like.

Instead, he smiled. If he hadn't visited Michael Found, reenacting that old Ghost of Christmas Present scam, the two of them wouldn't be together. In fact, Emma might not be alive right now.

Darius had almost forgotten that.

Michael bent over and picked up the cat, Darnell, who growled loud enough for Darius to hear. Then Michael and Emma walked toward Darius. Darius's heart pounded.

Emma didn't even notice him, but Michael nodded to him, clearly not recognizing him. Darnell, though, got a strange look in his golden eyes. He climbed up Michael's shoulder and continued to stare at Darius as the three of them walked toward the Union. Then Darnell gave the kitty equivalent of a shrug and slipped back into Michael's arms.

Emma scratched the cat on the head before slipping her arm around Michael's back. He rested his head on top of hers. They looked like the perfect couple, walking off into the sunset—at least until the cat yowled at them.

Darius grinned. Some things never changed.

Then Darius stood and walked in the other direction, toward a group of outdoor food vendors and more university buildings. He didn't understand Emma's attraction to the University of Wisconsin—especially with its hot, humid summers—but he did love a good bratwurst every now and then.

He bought one, along with a beer, and sat in the sunshine, watching the coeds and reminding himself that he had only one more couple to go.

One more.

One more and he would be free.

He found himself wondering if, once he were free, he'd be able to see Ariel again, and then he shook his head.

He couldn't think of that. He couldn't afford to. Even if she was the woman of his dreams, it wouldn't work. He would live for thousands of years, if he were lucky. She would live maybe to seventy-five. He'd known mortals who'd grown old and died on him. It was hard enough with friends.

He couldn't imagine how painful it would be with a lover.

No. Ariel was part of something that was not meant to be. And the sooner he understood that deep down, the better.

Eight

Ariel slid down the driver's seat in her rental car, her broken ankle throbbing. The Idaho morning was cool and cloudy, leaving the valley dark even though it was past seven A.M.

Emerald Aviation looked abandoned. There were no planes on the runway, and only three cars in the parking lot—the tiny car that Evelyn had used to drive Ariel to the hospital after the flight; a rusted one-ton pickup that was probably going to fall apart in the next good wind; and an expensive Mercedes roadster that looked like it wanted nothing to do with its poorer companions.

Cars passed on the highway, people staring at her. Or maybe she just thought they were staring at her. How often did a person sit in Emerald Aviation's parking lot, waiting for a single-engine plane to return from the wilderness? Probably not that often. Either that or the locals thought she was a hick tourist too scared to get out of the car.

There was some truth in that as well.

She'd been planning to come here for nearly a week now. The doctors had told her to go easy on the leg and not attempt the long drive down to Boise for at least a few days—even if she could find someone to drive her. The problem was that Idaho's north-south highway cut through some of the remotest parts of the state, and there were no really good places to stop between McCall and Boise.

Initially, she had pooh-poohed the idea. Then she had rented the car and discovered that driving across the tiny town was painful because of the way she had to hold her leg. Driving for hours would be excruciating.

Her leg throbbed now because she had made the drive to nearby Donnelly, where Emerald Aviation was. She couldn't get Duke's comments out of her mind—the fact that he hadn't known Darius, that Andrew Vari was a separate person, and that Vari had paid for her medical care.

She'd asked questions in McCall, questions about Vari and about Darius. Everyone who had met Vari remembered him and had some anecdote (usually negative) about him. No one remembered Darius. Since he was so gorgeous and so nice, no one who had seen him would have forgotten him.

It got curiouser and curiouser.

McCall was a resort town. Most of Boise's middle class—the ones who couldn't afford Sun Valley—visited McCall year-round. In the summer, they golfed, hiked, and swam in gorgeous Payette Lake. In the winter, they skied, skated, and made ice sculptures. They bought vacation homes and spent too much money. The locals tolerated them, and found ways to make a quick buck off of them, just like they did in any other resort town.

Ariel had been to McCall before with friends, but then she had camped. This time, though, she treated herself to a stay in McCall's best resort—Shore Lodge. Shore Lodge was over eighty years old, with gorgeous remodeled rooms and a spectacular view of the lake.

Ariel had taken breakfast every morning on the deck,

enjoying the summer flowers blooming in pots nearby and watching vacationers water-ski on the flat blue water.

She tried not to envy them. She wasn't having the athletic vacation she had planned. She was having a reflective one, though, in a beautiful setting, eating too much and spending too much time alone.

Amazing that hiking through the wilderness wasn't a lonely experience, but here, in the most beautiful hotel she had ever stayed in, surrounded by people she didn't know, she felt lonelier than she had in her life.

Part of it was because she was at loose ends. She wasn't used to being inactive. The cast on her foot prevented her from doing anything athletic—she couldn't even take a few relaxing laps across the lodge's heated swimming pool. No walking, no hiking, no running, no swimming, no golf. She could do nothing except sit and watch the people go by, and wonder what their lives were like.

Oddly, she wasn't feeling sorry for herself. Just a bit tired and out of sorts. She had too much time to think about that night with Darius, and then the next morning. She had reread his note a dozen times, and she still didn't understand it.

When she combined the events with the note and the conversation she'd had with Duke, she got even more confused.

So sometime during her solitary week, she'd gotten the idea to come and talk to the mysterious Andrew Vari. He would be able to answer a few questions for her. He would be able to tell her Darius's last name and how she could contact him. She had a few things to return to him, like his crutches. He might even be able to tell her what Darius's personal business had been that morning, and why he hadn't said good-bye.

Deep down, though, she was hoping that Darius would be with Vari, and she would get to see him one last time.

Ariel got out of the car. The ache in her ankle was deeper than she wanted it to be. She was never very good at healing. Healing required patience. She had probably done the most damage to her rotator cuff by trying to use her shoulder too soon after the injury. The doctors had yelled at her, then.

This time, she was trying to be careful, but it was hard. She hated being restricted. The fact that the drive caused her leg to ache irritated her. She wanted to snap her fingers and heal the bone, but that wasn't possible.

And if there was anything she hated, it was the impossible.

A wind blew across her face. It was damp and smelled of rain. She glanced at the clouds. They were darker than she had originally thought, and they looked ominous. In the distance, she thought she saw lightning.

Storms in the mountains were never pretty. They were violent and strong and dangerous. Mountain folk always prayed for rain with the storms because lightning was dangerous. Summers were dry up here, and when lightning struck, the wilderness burned. Wildfires destroyed hundreds of acres every summer and sometimes threatened remote towns like McCall and Donnelly.

She shielded her eyes with her hand while clutching the crutches to her sides for balance. Against the clouds she made out a tiny shape.

It looked like a plane, but she couldn't hear the engine.

Thunder rumbled overhead and lightning flared, illuminating the shape. Sure enough, it was a small plane flying just ahead of the storm.

Ariel shuddered. Flying with Duke had been a bad experience on a clear sunny day. She couldn't imagine what it would be like in the wind, with a storm on the plane's tail.

The plane pitched and dove, tilting first to one side and then to the other. Big fat drops of rain suddenly pelted Ariel, and she hobbled toward the building. As she did, a gust of wind came up, blowing dirt and gravel across the parking lot.

The plane pitched even more.

Her stomach twisted. These were the worst conditions in which to fly a small plane. She hoped Duke's skills were up to the landing.

She made it to the shelter of the building's back wall. Evelyn was standing there, hand shielding her face, much as Ariel had earlier, a look of strain on her face.

"Thought I might see you," Evelyn said, not taking her gaze off the plane. "Figured you'd want to meet Vari."

Ariel had told her the entire story on the way to the hospital. "I owe him."

Evelyn nodded, her expression tight. The rain was coming down in sheets now, and the plane looked like it was in trouble.

Ariel leaned against the building, trying to stay dry. She couldn't take her gaze off the airplane, tilting and rising on the wind. Lightning flared behind it again, and then a flash seemed to come from inside the plane itself.

She almost thought she heard a nasal voice utter a curse just before that last lightning flare. The voice sounded like it had come over a loudspeaker, but she didn't see any, and Evelyn acted as if she hadn't heard a thing.

But the plane leveled out. In fact, it didn't even seem to be getting wet any longer. Ariel could have sworn that the water was bouncing off an invisible barrier about three feet above the plane—like someone had raised a clear plastic umbrella over the entire area.

She didn't like that analogy. Umbrellas attracted lightning.

The plane positioned itself over the runway. Evelyn bit her lower lip. Ariel clutched her crutches tighter. A gust of wind pelted her with rain. The drops weren't big and fat anymore. They were thin and sharp and hurt as they slashed her skin.

But the plane didn't seem as if it were affected by the rain at all. It came down smoothly. In fact, the landing was a hundred times smoother than the one Duke had managed with her inside—on that clear, windless day.

Ariel frowned. No one flew better in dismal weather.

Evelyn ran toward the plane, her umbrella over her head. She slid the tiny stepladder up to the plane's door as she had when Ariel had been on board, and then she stepped back.

The plane's door opened, and Ariel's breath caught in her throat. She watched as a small leg, clad in pristine white, found the step.

The man who followed was tiny, just as Duke had said, and he did look something like a Disney character—or, more accurately, Edward G. Robinson from his more famous gangster movies shrunk down to half his normal size.

The small man—Vari, apparently—was wearing a white suit and a summer hat. In fact, he looked as if he had just left the *Casablanca* movie set. His clothes were pressed and extremely neat, considering the plane he'd just been in. They didn't seem disturbed by the weather either.

A spate of rain hit her face again, and she wiped the water off with one hand. Vari had stopped on the stairs. His gaze met hers, and there was something very familiar about it. In fact, she had underestimated his looks a moment earlier. She felt drawn to him, as if beneath those mushed features and oft-broken nose lurked the kindest man she had ever seen.

She had met him before. She was sure of it.

And completely unsure of it.

If she had met him before, she would have remembered him. She had never seen a man who looked that remarkable in her life.

Still, her heart was pounding as if he were as handsome as Darius. Perhaps she felt this way because she associated him with Darius—because she had been expecting Darius to get out of that plane as well.

Evelyn reached inside the plane and tugged on something behind the seat. Duke came around, head bent against the rain, and tried to help her.

Vari continued to stare at Ariel as if she were the first woman he had ever seen.

She stared back, unable to tear her gaze away from his.

He walked toward her, and she resisted the urge to hurry to his side.

It took all her strength to stay exactly where she was.

He hadn't expected her.

Darius had been concentrating too hard on the landing to pay attention to the people on the ground. Duke was a marginal pilot at best—used to the mountains, yes, but careless in the plane—and when the storm hit, it had taken all of Darius's magical powers to keep them from being killed in midair.

So he had sat for a moment after they stopped, gathering himself, pretending nonchalance and trying not to shake. Usually he was out of the plane and gone long before Evelyn could approach, but somehow she managed to get the ladder in place (making him feel smaller than he actually was) and the door open before he completely realized that he was safe.

Then he climbed out, trying to maintain what dignity he could, and he saw her, Ariel, standing next to the building as if she had been there all night.

Her skin was no longer ghost-white. The pallor was gone and so were the pain circles under her eyes. Even though her beautiful hair was wet from the rain, she looked prettier than she had at the house—and she had been stunning then.

She was watching him, her expression unreadable. It almost felt as if she knew who he was. But that was impossible. No one knew. His closest friends had never recognized him like this.

And she didn't dare either. How would he explain it? How could he? His job now was to stay away from her until he finished his sentence, so that he wouldn't have to help her find the person she was destined for.

He couldn't be polite. He couldn't give her any hint that he was the man who'd kissed her in the mountains.

He would have to be the Andrew Vari everyone knew and despised.

Darius swallowed hard. Usually it wasn't difficult to play the curmudgeon. In the early years, the dyspeptic attitude hadn't been made up at all. That had been his mood—angry, bitter, and caustic. Later, it became a shield, one that worked well for him.

He'd been doing it so long that it took no effort at all.

Except today. Today it would take all the energy he had left.

He walked across the parking lot, the wind whipping around him but not mussing him, the rain missing him too. He'd forgotten to remove the shield spell from himself and it was too late now. She'd notice.

She hadn't stopped watching him. She seemed to record each movement, as if she were trying to memorize it. He even got the sense that she was nervous.

What was she doing here? He had sent her away. He'd hoped that she would be back wherever she had come from, long gone, the episode in the mountains forgotten—at least by her.

He doubted he would ever forget.

He had almost reached her when he realized he didn't have the appropriate insult. In fact, he didn't have any prepared insult at all. He wanted to compliment her, to tell her she looked a lot better, to tell her he missed her.

To kiss her again.

If he could borrow Evelyn's stepstool.

That last thought sent a bolt of anger through him. Damn his sentence. Damn the punishment that made him small and ugly, looking on his best days like a lawn gnome and on his worst like some sort of hideous doll from a "Twilight Zone" episode.

No insult and feeling insecure. Wonderful. His plan to drive her away was failing even before he opened his mouth.

He'd have to play it somewhat safe then. He'd try to get past her without any conversation at all. And since she was waiting for her precious, gorgeous Darius, all six feet of him, she probably wouldn't even notice the troll walking past her.

As he reached her side, he caught the scent of her perfume, a trace of lilacs mixed with the clean smell of soap. He clenched his right fist, willing himself to keep moving.

"Excuse me," she said.

He stepped past her.

"Sir, please," she said. "Excuse me."

"Why?" he asked, making his voice even more nasal than it usually was. "Did you fart?"

She blinked at him in complete surprise, as if no one had ever asked her that question in her life. "No, I—"

"Then you don't need to be excused." He grabbed the glass door's handle and tugged. Until that moment, he had forgotten how heavy the damn thing was and how awkward it was to open for a person of his (current) height. He always had trouble readjusting after he changed back to Vari.

The wind made it worse. The door was nearly impossible to open. He would have to spell it too.

Ariel came up behind him and grabbed the handle. Apparently she had decided to assist him, but she couldn't get the door open either. The wind pushed on it, and she couldn't maintain her balance on her crutches and find enough force to pull the door open.

"If I wanted help," Darius said, regretting every word, "I'd ask someone competent."

She dropped the door handle as if it burned her. At that moment, Evelyn came up beside both of them and opened the door with astonishing ease.

The inside of Emerald Aviation had been the same for decades. Cheap brown paneling darkened the interior. Bad fluorescent lighting irritated his eyes. Shabby orange plastic furniture in the waiting area only made the room seem more offensive.

This morning, the entire place smelled of burned coffee. A styrofoam cup of the stuff steamed on Evelyn's metal desk, the blotter beneath it stained with rings from past coffee misadventures. A large radio set squawked in the back room, and a phone rang unanswered, as if voice mail had never been invented.

Even before Darius heard the shuffle of crutches on the cheap tile around the doors, he knew that Ariel had followed him inside. *Please,* he wished silently, *please go away. I don't want to be forced to talk with you anymore. Not like this.*

"I'm sorry to bother you," she said, apparently having rethought the excuse-me approach.

"Then don't." He kept his back to her. Usually he was witty and mean. This time, he wasn't even witty.

"It's just that I wanted to thank you."

He hesitated for a fraction of a second. There were a dozen ways to play this one, and since he hadn't thought he'd see her again—especially with his body in this condition—he hadn't analyzed which one was best.

He finally decided on the path of least resistance. Easier might not be better but it was—well, easier.

Darius turned to face her. "Thank me for what?"

Her eyes were wide and green, deep and filled with life. He could still see that hint of a future soul mate floating in them. Dammit, dammit, dammit.

"Calling for the plane."

His heart leapt. So she did recognize him, in some small way. Maybe she had overheard him. Or maybe she knew.

"Lady," he said, "impossible as this may seem, you have confused me with someone else."

She swallowed visibly. "You're Andrew Vari, aren't you?"

"Yeah." He crossed his arms.

"Duke and Evelyn said you're the one who called for the plane."

So she hadn't recognized him at all. He had to work to keep the disappointment from showing on his face. "Of course I called for the plane. How the hell do you think I'd get out of that godforsaken wilderness?''

"Not for you.'' She spoke carefully, as if she were afraid she wasn't being clear. "For me.''

"Lady, once again you are confusing me with someone else.''

"No,'' she said. "Duke picked me up at your house a week ago yesterday. I'd stayed there overnight, after I fell and broke my ankle. Your friend Darius rescued me. I was hoping you could tell me how to contact him.''

The anger Darius had felt earlier at the door, the circumstance, his size, himself, returned. She hadn't recognized him and she was only interested in beautiful Dar. She was as shallow as the rest of them.

"I don't know anyone named Darius. I have never seen you before, and I didn't call for a plane.''

"Yes, you did.'' Evelyn was standing near the door. He hadn't realized she was there. "When you signed off, you called me doll face like you always do.''

"Really?'' He made his tone cold. "I don't remember this phantom radio call.''

"Duke picked her up at your place.''

"A week ago yesterday,'' he said.

Evelyn nodded. Ariel was looking back and forth between them, confusion evident on her face.

"A week ago yesterday,'' he said, "I was nowhere near that house.''

He lied to her. He hadn't lied to a woman in need of a soul mate in more than a thousand years. It was one of his post-Camelot vows. No lies when he was trying to help people.

But he wasn't trying to help her, was he? He was running away from her. Or trying to, and doing a damn poor job of it.

Evelyn snorted. "Where would you have gone?''

As if he couldn't have gone anywhere on short stubby little legs.

He drew himself up to his full height—all four feet of him (well, three feet six of him)—and said, "Oh, I don't know. Down a hiking trail. To a hot springs. To a rafter camping site to meet the chicks. There's a lot to do in the mountains. Or have you forgotten?"

Evelyn raised her eyebrows. "I could've sworn it was you."

"If it wasn't you, then who was it?" Ariel asked.

He shrugged. "Maybe this mysterious Darius radioed in."

"Using your radio?" she asked.

"If he could find it."

Her eyes widened slightly. Apparently in that cursory search of the house she had done, she hadn't found it. "You really don't know who this guy is?"

"Why would I?"

"He was staying in your house. He knew how to use the stove. He cooked me dinner and breakfast. He seemed real familiar with the place."

Darius turned his back to her and walked to the desk. He had some paperwork to fill out before he left. "Maybe he was."

"A man you don't know?" Ariel asked, her voice rising.

He found the paperwork without Evelyn's help. It was the bill that would be dunned against one of the many accounts in the Andrew Vari name. On it, he noted, was $125 for Ariel's return trip.

"I'm only at the place two weeks out of the year," he said, scrawling his Vari signature on the paper. "It's quite possible some guy has been using the place as his own."

"But you were there, or supposed to be." Ariel had moved closer to him. He resisted the urge to move away. "How could you have missed him?"

"Sounds like it was pretty easy." He tossed the paper on the coffee rings.

"Mr. Vari," Evelyn said, "if you didn't call us, you might want to examine that bill."

"Already did," he said, working to keep his tone light.

"But there's a charge for Ms. Summers's plane flight."

"Steep, don't you think, for rescuing someone who broke her leg?"

Ariel gasped.

"You know the rules," Evelyn said. "If it's not life or death, the state won't pick up the tab."

"And suddenly you're a doctor?" Darius said.

"It was a broken ankle," Evelyn said.

"Something you could diagnose from the radio."

"You told us—"

He raised his eyebrows.

"—or at least whoever radioed told us that she needed hospital care, but that she was all right."

"And you trust the word of just anyone," he said.

"It sounded like you. He had your call letters."

"Posted above the radio," he said.

"And he knew how you signed off."

"Well, that's tough to know, ain't it, toots?" He glared at her, letting his anger show. It no longer mattered to him that Evelyn was in the right. He just wanted to get out of there. "I mean, every radio operator in this part of the state hears the communication between stations if they want to. And I have a hunch I'm known as a colorful character around here."

To his surprise, tough old Evelyn blushed. He wondered what she'd said about Andrew Vari, the most colorful mountain man of them all.

"It's okay," Ariel said, swinging herself between them. She had learned how to wield those crutches in the past week. "I'll pay for the trip. It's my expense. You obviously didn't know about it."

He glared at her. The last thing he wanted her to do was pay for anything. His treat, but he couldn't seem kind about it. How to take care of her and push her away? He had no idea.

"Look, lady, I'm richer than Croesus." Not that Croesus was all that rich. But no one still alive knew that except maybe a handful of other mages, most of whom liked to keep up the rumors of Croesus's wealth. "I can pay for this."

"But it's my expense," she said.

"Really? It's on my bill."

"Put there by a person you don't know."

He gave Ariel a sideways grin. "No matter what lies she's told you, I've known Evelyn for years."

Ariel's mouth thinned. "That's not what I meant."

"I know what you meant, honey. It doesn't matter who decided to put it on my bill. I'll pay it and you save your money. Or better yet, put it toward food. You look like you need some."

She looked startled again. Was no one ever rude to this woman?

"I'll pay it," she said to Evelyn.

Evelyn shook her head. "He can do it. Since he's being so rude in other ways."

"I don't take charity," Ariel said.

"Consider it payment, then," Darius said.

"For what?" Ariel asked.

"Shutting up and leaving me alone." He turned away from her and walked through the waiting area to the main door. The brown and gold shag carpet, matted from years of use and neglect, would slow her down.

Behind him, he heard Ariel sigh in exasperation. "Mr. Vari, doesn't it bother you that some stranger used your home?"

"No," he said. "Now that I've met you, I forgive you."

"I didn't mean me," she said.

He put his hand on the glass door, uttered a small spell so that his exit wouldn't be ruined by weight and wind, and then faced her. "Exactly what part of 'shut up and leave me' alone did you not understand?"

Her eyebrows went down in an elaborate frown. She opened her mouth to answer him, but he didn't wait for her words. Instead, he let himself out into the storm.

The wind buffeted him to the side and thunder boomed overhead. The rain was coming down in sheets. He patted his pockets for his car keys, realized he'd left them on the table in the house, and spelled them to his hand.

His steamer trunk sat in the rain behind his Mercedes. Duke had at least gotten it that far.

There was no sign of Duke anywhere, and the women were watching Darius from the inside of the building. He couldn't spell the trunk into the trunk. He would have to do it the old-fashioned, embarrassing way.

Dammit, dammit, dammit. He couldn't be elegant or sophisticated in this body. Even competent was hard.

He popped the car's trunk and stared at the steamer. Sometimes his sense of history got him in trouble. He liked using a steamer trunk most of the time, the stickers on it, the weight. He'd been using this one for more than a hundred years, and never before had it put him in a position like this one.

Oh, well. Watching him struggle with it would give Ariel a good laugh. If she despised him before, she'd probably hold him in contempt now.

Through the glass door, Ariel watched the little man struggle to put his steamer trunk in his car. The trunk didn't seem heavy as much as awkward. It was twice as big as he was, and wider as well. Yet he managed to lift it toward the car, staggering left, then right, as he tried to shove it inside.

"We should help him," Ariel said.

"You mean I should help him," Evelyn said.

"Or find Duke, maybe."

Evelyn snorted. "After that stupid discussion, I'm not helping him with anything. Vari's always been obnoxious and rude, but I never took him for a liar before."

Ariel looked at her. This entire meeting had left her unsettled. She had that same feeling around Vari that she'd had around Darius, as if he were going to say one thing when he would actually say another.

"What do you mean?"

"I talked to him," Evelyn said. "I know it was him. After twenty years on that horn, I don't make mistakes about the regulars. And no one can imitate that voice."

Ariel remembered the throat-clearing, the curse, and the whistling. She wasn't sure if she believed Evelyn or not.

"If he hadn't radioed in, then he wouldn't've paid for the plane trip. And he's nervous as a mountain goat about letting people into his place. He should've been bothered by it."

Ariel glanced outside. He'd gotten the steamer halfway into his car's trunk. Now he was pushing on it with his tiny shoulder. The rain that hadn't touched him before was drenching him now. His crisp white suit looked like clingy pajamas that were one size too big.

"Maybe if we help him, he'll tell us what's going on," she said.

"Naw." Evelyn crossed to her desk, picked up the paper that Vari had tossed, and sat down. "People keep secrets up here. Maybe he was meeting that guy for a reason."

"Like what?"

"How do I know? Maybe they're lovers, or maybe the guy's on the lam from something. Murder or evading child support or running drugs. It could be anything."

Ariel remembered the passion in that kiss. "They're not lovers."

Evelyn gave her a sideways look. "Then the guy's probably on the run, and you got mixed up in something you shouldn't have."

Vari was still shoving the trunk into the trunk. "I'm going to go ask him," Ariel said.

"I wouldn't," Evelyn said. "You don't know what kind of people live up here."

"I met Dar," Ariel said. "He saved my life."

"Yeah, and like as not would kill you if you got in his way."

Ariel shook her head. "Well, he's not here and Andrew Vari is. He won't hurt me. He can't."

Evelyn raised her eyebrows. "It's clear you haven't talked to him much."

Ariel ignored that. She crossed the tile and swung herself onto the carpet. That was slower going. It wasn't as flat as it had initially seemed. Her crutches caught in it. Or actually, Vari's crutches, if his story was to be believed. Darius had given her Vari's crutches.

Although that made no sense. The crutches were bigger than Vari was.

She reached the door. Vari had climbed onto his bumper and was using his entire body to shove the trunk forward. She grabbed the door handle, and only at that moment did she realize that she was going to have the same problem she had before.

"Evelyn," she said, "would you mind—?"

"Yes." But Evelyn got up anyway. Ariel stood aside as Evelyn pulled the door open. The wind caught it and slammed it against the wall. Rain drummed on the concrete.

"I'd rethink this," Evelyn said.

Ariel went out anyway. She wasn't afraid of the elements. She'd raced in weather like this. She swam in the Pacific, all the way to Alcatraz and back, in weather like this. She could hobble across a parking lot.

She was halfway to Vari's car when the wind rose again. The steamer trunk seemed to shrink slightly, then slide into the car. It was almost as if one of the trunks had been reformed to fit the other.

Vari slammed the car's trunk shut, then jumped off the bumper like a kid jumping into a pond—arms raised, legs bent. He looked almost exuberant.

When he landed, he ran to the driver's side and slid in.

"Mr. Vari!" she shouted, but he slammed the door behind him and started the car almost at the same instant.

The car's reverse lights went on, and he backed the thing up so fast, it took her a moment to wonder how he was driving it. She knew his feet couldn't hit the pedals, not when his tiny arm was hugging the back seat as he looked out the rear window.

The Mercedes stopped just short of her—as she somehow knew it would—and then went forward, out of the parking lot, spraying water in all directions. Somehow it missed her.

Then the car turned onto the highway and zoomed away, too fast for her to follow.

She did get a look at the license plate, though. She didn't get the numbers, but she got the state.

Oregon. There couldn't be a lot of Andrew Varis in that small state.

She stared at the now empty highway, rain flowing down her face. She got the very real sense that Andrew Vari was running away from her.

Maybe she had gotten closer than she thought. Maybe her initial sense of him had been right. Maybe he was a kind man, and lying to her had been painful to him.

His words had belied that, but his actions hadn't. He paid for the plane flight, after all.

She leaned on her crutches. "Andrew Vari from Oregon," she said, "I'm not done with you yet."

Nine

Darius drove like a demon until he reached Smith's Ferry, which was little more than a general store and a dot on the map. At least, that was how it had been for decades. Now a small development was attracting crazy Boiseans who didn't mind the commute or wanted to escape what passed for city life in a town that would barely qualify as a Los Angeles suburb.

He was a master at using the hand controls on the column to make the car function better than it would if he were using the accelerator and brake on the floor. His fingers were a lot more dexterous than his feet.

He parked the Mercedes in front of the general store— at least that hadn't changed much—and got out. The store was long and made of unpainted wood, with a wooden sidewalk in front of it.

The interior had the peculiar sweet odor of old candy, fresh plastic, and spilled soda. Tourist gew-gaws like painted mugs and bumper stickers filled the shelves nearest the window. Expensive groceries lined the remaining shelves, with cigarettes and magazines wrapped in brown paper on a shelf behind the counter.

A young girl, who had to be twenty-one because of the cigarettes and the sign warning in big bold letters that this store checked I.D!, leaned on the counter, reading the *National Enquirer* and twisting her long brown hair around one finger. She didn't look up as he walked past. She probably hadn't even seen him.

As he drove, he had spelled his white suit, changing it into a pair of blue jeans and a sweatshirt, the sleeves rolled up over his powerful arms. He also put on boots. He wasn't willing to drive in a storm like this dressed for summer heat.

His clothes as Andrew Vari were always flamboyant, a deliberate rebellion against the appearance the Fates had given him. If people were going to notice him anyway, he wanted to give them something to comment about besides his height. Clothes always did that.

He went deeper into the store, looking for something to snack on. He wasn't really hungry, just restless. He had to get out of that car. Inside it, all he could see through the rain cascading down his windshield was Ariel's surprised face as he backed toward her.

If she had gotten any closer to him, he would have talked with her and told her everything. So to prevent that, he shrank the steamer trunk, shoved it inside the car, and then hurried out of there faster than humanly possible.

He hoped no one noticed that part.

He had driven as far as he felt he needed to. There was no way she could catch him now, even if she had somehow flown to her car, which she couldn't do, not on those crutches. He had a few minutes now, anyway, and he meant to use them.

He needed them.

All that magic use had exhausted him. It had probably taken years from his long life. These past ten days, instead of being restful, had actually used more of his magic and his energy than the previous year had—and he had done quite a few parlor tricks to assist Emma and Michael in their budding romance.

And then there was the matter of the tiny mistakes he'd made. The broken ankle, the amount of time it took for the protect spell to kick in on the plane, the difficulty he had with the steamer trunk—none of that should have happened. All of those spells should have been easy, smooth.

After more than a thousand years, he found himself in need of a familiar. The last time had been disastrous. He didn't want to be burdened with an animal, but he would need one.

Maybe his search for it would take his mind off Ariel and his so-called vacation in the mountains.

And how very rude he had been to her. At least she didn't know that the Andrew Vari who had been so mean to her was really Darius. There was some small comfort in that.

"Hey, kid!" the girl said from the counter.

He sighed. He hated it when people made that mistake.

"Kid, come out where I can see you."

He waved his fingers in front of his mouth, creating a half-smoked cigar. Then he stepped into the aisle.

"What?" he said, making his stupid nasal voice as deep as it would go.

The girl studied him for a minute. She was so completely taken aback that her mouth hung open. "I-I-I'm sorry, sir. I didn't realize . . ."

She let the sentence hang between them. Good manners dictated that he speak next, accepting her apology and then allowing them to both move forward, he to buy what he wanted, she to blush in private.

He wasn't in the mood to be polite.

"I mean," she said when he didn't fill the silence, "all I saw was movement."

"Short movement."

She shrugged, her blush deepening.

"And you equate short with children."

"Well, usually," she said.

"I have news for you, Einstein," he said, "I haven't been a child in more than two thousand years."

She bit her upper lip, then offered him a small smile. "You don't look that old."

He had no idea why he was being truthful lately. Maybe it was a continued reaction to his time with Ariel. Or maybe it was because he'd had a conversation with someone he'd known his entire life—as rare as that was.

"I feel that old today," he said and walked back into the aisle. There he grabbed some beef jerky, Reese's Peanut Butter Cups, and some Rolaids. Then he went to the cooler and removed two bottles of water. He had trouble carrying it all to the counter, and even more trouble placing it there.

The girl, completely uncertain about how to react to him now, moved her hands forward to help, then moved them back. She did this several times, before he said, "I've got it."

She nodded, keeping her gaze averted, and he instantly felt sorry for what he'd done. She was clearly a good kid. She'd apologized, she'd tried to help, and he had made her pay for his foul mood.

"Sorry," he said around the cigar. It wasn't a very good one. Next time he conjured a half-smoked cigar, he'd have to make sure it was Cuban. "I've had a bad day. I just dumped the woman of my dreams."

"You dumped her?" The girl looked up from the register.

Little minds, he thought. Would he be so very hard to love? "Yes," he snapped. "She was chasing my car when I drove off."

"That's romantic." The girl bagged his groceries.

"It wasn't supposed to be romantic," he said, feeling the need to defend himself even though he knew the girl was being sarcastic. "I was *dumping* her."

She handed him his groceries but kept her fingers on the bag. "So you're such a popular guy that you can treat the woman of your dreams like that."

"You don't understand."

"Sure I do," she said. "You have women crawling out of the woodwork to see you. That would be the only reason to treat someone like that. Because you know you can replace her."

He tugged on the bag. "You really don't understand."

"You're right, I don't. Everybody I know has trouble getting a date but you. You're so popular that you can act like a jerk. I mean, that's gotta be the only explanation. You look weird *and* you're mean. Is that what women really want? I don't think so." She leaned forward. "Tell me you were nice to her once in your relationship."

He yanked the bag away from her, ripping one corner. "The best thing I ever did was let her go."

"Does she think so?"

He didn't answer that. Instead he stalked to the door and let himself out.

What gave that girl the right to lecture him? What gave anyone the right? How could she know what his life was like?

The rain had let up momentarily. He tossed the bag on the front seat of his car and slipped inside. The girl was still watching him through the windows.

What was it about her that rubbed him the wrong way? Her attitude? Her assumptions?

Or the fact that she was right?

Over all the years he'd been doing this work, the one thing he had learned was that few people were lucky enough to meet the person of their dreams, let alone talk to that person.

And he had kissed her.

Darius shook his head, trying to shake Ariel from his mind. He could do a spell to stop himself from thinking about her, but the way his magic had been going lately, he might make himself forget everything but her.

He reached into the bag, pulled out the bottled water,

opened it, and took a sip. Warm. He sighed, put the water in the cup holder, and grabbed some beef jerky.

Blackstone would have his head for eating junk like this, but Darius didn't care. Thwarted lovers were supposed to eat terrible food and drink too much and mope for weeks.

Of course, he couldn't tell anyone about what happened. Not that he expected the people in his life to notice anyway. He had a reputation for being difficult that looked like it was just going to get stronger.

He sighed and put the car in reverse, spraying gravel as he drove too fast. The girl was still watching, still judging. Not that he blamed her. He had behaved badly.

At the last moment, he stopped the car and sent a small spell her way. He created it, a tiny weave of lace, barely visible to the naked eye, and blew it toward her. It went through the window and brushed her face before disappearing.

Then he smiled, feeling better.

That spell was small enough and familiar enough that he couldn't screw it up. And he knew it was something she wanted.

A pretty girl in a dump like that could always use a bit of good luck.

Ariel sat in the Download Café, a latte to her left, staring at the screen before her. She sat at a counter that faced the wall, her laptop plugged into the access port beside her. The timer on the port clicked away, the minutes—and the cash they represented—disappearing quickly.

A handful of people sat at the tables in the café, and there was a line for service. But she was the only person sitting at this particular counter, and she hoped it would stay that way.

Her crutches lay on the floor beside her like a barrier. She'd learned, once she returned to Boise, that men seemed to think crutches provided an opening pickup line.

What happened to you? was the least offensive of them. They went down from there. *How could such a terrible thing happen to such a pretty little thing?* Or the most common, most sensitive one, *Didja trip?*

No, she always wanted to answer, *but if you're not careful, you will.*

Friends had told her that she should be thankful that men were so interested in her, and they were probably right. But most men who approached her with lines like that were single for a reason. They were obnoxious and difficult— rather like Andrew Vari had been.

They were probably fine underneath. He had proven to be kind—reluctantly kind, but kind nonetheless—and she knew that she was judging them only on a very small part of their personalities. But they were doing the same with her. She was female, passably pretty, at least to them, and that was all they knew about her. How could anyone have a relationship based on that?

She scrolled down the screen, reading the responses the search engine had found her. She was on her fifth directory— the kind that searched phone records and found people's addresses all over the country—and she had yet to find a listing for a Darius Vari. There weren't a lot of Dariuses either, although there were more than she expected, too many to go through.

She found herself wishing that these directories came complete with high school graduation photos or mug shots. Then at least she would know if she had found the right man.

Even when she limited her search to men named Darius in the Pacific Northwest, there were too many to play guessing games with. None of them were named Vari or any variation (no pun intended) of that name. And she had no idea what else Darius's last name could be.

She sipped her latte and worried about how much time she was spending searching for this man. Never mind the expense—downloading on someone else's service was pricey, but she had no choice, given that she had no apartment—the time this was taking spoke of an obsession. And usually the only thing she was obsessed about was her training.

Ariel closed her eyes. Training. Of course. Something had to fill the void left by her inability to exercise. She was doing physical therapy—sort of, not really enough to count, given the fact that she still had on her cast—but nothing was taking the place of all those hours spent swimming, running, and biking.

Finding Darius had become her hobby.

Not that she knew what to do once she found him. She was hoping for an address or a phone number so that she could contact him and thank him. That way, he would have her address and phone number and maybe contact her in return. She needed something to hope for.

Right now she didn't have a lot.

Part of that was her fault. The injury was going to prevent any kind of training at all. The doctors felt that she'd be able to run again, but that it would take time. They told her that she needed to be patient.

She also needed to figure out what she was going to do to make money. She had money in the bank, thanks to last year's endorsement deals (most of this year's canceled when they learned that she wouldn't be able to swim again), but it wasn't very much. Triathletes weren't that well known, and female triathletes were even less well known. The endorsement deals she'd gotten were small, and she'd had to repay some of the money sponsors had sent her to keep her training for the Hawaii Ironman. That, the unexpected time in the hotel, and all the changes had bitten deeply into her savings.

She was going to have to find some kind of job—and soon.

Ariel set her latte down and hit the link for advanced search. This time, she filled in the fields so that the search might have Darius, might have Vari, might have Oregon,

Washington, or Idaho. At the last minute, she added a might-have Andrew too.

If she was going to spend a bundle on computer time, she might as well get her money's worth.

The search gave her a lot of junk, but as she threaded through it, she found something interesting.

There was only one Andrew Vari in Oregon, and he lived in Portland. She found no listing for an Andrew Vari in Idaho, which made sense, considering these directories were based on phone company records and the house in the mountains had no phone.

Vari was her only link to Darius, and he had a car with Oregon plates.

She had found him.

But she wanted to make sure. She went back to the initial search engine and expanded her search to include newspaper articles and websites. She used the same parameters as before. By hitting "might" instead of "had to" she was getting a lot more information, some of it seeming to be relevant.

Instantly she got some strange hits, most of them with references to something called Quixotic, which, she thought, didn't describe Vari at all. One of the hits was for Quixotic's website, and she clicked on the link.

After a momentary darkness as her machine coped with the change, her screen revealed an elaborate website devoted to food. Apparently Quixotic was a restaurant in Portland, Oregon, and its owner, Alex Blackstone, was a well-known chef, if the reviews on the site were any indication.

The restaurant had been written up in everything from the *New York Times* to the *London Times*. Most of the articles were linked to the site, and she followed the URLs to interesting places. A few of the reviews had photos not just of the restaurant, which looked unprepossessing from the outside, but also of Blackstone.

He was a tall man with long black hair and sharp eyes. He was classically handsome, a type that didn't appeal to

Ariel at all. In many of the photos, his lawyer-wife stood beside him, a petite blonde who looked like she was still in college.

Ariel was confused. She had no idea why the Quixotic site kept coming up in her Andrew Vari search. She scanned the reviews, and while they told her about the excellent grilled salmon and Blackstone's way with recipes that had existed since the Middle Ages, they said nothing about an Andrew Vari.

Until she came across a *GQ* puff piece about the restaurant. In it, the writer mentioned Blackstone's assistant—"a diminutive man named Andrew Vari, who was so close to Blackstone that many of their friends called him Sancho Panza."

It was the word "diminutive" that caught her. A polite word for small. She searched farther, found more pictures, and finally saw one with Blackstone leaning against a bar and Vari beside him, sitting on one of the bar stools. They looked like an unusual pair of men—one tall and elegant, the other short and tough. Yet somehow their comfort with each other came through the photograph.

So she had found Andrew Vari. Ariel picked up her latte and studied the photograph. He seemed calmer than the man she had met. That man had looked panicked.

Vari had been lying about Darius. But why? Because they were involved in nefarious dealings, like Evelyn had suggested? Or because of something else? And how would she ever find out?

She went back to her initial Vari search and stored his home phone number and address on her computer. She would call him. If she couldn't get him at home, she would get him at Quixotic. And then he would give her a way to contact Darius.

If he refused, she'd send a letter to Vari and ask him to forward it to Darius. That couldn't be hard, could it?

She would get her contact. Not as smoothly as she liked, but it would happen.

And maybe she would get to see him again.

Maybe that would stop her thoughts about him, the way she found herself musing over his looks, dreaming of him, and tingling at the memory of his kiss.

She could find a new obsession—and finally move on.

Cupid's Revenge
(February)

Ten

Darius climbed into his chair and sat down next to the stainless-steel table so that he could watch the master chef at work. Blackstone had been experimenting with rabbit stew. He was trying to recreate a recipe he'd had in Queen Elizabeth I's court about 500 years before. In those days, rabbit stew was considered peasant food, but apparently one of her chefs had made it into a delicacy.

Over the years, Darius had watched Blackstone recreate hundreds of recipes. Unfortunately, by the time he found the right combinations, the staff was usually heartily sick of the main ingredient.

Right now, Blackstone was cutting leeks and carrots into very thin slices. He'd been debating about adding potatoes for the last hour. Darius had remained silent on the subject; he had a hunch the missing ingredients in the stew were rot and mold. Even in the palace in those long-gone days, the food was never very fresh.

Darius's chair was really a stool with a seat and a back.

Blackstone had had it made especially for him when he realized that no restaurant would get a five-star rating when its manager spent much of his time sitting on the counters talking to people.

Darius did like to be at eye level, and the kitchen was not set up for that—at least for him. Everything was built for Blackstone, who was at least six feet tall (Darius had never bothered to figure out by how much his friend towered over him) and so Darius often found himself staring at lips of counters and edges of stoves. He could see into ovens and pick things off lower shelves, and that was about it.

It was the middle of the afternoon. The lunch crowd had left and the dinner crowd wouldn't show up for another three hours. A few Power Lunchers lingered over dessert and coffee, their business not done, and some tourists had just arrived.

Darius didn't even have to open the swinging door to know that the new customers were tourists. They showed up after the lunch rush and ordered the swordfish, which had just been favorably mentioned in the new Michelin guide to Portland.

The assistant lunch chef was cooking the mid-afternoon meals, in addition to acting as sous chef for evening. The actual sous chef was on vacation—early February was not a busy time for restaurants in Portland—and everyone was doing a little extra to cover for her.

Except Blackstone, who had somehow gotten this rabbit stew in his head. Lately he'd been doing a lot of dish creation. Darius actually thought it might be a reaction to the fact that Michael and Emma had had their first child in January. Blackstone had decided not to have children a long time ago, but when his friends sent announcements of their little bundles of joy, his verbal response was always joy and his actual response was to create something new and wonderful of his own.

Rabbit stew didn't, in Dar's opinion, measure up to a

newborn daughter with raven black hair and stunning blue eyes. But he didn't tell Blackstone that.

What he was trying to tell his old friend was that they needed a better system for training and keeping their wait staff. Most waiters at upscale restaurants were used to temperamental owners. Blackstone was kinder than most, and although he was temperamental, he usually managed to hide it from his employees.

No, the problem the wait staff had with Quixotic was that they thought the place was haunted.

And why wouldn't they? Sometimes dishes magically appeared from the kitchen. Sometimes a burnt sauce repaired itself. Sometimes the flowers in the bud vases would change between lunch and dinner, and no one could remember doing it.

Blackstone, in his quest for perfection, would occasionally use his magic to alter things in the restaurant, and he was terrifying the staff. Darius had to admit that he was guilty of manipulation at times too, but he usually tried to keep the magic to himself.

"That's the third backup hostess we've lost in the past six months," Darius was saying.

Blackstone didn't seem to notice. He picked up a slice of carrot and held it toward the light. Darius knew what he was doing. If Blackstone couldn't see light through the center of the carrot, then he wasn't slicing thin enough.

"We really need a lunchtime maître d'," Blackstone said without looking at Dar.

"This is Portland." Darius suppressed the urge to sigh. They'd had this discussion off and on for the ten years Quixotic had been open. "You get too formal at lunch and our business will be cut by two-thirds. We're already pushing the price point. If we get snobby on top of it, people will only come here when they're trying to impress someone."

Blackstone set down the carrot and resumed cutting. "You've been saying that forever. Do you have studies that prove you're right?"

"Studies?" Darius crossed his arms. "We don't need studies. We could just do a controlled experiment. Spell this place, create an alternate reality for a few weeks, give us a maître d' at lunch, and see what happens."

Blackstone looked at him sideways. "You didn't do that, did you?"

Darius raised his chin. "Why?"

"Because you need a familiar. Any magic you do would be slightly off, and the results you get—"

"Would be off as well. Gee, thanks for the support, boss." Darius slipped off the chair. He was getting tired of this discussion. He'd been investigating different types of familiars. Blackstone's was a snake named Malcolm who kept himself hidden most of the time. His wife, Nora, would probably have a cat when she came into her magic.

But Darius didn't know what was right for him. And he didn't know why he was having problems with his magic now. He'd been without a familiar for centuries. Maybe the problems were occurring because he was so close to the end of his sentence. Maybe it was the Fates' not-so-subtle way of reminding him that his future would be very different from his past.

He had no idea, though, when the sentence would end. Aside from Ariel, he hadn't met anyone with a soul mate in the past year. Then he frowned. That wasn't entirely true. Emma and Michael's new daughter, Sabrina, had the sign of a soul mate buried deep in her beautiful blue eyes, but she was a bit young. Even if she wanted to be matched up, he would refuse until she was at least six months old.

Usually Darius saw a lot of people who were missing their life's mates. In fact, he often had his pick of people to work with. But since he saw Ariel Summers, he hadn't had a choice at all. Fortunately, she was far away from him. He thought of her often, but he didn't want to see her.

He didn't want to be tempted by her.

And he had been tempted—especially after she had made those phone calls. A whole series of them, spanning the last few months, each time asking him to put her in touch with Darius, each time saying she had a bit more information and she just wanted him to give her the last piece.

It took him a while to realize that she had been getting her information off the Internet, and it was unnerving to realize just how much information about him was available.

She found nothing about Darius, of course. He'd actually done a search on Nora's machine to see if he could find out anything about himself (never telling Nora why), and he found only one mention of his old self, listed as a winner on a website on the ancient Greek Olympic Games.

No other mentions of Darius existed, although he did find hundreds upon hundreds of references to some of his other old aliases. Merlin got the most press, Andvari the dwarf the least.

Blackstone and Nora thought Andvari was his real name. Blackstone had always believed that Darius came from Norway. While it was true that he'd had his interactions with Loki and Thor and the other Norse gods (enough that he got mentioned in more than one Norse mythology book as the dwarf whose fortune Loki had stolen. Actually, Darius had given Loki the fortune as a favor, and Loki had abused it—but that was a long and involved story, one he didn't like to think about much), he was never really part of their pantheon.

The closest he ever came to pantheons was his literary immortality. His influence on Shakespeare and Dickens created some of the more memorable characters in English literature, and he also could make that claim for a Spanish classic as well.

But websites on those characters didn't refer to Darius. It was all the references to Andrew Vari that made him nervous—some of them over a hundred years old.

It might be time to change the alias, or at least leave the Pacific Northwest.

"What's with you?" Blackstone asked.

He had put the carrots and leeks in a pot, along with some

kind of broth and fresh herbs. No rabbit yet. Blackstone couldn't decide if he wanted to use rabbit from one of his suppliers or see if he could find some actual Old English hare of long lineage to replicate the taste.

"What do you mean?" Darius asked, although he had a hunch he knew. He had started to stomp off, only to become lost in thought. These lapses of concentration had become common for him in the last few months, and they were beginning to annoy him.

"You snap at me, start to leave, and then you don't go much farther than the counter. Something's been bothering you, and I think it's got nothing to do with finding a familiar."

Blackstone usually wasn't that interested in other people's problems. Darius leaned against the stainless-steel table leg. If Blackstone noticed Darius's preoccupation, then it had to be really obvious.

"I was just thinking that I've used the Northwest as my home base for more than a hundred years. Maybe it's time to move on."

Blackstone set his knife down, spread his long fingers on the cutting board, and looked at Darius. "You getting tired of all of us?"

Darius shook his head. "It's just come to my attention that I've been here for a long time. Maybe the restlessness I'm feeling has something to do with that."

"Or maybe it has to do with Emma's new baby. Or my marriage to Nora. Things have changed drastically over the last ten years. Sometimes you find change unsettling."

Darius had never found change unsettling, but he'd often used it as an excuse to cover up some of his matchmaking behavior. He gave Blackstone a false smile. "That could be it."

Darius didn't want to continue the conversation, so he pushed open the swinging door and entered the dining room. Only one of the Power Lunchers remained, staring at the bill mournfully as he sipped European coffee in a demitasse.

Blackstone did cater to the trendy coffee crowd, but tradition lover that he was, he also provided old-fashioned types of coffee in old-fashioned ways.

The tourists were exclaiming over their salads and soups, staring at the cast iron wire sculptures on the walls, and rubbing their fingers over the linen tablecloth. Blackstone had decorated the place in Northwest modern—lots of cast iron and neon, with touches of class like the tablecloths and the bud vase on every table.

Quixotic had both a glassed-in balcony and a terrace on the second floor that overlooked the main dining room down below. Its interesting interior was just one of the many things that made people return to the restaurant. The main reason was, of course, the food.

Darius went to the maître d's station and made certain the correct menus were waiting to be handed out that evening. Then he went to the long bar near the front window. He'd found his stool so that he could reach the back bar where the main cash register lurked when he caught a movement out the window.

A faded blue Dodge Caravan was parked outside, its windows fogged. Someone was sitting in the driver's seat, reading a newspaper.

He tried to look away but found that he couldn't. Something about that Caravan caught his attention. It certainly wasn't the van. It was at least ten years old, boxy and covered with grime.

Then the person in the driver's seat set down the paper and rubbed at the condensation on the window with a sleeve. A face appeared in the cleared spot, staring at Quixotic with apprehension.

His heart stopped—or it felt as if it had stopped—or it felt as if it should have stopped.

He'd recognize those sharply defined features anywhere, that shock of auburn hair. He even knew that the eyes, which were too far away to see clearly, were green.

Ariel.

She was right outside.

He hadn't gotten rid of her after all.

Ariel pressed her nose against the cold glass. The rain had stopped, but the damp chill had gone all the way to her bones. Or, more accurately, her bone. Her ankle still wasn't 100 percent, and she felt the changes in weather in that broken bone.

The doctor who removed her cast told her she was lucky. He said, judging by the nature of the break, the injury should have been much worse. There should have been hairline fractures throughout the ankle and the bones of her foot, and there were none.

A miracle, he had said, especially considering how long it had remained unset and vulnerable.

She didn't see it as a miracle, at least not on days like this when it ached. She sighed, and her breath fogged part of the window again.

Time to make a decision.

She told herself she had come to Quixotic to apply for the hostess job advertised in that morning's *Oregonian*. She needed the work. She was becoming desperate. Her savings were gone, thanks to the fruitless move to Portland. A chain of sports stores had hired her to manage their Oregon branches. She'd accepted, moved, and the chain was bought out a month later by a competitor, who immediately liquidated the Portland stores, calling them redundant.

She wanted to call him a few names but had refrained, hoping he would hire her. He didn't, of course. She really didn't have enough experience for the position. She had been a prestige name, one designed to bring in the triathletes who seemed to congregate in this part of the Pacific Northwest, but that was it.

The new owner had seen her salary as a liability, not as an important investment in name recognition and advertising. So she was left with enough money to continue eating and to pay her rent for the next three months. She didn't even have enough money to move back to Boise. Renting a truck, paying first, last, and a security deposit on a new apartment would eat up all her cash.

Not to mention the fact that she didn't want to move back to Boise.

Ariel grabbed the newspaper and held it tightly, staring at the ad. She had driven by Quixotic every day since she had moved to Oregon. She had looked at the nifty calligraphic sign that rose up the side of the building, and the framing neon on top, and wondered what would happen if she walked in. Would she find Darius? Would Andrew Vari talk with her?

Vari had been rude to her on the phone—ruder than he had been in person. But his rudeness had been oddly tender, as if he was apologizing while he was saying terrible things. He did not encourage her—in fact, he made her feel as if she had been bothering him, which, she supposed, she was.

He kept denying that he knew Darius, and she still had the firm sense that he was lying to her.

Maybe she was deluding herself.

She kept telling herself that she had to forget Darius, but in truth, she hadn't stopped thinking about him since the moment she met him.

And now this ad appeared. She had lied to herself to get herself here, telling herself she was only here for the job. After all, how much training did being a restaurant hostess take? She'd waited tables in high school and had done some cocktail waitressing in college. Surely that would qualify her to seat rich patrons in a fancy restaurant.

Besides, if it didn't, she had a tailor-made excuse to talk with Andrew Vari.

She closed her eyes and rested her forehead on the steering wheel. She had been out here for half an hour. Either she went inside or she left.

And if she drove away, she had to promise herself that she would never contact Andrew Vari again.

She sighed, opened her eyes, and checked her hair in the rearview mirror. Then she opened the door and stepped outside.

It was colder than she expected. Chill air sent goosebumps up her nylon-covered legs. Her still-sore ankle complained about the high heels she wore, but she felt she had no other choice. She was very careful about where she put her feet. No sense tripping and reinjuring herself.

She closed the door and smoothed her green dress, thankful that it was made of some shiny wrinkle-proof material. She clutched a matching purse to her shoulder and saw herself reflected in Quixotic's glass door.

She had put on weight since the summer—all that inactivity—but her muscles were still toned and firm and the dress flattered her. It wasn't quite right for a job interview—a bit too cocktail party—but it was better than a business suit or a pair of jeans and a sweater, which were her other choices.

Ariel took a deep breath and grabbed the door's wrought-iron handle. It was cold to the touch. She pulled the door open and stepped inside.

No one manned the maître d' station or the front bar. Some people wearing jeans and turtlenecks laughed heartily at a table in the corner. A man, looking sad and depressed, sipped from a tiny glass cup as he made large slashes across a yellow legal pad on the table in front of him.

Her heart was beating hard. Somehow she had thought Andrew Vari would appear before her, his pugnacious face drawn up in a frown, ordering her to leave. Once or twice she had imagined the elegant Alex Blackstone—a man she had only seen in photographs—would stalk up to her and order her off the premises.

But she hadn't expected to be ignored. She glanced over her shoulder at the glass door. Rain had started to fall, light rain, something Oregonians called a shower. Oregonians had a hundred names for rain, she'd learned, much like Eskimos had for snow.

She was about to turn away when a woman came down

a curving set of stairs. The woman was a petite blonde who wore a bright red business suit. She seemed to be in her mid-thirties and had the kind of easy confidence that always made Ariel nervous.

Ariel couldn't tell if the woman was a customer or part of the staff. She was smiling at Ariel, though, and Ariel couldn't move away.

"Hasn't anyone helped you?" the woman asked, as if someone had committed a crime.

Ariel smiled. "Not yet."

The woman walked to the maître d's desk. It was almost as tall as she was. "Table for how many?"

"None," Ariel said. "I came about the job."

The woman smiled. The smile made her seem very young, almost as if she were a teenager trapped in an adult body. "I'll get my husband, then. It'll be just a moment. Go ahead. Make yourself at home."

She turned away and headed toward the back.

Ariel didn't move. The woman had to be Nora Barr, Blackstone's lawyer-wife who Ariel had read about on so many different websites. One of Portland's most important attorneys, acting as hostess in her husband's restaurant. How strange was that?

She probably wasn't really the hostess. Just making sure everything ran smoothly.

Ariel glanced at her van again. She hadn't given her name. She could still retreat. Drive away, pretend she hadn't been here.

Take Andrew Vari's hints and never see Darius again.

She bit her lower lip, unwilling to make that choice. Instead she walked to the nearest bar stool and leaned against it, waiting to meet the famous Blackstone.

Darius was peering through the crack in the swinging doors. Ariel was standing in the restaurant, wearing a dress that made her look radiant. The green accented her eyes, made her skin into a lovely shade of ivory, and highlighted her auburn hair. She no longer looked like she needed a good meal, and the extra weight emphasized curves he hadn't noticed before.

She was even prettier than he remembered.

Beautiful, actually. Even more beautiful than he remembered.

He groaned as Nora spoke to her.

Go away, he thought—he wished—he prayed. *Please go away*.

The Fates weren't going to be that kind to him. They were going to make him find that woman a soul mate.

Dammit.

"Okay," Blackstone said from behind him. "You have gotten stranger by the minute. What's going on out there?"

Darius jumped and let the door close. He tried for nonchalance as he wandered back to his chair by the table. "Nothing."

"Nothing? Nothing has you spying like a little boy who's afraid his mom will discover that he was the one who put the frog down his sister's dress?"

"I'm not real fond of little boy analogies," Darius said, resisting the urge to go back to the door.

"Well," Blackstone said, "it was the first one that came to mind. From the back, you could have been posing for Norman Rockwell's version of it."

"Then when I turned around, I'd be Andy Warhol's parody of it."

Blackstone grinned. He set down his knife and walked to the swinging door, peering through the diamond panes at his eye-level.

Darius held his breath. He didn't want Blackstone to see her. The reaction was partly defensive—he didn't want Blackstone to know what was bothering him so—and partly reflexive—in the past, women flocked to Blackstone, and Darius didn't want to see Ariel do the same thing.

Blackstone turned toward him, eyebrows raised. "A

woman? You're flustered by a woman? I thought you always flustered them.''

Darius shrugged. "I'm not flustered.''

Blackstone let out a low whistle. "Then I don't want to be around you when you are flustered.''

At that moment, the door swung open and hit him in the stomach. He let out an *oof!* and stepped back.

His wife Nora came in and grinned at him. "I saw you spying on me.''

"Actually,'' he said, apparently unhurt, "I was spying for Sancho.''

She looked at Darius. "You know that woman?''

"What woman?''

"The one who has you flustered.'' Blackstone grinned.

"Has *you* flustered?'' Nora said. "That's not possible.''

"That's right,'' Darius said, hoping Nora wouldn't press him further. He had promised her years ago that he would never lie to her. "Not possible. I have none of the softer emotions, and therefore I have none of the embarrassment emotions.''

"Embarrassment emotions?'' Blackstone said. "Is that what this is about? She embarrasses you somehow?''

"No,'' Darius said, feeling as if he were digging himself into a hole he didn't completely see, "flustering is an embarrassment emotion. One, I hasten to add, that I'm not having.''

Nora's grin grew. She obviously thought he protested too much. And he probably was. "Well, one of you should have some kind of reaction. She's here for the job.''

"Really?'' Blackstone's voice rose. "That's your province, my friend. She'd make a pretty hostess.''

Ariel would. But then he'd have to watch her every day, and he'd know when that one man walked through the door, the one she was going to fall in love with.

"Tell her the job's been filled,'' Darius said to Nora.

Blackstone crossed his arms and pushed against the door, apparently having forgotten that he'd been assaulted with it just moments before. "Lie to her? I thought she meant nothing to you. I thought you didn't know her. I thought she wasn't giving you any softer emotions, and their related cousins, the embarrassment emotions.''

Darius didn't look at him. He took a step toward Nora. ''Please. Tell her that. For me.''

''What's going on?'' Nora asked. ''Is she a friend of yours?''

He winced. ''It's just better if we don't pursue this any further.''

''I've never seen you like this,'' Blackstone said.

''And if you ask her to go, you'll never see it again,'' Darius said.

''Tell me what's going on and I'll stay here,'' Blackstone said.

''Alex,'' Nora said, ''if Sancho doesn't want to see her, maybe we should respect his wishes.''

''I've known Andvari for a thousand years and I've never seen him like this. He's been upset for the past few months. I think maybe I know why now.''

Darius shook his head. ''Aethelstan, please. Tell her to go.''

''Tell me who she is.''

Darius took a deep breath. He wasn't going to say any more. ''No.''

''Why not?''

''Because she's nobody.''

''Come on,'' Blackstone said. ''If she was nobody, then you wouldn't be so upset.''

''Really,'' Darius said. ''We've only crossed paths once before, and I just don't want to see her again. That's all.''

Blackstone peered through the door again. ''It couldn't have been that unpleasant. She's beautiful.''

Darius held his lips together.

''She'd make a great hostess.''

''Alex,'' Nora said again.

"I'm curious," Blackstone said. "You both know how I get when I'm curious."

"So," Darius blurted, "buy me a dog."

"What?" Both Blackstone and Nora spoke in unison.

"You heard me. Buy me a dog."

"What does that have to do with the woman?" Blackstone asked.

Darius was thinking fast. He didn't want to lie with Nora present, but he could mislead them if he was careful about it. "You said I needed a familiar. So buy me a dog."

"Did your magic go awry around that woman?" Blackstone asked.

"I didn't say that," Darius said, but he had purposely implied it.

"What happened?" Nora asked.

"A dog. Something small, so that I'm not dwarfed—so to speak. And not a yappy dog. Something that'll be friendly and is already housebroken."

Blackstone studied him for a moment. "I'm intrigued, Sancho. And you know what happens when I get intrigued."

"No, Aethelstan—"

But it was too late. Blackstone had already pushed his way out the door and into the main part of the restaurant.

"Oh, God," Darius said. "I've got to leave."

"Who is she?" Nora asked again.

"Someone I just can't see for a while," he said, glancing at the back door. But he couldn't make himself go through it, not without looking at her one last time.

He went to Nora's side, and together they peered through the crack in the door. Ariel was standing in front of Blackstone like a supplicant, and if anyone looked embarrassed, she did.

"She's nervous," Nora said.

"She's not the only one," Darius said, as he did a tiny spell so that he could hear the conversation occurring half a restaurant away.

* * *

Ariel hadn't expected Alex Blackstone to be so imposing. He was tall, with long black hair and silver eyes. He wore black jeans, a white T-shirt over a broad chest, and cowboy boots. The outfit suited him.

He made her feel small. Men usually didn't make her feel small, but he was the second one in a year. Darius had made her feel tiny as well.

Blackstone had a physical presence that she was sure women found attractive. But he didn't draw her in the way Darius had.

He stopped beside the maître d's podium and rested his elbow against it. He smiled at her. The look melded his sharp features and gave her a sense of a searing intelligence in a man that she would never want to cross.

"I'm Alex Blackstone. My wife says you're here about the job."

Ariel swallowed hard. "I am."

He tilted his head slightly as if he had heard something beside her words. "You sound uncertain."

He had caught her. She let out a small sigh. "Well, that's not the only reason I'm here."

"Really?" He didn't sound surprised. In fact, it seemed like he had already known. Maybe Andrew Vari had seen her and had warned him that she was a crazy woman, stalking him to find out about a man he swore he didn't know.

"Really." She threaded her hands together.

Behind Blackstone, the solitary man at the table stuck his legal pad into his briefcase, set the small leather folder with the bill inside closer to the bud vase centerpiece, and stood. He looked very disappointed.

"Then why are you here, Miss—?"

"Summers." She had to force herself to concentrate on Blackstone.

The other man had caught her attention. He picked up

the leather folder as if he couldn't decide what to do with it.

"Miss Summers," Blackstone said, and there was an implied question in his words. The question he had asked earlier, the one she kept failing to answer.

"I, um, met your assistant, Andrew Vari, in July." Her voice didn't sound as confident as it usually did.

The man slapped the folder against his hand. Was he waiting for someone to pick it up? Was service generally this bad in this famous restaurant?

"And what did you think of him?"

"He, um . . ." How to answer that question? These men were obviously friends. "He, um—"

"Is different," Blackstone said, as if he were trying to help her out.

"Yes," she said, "but that's not it, exactly."

The man walked toward the maître d's desk. Blackstone turned, almost as if he had known the man was going to approach, even though he had moved silently.

"Mr. Tucker," Blackstone's voice had extra warmth in it, as if warmth were an ingredient that could be added, like oregano. "How was your lunch?"

The man, Tucker, raised his head and seemed to focus on Blackstone for the first time. "Probably the last one I'll have here, Alex."

Blackstone seemed surprised. Ariel moved away, so that she wouldn't be perceived as part of this conversation. "Wasn't the food to your satisfaction? You know I would have prepared another dish—"

"No," Tucker said. "Those two people were my business's last hope, and they weren't buying. So no more expense account. No more business. I just wanted you to know that when I disappeared it was nothing personal. I just can't afford this place anymore."

Blackstone studied him for a moment. "I'm sorry to hear that."

Tucker shrugged. "Things change. I'm sure I'll get used to it in time."

He handed Blackstone the leather folder.

Ariel wanted Blackstone to tell the man the food was on the house, but he didn't. He took the money and, as he did, his fingers brushed Tucker's hand.

For a brief moment, a tiny thread of light formed over Tucker's knuckles. It disappeared so quickly that Ariel would have thought she imagined it, except for the reverse image it flashed against her retina—the way a camera's bulb left images after the photograph was taken.

"Sometimes," Blackstone said, "people just have bad luck. Eventually their luck changes."

He opened the leather folder and removed an already signed credit slip.

"I'm going to void this," he said.

Tucker shook his head. "There's no need."

"I'm sure you have better uses for the money at the moment." Blackstone shrugged. "And the restaurant is doing well. I can afford to serve a meal on the house now and then."

Tucker gave Blackstone a sad glance, almost as if he wanted to protest again but was afraid to push too hard. "Thank you, Alex."

Blackstone nodded. "My pleasure. I want you to come back when you can, Mr. Tucker. There're always ways to accommodate our very best customers."

Tucker nodded, thanked Blackstone again, and made his way to the front door. He still looked defeated, but not quite as destroyed as he had a moment earlier.

Blackstone stared after the man. Ariel watched Blackstone. She hadn't expected kindness from him. Somehow it put her at ease.

"Mr. Blackstone," she said, while he was still staring at the door, "do you know a man named Darius?"

He turned toward her, a frown creasing his brow. "Darius? Darius what?"

She shook her head. "I never learned his last name. He's about as tall as you are, with blond curly hair. He has a runner's build, very blue eyes."

"Darius?" There was something in the way he said the name, an incredulity, as if she were dredging a long-forgotten name out of his past.

"Yes," she said. "He was staying at Mr. Vari's house in the Idaho wilderness area, even though Mr. Vari denies it. He saved my life."

"Mr. Vari?" This time the incredulity was real.

She shook her head. "Darius. I'd like to thank him. But Mr. Vari says he's never heard of him. I'd just like a way to contact him."

"So you came here to see Mr. Vari."

She looked down at her hands. They were still threaded together. "I came for the job. I moved to Portland earlier this year and then my position got eliminated. When I saw the ad, I thought I'd apply. The fact that Mr. Vari's here is icing on the cake."

"Yet you brought that up first."

"Actually, you did."

His smile was gentle. "Have you worked in a restaurant before?"

She was a little startled by the change of subject. "Yes. I waited tables throughout high school and college."

Blackstone left the maitre d's station, placed the leather folder with the soon-to-be voided credit slip near the cash register, and reached beneath the bar.

Ariel glanced over her shoulder. The people at the remaining table were enjoying their entrées. She hadn't seen anyone serve them the food, a fact which she thought odd, since she had been staring right at them.

"Ms. Summers?"

She turned toward Blackstone.

He had set a slip of paper on the counter and held a pen. "Here's an application, if you're interested."

"Yes," she said. "I am."

"Mr. Vari handles the staff. I'll get him."

Blackstone seemed so professional, yet she had the sense that he was amused by her. He gave her the pen, then headed down the aisle between the tables, stopping to charm the people eating their entrées. They all seemed to perk up when he spoke to them, and as he moved on, they talked about him in an excited whisper.

She had forgotten how famous this place was. In the age of the celebrity chef, Blackstone had become an important person.

And she had spoken to him as if he were just anyone. He had made her feel at ease, as if everything were about her, not him.

Perhaps that was part of his charm.

She bent over the application. She had a résumé folded in her purse, but people usually didn't use résumés for simple restaurant jobs. Apparently not even for jobs at high-end restaurants. Still, she reached inside and pulled the résumé out, partly so that it would help her remember everything she needed to know.

Ariel glanced at the glass door.

This was her last chance to leave.

Darius had backed away from the swinging door. He was heading down the hallway to the employee break room, where he had hung his coat, when Blackstone entered the kitchen.

"Thanks for the echo," he said.

That made Darius stop. "Huh?"

"The echo," Blackstone said. "That spell you did so that you could hear our conversation created a lovely reverb that even now is making me slightly dizzy. Can you undo it, please?"

He was often polite when he was angry. Darius snapped his fingers and slipped inside the break room, grabbing his coat off the back of a chair.

Blackstone followed him. "You can't leave now. You have to go see her."

"Why? She's bothering me."

"That's clear." Blackstone crossed his arms and blocked Darius's way out of the break room. "Is Darius who I think he is?"

Darius's heart beat harder than usual. He made his expression as impassive as he could. "I don't know. Who do you think he is?"

"The guy who can't seem to find a hundred people who were meant to be together?" Blackstone's voice held a soft contempt. He had no idea who he was talking to. None at all.

Darius couldn't answer him. "I would like to leave."

"There's a woman waiting to see you."

"I don't want to see her."

"I think you should."

"Who are you? My boss?"

Blackstone's eyebrows went up. "In this restaurant, yes, I am."

"Fine," Darius said, shrugging the coat over his shoulders. "I quit."

"You can't quit."

"I just did."

"Because you're afraid of a woman."

"I'm not afraid of anyone."

"Oh," Blackstone said softly, "I think you are."

Darius felt a blush rise on his cheeks. Some of his emotions were apparently obvious and others were so hidden, not even his best friend knew about them. Not that it was Blackstone's fault. Darius hadn't told him about anything in his life that happened before the birth of Christ. He didn't think it was any of Blackstone's business.

At that moment, Nora opened the door and peeked her head inside. "Sorry," she said, "but there's a problem out front."

Ariel. Darius raised his head. Something had happened to her.

"What kind of problem?" Blackstone was asking.

"One of the diners has collapsed."

Blackstone hurried out the door. Darius followed, silently cursing himself. He should have used that moment to hurry out of the building, but he couldn't bring himself to do it.

The kitchen door was already swinging by the time he reached it. Blackstone's longer legs had gotten him to the table in half the time it took Darius.

Darius shoved his way through the swinging doors and stopped. Ariel was kneeling beside a man who was prone on the floor. She was doing CPR with the skill of an expert. Blackstone knelt beside her and touched the man's chest.

At that moment, the man coughed and seemed to come around. Darius clenched his own hands tightly together. He hoped Blackstone was careful in healing the guy. Ariel was too smart; she might figure a few things out that she shouldn't.

The man started to sit up, but she kept him down, holding his hand and talking to him. The other patrons were fluttering around him, looking useless. Nora was on the phone in the kitchen, apparently having called 911.

Darius wasn't needed here. Ariel was all right, the situation was under control, and he would only make matters worse. He slipped out the side door and stood under the eaves for a moment, feeling shaky.

She had described his other body with such precision: a runner's build, very blue eyes, curly blond hair. And as tall as Blackstone. She had said that part with awe, as if she preferred tall men.

She had been attracted to him. He should have felt flattered by this, but all he could feel was appalled.

He was not the man she thought he was. And the way things were going, he probably would only be that man for two weeks during every year of her lifetime.

He was as big a failure as Blackstone thought he was. He couldn't even do simple spells anymore.

And now the Fates were tempting him.

He didn't think he had enough strength to hold out.

Eleven

Ariel sat with her back to the wall near the kitchen door and watched the restaurant go through its late-afternoon rituals. In the front, the maître d', a slender middle-aged man who looked comfortable in a tux, spoke on the phone. The bartender sliced limes behind the bar, and three different waiters set tables for the dinner crowd.

The mess that had been the dining room half an hour earlier was long gone. The ambulance had come, the paramedics complimenting her on her quick thinking as they strapped the man to the gurney and plied him with oxygen. His family left with him, their meal unfinished, the bill not paid.

How did this place make any money?

Blackstone didn't seem concerned by any of it. He had been the picture of calm beside that dying man. It almost seemed as if his touch had awakened the guy.

In fact, once the ambulance left, Blackstone and Nora seemed more concerned about Ariel. They sat her at this

COMPLETELY SMITTEN   157

table, and Blackstone gave her some of the best stew she'd
ever had in her life. When she found out it was rabbit, her
stomach didn't churn as she would have expected it to.
Instead, she felt like asking for more.

The man really was a magician with food.

She was eating the last of her French bread and leaning
back in her chair. It felt good to be off her feet. Those high
heels did not agree with her ankle at all.

From the conversations she'd already overheard, she realized the first reservations of the evening were for five, and
by five-thirty, the place was going to be full. The kitchen
was bustling, with prep cooks and regular chefs and dessert
chefs and people who specialized in foods she'd never heard
of.

Blackstone was supposed to be cooking tonight, but he
seemed unconcerned. Nora had said that once he figured out
the rabbit stew, he felt his work for the evening was done—
even though it wasn't.

He was sitting across from her now, a frown on his face.
Nora sat next to him, her hand casually resting on his knee.
The two of them looked so affectionate together that it was
hard to believe they'd been together as long as they had.

It was, obviously, true love.

"Ariel," Blackstone said, staring at the side door, "I'm
going to hire you."

She blinked, startled at the turn in the conversation. She
had thought he'd do something to recognize her quick thinking, but not this. "You haven't even checked my credentials."

He smiled. "Credentials are a crapshoot. What matters
in restaurant work is how people handle themselves when
the boss is not around. You weren't even hired yet and you
dug right in."

She set down her bread. "To be honest, I would have
dug right in if he'd fallen on the street."

"I know," he said. "That's what I like."

"You don't know why I'm out of work or what I've done for the past few years or anything."

He faced her, put his elbow on the table, and rested his chin on the palm of his hand. It was a lazy movement that reminded her of Darius. "So tell me."

She glanced at Nora, who was frowning. For some reason, Nora didn't approve of his actions. And that seemed odd, because just a few moments ago, Nora had been very accepting of Ariel.

Ariel took a deep breath and decided to start at the beginning. She told him about the triathlons and the rotator cuff. She didn't tell him about the broken ankle, though. Just the need to rethink her future and the way she had come to Portland for a job that disappeared out from under her.

"I remember that merger. Even though I've lived in this country for . . ." Blackstone paused, as if choosing his words carefully. Nora gave him a sharp glance. ". . . what seems like hundreds of years, I still don't understand the need to merge and get larger. People contact me all the time with offers for the restaurant, ways we can make it a national chain, and I keep explaining that Quixotic is me, and I can't be franchised. No one seems to understand that."

"I do," Nora said, smiling at him. "I don't want you to be franchised. I'd have to share."

"And you don't share well." He smiled back at her. They stared at each other lovingly for a moment, and Ariel had to look away. She felt as if she were intruding on a private moment.

He leaned over and kissed Nora, then slipped his arm around her back.

"So you'll work for me, Ariel?" Blackstone said.

Ariel started. "I—I don't know."

"That's what you came here for."

She nodded.

"That and Andrew Vari."

She froze. What was Blackstone doing? Attempting to manipulate her somehow?

"Yes," she said. "Is he here yet?"

"He left." Nora's tone was flat, as if she were deliberately keeping emotion from it.

"When?" Ariel felt her shoulders tense. She already knew the answer.

Nora's gaze met Ariel's. "When he knew the man having a heart attack would be all right. An—" and she hesitated briefly, as if she were about to say something else "—drew didn't want to see you."

"Why?" Ariel asked, although she already knew the answer.

"He wouldn't say." Blackstone's strangely colored eyes met hers. "In fact, he'd never mentioned you before. Is there something I should know about?"

She looked away. Then she set her plate aside, her hands shaking. But she was the one who had brought it up. In fact, she was the one who started the whole thing by coming to Quixotic in the first place.

"This is embarrassing," she said.

"What is?" Nora asked.

"I've been a real pest." She shook her head, amazed at her own behavior. "I don't blame him for avoiding me."

All the good humor left Blackstone's face. "What happened?"

Ariel took a deep breath and then told him.

Darius was lying on the huge sofa sectional that filled his TV room. The leather upholstery stuck to his bare legs. He was wearing a pair of gym shorts and a torn T-shirt, having given up completely on his usual sartorial elegance.

The big-screen TV was on. He was surfing through the 100+ channels he got on his digital cable system and thinking of Springsteen's lament: 57 channels and nothing on. Or was that some other group? He couldn't remember anymore, and he didn't care.

The not caring was the toughest part. He usually cared

about being accurate in all things. But he had run away today, from his job, his best friend, and everything he cared about—all because of a woman.

And, if he told the truth to himself, he had also run from the contempt in Blackstone's voice.

The TV room was in Darius's basement, a space he had designed especially for solitary entertainment. The basement had no windows. He'd carpeted the walls, put in a fireplace for rainy days, and set up a theater-quality surround sound for the huge television set. He had a high-end DVD player as well as two VCRs, every movie channel in existence, and most movies available on video.

He had lived alone for almost 3000 years. He knew the importance of a comfortable hole to hide in when he was down and discouraged, like he was now.

He had run away from Quixotic. Sure, it had been in a moment of pique, but still. His stability for the past ten-plus years had been that restaurant. He had no idea what Blackstone would think when he realized that Darius had really quit, but he doubted his old friend would approve.

Darius had to find something new—somewhere else to go, some new city in which to reinvent himself. The problem was that he didn't want to leave Portland. He loved it here, and he loved the house.

He had built it to his own specifications. Everything in it was designed for a person less than five feet tall—including the stairs. In fact, he had insisted on making the stairs just right for him. Most staircases were designed for six-foot-tall people, and he tripped on them.

The staircases in this house were fit for his little legs, just like the shelves were in proportion to his little arms and the counters were in easy reach. Even the stove was artificially short.

Blackstone liked to call it Andvari's Playhouse, which in some ways it was. One of the reasons Darius left for his full-size two weeks was that he didn't fit in his own house anymore.

Suddenly he paused in his surfing. One of the pompous get-an-education-by-watching-too-much-TV channels was running a special on the facts behind Greek mythology. What caught his eye was a very famous statue of the Fates, as they had once appeared to Homer (the time Darius had dragged him along to one of his meetings).

As the announcer gave the Fates' names, the TV screen showed ancient portraits of the three of them in their long flowing robes. They were always depicted as they examined the thread of someone's life. Clotho held the spindle of thread, Lachesis carried rods, which she shook to decide a person's fate, and Atropos held a tablet on which she wrote the decision.

"Any good or evil men experienced in their lives," the announcer said, "came from these stern, gloomy, elderly goddesses."

"Oh, God," said a voice behind him. "Let's hope they never hear that description."

Darius didn't have to turn to know the voice belonged to Blackstone. Even though the house was locked as tightly as possible and the alarms were on, Blackstone had gotten in. He must have spelled himself to whatever place Darius was at.

"They've heard it before."

"And you wonder why they're mad at you," Blackstone said. "You bring Shakespeare to them and he portrays them as the witches in *Macbeth*. You take L. Frank Baum and he makes them the prototype for the Wicked Witches of the West and East."

"They were mad at me before that," Darius said.

"Oh?" Blackstone came around the sectional. He sat on the other end and stretched out his long legs on the leather. Then he peered at Darius as if he had never seen him before. "What happened to your clothing?"

Darius looked down at his shirt. The T-shirt was stained as well as ripped, and its logo had long since flaked and washed off. The gym shorts dated from the 1970s and were made of pilling polyester.

"It's the perfect couch-potato clothing," he said. "You know I always dress for every occasion."

Blackstone laughed. When it became apparent that Darius wasn't going to laugh with him, he stopped.

"Time to change, my friend. We have work to do tonight."

Darius shook his head. "I quit."

"You can't."

"I did."

"You run the restaurant."

"You can find someone else."

"You're good at it."

"I was good at it. I decided I don't want to be anymore."

"Because of the woman?"

"Because you were going to make me talk to her."

"What's wrong with her?"

Nothing, Darius thought. She was the most perfect woman he'd ever met.

"Is it because of your meeting in Idaho?"

Dar's breath caught. "She told you about that?"

"She says you lied to her when you got off the plane."

Darius sat up straight. She had recognized that? She knew him? Was that why she was pursuing him?

"She says that your friend knew things about that house of yours that no casual observer would know."

Darius leaned back on the couch. He grabbed a throw pillow and hugged it to his stomach.

"I certainly didn't know anything about it." Blackstone picked at the leather fabric. "I didn't know you had a house in Idaho, one that's apparently been in your family for a hundred years. Careless of you, Andvari, letting people take pictures of you for that length of time."

Darius clutched the pillow tighter and stared at the blank TV screen. Maybe he should just turn it back on and ignore Blackstone. Maybe he should tell his old friend to go away.

Blackstone was watching him closely. "You never told me you knew Hemingway or that you even liked the wilderness."

Darius closed his eyes.

"You never told me you knew Darius." Blackstone shifted his weight on the couch.

The movement went through the sectional, and Darius nearly lost his balance. He had to open his eyes, let go of the pillow, and brace himself with one hand.

Blackstone had a strange look on his face. "I always thought Darius and his inability to finish his sentence was a legend, you know. To teach us all a lesson. Like Sisyphus."

"Sisyphus is still rolling that rock uphill," Darius said.

"You're saying Darius does exist."

"All legends are based in fact. You know that, Aethelstan." Darius sat up and tucked his legs underneath him.

"Why didn't you tell me you knew him?"

"Why should I?" Darius looked at him. "You clearly hold him in contempt."

"I don't know him."

"This afternoon you said—"

"I know what I said." Blackstone ran a hand through his thick hair. "I've always thought he had it easy, considering what he'd done. All he had to do was put people together who loved each other."

"It's not easy." Dar's voice rose. "It's damn hard. People don't pay attention. They don't like to be united. They'd rather fight. Or pick the wrong lover. Or find an excuse to stay away from their beloved for ten years."

Blackstone's eyes narrowed. "This isn't about me and Nora. Any reason you tacked on that last sentence?"

Darius made himself take a deep breath. He couldn't afford to get any angrier than he was. "I don't want to deal with Ariel Summers."

"Why not?"

"She's obsessed with Darius."

"So?"

"It won't be good for her. I won't have anything to do with it."

"So don't tell her about him." Blackstone stood, went to the downstairs refrigerator, which stood in an alcove near the microwave and shelves full of popcorn, and took out a pale ale from the Rogue Brewery.

As he opened the bottle, he paused. Darius slid down among the sections, not wanting to see Blackstone's face, but the man was so tall his expression was unavoidable.

"You're in love with her," Blackstone said, with something like awe in his voice. "That's why you don't want to tell her about Darius. You're in love with her."

"I don't know her," Darius mumbled.

"That explains why you run from her, why you won't talk to her." Blackstone came around the sectional and sat down near Dar. "The man saved her life. She's going to be obsessed with him until someone or something else gets her interest."

"And you think that'll be me?" Darius swept his hands down his tiny body.

"Not in those clothes," Blackstone said.

Darius snorted. "She falls for a guy who looks like paintings of the angel Gabriel and you think she'll go for me?"

"Why not?"

"Have you ever seen me with a woman?"

Blackstone clutched the bottle, as if he didn't know how to drink from it. His epiphany had apparently interrupted his ritual. "I've never seen you interested in anyone before. You are usually so rude, you push them away."

"I was rude," Darius said.

"And she didn't leave."

Darius sighed. "She wants to find out more about Darius. It's not about me at all."

"Why couldn't it be?" Blackstone asked.

Darius pushed himself upright. "You handsome guys have no clue, do you?"

Blackstone blinked at him, clearly astonished at Dar's tone.

"It's never about guys like me. We're the villains of the piece. Or we're the comic relief. You see it everywhere. The evil trolls or the cute dwarves—the little men who take care of Snow White and sing 'Hi-ho!' And then, when Prince Charming shows up, we're supposed to step aside because a beautiful woman wouldn't want one of us when she can have you."

Darius stood and stomped across the cushions, careful to avoid the cracks between the sections. Blackstone watched from his seat at the edge of the sectional.

"And why wouldn't she want you?" Darius asked. "Look at you. Exactly what the fairy tale ordered: tall—"

"I can't help that," Blackstone said.

"Dark." Darius flicked at a lock of Blackstone's black hair.

Blackstone touched his scalp as if Dar's flick had burned him.

"And handsome. The whole package." Darius jumped off the couch and landed on the floor. He was shorter standing full height than Blackstone was sitting down. "You don't have to be smart or brave or funny. Those are just bonuses. All you need to be is pretty and you get the girl, every time."

"I only got the girl once," Blackstone said, clutching his unopened beer bottle as if it were his lifeline.

"Really?" Darius crossed his arms. "Just once?"

"Yeah," Blackstone said. "Nora. And, as you so kindly pointed out, that took ten years."

"Nora," Darius said with emphasis, "is your soul mate. I'm talking about all the other women around you."

"What women?" Blackstone asked. "I didn't see your Ariel make any passes at me."

"Emma thought you were good enough to kiss."

"A thousand years ago," Blackstone said. "Ten years

ago she was throwing dishes at me and begging you to take her out of my life.''

"The next time you go into a crowded room with me,'' Darius said, ''watch the women. See how they look at you, then see if they even notice me.''

"They notice you.''

"Sometimes,'' Darius said. ''They think we're Mutt and Jeff.''

"You have to update your references. No one remembers that comic strip.'' Blackstone retreated into sarcasm and superiority when he was nervous.

"Usually though,'' Darius said, ignoring the sarcasm, ''they don't notice me unless I say something rude. Then they look at me as if I'm a bug they want to squash.''

"Most people don't appreciate rudeness,'' Blackstone said in that same superior tone.

"Don't you think I know that?'' Darius asked. ''When I speak normally, rationally, calmly, they don't hear me at all. I could be talking to myself, although sometimes I even wonder why myself would listen.''

"That's not true,'' Blackstone said. ''I've never noticed anyone ignoring you.''

Darius let out an annoyed puff of air. ''Of course not. I'm always rude.''

"Even before you were always rude.''

"You didn't know me then,'' Darius said.

"I've been around you when you're not rude. People notice you then.''

"I'm only polite to friends,'' Darius said. ''And only when I'm having a bad day.''

"Well, you're not having a bad day today then,'' Blackstone said.

Darius clenched his fists. For the first time in their relationship, Darius felt like punching Blackstone. ''I'm having a terrible day. I found out that my best friend holds me in contempt.''

Blackstone raised his eyebrows. ''You?''

That was a slip. Darius hadn't meant that to come out the way it had. Blackstone had only obviously held Darius in contempt, without realizing Darius was before him.

"Yes, me," Darius said. "You seem to think I've been happy all these years, that I've chosen to live like this."

"I think every lifestyle is a choice," Blackstone said, pulling his beer closer to his chest.

"Really?" Darius leaned in and swiped the beer bottle. It was warm from Blackstone's hand. "You think I like looking like someone's lawn ornament? You think I planned to be the sarcastic sidekick?"

"You're not my sidekick."

"Oh?" Darius stalked to the small counter, found the bottle opener, and opened the ale. Then he walked back to the couch. "What do you call our relationship?"

"We're friends."

Darius shoved the bottle at him. "If we're friends, how come you're surprised I have a home in Idaho?"

Blackstone looked at the bottle as if it were a bomb. "Because you've elected to keep parts of your life secret."

"Have I?" Darius asked. "Or have you just failed to ask me about myself?"

Blackstone's dark gaze met his for a moment. There was something in Blackstone's expression that Darius hadn't seen before. A fear, a vulnerability, maybe even a sheepishness.

"I don't think friends have to quiz each other," Blackstone said.

"I'm not talking about quizzing." Darius pushed the bottle into Blackstone's hand, until Blackstone had to grab it in self-defense. "I'm talking about simple, ordinary, polite questions."

"I ask you questions," Blackstone said.

"Do you?" Darius asked. "Then when I go away for ten days every year, where do I go?"

Blackstone shrugged. "You take vacations."

"Yes," Darius said, letting sarcasm creep into his voice. "What kinds of vacations?"

Blackstone was beginning to look trapped. "You went to Cannes once."

"Once?" Dar's voice rose. "Once?"

"I think," Blackstone said. "You told me about the starlets, I'm pretty sure."

"Pretty sure? Does that sound like a man who is paying attention?"

"Well, you don't talk about yourself much."

"You don't ask much," Darius said. "Sometimes I think I could disappear and no one would care."

"That's not fair." Blackstone swung his legs around so that his feet rested on the floor. He braced the beer on his knee. "When it became obvious that you weren't coming back to the restaurant, I came right over here."

"On your own recognizance, or did Nora have something to do with it?"

Blackstone looked down.

"Nora said something, didn't she?"

"She's quicker about these things than I am. I would have come as soon as I realized there was a problem."

"There was a problem when you didn't respect my wishes, when you insisted that I see Ariel."

"What's with Ariel? Why is she so important?"

Darius grabbed Blackstone's beer and took a swig from the bottle. He wasn't a big pale ale fan—he kept those bottles for Blackstone—but right now the ale tasted good.

"She has a soul mate," Darius said, "and it's not me."

"Did Darius tell you that?"

"Knowing those kinds of things is Darius's specialty," Darius said with just a hint of irony.

"Is he attracted to her?"

"Who isn't?" Darius asked.

"Me," Blackstone said.

Darius glared at him.

Blackstone held up his hands like a man about to be

robbed. "She's not my type. No one has been my type since I met Nora. You know that."

"I thought guys just said that."

"Not this guy." Blackstone grabbed his beer back from Dar. "If he's attracted to her, maybe he's lying to you."

Darius gritted his teeth. Nothing seemed to change Blackstone's opinion. "He's not lying."

Blackstone must have caught the edge in Dar's voice because he inclined his head forward the way people sometimes did with the violent or the mentally ill. "All right. Has he ever been wrong?"

"Not since Napoleon and Josephine, and even that could be argued in his favor. After all, Napoleon wasn't entirely sane—"

"So he has been wrong," Blackstone said.

Darius went to the fridge and got his own beer, a Black Butte Porter. He struggled to open it, debated whether or not he should smash the mouth against the counter, and finally used his magic to get the cap off.

"Right?" Blackstone said. "He's been wrong."

"Not in a very, very long time."

"But everyone's fallible, and if you look at it, this guy's record isn't that good. I mean, he still hasn't completed his sentence."

"Stop harping on that!" Darius said.

Blackstone whistled in surprise. "You guys are close. How come I didn't know that?"

"*You didn't ask,*" Darius said, wondering how thick his friend was.

"I'm supposed to ask you which mages you know and which ones you don't?"

"You don't ask about my life. You never have. I've always counseled you on yours." Darius whirled. "It's part of my function. I'm supposed to celebrate when you get the girl because I'm asexual. I'm not supposed to have a previous history because my life started when I met you. I'm not supposed to have a life outside of yours because you're always the hero.''

Blackstone turned his beer bottle around in his hands. He was watching the motion as if he had just discovered it.

"Do you dislike me that much?" he asked quietly.

Darius closed his eyes. He supposed he deserved that. "You're my best friend."

"Who knows nothing about you. Who can't figure out when you're in pain."

"I'm as responsible for that as you are. You're right. I never told you these things."

Blackstone looked up. "You resent me."

"Why shouldn't I? You're everything I'm not."

"That's not true," Blackstone said. "You're a much better person than I am."

"Ah, the you're-a-nice-guy speech. Usually the sidekick gets that from the girl, but I guess it's okay to hear it from the hero."

Blackstone stood. "You can make as much fun as you want, but I'm very serious. You notice people. You told me for years that Emma wasn't right for me, but I didn't listen. You used your magic to help her in a very creative way when I kept telling her that something like that was impossible. You brought Nora to me that last night. You've saved my life twice and my sanity more times than that. And what have I done for you?"

Darius stared at him for a long time. "For the last thousand years, you're the only person who has treated me with respect."

"Nora does."

"She didn't at first."

"Emma does."

"She called me a little troll back in the Dark Ages."

"She's grown since then," Blackstone said.

Darius nodded. "Yes, she has. But you've been remarkably consistent. You've defended me. You've given me work. And you've been my friend."

"A poor one."

Darius shook his head. "The kind I needed."

"Past tense?"

Darius drank from the bottle. The porter tasted strange after the pale ale. He set the bottle down. "Ariel is different."

"Why?" Blackstone asked.

"Why is Nora different?" Darius asked.

Blackstone nodded. "Point taken."

He didn't say anything for a moment, then he took a swig of beer. Darius stared at him, wondering if he'd said too much. In all their years as friends, he'd never yelled at Blackstone, not about something personal. He'd only yelled at Blackstone when he thought the man was doing something crazy in his own life.

Did Darius hate his good friend? No. But he did resent him at times, and how easily everything came to him. Things hadn't been easy for Darius in a very long time.

"If you believe that Ariel is your Nora," Blackstone said, "then I don't understand why you're running away."

Darius shook his head. Maybe Blackstone would never understand him.

"I mean, you're not giving women much credit here."

"What?" Darius asked.

"Women," Blackstone said. "For every woman with a handsome husband, there are two who marry the homeliest guy in town. Haven't you ever seen gorgeous models on the arms of fairly ugly guys?"

"Ugly guys with money."

"That might be one explanation," Blackstone said. "But I think there might be other reasons. You think Ariel is gorgeous. I can see her beauty, but frankly, I think Nora's prettier."

"You think someone would find me better-looking than you?" Darius snorted. "You have a rich fantasy life."

"I think they might find you more appealing," Blackstone said.

"It hasn't happened in a thousand years," Darius said. "And I'm speaking from experience."

"Maybe you didn't give it a chance."

Darius frowned. "What's that supposed to mean?"

"You're the one who told me that you're always rude. Maybe you've chased women off before they could get close to you."

"Don't you think they should overcome the rudeness?" Darius asked.

Blackstone smiled. "Do you really want me to answer that?"

Darius grabbed his beer and walked back to the sectional. He sat down near Blackstone and grimaced when his tiny feet didn't reach the floor.

"We're not talking about some imaginary woman. We're talking about Ariel," he said.

"Who interests you," Blackstone said.

"Who has a soul mate she hasn't met yet."

"Who's to say that this soul mate is right for her?"

Darius rolled his eyes. "That's what a soul mate is."

"But sometimes we pick the wrong ones. I thought Emma was mine for the longest time."

"I didn't," Darius said.

"You could be wrong about hers."

"I'm not," Darius said.

"Prove it," Blackstone said. "Stop running away from her. Be nice to her. Charm her."

"Charm is your department, or don't you remember, Mr. Prince Charming Prototype?"

Blackstone grinned. "I've never been a prince."

"But you are charming."

"Sometimes," Blackstone said. "I'm not asking you to be me."

"Good," Darius said, "because that's clearly impossible for me. I couldn't be charming even if I were good-looking."

And he knew that based on personal experience. No matter how he looked, women didn't flock to him. They just came closer when he looked like his original self than when he looked like Andrew Vari.

"All I'm saying," Blackstone said, "is fight for her."

"Why?" Darius asked. "So that she can leave me when her perfect soul mate comes along?"

Blackstone finished his beer and set the bottle on the floor. "I've never heard you be so defeatist."

"Maybe you haven't listened."

"You always supported me. In fact, you pushed me at times. I seem to recall you were the one who took me to Nora and who wouldn't let me forget how I felt about her, even though I thought I was going to be with Emma for the rest of my life."

"That's you," Darius said.

"That's my point," Blackstone said. "You do this for your friends, but not for yourself. I bet you're being noble so that your friend Darius can have her. But I don't see him here. He hasn't contacted her. She's trying to find him and she can't."

"Darius isn't her soul mate," Darius said.

"You know this because he told you?"

"He knows it." Darius finished his porter and then burped. He shouldn't have had the beer on an empty stomach.

"All right," Blackstone said for what seemed like the thousandth time. "Then you're being noble for some unknown soul mate, which is even more inexplicable. Being noble gets you nowhere. I did it for Nora and Max, and all she has to show for it was a slightly unpleasant divorce."

"You don't understand."

"You're right. I don't understand why you won't fight for the woman you love." His gaze met Darius's.

Darius closed his eyes and flopped backward on the sectional.

"I hired her," Blackstone said.

"So?" Darius said. He didn't open his eyes. "I quit."

"I want you to come back."

"Not while she's there."

"So you'll get the woman you love fired?"

"Stop saying that." Darius put an arm over his eyes, blotting out the light that filtered through his eyelids.

"Fired?"

"The woman you love. It sounds so pathetic."

"It sounds romantic," Blackstone said.

"Like you know romance," Darius muttered.

"What?"

"Nothing."

Blackstone sighed. "If I have to fire her to get you back, I will."

"What if I say I won't ever come back?" The words were hard to say. He didn't know what he'd do then.

"I don't know." Blackstone sounded sad. "I'd probably nag you for the next thousand years."

"Your restaurant won't be around that long."

"Says who?"

"Says the rules. How're you going to convince the world that you're not Alex Blackstone who has looked the same for the past two hundred years?"

"I have some ideas," he said.

Darius brought his arm down and opened his eyes. "What kinds of ideas?"

"I'd let someone else run it for a while, maybe."

"In a pig's eye."

"Or maybe I'd be an absent owner, coming in only at night."

"As if that would work."

"Or maybe I'll get you to manage it for a while."

"People recognize me as part of the restaurant too."

"Not if you quit."

They stared at each other. Finally, Darius sighed. "You're not being fair."

"Sure I am," Blackstone said. "I'll get rid of Ariel at any moment on your say-so."

"Even if I say so right now."

"Even if." Blackstone didn't hesitate. He was very convincing.

"I don't want her there, Aethelstan," Darius said.

Blackstone studied him for a moment, then sighed and stood. "All right. I'll call her in the morning and tell her."

He picked up both beer bottles and tossed them in the recycling bag under the sink. Darius watched him, but he couldn't sense any posturing on Blackstone's part. The man seemed to mean what he said.

Ariel, who had no job and no money, would lose what little hope she had gained from this day. And it would be his fault, all because he was trying to prove a point. A rather childish point for a man who was nearly 3000 years old, trying to prove that his best friend really liked him by hurting someone else, someone who didn't deserve to be hurt.

"Don't fire her," Darius said.

Blackstone faced him, gaze impassive. He didn't smile triumphantly as Darius might have done. He didn't do anything at all. "I said I would. I keep my promises."

"I'll come back," Darius said. "Keep her on staff."

"I said I'd get rid of her if you came back," Blackstone said. "I mean it. We've been friends for a thousand years, even if I've been a poor one. I've only known her a day. I owe her nothing."

"I know," Darius said. "I appreciate the offer. Keep her."

"You have control," Blackstone said. "If you think she should go, just fire her."

Darius shook his head. "She's your employee. Treat her like the others."

Blackstone grinned. "Which means you can fire her, like you do all the other employees who need to be fired."

Darius propped himself on his elbows. "I don't want to have control over her."

"You won't have any more control over her than you have over our other employees." Blackstone shrugged. "No sense treating her differently."

"I can't be objective," Darius said. "I might fire her for flirting with someone tall, dark, and handsome."

"I won't flirt with her," Blackstone said. "I can promise that."

"Believe it or not," Darius said, "I didn't mean you."

Blackstone flushed. Then he shook his head ever so slightly. "Guess I deserved that. I really don't listen, do I?"

"Let's just say it's not one of your strengths."

Blackstone nodded. "All right. I'll be in charge of hiring, firing, and generally managing Ms. Ariel Summers. Deal?"

"Deal," Darius said.

"Come back to work, then?"

"Tomorrow," Darius said. "I have some gory, violent movies I've been saving up."

Blackstone grinned and picked one off the pile. "*Notting Hill* is violent?"

"Nope, just gory," Darius said. "Now would you get out of here before you embarrass me further?"

"You don't have to ask twice," Blackstone said, and waved his arms. He disappeared in a flash of light.

"Show-off," Darius muttered. Then he glanced at the DVDs. He wished he'd known Blackstone was going to study them. He'd have left out his guy flicks. The romantic comedies were there for research. A matchmaker always needed new tricks for ways to unite couples.

Even if the female half of one of those couples was a woman he cared about more than he was willing to say.

Twelve

Ariel's ankle ached. Acting as lunchtime hostess in a fancy restaurant was harder than she had expected. And she wasn't even the hostess in charge. She was the junior hostess, just learning her duties.

Hostess in Charge or Hic, as she jokingly had called herself, was Sofia Harney, a fiftyish woman who bore a striking resemblance to Sophia Loren. She was tall, big-boned, and big-busted, but surprisingly fit all the same. Her long brown hair was streaked with gray and she wore huge glasses over heavily made-up eyes.

She had a broad laugh and more energy than Ariel could ever hope for. And all the regulars seemed to know and love her.

"Can't believe you're retiring, Sofia," more than one regular said as she led him to his table.

"I'm not retired," she would say in response. "I'm moving to the weekends. At my age, you shouldn't have to work full-time."

Sofia's change to weekends, and the fact that the other junior hostess had quit before Ariel started, meant that Ariel would eventually become the Hic.

"I think any healthy twenty-year-old should learn the value of hard work," said the man currently in front of Sofia. She laughed, just like she had at every variation of this remark she had received all day.

"So do I," she said. "Which is why I'm training young Ariel here."

Ariel smiled, just like she was supposed to, even though she didn't want them to think she was too young for the job or only twenty. She didn't know why her age seemed important here, but it did. She found herself actually wishing for a few more years—or at least the wisdom those years could allow her to claim.

Sofia sat the man and his party at the table where the tourist had had his heart attack the day before. The tourist was doing surprisingly well, the hospital had told her when she called first thing that morning on Blackstone's behalf. In fact, the nurse had told her, he was doing better than any heart attack patient they had ever had.

"I'm beginning to think we should clone him," she had said.

Ariel straightened the menus behind the maître d's stand and looked out the door. The restaurant was gaining its midafternoon quiet. She was looking forward to it. She needed to sit down. Even though she had splurged and bought herself special shoes that would give her ankle good support, her feet hurt. She should have known better than to wear new shoes on the first day of the job.

"You look bushed," Sofia said as she approached.

"You don't," Ariel said, "and you did all the work."

Sofia gave her that lovely smile. "Go. Sit. After I finish here, I'll teach you the mysterious art of the cash register."

Finishing here was making certain that the all-important reservation log was up-to-date. New customers who had never been to Quixotic before were called to remind them about their reservation. The restaurant was so busy that if a customer was a no-show, after an hour, his table was given away.

Sofia said she spent a good part of the early afternoon on the phone, confirming reservations and making new ones. Indeed, the phone had started to ring at one-thirty, just like Sofia had predicted it would.

The afternoon bartender was stacking the bar's dishwasher. He smiled at her as she sat down.

"First rule of Quixotic," he said. "Never look like you're just resting."

Ariel started to stand and he waved her back down.

"All I meant was that you have to drink something if you sit here. What'll it be?"

"I don't suppose I can have a gin and tonic."

"Sure you can," he said, "but I don't advise it. You still have an hour or more."

She smiled, liking his easy affability. Everyone seemed content with their jobs here, and it didn't seem like an affectation. A few had talked softly about the building and how uncomfortable it made them—seems some people thought it was haunted—but everyone loved the restaurant and, as a rule, they liked Blackstone.

She had been warned, though, that he could be cold if something didn't go his way. Not angry, not violent. Cold, as if a withdrawal of his famous charm was enough to make people uncomfortable.

Andrew Vari hadn't shown up yet, which Sofia said was odd. He normally came in around eleven. But apparently he had left work early the day before and hadn't returned. The entire staff thought that was unusual.

The staff didn't have the same opinion of him that they had of Blackstone. They called him the Enforcer, saying he was the one who had all the terrible jobs. He hired and fired, and had called employees in for dressings down on several occasions.

No one disliked him, so far as she could tell, but no one

felt close to him either. A lot of the staff went out of their way to avoid him, considering him odd.

If his treatment of her had been any indication, she could understand why they were leery. He had been one of the rudest people she had ever met.

The bartender held up an empty glass. "First rule of Quixotic," he reminded her.

"Oh," she said. "Sorry. I'm tired and I'm not even done."

"First days'll do that to you."

"Yeah," she said. "I suppose." That and lack of exercise. She'd been worrying too much and not taking care of herself. Time to change that. Even her body was saying so.

He turned the glass so that it caught the light. "Um . . ."

"Seven-Up," she said.

He grinned. "I took you for a diet kinda girl."

"Nope," she said. "I like my sugar pure and unadulterated."

He laughed, and as he did, the main door opened. Ariel slid off the stool, the habit of attending to the door already engrained. She couldn't see who was coming through the glass, though, until he had stepped inside.

It was Andrew Vari.

He wore a dark gray pinstripe suit, a red tie tucked into his vest, and a single red rose in the buttonhole on his lapel. Over his shoulders he had casually slung a black raincoat, and on his head, he wore a fedora with a red hat band. The fedora was tilted rakishly to one side.

The entire look gave him a presence that more than compensated for his height. He looked like he had stepped off a movie set.

"How was lunch?" he asked Sofia, and he clearly wasn't talking about the food.

She smiled at him. "Good afternoon to you too, Mr. Vari. Got out of bed a little late today?"

"Just because you're going to reduce your time at the

restaurant, my dear, doesn't mean you can ask impertinent questions," he said, walking toward the maître d's desk.

"It's too late to change now," Sofia said.

Vari looked at her sideways, and Ariel held her breath. His eyes were blue. She had never noticed that before. They were the deep clear blue of an afternoon sky, and they were striking. She hadn't expected to find any part of him attractive.

"You know," he said to Sofia, "most people here respect me and would never speak to me that way."

Sofia shrugged. "They're just afraid of men who wear clothing as if it were a costume."

He stepped away from the desk and extended his hands down his suit. "What's wrong with my outfit?"

Ariel didn't move. She stood beside her chair, wishing she could disappear behind the bar. She still wasn't sure how to talk with him. She'd thought about it all night and had come up with nothing. She didn't want to apologize, exactly, but she didn't want to upset him either.

"Nothing's wrong with your outfit," Sofia was saying. "That's the problem. It's too precise. By two in the afternoon, most men would be a little rumpled. Their flower would have wilted—"

"Watch it," Vari said. "Most men hate public discussion of wilting."

"—or the creases in their trousers would have been ruined. Or they would be wearing the wrong color socks. Let me see your socks, Andrew."

He frowned at her. "My socks are personal."

"Andrew."

Ariel let out a silent breath. It was clear this was a game to them, a ritual that they both seemed to enjoy. The bartender leaned forward, his bar rag in his hand. He was smiling.

"Sofia, employees aren't supposed to harass the boss."

"You're not the boss," she said. "Blackstone is."

It almost seemed like Vari winced, but the movement was so quick that Ariel wasn't sure she had seen it.

"So I can harass you all I want."

"If that's the case," Vari said, "then I'll have to talk with him. There are laws against sock inquiries these days."

"But they're misdemeanors," Sofia said. "Let's see the socks."

Vari sighed and raised his trousers. His shoes were perfect, black leather with a single tassel. But his socks were an unexpected treat.

They were bright red, like the tie, the flower, and the hat band.

"Oh." Sofia's voice trilled downward in disappointment. "I was hoping for green."

"Green would be wrong," he said with complete seriousness.

"But green would prove that you're not wearing a costume."

"Green would prove that I'm color-blind, which I'm clearly not. You hate that I dress better than you do."

Sofia smiled. "I suspect you have a fashion coordinator on the payroll and I want you to share."

Vari smiled too, and the look was a revelation. His battered face had a warmth to it that Ariel had only glimpsed at the airport. She felt that shock of recognition again, as if she had spent a lot of time with this man at some point in her life.

Sofia had turned toward her. "Andrew," she said, her tone suddenly tentative, "apparently you haven't been introduced to Ariel Summers. She's our new—"

"Daytime hostess; I know." He faced her and bowed slightly, as if he were meeting a duchess. "Miss Summers."

No one had called her "miss" in years. "Mr. Vari."

He rose to his full height. He didn't even come up to her shoulder. "I see that your ankle is better."

Her mouth was dry. "Yes."

"Is it strong enough for you to spend all day on it?"

The bartender was peering at her as if she had grown a second head, and even Sofia's smile had disappeared. Blackstone had come out of the kitchen. Ariel could see him out of the corner of her eye, making his way through the tables toward the front.

Was he coming to protect her? Or to defend his position in hiring her without Vari being there?

"Yes," she said. "It's strong enough. Thank you for asking."

She felt like a schoolgirl meeting the principal. One false step and she'd be gone.

Vari's gaze met hers, and she felt that same flutter again. Something about him drew her forward. She had to struggle to stay where she was.

"Did you ever find your friend Darius?" he asked, and those striking eyes had an odd expression in them. Was it hope? If so, what kind of hope? That she would find Darius for him?

"No," she said.

"You still think I know him." That was a statement and not a question. He was standing awkwardly, his hands at his sides. She got the sense of contained energy, as if he felt like he needed to bolt.

Blackstone had reached them. He paused at the edge of the tables and watched, his entire expression wary.

"He knows things about you and your house that no one else should know," Ariel said.

Vari tilted his fedora back. "You know them."

"He told me."

"And then you somehow confirmed that no one else knew them?"

Sofia glanced over her shoulder at Blackstone, as if she were wondering whether or not to step in. He held out a hand, subtly enough to keep her from moving. Vari ignored it, but Ariel saw it all.

"I saw the pictures of your—grandfather?—with

Hemingway. I had to do a lot of searching before I found them. Darius knew all about it.''

"Mmm," Vari said, but he seemed taken aback.

"You look a lot like your grandfather," Ariel said.

Blackstone raised his chin ever so slightly. He watched Vari as if he were afraid the other man was going to say something wrong.

Vari shrugged.

"You know Darius, don't you?"

"This is not the place for this discussion," Vari said.

Ariel felt hope build. "What is?"

"Maybe after work."

"You just got here. I'm leaving soon." She sounded demanding and knew it. This man was supposed to be her boss and she was acting like she didn't care.

"You're not in a great hurry, are you?" There was a slight edge to his voice, as if the Andrew Vari she had met in Idaho were trying to get out, but he wasn't allowing him to.

She felt very uncomfortable. Everyone was staring and she could feel their concern, although she didn't think it was for her. It felt like they were closing ranks, like she had become an enemy suddenly, for attacking Andrew Vari.

What was it about this rude little man that inspired that kind of loyalty?

Probably the same thing that drew her to him.

"I used to be in a great hurry," she said. "But now so much time has passed that it would be silly to say that I am."

He nodded once, as if he were satisfied with her answer, and then he said, "You look a little pale. Are you sure the ankle is all right?"

She wasn't quite sure how to answer that. Was he trying to get rid of her, or did he actually feel concern? And if he did, why did he? Because she was working there now?

"I'm just tired," she said. "I haven't done this kind of work for a while."

"But she's very good at it," Sofia said in a hearty voice that Ariel hadn't heard from her before.

Vari didn't even turn around. He continued studying Ariel. "I'm sure she is."

She flushed. His tone was so ambiguous, she couldn't tell if he was patronizing her, being serious, or making fun of her, but she couldn't just let the sentence hang between them.

"Mr. Vari . . ." she said.

"Yes?" He had that look of expectation on his face again.

"I know you and I got off to a rocky start—"

"I wouldn't call it rocky," he said. "Bizarre, strange, stalkeresque, maybe, but not rocky."

"Andrew." Blackstone spoke for the first time. He did not sound pleased.

Ariel glanced at her new employer. He gave her a slight nod, as if he was encouraging her. "All I was going to say is that I'll be very professional here. I work until I get good at something. That's what I do."

Vari looked her up and down. Usually she objected to men who gave her the once-over, but she didn't feel he was doing that. Instead, he seemed to be taking her in, trying to see all of her.

"The poor start was partly my fault," he said. "I hate it when my vacation ends. I'm not pleasant."

"It seems that was a difficult time for both of us."

"Indeed," he said. "And now times will be better, right?" She nodded.

"Good." He turned, a sharp, masculine movement executed with the precision of an athlete, something she hadn't thought he was. Yet, as he walked around the maître d's desk toward Blackstone, he moved with an athlete's grace.

Blackstone was watching him too. He mouthed a "thank you" to Vari, a movement so faint that Ariel wondered if anyone else had caught it.

Thank you. For what? For being nice to her? Had Blackstone stepped in? She felt embarrassed. He was her employer, after all. She hoped he hadn't intervened in her life just because he had felt sorry for her.

She shook her head once. She had gotten herself into an interesting position. Nearly broke, working a job she thought she was too good for when she got out of college, living in a town with no family or friends—not that she ever had much support from her family.

She wasn't sure how she had come to this place, but she had seen herself reflected in Vari's eyes, and she didn't like what she saw. A woman who was obsessed with a man she'd only met once, a woman who had pushed so hard that the only contact she had with that man considered her bizarre.

Ariel took a deep breath. It was time to change that perception. She would do a good job here. A very professional job. And her personal life would be no one's business—especially at Quixotic.

Darius stepped into the kitchen and slammed the palm of his hand against the metal table leg before him.

Damn her. She looked so beautiful standing there in her dress. She spoke to him softly and asked about Darius as if he were a completely different person.

And he was, too. Darius knew he was, even though the man she wanted was him. The duality hadn't bothered him for centuries—not like this.

Never like this.

He kept expecting her to recognize him, and he wasn't sure why. She had such clear green eyes, such a sharp intelligence flowing through them, that he thought she, of all people, could see past this shell he wore to the inner man.

Apparently she couldn't.

"Stalkeresque?"

Blackstone had come into the kitchen and was standing behind him. Darius raised his head. The assistant lunch chef was huddled over the stove, stirring something that smelled of burgundy wine and garlic. The salad prep person and that day's busboy looked away when they saw him glance in their direction.

"Yes, stalkeresque," Darius said. "We have to have the problems on the table."

"We do?" Blackstone crossed his arms and leaned against the wall.

"Yes, we do." Darius walked down the narrow hallway past the break room. Just beyond it was the former closet that Blackstone used as an office.

Darius went inside. A table acted as a desk. A computer hummed on top of it. The single filing cabinet dominated the back wall, and a large analog clock rested above that. A transistor radio that had to date from the 1950s sat on a shelf and played 1970s rock and roll from one of Portland's less memorable radio stations.

"I thought you were going to be civil to her." Blackstone closed the door. Darius had known he would come this way.

"I was civil to her. I just had to define our relationship. That's all."

"Which is?"

"Manager/employee."

"Not lovelorn man/beautiful woman?"

Dar's back stiffened. She was lovelorn too—and for him. But he was the only person who knew it.

"When we're at work," he said slowly, "we're manager and employee."

Blackstone held up his hands, as if warding off the words. "All right. Do it your way."

"How would you do it, oh tall, dark, and handsome one?" Darius asked. Immediately, he wished the words hadn't come out of his mouth.

"I seem to remember a discussion about charm yesterday," Blackstone said.

"I seem to remember the sidekick telling the hero that sidekicks don't have charm."

Blackstone grunted and sat on the edge of the table. He

must have bumped it as he did so because the computer's screen saver clicked off, revealing an open recipe file.

"Hasn't anyone told you that each person is the hero of his own life?" he asked.

"Oh?" Darius asked. "Is that why women in those old movie serials always called their rescuers, 'my hero'? I'm sure that when athletes and movie stars are called cultural heroes, that's just a rhetorical term. I know it is when it refers to those broad-minded individuals who risk life and limb to save a child from a burning building. They're not heroes—at least to other people. They're only heroes in their own minds."

"Sarcasm," Blackstone said dryly, "is always the refuge of a person losing an argument."

"Is that why it's one of your favorite verbal tools?" Darius grabbed the computer's mouse and closed the recipe file. The computer asked him if he wanted to save it. He almost clicked no.

Blackstone stood behind him for the longest time, silent and unmoving. Darius had to play with the computer, even though he didn't want to, as if none of this concerned him. He opened the employee files and started a new one for Ariel, even though he didn't have her application in front of him.

"When most people say things like that, it's hyperbole," Blackstone said. "But with you and me, it isn't."

Darius typed in her name, his fingers caressing the keys.

"Over the centuries, you've been angry at me a lot. I've done a lot of stupid things."

Darius moved the cursor to the next line, asking for birth-date. He had no clue what hers was.

"But you've never been mad at me for who I am and how I look before."

Darius moved the cursor to the next line. Address. He didn't know that either.

"Yet twice in two days, you've yelled at me for things I can't change." Blackstone leaned his head against the wall.

"I mean, I could change them, I suppose. I could spell myself so that I looked different—at least for a while. Or I could dye my hair or hunch, or something. But I get a feeling that's not the real problem."

Darius moved the cursor to the line for phone number. He didn't have that either. He knew so little about this woman.

Maybe that was the problem.

He was as obsessed about her as she was about the tall handsome Darius she had met.

"If you want me to fire her, I can still do it," Blackstone said.

Darius sighed and closed the file. "I don't want you to fire her."

"Then what can I do?" Blackstone asked.

Darius shook his head. "It's not you, Aethelstan."

"You said that yesterday, but here we are, one day later, and you're still yelling."

"Yeah," Darius said, "I am."

He swiveled his chair. Blackstone was studying him.

"Have you ever met Cupid?" Darius asked.

"*The* Cupid?" Blackstone asked.

Darius nodded.

"*The* Cupid as in the little cherub in diapers who stabs everyone?"

Darius frowned. "Who taught you your mythology?"

"No one," Blackstone said. "I knew most of it was wrong, so I never bothered to learn it very well."

"No kidding." Darius crossed his arms. "Cupid doesn't stab people."

"Oh," Blackstone said. "He's one of us, I take it?"

Darius nodded.

"What does he do?" Blackstone looked at him.

"Shoots arrows at people," Darius said.

"To make them fall in love?"

"Yeah," Darius said softly.

"You think he's behind this?"

"Maybe," Darius said. "I saw him the morning that I met Ariel."

"Did you get hit with an arrow?"

"No," Darius said.

"Would you remember it if you did?"

"Oh, yeah," Darius said, remembering how startled Robin Hood had looked when he saw an arrow sticking out of his chest. He had stared at the arrow for a long time before he had looked at Maid Marian. Of course, by then the arrow had faded away—and the entire war against King John had, in a single moment, escalated.

"Then how can you blame him?" Blackstone asked.

"Because he may have new tricks," Darius said. "Like you said, I don't normally act like this."

"What are you going to do?" Blackstone asked.

"I'd love to choke the life out of the little weasel," Darius said, "but that's not going to be feasible. I'm in enough trouble as it is."

Blackstone nodded, apparently not realizing that Darius was referring to trouble with the Fates, not with Ariel. "Do you need my help?"

"Not yet," Darius said, "but if anyone asks, just say I was provoked."

Blackstone leaned forward. "You're not going to do anything rash, are you?"

Darius smiled. "When have you known me to be rash?"

And before Blackstone could answer, Darius clapped his hands and disappeared.

Ariel was following Sofia through the dining room, inspecting table setup for dinner. Suddenly a white light flared through the kitchen wall.

"What was that?" Ariel asked.

"What?" Sofia looked around, as if searching for something. "I didn't see anything."

"That light," Ariel said. "Straight in front of us. The kitchen wall."

Sofia stopped, then crossed herself. "You might want to do that."

"I'm not Catholic," Ariel said.

"You might want to convert," Sofia said.

"Why?"

"You're one of those."

Ariel frowned. This conversation had taken a strange turn. "One of whats?"

"The ones who can see." Sofia had lowered her voice.

"See?" Ariel was still staring at the wall. It looked normal now. "See what?"

"The ghosts." Sofia was whispering.

Blackstone had told Ariel about this. "I don't believe in ghosts," she said.

"Then how do you explain what you just saw?"

Ariel shrugged. "A power surge? Problems in the kitchen?"

"To cause a white light? Ariel, if that were the case, we'd hear sirens, fight off fire trucks, hear yelling and screaming. There's been nothing."

"Does everyone else see a white light?" Ariel asked.

Sofia shook her head. "Sometimes they see things disappear or appear. Or float. Sometimes they can see through the walls. Sometimes they hear voices."

Ariel did feel a bit disconcerted. The only other time she had seen lights like this, she had just fallen off a cliff. "What does Blackstone say about it?"

"He says if there are ghosts here, they are benign ghosts."

"Do you believe that?"

Sofia shook her head once. "That's why I try to be here only in the daylight, so that there are fewer of them. But in the winter, in the twilight, sometimes . . ."

She didn't finish her sentence. Instead, she headed toward the front of the restaurant, where the windows showed the darkening sky.

Ariel trailed behind her like a duckling. "I thought we were checking the tables."

"I'm sure they're fine."

"Then what are we doing?" Ariel said.

"Staying here." Sofia had reached the maître d's podium and she clung to it like it was a lifeline.

"Why?" Ariel asked.

"Because," Sofia whispered, "we're only a few steps away from the door."

Ariel resisted the urge to shake her head. She wasn't used to being around superstition. There had to be a scientific explanation for the lights.

She left Sofia's side and headed back through the restaurant, checking the tables as she went. The white linen tablecloths, the large bone china dish whose main purpose was to be whisked off the table as soon as the patron sat down, the expensive silverware, the napkins folded like tulips, all were in place.

This restaurant was like an old clock that had been kept in perfect repair; everything moved along in its time, just like it always had. When Sofia left, Ariel would take her place as a cog in a very big wheel.

Nothing was out of order and there were no more flashing lights. Yet the feeling of discomfort remained.

Ariel let herself into the kitchen, feeling her shoulder muscles stiffen as she did so. She was bracing herself for another encounter with Andrew Vari.

But she didn't see him. Only the cooks and the busboys, and the evening wait staff, who were just beginning to show up for their shifts.

Then Blackstone came out of the back room. He stopped when he saw her, looking like a little boy who had just gotten into trouble. As he walked toward her, he smiled, and his entire demeanor changed. He became the charming employer, the man who had befriended her the day before.

"Is everything all right?" he asked.

"I was just going to ask you that," she said. "I saw a light against the back wall."

"A light?" He sounded confused.

"Sofia said it was ghosts."

He laughed. The sound rang hollow. One of the chefs looked over, his pale skin blotchy from steam.

"I warned you about the superstitions around here," Blackstone said.

Ariel nodded. "I know. Only I'm the one who saw the white light."

"A white light," he repeated, sounding a bit stunned. "You saw it through the wall?"

Interesting choice of words. "I saw it against the wall."

He nodded.

"I'm worried that it could be a short or some kind of electrical problem."

He gave her a half-smile. "You have an analytical mind."

"Isn't that allowed here?" she asked, smiling in return.

"Of course it is," he said. "It might even be better."

"Better than what?"

He seemed surprised that she had heard his last comment. "Better than the rest of us."

He put his hand on her back and propelled her back toward the interior of the restaurant. "Come on," he said. "Let's go see if we can find that short of yours."

Somehow, though, she knew they wouldn't. And she knew that he knew they wouldn't. They were going through the motions, for a reason she didn't entirely understand.

"Shouldn't I bring this to Mr. Vari?" she asked as they left the kitchen. "I thought he was the one who took care of problems with the restaurant."

"He is, usually," Blackstone said. "But I think I'd better handle this one."

"Why?" she asked.

"Because Mr. Vari is gone."

Her heart fluttered. She resisted the urge to put her hand over that sore spot in her chest. "For good?"

Blackstone shook his head. "Only until he figures out what he should have known all along."

"What's that?" she asked.

"That there's more to him than snappy clothes and a pithy phrase."

"Excuse me?"

Blackstone glanced at her. "You have no idea, do you?"

She shook her head. "About what?"

"About what a great man Andrew Vari truly is."

Ariel stopped. "What are you trying to tell me?"

Blackstone studied her for a moment. "Something that's not mine to tell," he said, and walked toward the correct wall.

She found that amazing. She hadn't told him where she had seen the light, yet he seemed to know.

"I was supposed to meet Mr. Vari after work. Is that why he left?"

"I don't think he'll forget you," Blackstone said as he put his hand next to a particularly strange wrought-iron sculpture.

His words echoed the note that Darius had sent her. She felt an odd pang. "But you don't know."

He looked at her sideways, his expression speculative. "I'm beginning to know more than I should."

"Funny," she said, "since I met Mr. Vari, I'm beginning to feel like I know less than I ever did."

"Don't worry," Blackstone said, "everything will turn out just fine."

"That's precisely what I mean," she said. "I don't even know what just fine is anymore."

"You will someday soon," Blackstone said. "I'm sure of it."

Thirteen

Darius popped into the stall of a men's room. Graffiti had been scratched into the walls, all of it in English, and most of it crude. He stared at it, feeling disconcerted.

In the stall beside him, someone coughed. Darius glanced under the stall's side. A dirty pair of tennis shoes were half-hidden beneath a crumpled pair of polyester pants that were pooled at the bottom of a pair of hairy legs.

Darius stood quickly, nearly banging his head on the door's lock.

He was tall again. He hadn't used all his time in his original form this year. He rarely did, in case he needed it for personal emergencies. Most years he didn't. But he had learned this lesson during the Guinevere/Arthur debacle, when he hadn't been able to reappear to either of them as the blond stranger in order to put the record straight.

Since that incident had lasting historical repercussions, he vowed never to do anything like it again.

It felt strange to be tall and thin again. He was just beginning to get used to Andrew Vari. Darius sighed. He still wore his natty gray suit, but it had changed along with him. Now it was long, like he was, and as expertly tailored as it had been before. Only it didn't feel as if it fit him anymore.

The suit wasn't something Darius would wear. Darius had no need to be flamboyant. In fact, Darius, in his modern incarnations, was more of a blue-jeans-and-flannel man. Wearing the clothes of one identity when he was in the body of another felt very uncomfortable.

But he was in Monte Carlo—or he was supposed to be. At least that was where Cupid had said his casino was. But Darius had been to the casinos in Monte Carlo. They didn't have graffiti in the bathrooms, especially graffiti written in English.

Darius opened the stall door and stepped out. The bathroom was a pale industrial blue that had faded with time. A fluorescent light flickered overhead. A dirty mirror hung above the urinals, and the entire room smelled of ineffective deodorizers.

If this was a Monte Carlo casino, then standards had gone down in the five years since he'd been inside one. Normally in such a casino, this suit would be considered de rigueur. But Darius had a hunch that in this place the suit marked him as overdressed.

He found the exit and let himself out. The door led to a hallway that smelled of cigarette smoke. The air was blue, and it was clear that the air-filtration system had broken down a very long time ago. A bank of pay phones lined the wall. Two of them had phone books hanging from metal cords.

Darius picked up one of the books and looked at the cover. Las Vegas. He wasn't in Monte Carlo at all.

He frowned. He distinctly remembered Cupid telling him that his casino was in Monte Carlo. Darius had tailored his spell so that he would arrive near Cupid. Had the spell gone awry?

At that moment, the bathroom door swung open and a

short man stepped out. The man wore a stained T-shirt that barely covered his beer belly, and his polyester pants rode a little too low on his waist. He was balding, but what remained of his curly blond hair had turned silver.

It wasn't until he walked past that Darius recognized the man's distinctive gait. It was Cupid. Darius had never seen him in twenty-first-century clothing. He'd only seen the man in robes and sandals or in a loincloth and wings.

"Cupid?"

The man turned, looking surprised. When he saw Darius, he waved his arms and said, "Shhh!" as loudly as he could. If that didn't get other people's attention, nothing would.

Darius leaned against one of the phones. "Monte Carlo, huh?"

"So I'm ambitious," Cupid said, coming closer.

"Ambitious? I haven't been outside yet, but I assume we're on the outskirts of Vegas, right? One of those areas that development hasn't hit yet. This doesn't look like Monte Carlo at all."

"It's just a name," Cupid said.

"It's a country," Darius said.

"No," Cupid said. "Monte Carlo. It's a name."

"It's a country." Had Cupid lost his brains with his hair? "You told me you had a casino there."

"I said I have a casino, the Monte Carlo. You must have misheard me." Cupid sounded offended, which was Darius's first tip that he had been intentionally misled.

"This is your casino," Darius said.

"Yeah." Cupid crossed his beefy arms. He had a tattoo of a heart with an arrow going through it on his left biceps. Only instead of a name running through the arrow's shaft, there was a single word: *Nevermore*. "It has been for forty-five years."

"I see you've kept the place up."

Cupid nodded. "I do what I can."

"Is there any place we can talk?" Darius asked.

Cupid glanced over his shoulder. "I got some business I gotta attend to."

"Me too," Darius said. "And I'm on a short time schedule. So, where can we talk?"

"Later," Cupid said.

"Now," Darius said. "Or I tell people how you dress when you're not at the casino?"

Cupid's eyes narrowed. "So what's it to them?"

"I have photos." Darius extended his left hand. In it, he had Polaroids of Cupid at the Idaho house.

Cupid tried to grab them, but Darius pulled them out of his reach. "I don't remember you taking those."

"I didn't," Darius said. "Funny how well magic works, isn't it?"

Cupid cursed, loudly and creatively. Then he dug into the pocket of his pants and removed a cell phone. He held up one finger to keep Darius silent and dialed with the thumb of his other hand.

Darius heard some rings as Cupid put the phone to his ear. "Yeah," Cupid said, "it's me. I gotta situation here. I'll be there soon."

Darius could hear a tinny male voice responding, but he couldn't make out the words.

"Believe me," Cupid said, "if it takes longer than fifteen minutes, someone is gonna pay. And it won't be me."

He hung up, put the phone back into his pocket, and glared at Darius. "Let's make it quick."

"Let's make it private," Darius said.

Cupid shook his head, but turned and stalked out of the narrow hallway. It opened into a large room with a low ceiling. Smoke curled in the air. Players sat at kidney-shaped card tables, looking disgruntled. On the far side of the room, people sat before slot machines—the old-fashioned kind, which did not make electronic beeping noises, only the *ca-ching, ca-ching, ca-ching* of coins dropping into a coin tray.

Most of the people on the casino floor were over fifty.

Almost all of them looked like they hadn't left their chairs in days, maybe years.

Big gold signs covered the walls, declaring the casino to be the Monte Carlo, just like Cupid had said it was. There was an air of 1950s elegance gone to seed about the entire place.

Cupid led Darius around the cages to a door nearly hidden in the flocked wallpaper. They went through and immediately the smoke cleared some. The walls were a yellowish white and covered with promotional posters more than forty years old. Some had pictures of Sinatra, announcing a concert he had held in the casino's theater. Others had pictures of the rest of the Rat Pack.

After that, though, the string of famous artists turned into almost-rans and never-rans. The picture of a casino that had a short peak and somehow managed to hang on.

Cupid pushed open a presswood door and led Darius into an office filled with papers and poker chips. A wall of file cabinets blocked the door.

Cupid pushed some newspapers off a chair and pointed to it. "Sit."

"Do you want me to jump and beg too?" Darius asked, not getting anywhere near the filthy plastic.

"Hey," Cupid said, grabbing another chair and sitting on it backwards. "You're the one who came to me. Whazzup?"

Darius shook his head. "You know, for a man who is written about as a semideity in many mythology books and who makes guest appearances on Hallmark cards every February fourteenth, you don't have a lot of dignity."

"Don't need it," Cupid said. "The image is already established."

He grabbed a box off the desk. Cuban cigars. He opened it, and the scent wafted toward Dar. When he was in his Andrew Vari mode, he'd been known to enjoy a cigar or two. But right now, the smell sickened him.

"What did you do to me?" Darius asked, deciding he didn't want to stand in this small, sad room any longer.

"What do you mean, what did I do? You did something to me, pal. Seems to me that's why you got your sentence. Tampering with a semigod, you know. Very bad form."

"When you came to my cabin, you did something to me."

"Oh?" Cupid sat up. "You base this on what?"

"Ariel," Darius said.

"Aerial what? Acrobatics?"

"No," Darius said, speaking precisely. "My feelings for Ariel."

"Aerial what?" Cupid asked again. "Stunts?"

"Ariel Summers," Darius said.

"Aerial summersaults?"

"Are you being deliberately dense?" Dar's fists were clenched. He was going to punch this little fraud if this conversation went on like this much longer. "Ariel Summers is a woman."

"Oh!" Cupid grinned. "The redhead."

"Yes," Darius said. "The redhead."

Cupid got a silly grin on his face. "I love athletic women. Not that Psyche isn't athletic, but you know what I mean."

"I don't want to think about what you mean," Darius said. Then he frowned. "How do you know Ariel? Were you supposed to zap me so that I'd fall in love with her? Was this the final test of the Fates? Let's see if Dar can overcome his own lust and still give the girl the man of her dreams, even if that man is someone else?"

"What?" Cupid asked.

"What do you mean what?" Darius asked.

"I meant what," Cupid said. "As in what the hell are you talking about?"

"I'm talking about my feelings for Ariel."

"*Your* feelings."

"Yes," Darius said.

"*Your* feelings?"

"*Yes,*" Darius said again.

"Really? Your feelings?"

"Well, who else's feelings would we be talking about?"

"Her feelings." Cupid had tucked his knees underneath himself, so that he was sitting up higher.

"Her feelings?" Darius was confused. "What about them?"

"She's supposed to be in love with you."

"What?" Darius asked.

"I shot her. She's supposed to be in love with you."

Darius sank into the filthy plastic chair. He was feeling dizzy and it wasn't from the cigarette smoke. "With me?"

Cupid nodded. "I guess the Fates didn't think anyone could fall in love with you, so I was supposed to intervene. I did, finishing out the last of my new sentence, and then I came to your place for breakfast. You're a hell of a cook, Dar."

Darius reached for one of the Cuban cigars. It felt smooth and small in his long fingers. "But you didn't do anything to me?"

"Did you see an arrow?"

"An entire quiver of them, actually," Darius said. "Hanging between your wings."

"I mean in you, stupid."

Darius glared at him. "I'm not stupid."

"It's beginning to sound like you are. I mean, if you're in love with her and she's in love with you, then where's the problem?"

"She was supposed to fall in love with the next man she saw, right?"

"Yeah, right," Cupid said. "How dense are you?"

Darius ignored the way Cupid had turned his own words against him. "And when were you supposed to shoot her?"

"Before she saw you, which I did."

"Why?" Darius asked.

"What do you mean why?" Cupid asked. "So that you could live happily ever after."

"No," Darius said. "If you were supposed to do that, then you should have shot me too, which you deny."

"I didn't need to," Cupid said. "You're in love with her. You said so yourself."

"I didn't know her when I saw you."

"Sometimes these things just work out." Cupid grabbed a cigar for himself, bit off the end, and conjured a flame on the end of his finger, lighting the cigar. Foul blue smoke filled the room.

Darius set his cigar down, no longer tempted. "This thing isn't working out."

"Oh, sure," Cupid said. "Because you worry too much. Go home, Dar. Kiss the girl. Get married or whatever it is people do these days. It's not my concern anymore."

"No," Darius said. "It's mine. She's obsessed with Darius."

"Darius?" Cupid said. "Since when did we start referring to ourselves in the third person?"

Darius took a deep breath, then coughed, realizing his mistake. He still thought of himself as Andrew Vari. "You know what I mean."

"Actually, no." Cupid took another puff of his cigar. His cell phone rang. "Excuse me," he said, pulling the phone out of his pocket.

"No." Darius grabbed the phone. "We're going to finish this conversation."

"Yeah," Cupid said, his voice rising in panic. "After I get that."

Darius flipped the phone open. "Cupid is busy right now," he said into it and hung up.

"Oh, that'll help," Cupid said. "They think my name is James."

"Then you'll have a bit of explaining to do, won't you?" Darius asked.

The phone started ringing again. Darius slipped it into his pocket.

"I could spell that phone to me," Cupid said.

"Do it," Darius said, "and I'll make sure they can't understand a word you're saying."

"You came to me for a favor," Cupid said, "so stop being a butt."

"I came to you for an explanation," Darius said. "And I specialize in being a butt."

The ringing stopped.

"All right." Cupid put the still-smoldering cigar in a full cut-glass ashtray on the side of his desk. "The Fates were afraid the girl wouldn't fall in love with you, though for the life of me, I can't figure out why."

"I don't need the sarcastic side commentary," Darius said.

"So they gave me the job. I had to shoot her and guarantee that she'd see you next. Which I did, quite efficiently, I might add. I shoot her, she sees you, and falls in love. You see her and fall too, which kinda surprises me, considering all the women you've known. What is it about her? I thought you swore off redheads after Anne of Austria."

"She wasn't a redhead," Darius said.

"Whatever." Cupid held out his hand. "Phone."

"Did the Fates say why her?"

"Oh, you know. The usual crap. Destiny, life's journey, personal growth, blah, blah, blah."

"Hers or mine?"

"Hers or mine what?"

"Destiny. Was it her destiny or mine to fall in love?"

"Well, how am I supposed to know? I'm just the messenger. Literally."

"What about her soul mate?" Darius asked. His heart was pounding. If they had Cupid shoot her, then maybe, just maybe—

"What about him?" Cupid picked up the still-smoldering cigar, stared at it for a moment, and then stubbed it out.

"She has one."

Cupid gave him a disbelieving look.

"Trust me," Darius said. "Being able to see soul mates is one of my many gifts from the Fates."

"Such lovely women they are. Generous. Kind. Manipulative as hell.'' Cupid coughed. It was a smoker's cough, deep and throaty.

"Well?" Darius asked.

"Well what?"

Darius clenched his other fist. If he didn't see Cupid for another thousand years, it might be a thousand years too soon. "What about her soul mate? Didn't the Fates consider him?"

"I assume, since I was instructed to shoot her before she saw you . . .'' Cupid's voice trailed off. "Wait a minute."

Darius stood. He couldn't sit still for this.

"They were very insistent on the arrow."

Darius turned. "The arrow?"

Cupid nodded. "You know. I had various types."

"Right," Darius said. "Gold and lead."

"Oh, man. You are behind the times."

"I am?"

Cupid nodded. "Those were the first crude versions. By the end, I had a hundred different kinds, from the thick Everlasting arrow to the slim Lust-at-First-Sight arrow."

Darius felt his breath catch. "And?"

"And what?"

"What type of arrow did they want you to use?"

Cupid slid back down on the chair. He rubbed his knees as if sitting on them had made them sore. "I forget."

"You just said—"

"I know." Cupid was looking down. "But I forget."

"I take it that the arrow wasn't an Everlasting one," Darius said.

"No moss grows on you." Cupid stood. "Ah, hell, Dar. I thought, what could it hurt? She was pretty and you're not known for your serious relationships. When we met, you didn't even believe in love."

Darius felt as if the air had been knocked out of him. "Three thousand years ago. My life has changed a little in that time."

"Well, you know. I owe you."

Darius nodded.

"I mean, you got punished and all, but I wasn't above feeling a little satisfaction when they said . . ." Cupid shook his head. "I don't feel that way now. I saw you that morning and thought, jeez, you turned into quite a guy, you know. You didn't throw me out or nothing, and you wanted to. I could tell. I mean, we have history, you know?"

"What kind of arrow?" Darius asked.

"It wasn't a bad one. You know. I got the Love Is Blind ones, which I think should be trashed, and the Love the Next Thing You See ones, which can sometimes get ugly and really explains how people can get hung up on, say, a car or something. It wasn't one of those."

"What was it?" Darius asked.

"And it wasn't lead. I haven't used a lead arrow in two thousand years. They got banned."

"Cupid—"

"James. Just call me James. I'm so sick of that little dimpled boy that they draw me like. I mean, I haven't looked innocent, maybe ever. You know?"

"What kind of arrow?"

Cupid bowed his head. "Lustatfirstsight," he mumbled.

"What?" Darius asked, even though he thought he knew what Cupid had said.

"Lust at First Sight." Cupid raised his head. He had a pleading expression on his face. "It's a sweet little spell, really. It's not powerful, not like it could be, you know, overwhelming, because that leads to things people could get arrested for. This was just one of those zippy little spells that sent shivers through the recipient, and it usually leads to love—"

"Usually?" Darius asked.

Cupid shrugged. "Sometimes it goes awry."

"When?"

"When the object of the affection doesn't return it. But you have. I mean, you love the girl, right? That's why you're here, because you've never been in love before and you

wanted me to undo a spell I didn't even do. But I can give
you advice. I mean, I know how to handle this sort of thing,
you know? It was my job, before this place. And after,
actually. For a while, anyway. You know."

"Awry how?" Darius asked.

Cupid frowned. "What is going on with you and that
girl?"

"Woman," Darius said. It was a reflexive comment.
"Awry how?"

"I mean, you shouldn't be having any problems. In fact,
by now, you should be married or at least getting some."

"Cupid—"

"James."

"Eros," Darius said.

"Shh!" Cupid swore. "That's powerful magic you're
just floating around. If someone around here hears that, then
I'm screwed."

Darius crossed his arms. A mage's real name often made
him nervous. "I'll call you that again, Cupid, if you don't
answer me."

"James," Cupid said.

"I'm not calling you James," Darius said.

"Okay. Okay. I forgot now. What did you ask?"

"How can the spell go awry?"

"Oh, yeah." Cupid stood and walked behind his desk.
He was almost hidden by the stacks of papers. "If the lust
is unrequited and unresolved, meaning if the two parties
never get together and if there's no resolution to the initial
attraction, like say if one of them disappears or dies or has
a girlfriend . . . ?"

His voice trailed off and he peered at Darius over the
papers.

"You got another girlfriend? You been screwing around
again? I heard about Anne Boleyn. I have no idea why a
woman with six fingers would appeal to you, but—"

"I never got involved with Anne Boleyn," Darius said.

Other Annes, yes, but not Boleyn. "And I don't have a girlfriend."

"Shame," Cupid said. "You know, you should always have a relationship. The wife taught me that. It's healthier, both mind and body, you know?"

"Cupid!" Darius said. "If the relationship ends at the wrong point, then what goes awry?"

"Well, not if it ends, really, because that means that there was a relationship. But if it never really is one, like if no one does the nasty or declares undying love or has a long romantic weekend on some boat in the Mediterranean, then the spell turns sour."

"How sour?" Darius asked.

"The shootee gets a little obsessed."

"Obsessed?"

"Yeah. You know. Daydreams, focuses on the lustee for a while, maybe has fantasies that should by all means remain private."

Darius closed his eyes and leaned against the door. Make phone calls, look things up on the Internet, pursue the man's friend, who really wasn't his friend but was him, but in a way that couldn't be explained.

"Is this a permanent condition?" he asked, feeling very tired and more than a little sad.

"No," Cupid said. "Just like the lust isn't. It's got to become something else."

Darius opened his eyes. Cupid was watching him a little too avidly. Darius hoped to hell Cupid wasn't playing more tricks on him. If the little guy was, then Darius might just take him to the Fates, whether they were behind the whole thing or not.

"What do you mean, become something else?"

"Well, you know. Lust becomes love or hate or sometimes revulsion, usually friendship. Never indifference. And if it isn't requited, it becomes obsession for a little while. But it turns. You know, becomes something else. Even becomes forgotten after a while."

"How long a while?" Darius asked.

Cupid shrugged. "Varies from individual to individual. You know that."

"How could I know that?"

"Like love. I mean, how many of your clients end up in the Las Vegas Church of the Royal Elvis on their first date?"

"None of my 'clients,' as you so quaintly call them, have ever ended up there."

"Jeez." Cupid ran a hand across the evening shadow on his fleshy chin. "A lot of mine do."

Darius raised his eyebrows but bit back the comment he was going to make. Cupid wouldn't appreciate Darius's analysis of his abilities—especially now.

"Well, you get my point anyway," Cupid said. "Every couple is different, every person is different, every case of lust is different. Hell, some of them are sated in just one night. One very long night, but one night just the same."

"We're not talking about lust," Darius said. "We're talking about obsession, and one woman in particular."

Cupid reached for the stub of his cigar, nearly tipping the filthy ashtray, and caught the whole mess with his left hand. "What did you do, Darius? You had the perfect setup. She comes to you, what, a few hours after I leave, and you have that lovely remote hideaway, and you cook her something delicious, ply her with some wine—hell, with the spell I used, you wouldn't've needed the food or the wine—and you got instant sex, man. Instant. I mean, you could have had a great time for weeks. You could *still* be having a great time."

He set the ashtray back on the cluttered desktop and peered at Darius.

"You're not one of those nuts, are you? That whole courtly love thing back a thousand or so years ago—you didn't believe that garbage, did you? I mean, I had nothing to do with it, and I know you didn't. Psyche said the whole thing was damaging, that worshipping from afar thing was bad for marriages, bad for the knights and their shining armor."

He shook his head.

"You ever notice any of them to have shining armor? I think that's more of a myth than we ever were. Or I ever was, since I never heard of the great god Darius. In fact, I never heard of the great matchmaker god in any religion. You should really try to achieve more. Most of us with magic powers left our footprints in legend."

Darius had nearly had enough.

Cupid frowned. "Although seems to me you did. What was that loving and leaving of Guinevre? I hear that this Lancelot guy really had nothing to do with it and the guy she got involved with looked vaguely like you. In fact, I always thought it was you. You know, you and I were supposed to work the Arthur gig together, but I had to tend to his sister Morgaine first. Talk about your lust turning to obsession, jeez. That woman could hate with the best of them. Or the worst of them, as the case may be."

"Cupid," Darius said.

"So, give, Dar. What'd you do to that poor girl? How come she's obsessing, not lusting?"

Darius didn't want to answer that question because his answer would lead to too many other questions. Instead, he asked, "How long will she be obsessing?"

Cupid shrugged. "Like I said, everyone's different."

"Guess."

"The spell's supposed to last a year. She should get through that and then her head will clear."

"Wonderful." Darius leaned his head against the wall.

"I gotta tell you," Cupid said, "once we've evolved to obsession, a one-night stand won't work. You see, she's been imagining how it would be with you for so long that the real thing can't measure up. Not that I'm saying you couldn't measure up normally, but you know what I mean. And magic isn't going to solve that either, if you know what I mean, because there's no way that you can know her fantasies down to the most intimate detail, if you know what I mean.''

"I know what you mean,'' Darius said through tight lips. "I also know that a man who has been alive as long as you have should be able to speak without using a cliché.''

Cupid grinned. "English ain't my native language. I'm proud of my use of idioms.''

"Yeah, right.''

"Like that one. See, you even got the right inflection—''

"Cupid, she's ruining her life. She's not living her dreams anymore. She's chasing after someone who doesn't exist.''

Cupid leaned forward. "You exist, bud. You're standing right here.''

Darius shook his head. "I'm not the man she thinks I am. You just said it. I can never measure up.''

"And it's not worth the try now.''

"So what do we do?''

"What do you mean, we?''

"I mean 'we' as in you and me.''

"That's what I thought you meant.'' Cupid sighed. "I can't do nothing. It's part of my plea bargain with the Fates. I've done my penance, and to undo it would be tantamount to undoing my entire sentence.''

"I can't believe that the Fates would sacrifice one innocent mortal life for some greater magical plan.''

"They always say they're righteous, but I don't know,'' Cupid said. "They seem spiteful to me.''

Darius shook his head. "What can we do to help Ariel?''

"We already had the 'we' discussion,'' Cupid said. "Ask me again. Use these words: 'What can *I* do to help Ariel?' ''

Darius sighed. He knew Cupid well enough to know the little bastard wouldn't answer the question until Darius asked it correctly. "All right. What can I do to help Ariel?''

"I'm so glad you asked.'' Cupid stretched out his short legs, revealing bright orange socks under those ugly polyester pants. "You give her a new obsession.''

"I thought that's your job."

"No, no. Obsession is just focus. As long as she focuses on you—Darius, as you so royally call yourself, as if you're not here at all—she'll obsess about you. But if you can get her to concentrate on, say, chocolate, or the novels of Dostoyevsky, then maybe she'll switch the obsession to that."

Darius straightened. "Can that happen?"

"Sure." Cupid sat up on the back of his chair, his feet firmly planted on the seat so that the whole thing kept its balance. "So long as she loves the thing you want her to obsess about and she only lusts after you."

"Meaning what?" Darius asked.

"If she loves you," Cupid said, "she stays obsessed."

"Then what do I do?" Darius asked.

"Wait until July and hope that the damage isn't permanent." Cupid's phone rang again. He held out his hand. "It's been over fifteen minutes. Can I talk to the kneecap breakers now before they go after my casino?"

"You're in with the mob?" Darius asked.

"Where've you been?" Cupid asked. "The mob left Vegas in the Nineteen-seventies."

"Then who?"

Cupid frowned at him. "Faeries."

Darius raised his eyebrows. "Faeries? What did you do to them?"

"I made their queen fall in love with an ass."

"I don't think Oberon would want to be described that way," Darius said.

"Oh, c'mon," Cupid said. "You're the one who knew Shakespeare. I always thought you fed him that story."

"You mean about Bottom?"

"Who else?"

Darius pulled the phone out of his pocket and shook his head in wonder. "I always thought that was the only one he made up."

* * *

Ariel couldn't remember being this exhausted in a long time, at least not from physical work. From a race, yes. Only that kind of exhaustion felt different. Then she felt as if she had drained all the energy from her body and rest would replenish her. Her mind was always excited, and she looked forward to the next day.

Here, she felt as if everything was tired, not just her body, but her mind, and that no amount of sleep would cure it. Some of the feeling, she was sure, came from disappointment. The rest from the fact that she was back where she had started all those years ago: a hostess in a restaurant. A job that had little distinction and where she was completely replaceable.

Of course, Sofia did the job well enough that everyone would miss her. But she had put a lot of effort into it. Ariel couldn't imagine feeling enthusiastic about days spent leading people to tables, handing them menus, and ringing up their bills.

She pushed open the door to the kitchen. It smelled heavily of garlic and burgundy wine, along with something breadlike and sweet. The ovens were running as well as the stoves. Someone was baking.

The chefs were busy with the handful of late-afternoon orders, and the salad prep workers were just finishing up. No Andrew Vari.

Ariel sighed. She had really destroyed that relationship. Who could blame him for avoiding her? She had treated him badly, and he hadn't accepted her apology. She wasn't sure if she would have either. She had probably made him feel very insignificant.

She had put as much effort into her pursuit of Darius as she put into anything she wanted. People in the tri-circuit thought she was extremely aggressive, in a sport that encouraged aggressiveness. She could only imagine how it felt to be on the receiving end of her drive when it had to do with another person.

Her cheeks flushed. She slid down the main hallway to the employee break room. The time clock was located there, probably to keep it out of view of all those snobby restaurant reviewers who seemed to line up to investigate Quixotic. Not that a time clock would have been embarrassing, but it wouldn't have the right level of class.

The break room was empty, but it smelled of cigarettes. A large sign above one of the file cabinets read NO SMOKING, and she wondered who was going to get in trouble, or if she was the only person who noticed the smell.

Coats hung on a wire rack, and on top of it, beside the hats, someone had left a hardback copy of the latest John Grisham novel. A bookmark with a chewed tassel marked a spot halfway through.

Ariel went over to the time clock and grabbed her punch card. She slid the card into the machine, hit the button, and heard the machine click as her log-out time registered.

One official day done. Who knew how many more to go.

A light flared, nearly blinding her. For a moment, the time clock vanished and she was staring into a large room filled with slot machines and blue smoke. The stench of cigarettes, body odor, and sweet cleansers nearly overwhelmed her.

Then it vanished—all but the urge to sneeze, which she did. She put a hand to her forehead. No fever. Nothing. Then she braced herself against the wall. It was as solid as it had been before. The time clock was back and the minute hand hadn't changed positions.

No wonder they said this place was haunted, if this was the experience everyone else had around here. Whatever it was seemed real enough. The stench of cigarette smoke, faintly present in the room before, was much, much stronger now.

She put her punch card back and turned around.

Andrew Vari was standing behind her, an expression of

panic on his mashed face. His natty suit was too long for him, and as she watched, it seemed to shrink to fit his form.

She closed her eyes. When she opened them, he was still standing there, only he was tailored as he had been before. Sofia was right; the man's clothing was almost too perfect.

His beautiful blue eyes met hers. Her heart was pounding, as if he'd found her doing something wrong.

"I didn't hear you come in," she said.

He didn't say anything, and she wondered if she was hallucinating him too.

"Did you see a bright light just a minute ago?" she asked.

He seemed startled. "Did you?"

So he was real. Or at least the hallucination was reacting to her properly.

"I saw a light this afternoon too," she said. "I told Sofia about it and she nearly ran to the front of the restaurant."

"Yeah," Vari said. "I think we're losing her because she believes this place is haunted."

"She says she's staying on the weekends."

His smile was small. "That won't last."

Ariel's heart was still pounding, as if she'd just come off a twenty-six-mile course. "Is there that much wrong here then?"

He shrugged. "Nothing's wrong here, but people do see things. Tell me about the light."

"It flashes, like sheet lightning, and then it's gone. Only this time . . ." She didn't want to finish that sentence. He thought she was crazy enough.

"Yes?"

"I thought I caught a glimpse of someplace else."

He raised his eyebrows. That was when she realized his fedora was missing. His outfit looked incomplete without it, but he looked a little more human, as if he could make a mistake or two. She liked him better this way.

"What kind of place?"

She shook her head. She wasn't going to go that far. "It was just a sense impression."

He studied her for a moment. It seemed as if those blue eyes could see all the way through her.

"You punched out," he said after a moment.

"Yes." Her throat was suddenly dry. "Wasn't I supposed to?"

"I promised you that we'd talk after you got off work."

She had thought he had forgotten that. Was that why he was here? Had he followed her into the break room, snuck up on her so silently that she hadn't even heard the door open and close?

She grabbed a chair and was pulling it out when he shook his head.

"There's a deli across the street. Let's go there." He grabbed his raincoat from the coat hanger, reaching up as if it were the most natural thing in the world—which it probably was for him—and letting the hanger swing awkwardly.

She resisted the urge to catch it. Instead, she took her own coat off the hanger, grabbed her purse, and slung it over her shoulder.

"I'll follow you," she said.

He led her to the back exit. The main room of the restaurant was dark. The neon art on the walls flared softly. Someone had lit all the candles on the tables, giving the place a modern, elegant, and intimate air.

Up front, she could make out a man standing at the maître d's post. Sofia had told her that good maître d's were so hard to find that Blackstone had put theirs on salary.

Lucky man.

Vari pushed open the exit door, turned up his collar, and stepped out into the rain. He hadn't put on his hat and didn't seem to notice that it was missing.

She followed, the cool air caressing her face, startling away some of her exhaustion. Vari went to the light and crossed the street, not waiting for her. She had to struggle to keep up.

The deli was of a kind that only existed in the Northwest.

No ethnic foods, no unpronounceable dishes. The salads were all recognizable, from the standard iceberg lettuce fare to the potato and various pasta salads. There were a few dishes that could be heated, and a sandwich bar that had nothing more exotic than turkey and beef.

The coffee bar was more elaborate than the sandwich bar, offering more choices—and some of those were unpronounceable. There was also a wall of desserts, all of them too large and sumptuous.

She ordered a turkey sandwich and a brownie, along with an iced tea, and was surprised when Vari paid for it before she had a chance to whip out her wallet.

"That's all right," she said. "I can get it."

"I know you can." His voice was gruff, and seemed to grow gruffer whenever he did a kindness. She had noticed that in Emerald Aviation.

He ordered a large blueberry muffin and one of those unpronounceable coffees. By the time he'd paid for everything, their order was ready.

She bussed one of the plastic tables and wished for a rag to wipe it off but couldn't find one. So she grabbed a handful of napkins and knocked someone else's crumbs to the floor.

Vari set the tray down and they divided up their food. She took a bite of the sandwich. Her stomach growled as she did so, and she realized that part of her exhaustion had been hunger. She hadn't eaten a thing since breakfast—and that had been half an English muffin and an orange.

"I promised you we'd talk about Darius," he said and took a deep breath, as if the topic made him nervous.

"I'm sorry that I was so pushy. I just want to thank him—"

Vari put up a small hand. It was calloused and scarred, as if he had done a lot of hard labor. "Save it. We both know that if a thank-you was all you wanted, you'd've given up by now."

His bluntness made her gasp. She felt heat rush to her cheeks all over again. "I'm not like that—"

"Not usually, I'm sure." He took another deep breath. He was like a drowning man who couldn't get enough air.

He glanced out the window at the dark, rainy twilight street. She followed his gaze. Cars went by, headlights flaring. Quixotic's neon sign reflected on pools of water covering the sidewalk.

Finally, Vari let out a sigh, as if he had resigned himself to this conversation. He pushed away the untouched blueberry muffin and cradled his tall cup of fancy coffee.

"I've known Darius . . ." His gaze met hers, and she felt a shiver run through her. ". . . his whole life. I guess it's fair to say that. You can say I told you so now."

She sipped her iced tea, not trusting herself to say anything.

"He's . . . prone to disappearing."

She got the sense that Vari was choosing his words carefully.

"And he's been involved in some . . . shady things."

She gripped her own glass tightly. "Is that why you wouldn't tell me about him?"

"I wouldn't tell you because no one is supposed to know he exists." Vari grabbed a bit of muffin, picking the top layer off but not eating it.

"What do you mean? Is he some kind of criminal?"

Vari kept his head down, but he smiled. The smile was both sad and reflective. "Yes."

She couldn't believe it. The man she had met? The man who had rescued her? The man who had kissed her with such tenderness? How could he be some kind of criminal?

"What did he do?" she asked.

Vari closed his eyes, as if the subject pained him. "He ruined a lot of lives."

"How?" she asked, unable to believe him.

Vari got that same sad smile again, shook his head, and opened his eyes. They looked past her, as if lost in memory. "It's too complicated to explain. Let's just say he's very good at manipulating people's emotions."

She felt her breath catch.

Vari looked at her this time, and she got an odd sense that he was very vulnerable. She hadn't thought of this brash man as vulnerable before.

"Including yours?" she asked.

He seemed startled by the question. "I suppose you could say I've been a victim of Dar's actions for a very long time."

"Why didn't you want to tell me that?"

He picked at the muffin again. "You thought he was some kind of hero. That's rare. I didn't want to spoil it."

"Giving me his address wouldn't spoil it. I would just send him some kind of thank-you—"

"Would you?" Vari asked. "Really? Was that what you wanted? Because I think you wanted a lot more."

The heat in her cheeks got worse. "I thought, maybe, there was a bit of interest, but I can live without that. I mean, I'm an adult."

"See?" Vari looked away from her. "He manipulated you too."

"How can you say that? You weren't there."

"A lot of people believe that Darius is incapable of the softer emotions—love. Even friendship."

She frowned. "Do you believe that?"

He broke the entire muffin in half. "Sometimes."

His voice was soft. She got a sense he never opened up like that to anyone.

"So you're not telling me to protect me?" she asked.

"And me." He grabbed the butter and slathered some of it on the half of the muffin he hadn't ruined. "If he hurt you, I don't want to be the one responsible."

"How would you be responsible?"

"If I let him near you." He took a bite of the muffin, then set it down. "Besides, he's gone now."

"Gone?"

Vari nodded. "I have no idea when he'll be back."

"And you wouldn't tell me if he did come back, right?"

She sounded bitter and she knew it. She tried to sound calmer, but his matter-of-fact tone was destroying any hope she had. In some ways, Darius had been her focus since she'd come out of the mountains, his kindness all she'd had to hold on to, his kiss what she dreamed about at night. Without that, what would she have?

"You know, there was an Ariel Summers who was a world-ranked triathelete," Vari said, not answering her question. "Is that you?"

She blinked at him in surprise.

He lifted his cup toward her in a mock toast. "Just because I'm short and ugly doesn't mean I can't dream a little. Triathlon is the ultimate sport. Ironman tests endurance like nothing else. And I remember watching an Ariel Summers surprise the world in Australia a few years ago."

The turkey sandwich had lost its flavor. She set it on the plate, resisting the urge to stand up and leave. "Yeah," she said, and it cost her more than she thought it would. "I used to be a triathlete."

"Used to?" He leaned his chair back on two legs. She got the sense that he was calmer now that they weren't discussing Darius. "I can't believe that an ankle injury would ruin a triathlete's career."

"That happened after."

"What did?" He was watching her, as if she were a test subject, but for what she couldn't tell.

"The ankle injury. I was done before that."

"Why?"

"I tore my rotator cuff." And in this rainy weather, her shoulder was constantly sore.

"I thought things like that heal," he said.

"Sometimes," she said, "but they run the risk of permanent disability. And I couldn't seem to get my strength back up. The swim was always the worst part of my tri career. The shoulder injury sort of sealed my fate. And then the ankle . . ."

She shook her head, not willing to go on. The ankle had

been the last straw. She felt as if she had been betrayed by her entire body.

"What about the ankle?" He brought his chair back down on all four legs, his expression avid.

She shrugged. "It was just one more thing."

"But it's healed, right?"

"Enough to wait tables."

"What about running?" he asked.

"What about it?"

"Is the ankle healed enough for that?"

"I suppose. The doctors said it would be fine."

"So why aren't you?"

"What?"

"Running."

"Why should I? I can't race anymore."

"There're marathons," he said. "And bike races. You don't have to be a triathlete to compete."

She touched the sourdough bread on top of her sandwich. The bread was flaky and light, very good. But she still didn't want it.

How could she explain to him that marathons were nothing? She excelled at much more than that. She swam 2.5 miles, then biked 120 miles and then ran a marathon all in one day. That was what she thought competition was. To break it down into a single tiny piece was silly. It wasn't competition at all.

He tilted his head. "You have an opinion you're not sharing."

She picked up her sandwich and took another bite. It was good and she was still hungry. She ate a bit more, savoring the way the sharp cheddar blended with the smoked turkey.

"You think it's too easy to run a marathon." He gave her a half grin. "You see it as part of a race and not the entire race."

She shrugged, amazed that he could see through her that well, this man who obviously didn't run marathons or race.

"What about extreme marathons?"

She knew about them, but they were part of another sport, something she didn't do and didn't care to do. When she had been racing, she had been very focused on her sport. She hadn't had time for the others.

"What about them?" she asked.

"You think twenty-six-point-two miles is an easy length to run in an afternoon," he said. "It's not a challenge for you."

"I've done it," she said. "More times than I care to think about."

"So what about a hundred miles?"

"Running?" she asked.

He nodded. "They've been doing those races for years now. It's been the subject of some controversy in the sports field. Is that pushing the human body too hard? Too far? Rather like the early days of Ironman, when everyone was considered a nut."

She stared at him. How did he know all this?

"In fact, it's like the early days of marathoning before everyone and his dog decided to try it. In those days, marathoners were considered fringe. Remember?" Then he shook his head. "Of course you don't remember. You're a baby."

She felt a flash of anger. "And how old are you, oh ancient one?"

His gaze met hers, and she saw a challenge in it. "Two thousand, eight hundred and one years old."

She let out a puff of air. "I didn't ask how old you felt."

"Isn't that the truest judge of age?" he asked.

She shook her head, unable to believe the way this conversation had gone.

"So what about it?" he asked.

"What about what?"

"Extreme marathoning." He put his elbows on the table and studied her. "One hundred miles in one day. Could you do that?"

She felt a surge of anger, followed by a feeling she hadn't

had in almost two years. "I can do anything I put my mind to."

"You know that for a fact?"

"Yes," she said.

"So you don't have to run a hundred miles in one day to know you can do it."

"That's right," she said, finishing the sandwich and grabbing the brownie plate. "I know I can do it."

He leaned back and studied her. "But can you win?"

Her gaze met his, and she frowned. She hadn't expected the conversation to go this way. "Why are you asking me this?"

"Because," he said softly, "I sponsor athletes, and I'm looking for a greyhound. Someone who can train and try this new sport, test its limits. I'm willing to bet one has just fallen into my lap. Are you game?"

Her hands were shaking. She hadn't thought about returning to sports. Not at all, and she wasn't exactly sure why. Suddenly she had an offer of a sponsorship and something to train for.

"Why are you doing this? So that I won't nag you anymore about Darius?"

His eyes glinted. "If I sponsor you, you won't have time to nag."

She stared at him. How long had it been since she'd had purpose? She'd tried to make the hike her purpose and that had failed. Then she lost her management job—her attempt at a real life, as most people called it—and all she had left were her fantasies.

They weren't taking her very far.

But she didn't know this man, and the few times he had talked with her, he had been rude to her. Suddenly he was offering her a life on a silver platter.

It made her nervous.

"Well?" he asked.

"I'll think about it," she said.

His smile was wide and real, and she got the odd sense

that he was relieved. "Thank you," he said, as if she had done him a favor.

"I haven't agreed to anything."

"But you're going to think about it," he said. "That's more than enough for me."

She frowned at him. "You act as if this matters to you."

"It does," he said softly. "It matters to me more than I can say."

She studied him for a moment, and saw the light behind his eyes close. He wasn't going to tell her any more. She wasn't sure she wanted to stay here. He made her nervous. Not just because he was strange—he was—but because he made her feel warm and attractive and crazy all at the same time.

"I should be heading home," she said. "Thank you for dinner."

"You're welcome." He made no move from the chair.

She gathered her coat and left him. As she stepped outside the deli, she glanced through the rain-streaked window. His back was to her, and he was hunched forward, as if protecting himself from the world.

What an odd, lonely little man. Then she shook her head. Oh, no. She wasn't going to trade her fascination with a Greek god for someone like Andrew Vari. She'd find something else first.

Maybe he was right. Maybe she should think about running again.

After all, she had nothing else.

Fourteen

Darius sat in the deli for a long time, staring at the mutilated muffin. His large double tall had grown cold, but he didn't have enough energy to get up and buy himself a new one.

Ariel had left, a bounce in her step that hadn't been there before. He hoped the bounce would stay.

He couldn't believe what he had just done. He had told her parts of the truth to take her attention away from her precious Darius, and he had tried to redirect her back to sports.

He'd planned, as he left Cupid, to talk to her about marathoning. It was an accepted sport. The top athletes were well known. There was some good prize money and there were good endorsement deals.

But he'd seen that contempt in her gaze and knew that marathons wouldn't hold her. She thought they were for wimps. He shook his head. They weren't, but she had been one of the top female Ironman athletes in the world. She ran marathons for *practice*. No wonder she had looked at him that way.

He had only seen her weak and broken, as in the mountains, or listless and lost, as she had been here. He had only seen hints of the woman she really was, the one who had enough physical strength to be a distance athlete in three different sports, and the one who had enough mental toughness to compete in all three on the very same day.

Except for the moments during her fall. Then he had truly seen what an exceptional woman she was.

That expression on her face when he had mentioned marathons had startled him, and he had spoken without thinking. He knew that groups of runners who no longer felt challenged by the marathon had started the 100-mile races, but he had no idea if those races were sanctioned or if they were taken seriously.

He kept up with sports, but until now it had been an idle curiosity, not a passion.

If he was going to sponsor Ariel, it had to become a passion.

Sponsor. He sighed, slid his chair back, and walked to the counter. There he bought himself a meatball sandwich and another large double tall. This time he was going to eat, not pick at his food.

He needed to think.

He wasn't sure where the sponsorship comment had come from. Being at Ariel's side for the next six months was certainly not something he had planned on. The more he thought about it, the more the idea made him feel uncomfortable.

After all, he was the cause of her problems in the first place. If the Fates hadn't needed someone to fall in love with him or lust or whatever it was—to test him—then she wouldn't have been shot by Cupid, and she probably wouldn't have been on that mountainside at that time, in that place. She wouldn't have broken her ankle, become obsessed, and moved to Portland.

She would have found something else on her own, something to fulfill her and give her life meaning.

Instead, she would have him, the cause of it.

Darius sat back at the table, pushing the ruined muffin away and setting his meatball sandwich in its place. He put his head in his hands and closed his eyes. His fingers smelled of the marinara they had put on the meatballs, and he was tired.

So very tired.

Maybe this was what the Fates wanted him to feel about his entire life. Guilt, remorse, and unworthiness. Emotions he didn't even know existed in his arrogant youth. People, he believed then, had an obligation to *him* because of his magic, his talent, his natural athletic abilities, and his clear superiority.

What he had learned in the intervening years was that he had no clear superiority, that for all his talent, his magic, and his natural athletic abilities, he was more of a screwup than anyone else he had ever met.

Maybe he was humble enough now. He wondered if he should go to the Fates and ask.

He raised his head and picked up his sandwich. He'd seen Cupid; that was enough for one day. Maybe he should stop focusing on himself and try, instead, to focus on someone else.

On Ariel, and helping her rebuild her life.

Ariel unlocked her front door and stepped inside. She flicked on the overhead light, closed the door, and leaned against it.

The building she lived in was actually a guest cottage behind a house built in the 1920s. The cottage was small—one main room, plus a small bedroom and a bath—but it was private, and she didn't share her walls with anyone.

The owners had recently remodeled the cottage and she was its first tenant. It had a large main room, with a kitchen area and a dining area, as well as a place for a couch and a few chairs. Above the kitchen's bar was a skylight that she really valued on gray Oregon days.

A narrow hallway led to the bathroom and the bedroom, which was barely large enough for her queen-sized bed. She had brought some of her furniture from Boise: the L-shaped couch, the overstuffed chairs, and a kitchen table that had been with her since college. A TV with cable, her best friend since she had gotten laid off, sat on a built-in shelf in the corner, beside the stereo system she had purchased at one of the outlets for less than a hundred dollars.

Small, intimate, and hers. Yet it meant so little to her that if someone told her she had to move tomorrow, she would find a truck and pack her things.

She had never really had a place that she called home, only a place where she rested when she was done training, or hid when she was feeling bad. She had never had a place she valued so much that she would do anything to stay there.

Ariel sighed and came all the way inside the cottage, dropping her purse on the end table near the door. She was tired from being on her feet all day—something that she never would have admitted to herself six months before.

She walked into the bathroom, peeling off the clothing that still smelled of the restaurant. The conversation with Vari had left her unsettled. The things he had told her about Darius were things she had worried about in the darkness of night.

It wasn't normal for a man to disappear the way he had, or to be so very hard to find. Usually people who were hard to find were that way on purpose—hiding from family or friends or child-support payments.

Or trouble with the law.

She plugged the tub and turned on the faucet, sticking her hand in the water to set the temperature. When she got it right, she grabbed the bottle of expensive bubble bath she had indulged in the day she got laid off and poured it liberally in the tub. Instantly, the small room filled with the scent of vanilla.

Darius hadn't seemed like a man who would be in trouble with the law. He hadn't seemed like someone who manipulated other people's emotions to get what he wanted. She had met men like that, and they were usually very obvious— at least to her.

But, she supposed, the good ones, the real confidence men, had to be so subtle that most people wouldn't suspect. And she hadn't been in the best condition to judge him at the time.

After all, she had just fallen off a cliff. She had broken her ankle and she had been in a lot of pain. And she just might have injured her head.

She brought a hand up to her hair. Those flashing lights bothered her, but she wasn't sure she wanted to see a doctor about them. Not yet. She'd see if there were other symptoms first.

The tub was full of steaming water. The bubbles piled high over the edge. She grabbed Peter Robinson's *In A Dry Season* off her bedside table—she'd been reading a lot of mysteries lately; she suspected that was because of her search for Darius—and took off the last of her clothing.

Then she went back into the bathroom, put the book on the rug, and sank into the water, leaning her head against the side of the tub.

Extreme marathons. She had lied to Vari. She knew about them. She even knew people who ran in them.

He was right—the races were still on the fringes of legitimacy. And even though he had also been right about the history of Ironman, she had joined the sport after it had gained a measure of respect.

She couldn't imagine being a pioneer. She'd read about the history of all her sports, about how women weren't allowed to run marathons (it was considered bad for their health) and how they snuck into the races. She'd even seen the famous footage of the female runner who was attacked by a marathon official during the Boston Marathon in the late 1960s.

One of the reasons Ariel participated in her sport was because she was an athlete. She wanted to make a good living at what she did. She wanted to be recognized, get endorsements, while stretching her body to its limits.

The bubbles popped around her. Lance Armstrong had gone from being a tri-geek to being a cyclist. But he didn't do day-long races. He excelled at the Tour de France, considered the most grueling race in all of sport.

He had gone to something harder, not something easier.

But she didn't want to sit on a bike for the rest of her career. Even though the 120-mile bike length of the Ironman was difficult, it still felt like cheating to her. After all, she had a machine beneath her. Wheels that carried her food, her water, and her sports drink. She was sitting down. Even though it wasn't rest—and didn't feel like rest—it wasn't grueling either.

Cycling didn't excite her.

Swimming in oceans excited her. Running excited her— that feeling that she could do anything while she was on her feet. That was why she had gone hiking in the first place. It was just her and her body against the elements. Swimming felt like that too, even when she was wearing a wetsuit. *She* was struggling against the water, dealing with the dangers that lurked in the darkness and the waves and the salt and the rain.

When she rode, the bike touched the pavement, protected her from the bumps, allowed her to catch a snack.

She couldn't do that if she ran. It would be her against the road.

But the hundred miles felt like a publicity stunt, not a real race. Yeah, she would have to push herself to do it, but she really didn't want to.

Maybe the key wasn't the distance.

Maybe it was the speed.

She was a good marathoner, but not as good as the women

who won the Boston or the New York or the other big international marathons. She wasn't that fleet. Of course, she had run all her marathons in competition *after* the swim and bike leg.

She'd never competed in a marathon as a race. Only as practice. She'd never tried to win.

Excitement flared inside her. She sat up, sloshing water against the rim of the tub. The bubbles surrounded her, covering her skin.

She hadn't felt like this in months, maybe in a year. Maybe not since she felt her shoulder rip on that horrible morning in Canada.

Who would have thought that Andrew Vari would revive her interest in sport? When she had gone to the deli with him, she had expected a lecture about her behavior in the restaurant. She hadn't expected an offer of sponsorship.

He was a lot more complicated than she ever could have imagined.

She smiled, dried her hand on a nearby towel, and picked up her book. For the first time in months, she felt as if she had the ability to relax.

The next morning, Darius sat at his favorite table in Quixotic. The restaurant wouldn't open for another two hours. He was sipping much-needed coffee and eating a piece of freshly baked apple pie as his breakfast. Over the table's surface, he had spread the quarterly reports. He was going over the accountant's work, detail by detail.

As Quixotic got bigger and its holdings diversified, Darius had discovered more and more people who wanted to siphon funds from it. Not the least were its first group of accountants, who had believed that a successful restaurateur like Blackstone wouldn't have time to monitor his own books.

The accountants were wrong—and they had some very nasty hours spent as slugs in Dar's garden. He usually didn't punish that way, and he wouldn't have done it that time if they hadn't pissed him off by insulting his height as well as his intelligence.

The accountants remembered their slug existence as very nasty dreams. But the dreams had been effective enough to make them all choose new professions.

The accounting firm that did Quixotic's books now was highly competent. Still, Darius went over everything. He felt that he shared some responsibility for the slug incident by feeling a little too much trust. He hadn't checked the books as often as he should have.

Usually he didn't mind the task, but this morning the numbers blurred in front of his face. He hadn't gotten much sleep the night before. His meeting with Ariel had left him too keyed up, and so he had tried to calm down by watching *Gladiator* on video.

That had been an even larger error. He liked spectacle movies, but he should have remembered that Roman epics always made him angry. Hollywood got everything wrong.

Darius should know—he had been there.

Commodus was a loathsome man, but he didn't murder his father. He did, however, execute his sister. And he didn't die at the hands of a gladiator. He died at the hands of his own ministers, who had him strangled in his bath.

Darius had tried to watch *Gladiator* as the fictional adventure that it was, but the screwed-up, Hollywoodized details made him angry. And not just on the history stuff. Usually he didn't mind that they wore togas from one period and sandals from another. Heaven knew, he didn't get upset over all the Arthurian sagas, none of which were right. But for some reason, the liberties taken with Rome irritated him.

Maybe he had put in the movie on purpose. Maybe he wanted to be irritated after his meeting with Ariel. Maybe he felt that he had no right to enjoy the evening.

Maybe he felt that he should stay awake all night.

He rubbed his eyes with his thumb and forefinger, but the sandy feeling remained. He could spell himself awake, but his magic still wasn't on solid ground. He still hadn't solved his familiar problem. No animal appealed to him.

Maybe he should get a tame bear and be done with it.

Then, at that moment, he felt her, as clearly as if she had spoken his name. She was standing behind him. The hair on the back of his neck rose and his breath quickened.

He closed his eyes and forced himself to take a deep breath—to calm down.

Only as he did so, he caught a whiff of her clean, fresh scent. The calming techniques of centuries no longer worked.

"Mr. Vari?"

He opened his eyes, starting at the use of his name. Part of him had expected her to call him Dar.

He turned toward her.

She looked radiant. Her porcelain cheeks were flushed with color and her green eyes sparkled. Her auburn hair fell in soft waves across her face.

He said, "Call me Andrew, Ariel," and somehow it sounded like a command.

She nodded in the way that people had when they had no intention of doing as they were instructed. "Do you— mind if I sit down?"

He flushed—or would have, if he hadn't caught the reaction so quickly. "No, by all means, please sit."

She smiled, then sat down across from him. He gathered the papers and set them aside. Employees weren't supposed to see the books.

"I wanted to thank you for your generous offer," she said, and he could tell just from her tone that she was going to refuse. "I thought about it all evening."

He folded his hands over the papers, resisting the urge to talk over her, to defend the offer, to refuse to let her finish.

"But I'm going to turn you down."

He nodded, then sighed, picking up the papers and thumping their edges on the table to straighten them. He would regret that later, when he was trying to sort out the various piles.

"It's not because I don't want your help, it's just that . . ." Her voice faded and he could finish the thought for her. *It's just that I don't want anything to do with you.*

"It's all right," he said. "You don't owe me an explanation."

"But I do." She leaned forward, her hands folded on the table as well. "You've been very kind to me despite my behavior. Yesterday, you offered me an incredible opportunity."

And she was turning him down. She looked radiant while she was doing it. Better than she had since she'd come to the restaurant. What did that say?

"I know something of the ultra marathons," she said, using their real name.

He felt that flush return. He had lectured her about something she was already familiar with.

"I know they'd be a challenge. I've never run that far. But I'm not a fringe athlete. I really don't want to work on the edge, even if it is a challenge."

"I understand," he said, and he did. He was a fringe athlete—or had been, thousands of years ago. Back when people thought the games he participated in were silly and a waste of time, even though they attracted huge crowds.

Even though they had made him both famous and arrogant.

"But you got me thinking." She had leaned even closer, as if she could sense his withdrawal.

He rolled up the papers and clutched them in one hand. His hand was too small to hold them, and they fanned out, spilling across the table like leaves in a wind.

This time, the flush heated him all the way through. What a thing to do in front of her, to remind her about how different he was, how inadequate—

"Let me get that," she said, rising.

"No," he said, standing on his chair just so that he could reach across the table. "I got it."

He scooped up the papers, which were now more out of

order than they had been before, and set them on the chair beside him.

She stared down at him, then seemed to realize that she was towering over him, and sank into her seat.

"As I said," she went on, "you got me thinking. I miss competing. And while I've run marathons, I've never tried to win one."

He was still standing, like a little boy waiting for his mother to reprimand him for putting his feet on the furniture. But he didn't want to sit down. He didn't want to call any more attention to his own awkwardness.

He hadn't behaved like this in years, maybe even centuries. Usually he flaunted his short stature, dared people to attack it. With her, he didn't want to. He sat down slowly, kicking his feet out in front of him like he always did in chairs built to real-people height.

"So, I was thinking I'll enter the Portland marathon this fall and see if I can win. I've never really given my all in a real marathon—in the Ironman I was always trying to survive them, so in practice, I was going for pace, not for winning."

Why was she telling him this?

"You'd have to pace in a regular marathon." His voice sounded even gruffer than usual. He wasn't hiding his discomfort well.

"Yes, but it would be a different tactic, one I have to learn. And every runner dreams of qualifying for the great marathons, like the Boston." She smiled at him. The smile was gentle, and it softened her face. "I had forgotten that dream until I talked to you."

He let out a small puff of air. Maybe the conversation had worked. Maybe he had managed to refocus her obsession on something else.

She was looking down at her hands. "So I actually went out and ran this morning."

"You did?" He couldn't keep the surprise from his voice. "What about your ankle?"

"It's weak," she said, "but not because of the injury. Because I haven't worked to strengthen it. And I didn't go far. Just three miles."

Just three miles. He couldn't do three miles to save his life—at least not in this form. His Darius form could go much farther, but only because he always reverted to the body he wore when he had gotten in trouble all those millennia ago.

"Besides the ankle, how did it go?" he asked.

"It went all right," she said. "I have a lot of work to do to get back into shape, but I can do it. I've done it before."

He smiled at her. "So you'll still need a sponsor."

She shook her head, and he felt his smile fade. "I can train for a marathon on my own time. This job will pay for all my needs. I have most of the equipment."

"But running while you're standing all day—don't you think that'll be harmful—?"

"I couldn't hold this job and train for an Ironman, but I can train for a marathon. People do that all the time. Not that I don't appreciate your offer. I do. Really. But I would be cheating you if I told you I needed it, and not having a sponsor takes some of the pressure off me."

"But what about rehabilitation for the ankle? Weight training, all the prep that goes into modern athletics?"

"My ankle is rehabilitated, according to my doctors. It's just weak. And I can fit in the training around this job. It's not like there's much else for me to do."

Then she bit her lower lip, as if she hadn't meant that last sentence to come out.

She still didn't want his help. But she was determined to return to her calling. He had done that much.

"Thank you for telling me," he said, wondering where that cool polite voice had come from.

She looked down at her hands. Her hair shone in the thin light. "I guess I owe you for pointing me in the right direction."

"You don't owe me anything." Then he rethought the

statement. "Except that you'll come to me first if you change your mind about sponsorship."

She nodded, then raised her head and smiled at him. It seemed like a rehearsed move, as if he still made her nervous.

"I'll do that," she said quietly. "I won't make you regret that you asked."

And then she was gone, leaving a faint scent of soap and woman in her wake.

He stared after her for a long time. Being near her was going to be a lot harder than he had thought.

Familiar Things
(March)

Fifteen

Ariel had forgotten the way exercise made her feel. She had forgotten the pleasant ache in her muscles, the expansion in her chest as she used her lungs to their fullest capacity. She had forgotten that exercise put color in her cheeks and confidence in her walk.

She had forgotten how it lifted her spirits and made her feel strong.

In the weeks since she had started running, she hadn't spent much time thinking about Darius at all. One morning, she had awakened to find that she had dreamed of him. She felt odd, as if she were a recovering alcoholic who had relapsed. Instead of falling back to sleep, she had crawled out of her warm bed, pulled on her sweats, and run her three-mile circuit. That had cleared her mind and taken away the uncertain, queasy feeling she had had when she woke up.

These days, she thought mostly about running. Every Sunday, she outlined the week's workouts and posted them on the refrigerator. Her goal was to hit the marathon length by the beginning of April. But she was adding in splits and track workouts of a type she had never done before.

She also designated her courses—some days running hills, other days making certain she stayed on flat ground. And once a week, she timed herself.

When she had started triathlons, she had worked her way to the Ironman—starting with sprint tris, moving up until she hit Olympic length, and finally, after about two years of training, planning for her first Ironman.

She wasn't going to take two years to get to her first marathon, but she was going to take her time on striving to win her first. Since she hadn't worked the kinds of strategy it took to win running events, she had to concentrate on that and, she believed, small victories would encourage her to continue.

Small failures wouldn't set her back. They would just make her work harder.

Even though she was now running ten miles on her longest days, she planned her first race to be a 5K. Three miles would test her strategic planning—her first instinct, she knew, would be to run flat out because, to her tri-geek brain, three miles was nothing. But in her condition, it was long enough, and she had to treat the distance with respect.

Maybe that was what she was working for the most: learning respect for a sport she had once considered too easy.

It wasn't easy at all. It was just different from what she had done.

Running, and running related activities, such as her weight workouts and weekly cross-training (which she did in the pool so that she wasn't riding her bike on Portland's rain-covered streets) took up her free time. The rest of her life centered around Quixotic.

She had learned the job quickly. Sofia had gone to the weekends and then, as Andrew Vari had predicted, had quit a few weeks later, after another incident.

In addition to Sofia, that incident had cost the restaurant two busboys and the relief bartender. They all believed that they had finally seen the ghost.

Ariel had never gotten a coherent story from any of them, but what she had been able to piece together was that a short balding man wearing polyester pants and smoking a stinky cigar had come into the restaurant in search of a friend. When it turned out that no one had heard of his friend, the short man had vanished.

Literally. One moment he was standing in front of Sofia. In the next moment, he cursed, waved his arms, and disappeared.

Most of the customers didn't seem to notice. Those who did talked with Blackstone, who had calmed them down. But Sofia, the busboys, and the bartender, all of whom had been standing close to the man when he disappeared, could not be calmed. Sofia claimed that her outfit smelled of cigar smoke, and that there was ash on the floor.

Ariel had thought the incident curious, but she hadn't taken a lot of interest in it. Sofia had proven herself superstitious, the busboys were young and impressionable, and Ariel suspected the relief bartender had been sampling the wares long before he saw the so-called ghost.

It wasn't until Sofia came to Quixotic to pick up her final check that the incident took a new significance in Ariel's eyes.

Sofia had refused to come inside the restaurant. Instead, she had parked out front and signaled Ariel through the door, asking her to send Blackstone or Andrew Vari outside with the check. Ariel, in turn, sent one of the waiters back for Blackstone, who had been working lunch that day.

She wanted to talk to Sofia, to see if she could get Sofia to return just for the weekends. Since Sofia had quit so quickly, no one at Quixotic had had time to hire a new weekend hostess, and the extra work (which Ariel was splitting with one of the waiters) was cutting into Ariel's training time.

Ariel had stepped out into the warm afternoon, reveling in the early spring sunshine. Sofia stood by the curb and wouldn't listen to Ariel's arguments about returning to work. Somewhere in the entire discussion, Sofia had started telling Ariel the story of the ghost.

Ariel mostly tuned it out. She had heard the story from the other sources and she was getting tired of it. The cigar smoke, the ash, the sudden disappearance felt like a rehearsed script to her. But this time, Sofia added something Ariel had never heard before:

"He was nasty," she was saying. "He kept shouting for his friend Darius and telling me that I was protecting him. As if I know anyone with that name. And the more I denied it, the angrier this man got. Then he said something about the fact that this Darius had caused him to have trouble with the little folk, which I thought particularly offensive, given Mr. Vari, and—"

"Darius?" Ariel felt her entire body stiffen. "Are you sure?"

Sofia looked annoyed. "Of course I'm sure. But no one knows who he is. Mr. Blackstone had never heard of a Darius, and Mr. Vari seemed very upset when I mentioned it, probably because of that little folk comment."

"Probably," Ariel said absently. "Did the man say why he thought someone named Darius would be in the restaurant?"

Sofia frowned. "Why? Do you know a Darius?"

"I met a man with that name in Idaho."

Sofia grunted. "It couldn't be the same man. Besides, the man who asked the question was a ghost. He *vanished,* Ariel, or weren't you paying attention?"

Ariel had forgotten that part. It made the request even stranger. She had been about to ask more questions when Blackstone had come out front with Sofia's final check. He had asked Ariel to excuse them, and she had, leaving Blackstone to try to convince Sofia to return.

But Ariel had seen Sofia's shaking fingers and had known that Sofia would never enter the restaurant again.

Ariel wasn't certain why she wasn't afraid of the so-called ghost. She had seen a number of strange things at Quixotic herself since the day the lights had flashed all over the building.

One afternoon, a customer had complained that he had the wrong meal while Blackstone walked past. Then the customer squealed and pointed to his dish, exclaiming, "It was different a moment ago."

Blackstone, to Ariel's surprise, had smiled.

Then there had been the bills that had been mysteriously paid, even though Ariel, who handled the money on her shift, hadn't taken cash from anyone. And there was the one day when a customer had started screaming for no reason, his apologetic wife trying to hustle him out of the restaurant.

The man had been pointing at Andrew Vari at the time, saying he looked just like a man who had cursed his father fifty years before.

Vari had seemed quite calm about it, and Blackstone had shaken his head. It had been the employees who were unsettled by it, even Ariel.

She thought about that moment often when she ran, and wondered about Vari's family. The appearance must have gone down through the generations. The man she'd seen pictured with Hemingway had looked just like Vari as well.

At first she tried to put Vari out of her mind, but he seemed to creep in at the oddest moments. When she was running. When she was cooking. When she was reading.

And those blue eyes of his were mesmerizing. She found herself thinking about them most of all.

He was the first human being she'd ever met who intrigued her like this. He was a puzzle, an intricate puzzle that she felt she might never find the key to.

But she was searching. The man was simply too interesting to ignore.

* * *

Darius shouldn't have come to the race.

He dressed down for it—a white bowler hat, a blue shirt with a white collar, and faded blue jeans, which he'd had to conjure up because Andrew Vari didn't own a pair that wasn't crisp and perfect. He wore deck shoes to complete the outfit, and felt, oddly, like a crusty elderly man who was heading out on his daily constitutional.

He'd spent another fifteen minutes in front of his closet, trying to rethink the outfit. He didn't want to be noticed. He didn't want Ariel to know he was there at all.

Which created a problem. Because in order to see, he would have to stand in front of the crowd, or sit up high on something, or use some magic. He didn't want to use the magic.

His abilities was getting shakier and shakier, and he still hadn't found a proper familiar. He'd even gone to the local pound with Blackstone, hoping to find some creature that would suit him and his abilities, but none seemed right. On his own, Darius had tried a few pet stores and, other than spell the animals so that nice people would take them, he did nothing.

He did, however, buy a hundred-gallon fish tank and fill it with interesting fish. But fish, Blackstone told him with great authority, did not count as familiars. It seemed that Houdini had substituted an aquarium full of fish for the mouse he kept carefully hidden from his friends and compatriots (after the mouse died, of course), and it was that aquarium, Blackstone believed, that caused Houdini's untimely demise.

The proof, Blackstone would say whenever he saw Darius's aquarium, was in the method of death: Houdini, always arrogant, had tempted the Fates by revealing himself as a magician, and the moment he slipped up, they got their revenge—by drowning him.

Darius knew he was tempting the Fates by going so long

without a familiar when he so desperately needed one, but his old mentor Bacchus had told him that a familiar could not be summoned. It had to appear in its own good time.

Darius felt like time was running out.

He had arrived at the race grounds late, barely finding a place to park. The athletes were already milling near the starting area. All of them were wearing shorts and T-shirts despite the chill March morning, and they were jumping on one leg, then the other, like children, trying to keep warm.

The race was being held in Tom McCall Waterfront Park, with its lovely view of the rivers and bridges. It was a new race—called the In Like a Lion 5K (which, if they had known where that phrase actually came from, they would have changed the race's name)—and was going to be an annual on March 1 of every year.

He could tell the serious runners from the weekend warriors. The serious runners were lean and focused. They stood closest to the starting point, their low singlet numbers revealing their quick 5K times.

The weekend warriors, as a group, were not lean. They were becoming lean. They milled around each other, talking, or getting encouragement from friends on the sidelines. Most of them clutched their water bottles like lifelines, and they all wore watches the size of sundials. The watches probably had more features and alarms than his computer—set to run a few minutes, walk a few minutes, pant a few minutes.

He shook his head. The old arrogance was hard to shake, especially when it came to sports that allowed amateurs. He loved sports, but he still had trouble dealing with the folks who didn't commit to them heart and soul.

When he finally fulfilled his sentence, he would have to be careful about restarting his own athletic career. The last thing he wanted to do was rekindle the arrogance that had gotten him into trouble in the first place.

It took him a while to find Ariel. She was standing on the sidelines, looking extremely calm. A water bottle dangled from her hand as she listened to a tall rangy man talk to her.

She watched the man with rapt attention, a smile on her face. Darius's mouth went dry. In all his concern for her obsession, he had forgotten what he had learned so painfully in the mountains—she had a soul mate, one she hadn't met yet.

Perhaps this man was him.

As if confirming Darius's thought, the man leaned forward and brushed Ariel's lips with his own. She reached her arms around his neck and pulled him close.

They held each other for a long moment, rocking back and forth together as if they were attuned to the same rhythm. Then the man stepped back, held Ariel by the upper arms, and smiled at her. He seemed to be encouraging her.

She certainly didn't need Darius.

Not that she would have known he was there anyway. He wasn't about to tell her. When he had overheard her mention the race to one of the waiters, he had vowed to come. He wanted to see how her new obsession was working.

Obviously, it was working just fine.

He pushed his way through the knot of people that had formed behind them. Most of them acted like trees—immobile, ignoring him. The rest seemed to think he was a weird, overdressed child who had wandered into the wrong place.

He had almost made it through the knot when he heard one of the organizers tell everyone to get into position. They had to line up, fastest runners up front, the laggers behind.

In spite of himself, Darius turned around, wondering if people were really that cooperative. They seemed to be. Ariel was right up front, her body ready, her face a mask of concentration.

She had never looked more beautiful.

The man who had talked with her was sitting behind a nearby table, writing down figures. He wasn't even looking at her, and she didn't seem to be thinking about him either.

Her entire body was poised at the edge of something—a moment that might change her forever.

Then the starting gun went off, and she lit out, immediately ahead of the pack.

Darius walked back toward the starting area, willing her to slow down. She had to pace. He knew she thought of this as a sprint, but it wasn't. Even though she was used to the five kilometers—it was the three miles she had told him she had started with—she didn't dare take it for granted.

Not at all.

If she burned up all at once, she'd be disappointed by the end.

Almost without thinking about it, he wrapped his hand into a fist as he started a spell. He'd slow her down. He'd keep her ahead of the pack but paced, so that she didn't burn out, so that she didn't get disappointed—

And then he realized what he was doing. He was taking away her opportunity to succeed or fail. He was taking away her opportunity to learn from her experience, to set her expectations properly, and to react to them with the strength that he knew she had.

He unclenched his fist and let his hand fall to his side. He couldn't see her anymore. The runners were still fanning out along the course, but she was long gone, not even a cloud of dust rising behind her.

He could spell himself to the turn-around point, but he didn't dare. If he did something wrong, then he would interfere with the race as surely as he would have if he had cast the spell.

Darius sighed. He was hooked now. He couldn't go home if he wanted to. He walked toward the starting area—which was now being converted into the finish line by the man who had hugged Ariel—and watched as the man strung the ribbon between two poles.

Around Darius, the small crowd talked nervously. He caught snatches of conversation: how Suzy had lost fifty pounds and thought she was ready for running; how Dan felt he was ready to try a real race; how Julia had always dreamed of winning something. The real athletes didn't seem to be a topic of conversation—maybe they didn't bring supporters. Or maybe there were no real athletes in this race aside from Ariel.

Darius slipped his hands in his pockets, staring at the path through which, someone had pointed out, the runners would return. Nothing yet, not that there should be. He'd only been watching for a few minutes.

He inched closer to the finish line. Some people who had stood farther out in the earlier part of the race were inching back toward the end, and he wanted to be in front of them.

The man who had hugged Ariel was talking to another woman, older with a mane of gray hair. She laughed and touched his arm as they spoke, and then, suddenly, the man enveloped her in a hug.

Darius's fist curled again. If that man was going to hurt Ariel, he would have to answer to Darius.

The man rocked the woman the same way he had rocked Ariel, and their bodies seemed just as attuned. Finally the man pulled back, held her arms, and talked to her. She laughed again, kissed him on the cheek, and went to the sign-in table, where she seemed to go back to work.

Darius nudged the guy next to him. The guy looked down, surprised.

"Who is that man?" Darius asked, pointing at the serial hugger.

"He's the guy who organized this whole thing. Used to be pretty good himself, I heard, until he blew out his leg."

Darius raised his eyebrows. An injury? "He blew out his leg?"

The man next to Darius nodded. "I think. Or maybe it was his back. Or something. All I know is that he doesn't compete any more, and my girlfriend is glad of it. She said he used to be real shovey on the course. Real arrogant. People put up with him because he's, like, important, but I don't think any of them like him."

Darius frowned. He thanked the man beside him, then stared at the serial hugger. Sure enough, he was hugging another woman. She had a pained expression on her face as she let him hug her. Then, just as he had done before, the serial hugger pulled back, held the woman by the upper arms, and talked to her as if he were her coach. The woman gave him a polite smile, patted his cheek, and moved away.

Had Ariel been humoring him? She didn't seem like the kind of woman who would humor anyone.

A wave of discomfort ran through Darius. If she didn't humor anyone, then she welcomed the serial hugger's attention, which Darius liked even less. He didn't want her soul mate to be a man whom everyone else took as an annoyance.

"I see them!" someone yelled, and Darius whirled toward the path, amazed that he had forgotten to watch for Ariel.

He saw a flash of color through the trees. His mouth was dry and he wished he had thought to bring something to drink. He hadn't expected to be this nervous, or this uncomfortable.

A man charged down the path, running as if he were in Spain and a bull was behind him. The man was red in the face, his shirt wet with sweat, his arms pumping, wasting energy.

Ariel was right behind him, moving gracefully. She looked like she could run all day. Her shirt was damp, but not doused like the man's was, and her skin was flushed, but not red with overexertion.

They were the two leaders. No one else was even close.

The man glanced over his shoulder, panic on his face, as if Ariel were a hound let loose from hell to pursue him. She didn't seem to notice him. She passed him as if he were a rock in the road and continued toward the finish line with those easy, graceful sprints.

She was made to run. If Darius had thought she was stunning before, he thought she surpassed it now—becoming, simply, the most perfect human athlete he had ever seen. Her entire body moved together, without effort, like

the giant cats of the African plains, running after prey. She
had been born to run, and she probably hadn't realized it,
with her focus on the Ironman.

She had no idea how wonderful she looked.

She broke the tape, someone took a Polaroid, and she
slowed down, grinning like he had never seen her grin before.
The man came in after her, looking dejected.

Ariel still didn't acknowledge him. She was doing a small
celebratory jig all by herself, near the aid station. Other
runners trickled in, many of them red-faced and exhausted,
having given their all to the 5K distance. A few, even farther
behind, didn't look as tired, but they were clearly out to
finish, not set a personal record.

The serial hugger approached Ariel and congratulated her.
Darius moved closer so that he could hear their conversation.
The serial hugger held out his arms, but Ariel shook her
head and danced away from him, saying something about
being too sweaty.

Then, as she turned her back on him, her mouth pursed
in distaste.

Her expression sent a shot of joy through Darius. He tried
to quell it—she had a right to be attracted to other men.
She would be someday. He knew she would be. She had
that soul mate in her future—but he was so glad the serial
hugger distressed her as much as he distressed the other
women.

Darius smiled, not just because Ariel had rejected the
serial hugger but because her joy at winning was so palpable.
He was glad she had focused on the running, glad her atten-
tions had turned away from him. She seemed so much healthier, so much more vibrant now, as if she had been in a dark
place and had suddenly stepped into the light.

Darius turned away, heading toward his car. For the first
time, he'd watched a race and hadn't regretted that he had
short legs and no discipline. The race hadn't been about
him.

It had been all about her.

"Mr. Vari!"

Ariel's voice carried over the murmur of conversation and the shouts of congratulations from friends of the runners now crossing the finish line.

Darius kept walking, pretending he didn't hear her. He hadn't wanted to get caught. This was her moment; she didn't need him lurking around.

"Mr. Vari!"

Her voice was closer, and he couldn't pretend he didn't hear her anymore. He turned. She was running to catch up to him.

Her joy was unmistakable up close. She grinned, and the entire world got brighter. "What are you doing here?"

He could lie, he supposed, but he couldn't think of anything convincing. "I came to watch you race."

"You saw it?" Her voice rose with pleasure. "Really? How did you know I'd be here?"

"You mentioned it to someone at work and I overheard." He shrugged, feeling out of place, like a voyeur who'd been caught. "I wanted to see how you did."

"I did very well." She was bouncing on both feet, as if she couldn't stop moving.

"I know." This time, he couldn't keep the smile off his face. "I saw. Your race was spectacular. You sure pissed off that other guy."

Her grin became mischievous. "He *hated* losing."

"I think he hated losing to a woman."

"That too," she said. "You know, he arranged this race so that he could win."

Darius leaned his head back in surprise. "He did? How do you know that?"

"You know the guy who fired the starting gun?"

"I saw him. I don't know him."

"He's one of the biggest gossips in all of sport. Not to mention the oogiest toucher." She shuddered. "When I asked him how the race got organized, he told me who was behind it, and I knew. The races he organizes get shorter and more obscure, and he usually moves on to a new venue for the next year, leaving the other partners behind. I suspect this year he'll really be gone. He hates losing to anyone, but this'll be fun. Watch how he posts the results: it'll be men first, with him as winner with his slow time, and women second, with me as winner with the better time. And there won't be any overall winner.''

"Doesn't that bother you?'' It bothered Dar. He wanted to find the bigot and set him straight.

Ariel shook her head. Her eyes twinkled. "Doing well is the best revenge. And no matter how he manipulates the numbers, I *won.*''

Dar's grin matched hers. "You did, didn't you?''

He wanted to hug her but didn't know how, especially after her comments about the serial hugger. Not to mention the height difference. He would have the disadvantage of hugging her waist, with his face buried in a private part of her anatomy.

Not that he would mind that, but she probably would.

"I'm so glad you came,'' she said again, flapping her arms as if she didn't know what to do with herself.

"What are you going to do to celebrate?''

She wiped a damp strand of hair off her forehead, then shrugged. "Gee, I don't know. Take a shower?''

He'd invite her to lunch, but it was 9:30 in the morning. "Beer's not appropriate this early, but we might be able to scrounge up some champagne. Add a little orange juice and it's perfectly legal.''

"I'd love it,'' she said, "but I don't do alcohol when I'm training. It dehydrates the body and puts the wrong kind of chemicals in.''

Then she rolled her eyes.

"Listen to me. I'm such a tri-geek. I appreciate the offer, really.''

He nodded, feeling awkward again.

"Breakfast would be nice, though. But I have to wait for everyone to get done. They have a ceremony.''

It felt like she was throwing him a bone. He struggled to keep the smile on his face. "I—um, have to be at Quixotic at ten. Maybe the next time?"

"Sure." She didn't seem at all upset by his inability to stay. Then she bent and kissed him on the cheek. "Thank you for coming. Really. It meant a lot."

And she danced off, her joy sparking off her like a candle shedding light.

Darius touched his cheek. The kiss had been meaningless, a gesture of thanks, nothing more. But it had sent a shiver of desire through him, followed by a thread of hope.

Which he quickly buried.

She was making the transition away from her obsession to a new and healthier fascination. He had to do the same thing.

He threaded his way through the crowd to his car and headed to Quixotic, even though it was his day off.

Ariel's limbs tingled and her lungs burned. Even though 5K was an easy length for her, she wasn't used to going so fast. The race had drained her more than she had thought.

She clutched the small trophy, the certificate done by a local calligrapher, and the free T-shirt she got automatically as the winner, and headed to the parking lot. She had used the showers provided by the organizers, but she had forgotten to bring her own soap. Her skin smelled of industrial cleansers and was already starting to itch.

Still, she had enjoyed herself, more than she ever thought possible.

The race had left her in a good mood, but the cap on her experience had been Vari's presence. She had been feeling sad and a little sorry for herself when she had arrived at the race location. It seemed she was starting this athletic career the same way she had started the other one—alone.

Throughout her triathlete career, she had raced for herself and herself only. When she had dated, she usually dated men who were also competitors and often were in the same races she was. She dated few non-athletes. The ones she had dated, like that lawyer in Boise, had been completely uninterested in triathlons. If she could drag them to a race, they would get bored because the triathlon (particularly the Ironman) was an all-day affair. It wasn't like football or basketball, where the spectators constantly had something to watch.

As a consequence, no one had ever willingly stood on the sidelines and rooted for her. Until today.

Vari's presence had touched her deeply. She was even more touched because he had tried to leave without being seen. He had been interested, and the interest had been pure.

So had the support.

Ariel smiled to herself and got into the car, feeling restless. She needed to do something to celebrate. Too bad Vari hadn't been able to go to brunch with her. Maybe she would invite him to the next race, with the idea that they could go somewhere afterward.

Then she hesitated. Her relationship with him had been so strained because of her obsession with Darius. Would Vari be uncomfortable if she asked him?

There was, of course, only one way to find out.

And she had two weeks before the next race, so she had some time to think about it.

She pulled out of the parking lot and paused. She deserved a nice meal and something fun. Normally, she would have stayed downtown, but this time she wanted to do something different.

This time, she was going shopping.

She grinned, knowing there was good shopping in Portland's downtown. But good shopping wasn't what she wanted. She wanted kitsch and noise and the camaraderie of a bunch of people she didn't know. She wanted an Orange Julius and a Cinnabon.

She wanted a mall.

Ariel knew of two (even though there were probably

more)—the Clackamas Town Center, where Tonya Harding used to practice her skating in the built-in ice rink, and the Washington Square Mall, which had nothing whatsoever to do with athletics. The malls were on different sides of the city.

So she drove west, to Washington Square, where she wouldn't have to think about anything. She could join the hordes of Saturday shoppers and pretend that her life was just like theirs, whatever that meant.

Besides, she thought she had seen an Orange Julius stand the one time she'd been in Washington Square.

The drive was congested—all of Portland shopped in the suburbs on Saturdays—but she didn't care. She was enjoying her time out. Her mood was better than it had ever been.

Portland, she was beginning to realize, was a runner's paradise. It was Nike's hometown, and as such, had a great deal of respect for athletes of all stripes. The city and the outlying areas also had a lot of casual races, which was what she needed to get into her new mindset.

Boise was an athletic city as well, but it didn't have the same traditions as Portland. Portland's weather made running a year-round sport. Locals, if they were involved in athletics at all, were usually runners.

If she wanted to, she could talk to anyone passing on the street about running.

She liked that.

She pulled into Washington Square Mall's parking lot and circled for a while, looking for an available space. Even though this mall was older and hadn't really expanded enough on its latest remodel, it was still very popular on the weekends. She finally managed to find a parking space near the Barnes & Noble on the other side of the access road. She got out of the car, locked the precious trophy inside, and headed toward the mall.

Ariel didn't find her Orange Julius, but she did find Cinnabon. She had a real lunch, followed by a tiny cinnamon roll covered with too much wonderful frosting, and she shopped for two hours without buying anything more expensive than a book.

On the way back to her car, she wandered past the shops in the strip mall that had sprung up across the road from the mall. Most were business-related stores, like Kinko's, but some were older. There was a for-rent sign in one window, and she got the sense that the turnover among the non-business shops was higher than the strip mall's owners anticipated.

As she passed a pet store she had never seen before, she spied a puppy in the window. The puppy was a basset hound with liquid eyes, and ears so long that he kept stepping on them. He looked sadder than the average basset hound, and her heart went out to him.

Usually, she didn't go into pet stores. Her tri-geek lifestyle hadn't allowed her to keep pets—she was on the road too much—and if she got a pet, she would have gone to the Humane Society and saved one's life.

But she couldn't pass up the puppy. He was darling. Almost before she knew what she was doing, she pushed open the pet store's heavy glass door.

To her surprise, the store's interior had an odd twilight quality. Fish tanks of all sizes lined the walls, and their lights provided most of the illumination. They were filled with fish of all sizes and shapes. Some of the fish had tanks to themselves. Others were in large groupings.

A desk in the center had a cash register and all sorts of fish paraphernalia, from pretty colored gravel to multicolored glass seashells. Empty tanks filled a center aisle, along with other tank supplies: hose, bubblers, and heaters. Fish food and chemicals lined another aisle.

The puppy was the only mammal in the store—besides Ariel and the man behind the counter. He looked up from his newspaper as she let the door close behind her.

"Help you?" he asked.

"The puppy caught my eye," she said.

He smiled knowingly, apparently seeing her confusion.

"The puppy's on loan from the Humane Society. We help them out when they have too many dogs to get rid of. Sometimes people are willing to buy from a store but never go to the pound."

Ariel felt her cheeks flush. "He just caught my eye."

"He's a cute little bugger," the man said. "It's his first day here."

She walked over to the large cage the puppy was in. He followed her every move, his tail wagging. His ears trailed alongside him.

"He looks purebred," she said.

"Oh, he is." The man sounded bitter. "One of the local puppy mills got shut down. A hundred dogs, all living in their own filth. I guess they had to put twenty to sleep."

Ariel winced. "I hadn't heard."

"Happens a couple of times a year around here. That's why I don't carry pets. It encourages these idiots who are just into breeding for the money. With so many animals going homeless or being put to death because no one will adopt them, animal breeders are just perpetrating a crime."

"All of them?" she asked.

He shrugged. "There are legit folks. But why get a pure-bred dog? They're usually nervous and high-strung, with a ton of health problems. Mutts live longer and are much happier."

She put out her finger and the puppy licked it. His big sad eyes reminded her of someone.

"Is this guy okay?" she asked.

"Oh, yeah. He was one of the lucky ones. They nursed him back to health. Now they have eighty dogs to get rid of. Some of the pet stores are helping, and they've put out big notices in the papers and stuff."

The puppy wagged his stubby tail.

"How much is he?" she asked, unable to believe the question had come out of her mouth.

"He's free. But there's a $25 adoption fee that goes to

the Humane Society for their costs, mostly for his shots. It's all on the sign.''

She looked for a sign, and finally saw it above her eye level. It explained the situation and the fees. It also said she got a free leash and a bag of food with the dog.

''Is he housebroken?''

The man shrugged. ''The Society says he is, and he does his business when I take him outside. But I'm not guaranteeing anything.''

She nodded. The puppy sat down and watched her. He seemed not only sad but wary; even his little overture in the beginning had been cautious, not effusive, the way most puppies were.

Ariel crouched in front of the cage. He came toward her, tail wagging again, but he didn't get too close.

That sadness—it was so deep. And finally, she had it. The dog reminded her of Vari. Andrew Vari's eyes were that wary and that sad, especially when he looked at her.

Just last week, she had overheard Blackstone tell Vari he needed some kind of pet. Vari had said he was looking for one but couldn't find the right thing.

This basset hound was right; she knew it.

She also knew that a person should never buy an animal as a gift, in case the recipient didn't want the pet. If she was going to buy the dog and offer him to Vari, she had to be prepared to keep the dog herself if Vari didn't want it.

The dog whimpered. She reached through the bars of the cage and scratched the puppy's chin. The tail wagging grew steadier.

Running wasn't like Ironman training. She wouldn't be training ten-plus hours every day, coming home only to do laundry, a few reps on the weight machines, and sleep. She would have time to care for a pet, even with her job.

Although bassets weren't running dogs. They didn't have the legs for it. Sometimes bassets had trouble walking fast.

Not that it mattered. If she kept the dog, it wouldn't be as a running companion.

"I'll take him," she said.

"You will?" The guy sounded surprised. "You know, dogs aren't something you buy on the spur of the moment. You're making a ten-, maybe fifteen-year commitment here."

"I know," she said. "It's time I make a commitment to something."

The man frowned. He reached under the counter, pulled out the leash and collar, as well as a bag of Science Diet puppy food, and some baggies. It took her a moment to realize what the baggies were for.

"Full service place," she said with a smile.

He didn't smile back. She had a hunch he'd come after her if she didn't give this dog a good home.

She wasn't about to tell the man she planned to give the dog away.

He reached inside the cage and slid the puppy out. The little dog struggled against him, the tail between his legs.

"He doesn't like to be touched," the man said. "He was pretty badly abused. Can you handle that?"

If she had to, she could. She was pretty sure that Vari could handle it even better than she could.

"Does he have health problems because of it?"

"None that we know of." The man set the puppy on the counter. The little dog's tail started wagging the minute the man let go of him. Then the puppy bent his long snout and started sniffing, investigating every square inch of the tile as the man slid the collar around the dog's neck.

"Now," the man said to her, as if she were a child, "you get his name and address on this collar first thing. Too many dogs get lost and their owners never find them again. If you have any problems, you call me or the Humane Society. If for any reason you decide you don't want him, bring him back here. Don't just abandon him."

Ariel gasped. "I would never do that."

The man grimaced. "You'd be surprised at how many

people do. Dogs and puppies are two different creatures, and once folks realize that dogs aren't as cute, well . . ."

He put everything in a bag. Ariel scratched the pup's ears. The dog's tail wagged even harder.

"At least he likes you," the man muttered.

"What?" she asked.

"Oh, you'd be surprised how many people came in here because they saw him in the window. He growled at most of them."

"Really?"

The man nodded. "But he likes you. That's a start."

Ariel took out her checkbook. "Check to the Humane Society?"

"Yep." The man shoved the bag toward her. "I'll call them first thing. Time to get another of the dogs."

"I'm amazed you don't offer to do this more often," she said. "Think how many animals you could save."

The man raised his head and looked directly at her. "I used to, before I knew that I was supporting places like the one that damaged this little guy. Then I only took strays and animals that people brought in. I'd inoculate them, make sure everything was fine, and sell them for the vaccination fees."

"But?" Ariel asked.

"I couldn't part with them." He ran a hand on the puppy's back. The dog shivered but didn't pull away. "I never knew if they were going to good homes. I always wanted to tell people that if they treated the animal badly, I'd hunt them down and shoot them."

"Always good for business," Ariel said.

He looked at her. "I'm serious."

"I know," she said, not at all offended. "And I promise. I'll make sure he has a great life."

The man studied her for a moment, then nodded. "I believe you."

"Good." Ariel smiled. She attached the leash to the puppy's collar and picked him up. He didn't struggle against her like he had struggled against the man.

The puppy let her set him on the ground; then he began sniffing the floor like he had sniffed the countertop, inch by inch.

Ariel picked up the bag and stuck it under her arm. Then she clucked at the puppy who, to her surprise, stopped sniffing and heeled as if he had been doing it all his life.

"Well, I'll be," the man said as she led the dog to the door. "Remember, come back if there are problems."

"I will," she said and stepped outside.

The brightness made her blink after the gentle light in the pet store. The puppy looked up at her as if her hesitation made him nervous.

Then a car drove past and the puppy shied. He hid behind her leg and whimpered again. She wouldn't be able to walk him across the parking lot. He was too little and probably would be startled by the strangeness of it all.

So she bent down and picked him up with one arm, cradling him against her as she walked to her car. He leaned his head on her wrist, his little body trembling. But the expected struggle never came.

She used her keyless entry to unlock the car, then set the bag in the backseat. She didn't have a dog carrier. She hoped the puppy would do all right beside her.

He went inside the car as if he knew it was the right thing to do. Then he sat in the passenger seat, unable to see over the dash. He had a calmness about him that was simply unnatural in any creature that young.

She climbed in beside him, closed the door, made sure the windows were up, and stuck the key in the ignition. The roar of an engine coming to life would scare him—she was certain of that. But she started the car, and the puppy's tail thudded against the seat. He looked at her as if he was ready for the adventure of his life.

She wasn't. As she pulled out of the parking lot, she

began to regret her decision—not buying the puppy, but her decision to give the dog to Vari.

He would never know if she didn't show him the dog. But she had the oddest feeling that the puppy had been waiting for him and she was merely the delivery service.

She would stop at Quixotic and see if Vari agreed.

Sixteen

Darius sat on his stool in the kitchen, watching Blackstone create his latest dish. He was struggling to recreate some kind of vegetable pie he'd had during the Depression, and had made one of his assistants go to the store for lard not half an hour earlier.

Blackstone was leaning over the steel table, muttering, trying to remember which items were rationed and which ones weren't, which ones were cut so that the ingredients went farther, and which ones remained the same.

Darius supposed he could help—he had vivid memories of the Depression—but he didn't feel like helping. The kitchen was hot because the pastry chef had just finished her morning baking (she had stayed longer because Blackstone expected a rush on pies for reasons Darius couldn't fathom) and smelled of fresh bread.

Usually being in Quixotic calmed him, but not this morning. This morning, he wished he had taken up Ariel's offer and gone with her to brunch, even though she had only done it to make him feel better.

He was beginning to think he'd take her company no matter how grudgingly she offered it, and that attitude was dangerous. The jealousy he'd felt at the race this morning was improper. He had to do his job as impartially as possible—and impartiality meant a lack of involvement.

"You listening?" Blackstone asked.

"Obviously not," Darius said, "or I would have been rudely ignoring you."

"As if that's far-fetched," Blackstone said. "I was wondering if they could have used near-beer. Was it still being made in Thirty-three?"

"Are you sure you ate this in Thirty-three?" Darius asked. "Because Prohibition was still going on in Thirty-one, so there would have been near-beer then."

Blackstone frowned as if he were trying to remember. As he did, the back door opened. Ariel leaned in.

She looked hesitant. Maybe she was in some kind of trouble. Darius slipped off his stool and instantly lost sight of her.

He suppressed a curse.

She stepped inside, and her face brightened when she saw him. Then that look vanished and the uncertainty returned.

"Hi," she said, completely ignoring Blackstone.

"Hi," Darius said, stepping out from behind the table's shadow. "Is everything all right?"

She bit her lower lip. "I may have made a mistake."

That got Blackstone's attention. "What happened?"

She smiled at him, the look so radiant that Darius felt another curse rise inside him. He held it back. "Something I need Mr. Vari's help with, actually."

Blackstone bent toward Darius, raised his eyebrows, and grinned. Darius ignored him. "What do you need me for?"

"It's in my car," she said and walked toward the door. "Hurry."

He hurried as best he could on his stubby legs, his stomach

twisting. What kind of trouble had she gotten into and why had she come to him for help? Was she beginning to see him as the kind, neighborly man whom everyone befriended and no one noticed was really lonely?

She was out the door long before he reached it. As he stepped into the bright sunlight, he blinked. He had been inside longer than he thought.

Her car was parked near the Dumpster. Something was standing on the driver's side looking out.

Not something.

Someone.

His breath caught in his throat. For a moment, he had dual images—a young boy, barely old enough to stand, and a puppy, its paws on the armrest, its head looking out the window.

She reached the side of the car and opened the door. The dual image vanished. She bent down and picked up the puppy, cradling it against her.

Darius could feel the dog's magic crackling from his spot near the restaurant.

The puppy licked Ariel's face and squirmed, clearly wanting to get down. Ariel held it tightly and watched Darius.

He wanted to squirm too, but he held himself motionless. Did she know what she had? He said, "I don't understand. What's the problem?"

The puppy was wriggling even harder now. Ariel wrapped a leash around her wrist, an obvious precaution in case the puppy got away.

"When I saw him, I thought of you," she said softly.

He stared at her. No one had ever done this for him. She didn't even know that he needed a familiar, and yet she had brought him one.

How had she known? She had no magic; that was obvious. She was as mortal as Emma's husband, Michael.

Yet she had recognized a dog with a bit of magic.

"I know you're not supposed to give pets as gifts," she said into his silence, "but if you don't want him, I'll keep him. Only it feels like he belongs to you. He seems like the perfect dog for you.''

The puppy swiveled his head at that moment, as if he had understood her words. He was a basset hound, a particularly mournful-looking version, with ears so long that they hung past his feet.

''I can't take him from you,'' Darius said, trying not to sound ungrateful and trying to hide how unnerved he was. ''I mean, you're the one who found him.''

''And bought him on impulse.'' She shrugged. ''The guy at the store warned me not to do that. But you said you were looking for a pet.''

''You heard that?'' This time, he couldn't keep the surprise out of his voice.

''Well, you were having a rather loud conversation about it the other day with Mr. Blackstone.'' She shrugged. ''I thought maybe this puppy would work for you. But if he doesn't, I'll keep him.''

Darius took a step closer. The puppy was wriggling so hard, Darius was amazed Ariel didn't drop him. Darius stopped in front of the dog. Ariel bent so that the dog could see him better.

The puppy licked Darius's face. The pup's breath was amazingly sweet—probably because it was still young.

The dog scrambled onto his shoulder. Ariel braced the dog until Darius took its solid belly between his own small hands. The dog weighed more than he thought it would. It was all muscle and sinewy—and verged on being too thin.

''Didn't they take care of this creature?'' he asked, sounding more belligerent than he intended.

''He was rescued from a puppy mill. I guess he was abused. He may be a bit high-strung because of that.'' She hovered close, still holding the leash ''You don't have to take him just because I gave him to you. I know it was inappropriate—''

''Stop apologizing.'' Darius nuzzled the dog. It did feel right. This was the familiar he'd been waiting for. Small, stubby, slightly broken but with an irrepressible spirit. "I like him. I like him a lot."

"They say he's housebroken, but they're not sure it's a hundred percent. And I have some dog food in the car—"

"All right." Darius extended a hand for the leash. She handed it to him. He set the puppy down. It immediately leaped up to try to kiss him again, but it jumped no better than Andrew Vari did.

Ariel laughed fondly. "He's a good dog."

"I can see that." Darius crouched and patted the puppy. He'd always thought dogs were too simple for familiars. Loyal, trusting, somewhat dumb. But this dog had learned not to be trusting, and he certainly wasn't dumb.

Darius had a hunch the puppy would be loyal, too. Ariel was right; he felt a bond to the pup almost immediately.

"What's his name?" Darius asked.

"I haven't given him one," Ariel said. "Names are important. I figured you'd want to name him yourself."

He glanced at her again. How had she known that magic tenet? "What makes you say that?"

She grinned. "People always name their dogs, silly."

"No, I mean about names being important."

She shrugged. "I don't know. If I named him Sparky and you thought that was a dumb name, you'd think about that every time you called him. His name wouldn't be Sparky. It would be Sparky Whatadumbnameforadog."

She said that last all as one word. He laughed.

"You weren't thinking of naming him Sparky, were you?" he said with a little more alarm than he intended. It was a dumb name for this dog. "I mean, he's a basset hound. Somehow Sparky doesn't seem lugubrious enough."

"Oh, you're not going to give him some slow wimpy name, are you?"

"Slow, wimpy?"

"You know, like Homer."

"Homer. For a dog." Darius grinned. He doubted the

legendary Greek poet had any idea that dogs were now named after him.

Ariel smiled. "You know."

"So what do you think he should be called?"

She looked at the dog. Darius followed her gaze. The puppy was sniffing the asphalt, making snuffling noises so loud that it sounded like he was going to inhale the entire parking lot.

"Nosy?" she said.

"Where's the dignity in that?"

"Who said a dog needed dignity?"

"I do." Darius patted the puppy's neck. Ariel did seem pretty involved with all this. He didn't want to give up the dog—she was right, the pup was perfect for him—but he didn't want to upset her either. "Are you sure you don't want to keep him?"

The pup looked up at him. If a dog could look startled, this one did.

"You don't like him, do you?" Ariel's smile faded. "Well, that's okay. I mean, he and I—"

"I like him," Darius said. "I just don't want to take him away from you."

"I'd like to visit," she said. "Can I have that? I won't be his mommy. I'll be like—his aunt. Or his godmother."

"Do dogs have godmothers?"

She laughed. It was a sound Darius didn't hear often enough. "He does. So what are you going to name him?"

"Well," he said, "I think Lugubrious is too long."

Ariel pushed at him with her hand. "You wouldn't call him that."

"As I said, it's too long. Maybe I'll call him Mournful."

"That's terrible," she said.

He smiled. "Yes, it is."

"Come on," she said. "You can do better."

The pup had wrapped himself around Darius's leg. Darius moved the leash to untangle it. The pup watched him as if he were studying what Darius was doing.

"Munin," Darius said.

The pup barked, then wagged his tail. The dog clearly approved.

"What?" Ariel said.

"Munin," Darius said again. "It's from Norse mythology."

Like Andvari, which had become the corrupted Andrew Vari.

"I don't know much about the Norse," she said.

"It means memory," Darius said. It was more than that. His dour old friend Odin kept two ravens in those days. He had jokingly named one Hugin, or Thought, and the other Munin, or Memory. Odin let them free during the day and used their bird eyes to spy on his enemies.

That practice became mythologized —as so many practices had—in an entirely different manner. According to the Norse myths, the ravens would perch on Odin's shoulders. During the day, the birds would fly all over the world and bring back the news of all that human beings did.

The birds never did that. Hugin had been plain nasty. He loved mind games and often toyed with Odin's sensibilities. But Munin had been a gentle bird for a raven, and remembered everything, which seemed to inform his perspective.

Darius hoped for that from this puppy. He also hoped it wasn't too much to ask.

"Why memory?" Ariel asked.

"Because I never want to forget that look of joy you had on your face this morning," he said, and then drew in a breath. He hadn't expected that to come out of his mouth. No matter how hard he tried not to tell her things, he couldn't seem to help himself.

She blushed. Her blushes accented her pale skin and auburn hair. If anything, the expression made her even more beautiful.

She sat down and reached for the dog, as if he were both her lifeline and her excuse to stop towering over Dar.

"You're such a kind man," she said, her gaze meeting his. "Why do you hide it?"

He started. "I'm not kind."

"Yes, you are. And you pretend to be so gruff and mean. Why?"

He shrugged with one shoulder and concentrated on the dog. Maybe Munin wasn't her lifeline; maybe the dog was his. "People see what they want to see."

Ariel scratched between Munin's ears. The puppy was in doggy ecstasy, receiving attention from two different humans. "You think people want to see a grumpy man?"

"A man who looks like a leprechaun either has to be grumpy or very gregarious." Darius shook his head. "I have never been gregarious."

"You cater to it?"

"It's easier."

Her fingers brushed his and sent a jolt through him. Her flush grew deeper, but she didn't move away. "It must make life very lonely."

Was she coming on to him? Whyever would she do that? No well-adjusted woman had ever come on to him. Ever. Although a number had used him, particularly when he served in various courts.

"Actually," he said, trying to sound lighter than he felt, "it's a good weeding-out process. The people who can stand me grumpy are going to be truer friends than the ones who stay beside me because I'm easy to get along with."

Ariel nodded, and he realized that he wasn't the only lonely person here. He had never seen her with friends. No one had come to her meet except for him. The people she had seen there had been acquaintances and nothing more.

"What about you?" he asked. "Why do you keep yourself distant?"

Her fingers moved on Munin's loose doggy skin. The puppy kept looking back and forth between them, seemingly unable to handle this embarrassment of riches.

"I guess I'm not good with people," she said.

"I've watched you in the restaurant," he said. "You're great with people."

"Superficially, maybe. But no one hangs around for long."

"Because you don't let them in."

She smiled down at her hands. Munin laid down, as if his joy had collapsed his tiny legs. Darius kept one hand on the dog, thankful that Munin didn't have that high-strung energy some of the larger breeds did.

"I'm not even sure what that means," she said. "How do you let someone in?"

By admitting something like that, he almost said, but didn't. He didn't want her to become more self-conscious than she already was.

"By letting him buy you lunch for finding him the best dog in the whole world?"

Munin's tail thumped. Already he understood that phrase.

"I thought you had to work," Ariel said.

"Blackstone can handle it. Besides, he's trying to make some terrible vegetable pie and I don't want to be a guinea pig." Darius said that last with a smile so that she knew he was kidding.

"Well," Ariel said, "in that case, let me save you."

She stood and dusted herself off. Darius handed her Munin's leash. "I have to tell Blackstone I'm leaving."

"Let him meet the dog," she said. "After all, he's the one who has been nagging you about getting some kind of pet."

Darius hadn't realized the staff had overheard so many of those conversations. He wondered what they thought about that, and then decided that he didn't care.

"All right," he said. "Let's hope there's no health inspector inside."

"Guide dogs are exempt." Ariel gripped the leash and tugged softly. Munin got to his feet as if he had been to obedience school.

"He's not a guide dog, is he?" Darius asked. He thought

that only big dogs got to be guide dogs. He couldn't imagine a blind person being led by a sad, mopey little basset hound.

"Sure he is," Ariel said with a grin. "He's your guide dog for the next part of your life."

Darius gave her a stunned look. How did she know this stuff? It was too much of a coincidence. "What do you mean?"

"You know. Man's best friend. What's the saying in politics? If you want a friend, get a dog?"

Darius blinked at her. That was what she meant? She unnerved him. It was almost as if she saw edges of the magic without seeing all of it.

"What?" she said. "Did I say something wrong?"

He shook his head. "No. Sometimes you're just a little too right, that's all."

She frowned, and he turned away from her, pushing the kitchen door open. Blackstone was still poring over his recipe, muttering to himself. The sous chef seemed to be making a roux on the stove which, if Darius remembered right, was not the basis of any night's main dish.

"Alex," Darius said to Blackstone. "Come here."

Blackstone looked up at Ariel, then looked down at Darius, and then looked farther down at Munin. "What's that?"

"The bear I promised you," Darius said. "Come here."

Blackstone grinned, leaving his recipe behind him. "Finally. He looks perfect too."

Darius knew that Blackstone could see the overlying personality, just like he could, and he prayed that he wouldn't say any more. Sometimes Blackstone could be incautious.

"Where'd you find him?" he asked.

"Ariel found him."

Blackstone raised his eyebrows and looked at her intently. "Indeed."

He sounded like one of those 1930s movie detectives— a Sherlock Holmes rip-off.

Ariel flushed again. "I just saw him and thought of Mr. Vari, and, well, here we are."

"Yes," Blackstone said. "Here you are."

He gave Darius an inscrutable glance, then crouched by the dog. Munin watched Blackstone as intently as Blackstone watched him. They were sizing each other up. Both knew that the other was important to Darius—they were vying for head dog of the pack.

Darius crouched and put a hand on Munin. "He's going to be perfect."

"I see that," Blackstone said. "It's amazing, really. How *familiar* he seems."

That word, and so fast. Darius resisted the urge to shush him. "Well, yes."

"So you were with her?" Blackstone asked, speaking as if Ariel weren't even in the room.

"No," Darius said.

Blackstone stood, frowning at her. "You just knew this dog was for Mr. Vari?"

She nodded, looking confused by the direction of the conversation. Darius stayed beside Munin, who was the only one who didn't seem to sense the undercurrents in the room.

"And you just happened to see lights?" Blackstone asked.

"So I'm a little crazy." Ariel's voice was tight. "Isn't everyone?"

"No, thank God," Blackstone said, and at that, Darius stood. Not that it mattered much.

"Alex," he warned.

But Blackstone shook his head. "It doesn't work like this, Sancho."

Darius clenched one fist. He wasn't going to shush Blackstone. That would call attention to his words.

"This time, apparently, it has," he said.

Ariel was watching both of them. "Did I do something wrong?"

"No," Darius said quickly. "You did something right. Alex is just jealous."

"Of a dog?" Ariel said.

"Strange as that may seem," Darius said. He tugged on Munin's leash. "Let's take the little guy to my place and see if he likes his new surroundings."

Ariel gave Blackstone an uncertain glance. "I don't understand what's going on."

Blackstone hesitated, then he gave her his most charming smile. "My old friend is right," he said, using that smooth voice that usually made women melt. "I'm not used to sharing him."

"You're threatened by a dog?" Ariel asked. "You need to get out more."

And then she walked into the parking lot.

"Cheeky," Blackstone said.

"Accurate," Darius said.

"Something's going on," Blackstone said. "She's not supposed to see fringes."

"I know," Darius said.

"I was worried when she saw the lights, but a few of the employees have seen some of the trace magic before. But nothing like this. Only we're supposed to see familiars." Blackstone was speaking in soft, hushed tones.

"I know," Darius said.

"She's not one of us. That's obvious. But there's something—"

"I know," Darius said.

"Is that all you can say?" Blackstone asked.

Darius nodded. "I'm as surprised by it as you are."

"Have you ever figured out where her friend Darius is?" Blackstone asked.

"Yes," Darius said and glanced over his shoulder. Ariel was standing by her car, watching the door and shifting from foot to foot. She looked unhappy. Darius didn't want her to be unhappy in any way.

"The mage who came here and scared Sofia was also looking for Darius."

"I know," Darius said.

"So where is he?"

It would have been so easy to answer and so very hard. Because the two-word response—right here—would have led to a day's, maybe a week's, long conversation.

"I'll tell you when Ariel's not waiting," Darius said, and tugged Munin toward the door.

"She has a soul mate," Blackstone said, even more softly than he said anything else. It was clearly meant as a reminder, a way of preventing Darius from further hurt.

"I know," Darius said. "I don't want to think about it."

Blackstone studied him. "You'll have to think about it at some point, my friend."

Darius glanced at Ariel again. Her gaze met his, and he could read the question in it, even at this distance. She wanted to know what was going on.

"I'm not going to think about it today," Darius said.

This one day was theirs. He was going to enjoy it as long as he could.

The spring air had a bite to it. Ariel wished she had worn her jacket after all. Goosebumps had risen on her arms, and she resisted the urge to hug herself.

What was Blackstone saying to Vari? That she was crazy? Dangerous? Both?

She had seemed like an unbalanced woman right from the start, and she knew it wasn't normal to give gifts to men she worked with. It's just that the dog seemed so perfect. But Vari had been giving her uncomfortable looks since she had done it, and then Blackstone had given her the same odd stare.

Come to think of it, even the dog had looked at her strangely at one point.

She shook her head. Maybe she was getting paranoid.

The wind shifted slightly, bringing the stench of rotting food with it from the nearby Dumpster. Ariel leaned against her car, feeling the cold metal through her thin shirt. Maybe

Blackstone was trying to talk Vari out of spending time with her.

Maybe he was trying to talk him into giving the dog back.

But why would he? It was obvious that Munin was perfect for Vari, and that they liked each other. How could a man be jealous of a dog?

Everything was strange at Quixotic. Sofia had warned her about that, and Ariel hadn't listened. Everything had been strange in her life since she fell off that cliff. Nothing had been the same.

Sometimes she dreamed about it. The dream would seem so real—like a memory. She would be falling, trying to save herself, and in one silly Wile E. Coyote moment, she would look over her shoulder and see nothing beneath her.

Nothing except the river water glistening in the July sun.

Then she would struggle even harder to save herself but feel herself free fall anyway and know that she wouldn't survive the impact, so she might as well enjoy the ride. The wind would whistle through her hair, her body would stiffen in spite of herself, and she would look down one final time—

—and see a ledge form right beneath her.

She always woke at that moment, the falling sensation still with her, knowing that the impact would hurt more than she could bear.

Yet all she had done was break an ankle.

Odd. Just like the flashes of light were odd. Just like people disappearing was odd.

Just like the way she knew—she *knew*—that the dog had to come to Andrew Vari.

On those reality TV shows they sometimes talked about people gaining psychic powers after near-death experiences. Was that what had happened to her?

Only that wasn't right. She clearly remembered seeing a strange man in a diaper the morning of her fall. He had shot at her with an arrow—and he had missed.

That had been hours before she hit her head. Right? Or had the memory come after the fall?

Vari nodded to Blackstone, then stepped all the way out of the restaurant. Blackstone disappeared back inside. Munin heeled beside Vari, as if he'd been doing it all his life.

The garbage smell had grown stronger, and so had the wind. Ariel rubbed her arms, trying to make the goosebumps go away.

Vari watched the movement. Nothing she did seemed to miss his scrutiny. Was that because she made him nervous or was it something else?

"I'm sorry about Alex," Vari said as he got close to her. "He can be weird."

She was always startled at how short Vari was—at the fact that she had to look down at him. He had such a large presence. Sometimes she even thought he was taller than Blackstone.

"I guess today's the day for it." Even she had been weird today. "Are you still up for lunch? Or are you just going to take Munin home now?"

Vari studied her for a moment, his beautiful blue eyes serious. "How about lunch at my place?"

A shiver ran through her, a pleasant shiver that she was certain just came from the chill breeze.

"Lunch at your place would probably be best," she said, "considering we have a dog to settle."

He smiled as she said "we" as if the word had pleased him.

"Do you need to come back here?" she asked. "If you do, we can take one car."

He shook his head. "I'm done for the day. I'll meet you there."

He started across the parking lot.

"Mr. Vari," she shouted after him. "Where?"

"Andrew," he said.

He had told her that before, but the name just didn't suit him. She had trouble fitting her mouth around it. "Andrew. Where do you live?"

She knew the address from her Internet searches, but she

didn't know where it was. She had never really stalked him. She had never gone to his house.

He gave her the address and the directions. Then he led Munin to the employee parking lot.

Ariel watched them go, man and dog. They had similar walks, slow and comfortable, as if they knew they weren't beautiful creatures but had enough personality to make up for it.

Personality was really what counted, wasn't it? After all, people grew older, put on weight, lost their hair or their teeth. The beauty never lasted. The personality did.

The kindness did.

She got into her car and started it up. It smelled of dog and dirty running clothes. Familiar scents. She felt an odd pang, wishing she could have kept Munin. But Munin's reaction to Vari proved that Munin was never meant to be Ariel's dog.

As she pulled into downtown traffic, she thought it strange that she was sad she wasn't going to have a dog. That morning, she had woken up with no idea of getting a pet. Munin had changed her as well—or perhaps opened up a part of her that she hadn't acknowledged before.

She was lonely. Deeply lonely. She had been thinking of Vari as lonely, but he had Blackstone, his work, and his friends of long-standing. She had no one. Her family saw her as an obligation, and she had never made close friends.

She had been in Portland for months, and the only people she knew were the people she worked with.

It was time to change that.

The drive to Vari's house was an easy one, but he lived quite a distance away from downtown. She was surprised, as she pulled up to the address he had given her, at the size of his house. Somehow she had expected him to live in an alpine cottage, complete with a gabled roof and an arched doorway.

Instead the house was Northwest Modern, somewhat conventional despite its size, with a manicured garden out front and large trees flanking its sides. The house blended with the other houses in the neighborhood. Somehow she would have thought that Andrew Vari's house would have been so distinctive she could have seen it from miles away.

So much for predictions.

She parked on the street, and as she got out of the car, Vari opened the front door. Ariel felt her mouth open in surprise. She had left before he had. She hadn't expected him to be there yet.

He leaned against the doorjamb as she came up the walk. Daffodils were blooming beside the sidewalk, and a camellia bush on the side of his house was ablaze in pink flowers, their soft scent coming toward her on the breeze.

"Where's Munin?" she asked.

"Investigating the dog food bowl in the kitchen, last I checked," Vari said.

"He's a puppy. You might not want to leave him alone. They chew, you know."

Vari grinned. "I'm sure he'll be fine."

"I had no idea you put such faith in the creatures around you." She walked past him inside the house.

The foyer was light. A short table, covered with flowers, stood against the wall, a mirror behind it adding size to the room. A staircase curved up the right side of the foyer. A skylight above the landing illuminated the entire area.

The living room, off to the right, had a wall of windows not visible from the street. The place obviously had a lot of light—perfect for a gray Oregon winter.

The furniture was all low, built more to Vari's specifications than hers. But that made sense. This was his house. What caught her eye, though, was that the furniture was all custom made, leather, and clearly expensive.

Apparently Blackstone paid Vari well.

Vari closed the door behind her. He led her through the hallway and into the kitchen. Munin was eating out of a large dish, his little puppy tail wagging ecstatically. A half-empty bowl of water sat beside the dish. There were large puddles around the bowl.

The kitchen smelled of spaghetti sauce, and her stomach rumbled. A sense memory came to her—the spaghetti she'd had in the mountains. It was the best sauce she had ever tasted, and it smelled like this.

"How did you get here so fast?" she asked. "You even managed to put a meal on the stove."

For a brief moment, he looked guilty. Then he shrugged. "Back roads. I know all the shortcuts."

Portland was crisscrossed by rivers and limited by mountains. There weren't many shortcuts in the city. The distances remained constant.

"Someday you'll have to tell me what the shortcut is."

He nodded, but she could see that he had no intention of telling her.

She glanced at the stove. Water boiled on top, and the sauce was bubbling in another pot.

"And you managed to put on lunch."

"Freezers and microwaves," he said. "Modern miracles."

It was her turn to grin.

"It'll be ready a few minutes after I put the pasta in. What would you like to drink?"

"Just some water." She glanced at the floor. "I've been inspired by Munin."

"He's nothing if not enthusiastic." Vari grabbed a glass from a nearby cupboard. He didn't have to reach very high. Even the kitchen had been built to his specifications. The stove was lower than most, and the cupboards and counters were at his waist level. Only the refrigerator was normal-sized. It had ice and water in the door.

He filled the glass and handed it to her.

"I've never been in a house like this one. You had it custom-built?"

"Naw," he said. "I got it from the leprechaun who did promotions for O'Hallerans. He was only here for the two weeks around St. Patrick's Day, so he felt that he didn't get enough use out of the place.''

She chuckled and sank into one of the kitchen chairs.

He shook his head. "Sorry. That just came out.''

"Small wonder,'' she said.

He raised his eyebrows. "Was that a slight?''

"The puns are flying thick around here,'' she said, and hoped he wouldn't be offended.

"Fortunately they're short puns,'' he said, and sat down beside her.

"Not to mention redundant.''

He leaned his head back and laughed. It was a hearty sound, one that seemed almost too big for him. The sound startled Munin, who scrambled under the table.

Vari reached down and patted the dog, comforting him.

"Most people hate it when I joke about these things,'' he said. "They don't know whether they should laugh or not.''

"You do,'' she said, "so I figured I could.''

"Took me a long time to be able to laugh at myself.'' He picked up Munin, who licked his face, and then wriggled to get down. "It's not a skill I'm going to give up just because it's no longer politically correct.''

"It's no longer politically correct to laugh at yourself?''

"Short jokes, personal jokes, jokes about character,'' he said. "Somewhere along the way they became as verboten as the truly ugly racist jokes that were popular fifty years ago.''

"You don't think they're the same.'' She sipped the water. "After all, they're about how a person looks.''

"Or thinks or acts.'' He leaned back in his chair. "If we can't laugh at ourselves, what's the point of living?''

"I always think there's a point in living,'' she said.

He gave her a sideways glance. She got a sense that at one time, he might have questioned that.

"You've been through a lot, haven't you?'' she asked.

"No more than some,'' he said.

"But more than most."

"You could say that." He sighed, then bowed his head. "Look, Ariel, I'm not—"

Munin barked. The sound was small and deep, rather like a six-year-old boy with a bass voice and no way to project it.

Vari shook his head, clearly startled. "You're starting in already, aren't you, buddy?"

He was speaking to the dog, although Ariel wasn't sure why. "What do you mean?"

"Pets protect you," he said.

"What was he protecting you from?" she asked.

"Making an ass of myself." He stood and walked to the refrigerator. He opened it and took out a package of fresh pasta, dumping it into the boiling water. "Lunch in two minutes."

She frowned at Munin, wishing the dog hadn't barked. Until that point, Munin had seemed very well behaved. Now he was licking the spilled water off the tiled floor, just like any dog would do.

Vari moved around his kitchen with the grace of a dancer. He got out a colander and put it in the sink, then grabbed dishes from a cupboard and set the table.

"You don't have to worry about making an ass of yourself with me," she said. "I've been asslike enough for both of us."

He paused and looked over at her. Those blue eyes of his made her breath catch. She could see all the way through them. And she had been wrong about beauty and personality. He had both. His beauty was just hidden, something that only a person who really looked for it would see.

"I never thought you were an ass," he said. "Just a bit obsessed."

"Stalkeresque behavior?" she said. "Not asslike at all, huh?"

His cheeks colored. "I was trying to piss you off so you wouldn't ask more questions about Darius."

"I didn't get mad," she said. "Just embarrassed."

Munin had stretched out on the tile, his head between his paws, his long ears flopped over them like rags. His eyes were closed and his breathing was heavy.

Vari stepped over him on his way to the stove. The puppy didn't even wake up. Like all puppies, he slept suddenly and hard.

Vari stirred the sauce, then stirred the pasta, shutting off the burner. The muscles in his back rippled as he moved. Even his body, compact as it was, was beautiful.

She had just been trained not to look at men like him too closely. It was all over the culture. Never look at someone who is different—you might draw attention to them. You might embarrass them. You might become like them yourself.

He picked up the pot of boiling water and carried it around the dog, careful not to trip. Then he poured the contents into the colander.

Maybe the problems had always been hers. Her parents had died and her aunt had seen her as an obligation, so Ariel had remained distant from everyone else, afraid that they'd see her as one as well.

But she wasn't anyone's obligation. She was her own person. And she could remain like that even if she spent time with someone.

For the first time since the mountains, she had found someone she wanted to spend time with. And she wouldn't mind touching him, either, to see what the look in his blue eyes would be as her hand caressed his skin, her fingers massaged those muscles in his back, moving down—

She shook herself out of that thought.

He turned and apparently saw the movement, because he smiled. "Penny for them," he said. "Or has inflation hit that too?"

She didn't smile. Instead, she took a deep breath. If sports had taught her anything, it was this: The only person who really failed was the person who never tried.

"Could I ask you a question?" she asked.

"How many?" he asked, still in a playful mood. Obviously, he hadn't caught her shift. "Because that counts as one."

"As many as it takes."

This time, he must have caught the change in her tone because he frowned. His eyes shut down and all the beauty that had been in his face vanished.

"Ask," he said.

She swallowed. Munin raised his head and watched her. Apparently he hadn't been as deeply asleep as she thought.

"Does Quixotic frown on relationships between employees?"

His face shut down even more. "Why? Is there someone there who interests you?"

"Yes," she said.

He nodded, then turned back toward the food. "When you ask about Quixotic, do you mean is there a company policy?"

"Yes," she said.

"We've never needed one. We're a small operation." His words were clipped.

"But would it create problems?"

"With me or with Alex?"

"What's happened in the past?" she asked.

"It's never come up." His words were curt.

"You've never had employees who've gotten involved with each other?"

"It's not that kind of place." His reaction was puzzling her. He had no idea what she was talking about. He obviously thought she was interested in someone else.

Munin was sitting up, looking at her with vast disappointment. She had no idea that a dog's face could be so expressive.

"What kind of place is that?"

"A place where people get involved with other people."

"Oh." She spoke quietly. "You think it would disrupt things, then?"

"Probably."

She nodded, glad to have his honest assessment before she told him how she felt. She didn't want to create problems for him at work.

"What if I quit?" she said.

He whirled. Spaghetti flicked off the tongs he held in his left hand and landed next to the dog. Munin seemed to debate a moment between the food on the floor and continuing to let Ariel know about his displeasure.

The food won.

"We don't want you to quit." Vari looked ferocious. "The other guy will have to quit."

Ariel suppressed the urge to smile. "I don't think he can quit. He's a fixture at Quixotic."

"No one's a fixture there." He brandished the tongs as if they were a club.

Munin had devoured the spaghetti and was watching Vari again. This time, the dog seemed worried.

"Not even you?" Ariel asked.

"Me?" He shook his head. "I don't count. Alex and I are a team. We have been forever."

She took a deep breath. When it came to himself, he was so dense. "And if I got in the middle of that team?"

Vari snorted. "Fat chance. Alex is a happily married man. In fact, not many people are more happily married than he is. He wouldn't even give you a second glance, not that you're not deserving of one—you are—but he wouldn't because he doesn't, not anymore—"

"I wasn't talking about Alex," she said.

Vari brought the tongs down. Then he sat down and peered at her as if she had lost her mind. "You're talking about me?"

"What's so hard to believe about that?"

"You're interested in me?"

She smiled. "Yes."

"For God's sake, why?" Then he shook his head. "I know why. Cupid. Dammit."

"Cupid?" Her smile grew. "You believe in Cupid?"

"No, I don't believe in him. I know hi—um, I think he might have gotten his arrows crossed."

She reached for Vari's hand. It was as strong as she had imagined it would be. "Is it that hard to believe that I would be attracted to you?"

"Yes." He tried to pull away, but she held on to his fingers.

Slowly he raised his eyes to hers, and she saw pain in them. Deep, old pain. And with it, something else she recognized. He was too vulnerable. He couldn't take more hurt.

"Ariel," he said, "I don't know if you're trying to get back at me for the whole Darius thing, but this isn't something you should play with."

"I'm not playing." She scooted her chair closer. His eyes were beautiful, but so were his lips. Thin and fine, perfectly formed. If his nose didn't look like it had been broken dozens of times and his cheekbones weren't in the same condition, his face would be conventionally attractive. As it was, he was very attractive—to her.

"Ariel," he whispered. "Don't."

She let go of his fingers. He flexed them. Then she slid her hands around his face and pulled him close, her lips touching his.

The kiss was electric. He tasted fine and familiar, and as his mouth opened beneath hers, she could sense his longing. Hers matched it. She wanted nothing more than to keep kissing him for a very long time. This was where she was supposed to be. This was the man she was supposed to be with. This—

"No." He said it against her mouth and then pulled away. The pain in his eyes was deep. He rested his forehead against hers. "I'm so sorry, Ariel."

This was the second time in six months that a man had

apologized to her after kissing her. And around a spaghetti dinner too.

What was wrong with her? Why wasn't anyone interested in her?

"I'm not sorry," she said.

He shook his head and pushed away from her. "It won't work."

"Why not? I asked about Quixotic."

"There's so much you don't know about me. I can't tell you."

"Why not?" she asked.

"Because," he said, standing and walking away from her. "I'm not supposed to be the one who falls in love with you."

Munin whimpered.

"Excuse me?" she asked.

"I'm not the right person for you, Ariel."

She clasped her hands together, twisting them. "I think I'm supposed to be the one who decides that. Who's right for me and who's not. That's my decision."

"Usually, yeah, but sometimes circumstances—"

"You're talking about Dar, aren't you?" she asked. Munin whimpered again.

"In a way." Vari bowed his head.

"Dar doesn't matter to me," she said. "You were right. It was an infatuation. A reaction to the accident. Nothing more than that."

"Nothing?" His voice was hoarse.

"Maybe an attraction, but that was it. I'm past that."

"And attracted to me now." He made it sound like she didn't know her own mind, as if she was attracted to any man who was kind to her.

"It's not like that," she said.

"How is it, then?"

"I think I'm in love with you," she whispered.

He raised his head. For a moment, his expression was

unguarded and in it she saw longing—and anger. "You can't be."

"What does that mean, I can't be?" Now she was getting angry. "I am."

"No," he said. "You just think you are."

"What?"

"You just think—"

"I know what you said. And I know how I feel. How dare you minimize it just because you're not interested? You should say something polite, like, 'Gosh, Ariel, how nice of you, but you know, you were right, it wouldn't work because of work' or 'Gee, Ariel, I'm flattered, but I don't have those feelings for you.' You're not supposed to say, 'Hey, lady, judging by your past behavior, you're too stupid to know how you really feel. Maybe you should get some counseling.' "

"I didn't say anything about counseling."

"No," she snapped. "I did. Maybe I can find out why I'm falling in love with inappropriate men."

She stood, stalked past Munin, who didn't even try to follow her, and headed for the front door.

"Ariel."

She stopped.

"Stay for lunch." His voice got softer, gentler. "Maybe we can sort this out."

Her heart ached. She should have known better than to open up to him. He was kind and he was nice, but he wasn't interested in her, and she had just embarrassed herself even more than she had before.

"No, thanks," she said. "I've just realized that spaghetti is a very unlucky meal for me."

And then, as quietly as she could, she walked out of Andrew Vari's house.

Seventeen

She didn't even slam the door. He would have slammed the door if someone had spoken to him like that. He would have screamed and shouted and made a horrible scene, and then slammed the door just for effect.

Munin was staring at him.

Darius glared back. "All right. Now you know who the stupid one is in this relationship."

The puppy cocked his head.

"But you don't know the whole story. There's Cupid, you see, and his damn arrows . . . ."

The puppy tilted his head back, as if he were listening but not believing.

"Well, it is his fault. If he hadn't shot her, then she wouldn't think she was in love with me. And if she didn't think that, then she'd be free to find her real soul mate."

Munin grumped and slid onto the floor as if all his bones had turned to water. A familiar yes, but a real dog too, with all of a real dog's traits. His human was talking gibberish, so he had clearly decided that he didn't need to listen.

And, frankly, Darius was getting tired of listening to himself. The Fates hadn't treated Ariel fairly. They had tampered with her in order to get to him, and that wasn't right. He didn't care if they were what passed for law among his people. They had misused it, and at great cost to Ariel.

He put his finger to his lips. She could kiss, though. The way he had felt when she touched him, when she put her hands alongside his face, her thumbs and forefingers around his ear, her hands spread down to his jaw, had sent tingles through him.

He had never wanted that moment to end.

And the moment he had that thought, he had ended it. He had been stealing from her ever since he met her. Her kisses, her focus, and now her love.

It wasn't right.

And he was going to put an end to it.

He looked at Munin. Munin gazed up at him from his wrinkled puppy brow, the picture of dejection.

"If I go see the Fates, will you promise not to trash the house?"

Munin didn't move. Darius took that to mean that Munin wasn't promising anything.

"Do you have to go out?" Darius asked. "We can tend to your needs real quick before I leave."

Munin continued to stare at him.

"Of course, you need a collar." Darius snapped his fingers. A red collar with a name tag appeared around Munin's neck. Darius bent down and double-checked the tag. All the information was correct. "We could just leave you tied up in the back yard."

Munin whimpered. This dog wasn't even two months old and he already knew how to tug heartstrings.

"You don't want to come to the Fates. They're capricious, and they're probably mad at me, and they might just take it out on you."

Munin closed his eyes, as if the thought pained him.

"Tell you what," Darius said. "I'll spell a doggy door into the garage. If you need to use the facilities, you can do it out there. We can rinse off the concrete. Deal?"

Munin sighed.

"I'll take that for a yes. I won't be long, I promise."

Munin sighed even louder. Darius had to get out of there quickly or the puppy would manipulate him into making an unwise choice. No creature should visit the Fates on his first day as a familiar. Especially when his human's history with the Fates was so very bad.

If something happened to Darius while he was with the Fates, he would make sure they took care of Munin. It was the least he could do.

He took a deep breath, steeled himself, and then clapped his hands together. As he vanished, he realized he was making his first trip to see the Fates in more than four hundred years.

Somehow, Ariel found herself back in front of Quixotic. She didn't remember much about the drive. She kept replaying that horrible scene in the kitchen over and over again in her mind.

Maybe she really didn't understand men. Maybe she didn't know them at all. She had thought Darius had enjoyed the kiss they shared in the mountains, but he'd let her go to bed alone, and when she'd awakened the next morning, he had disappeared.

That behavior had made sense when Andrew Vari had explained that Darius was irresponsible. But Vari wasn't. He was a good, kind man who must have pretended to enjoy that kiss and then realized he couldn't take it any longer.

He had tried to tell her. Tried to keep her from going too far. She should have realized that he wasn't interested when he didn't understand who she was talking about. When he hadn't known he was the one at Quixotic who'd captured her attention.

She had thought he was just humble. And maybe, just maybe, she was arrogant enough to believe that no one else had been interested in him the way she had, so of course he wouldn't know such interest when he saw it.

But no. He hadn't looked at her that way. He saw her as a nice woman, a co-worker, someone he would support like he supported the other employees at Quixotic. And she had gone overboard—first with the dog, and then with the kiss.

He was polite enough to keep the dog, but the kiss had probably been too much.

It had been too much for her too.

She opened the car door and got out. The air had grown even colder, and she could see clouds peeking over the tops of some of Portland's taller buildings. It would rain by evening.

This day already seemed too long by half.

She pushed open the glass doors. The familiar smells of Quixotic—garlic and wine and freshly baked breads— threatened to overwhelm her. The restaurant was full. The clink and jangle of glasses and silverware was the underpinning of a hundred conversations. Jazz played softly in the background.

Waiters moved through the tables carrying trays. Busboys worked at being invisible, and the new afternoon hostess gave Ariel a nervous smile, just like Ariel must have the first time she saw Sofia come in on a day off.

Ariel smiled back at her and made her way through the aisles between the tables. She hoped Blackstone was still there. Her right hand had clenched into a fist.

She couldn't come in here again. She couldn't face Vari again. She had embarrassed herself in front of him one too many times.

Ariel pushed open the kitchen door and stepped inside. The subtler scents of prime rib mixed with the sharp smell of cayenne and olive oil. One of the chefs was making a spicy dish on the top of the stove while another carved the prime rib over in the corner.

Blackstone was leaning against the counter, talking on his cell phone. His head was bowed, but she could see a soft expression on his face, one he reserved for only one person—his wife Nora.

As Ariel let the kitchen door swing shut behind her, Blackstone looked up. His expression changed, and she remembered what Vari had said about Blackstone not caring for any other woman.

Vari had been right. Blackstone and his wife were a perfect match.

Ariel wondered if she would ever find hers. Maybe she was one of those people who was destined to go through life alone.

Blackstone hung up the cell phone and gave Ariel a puzzled glance. "Everything all right?"

His voice carried over the din in the kitchen. The staff looked at her, but she couldn't meet any of their gazes. She kept her eyes on Blackstone, because if she looked anywhere else, she might fall apart.

"Can I talk with you in private?"

"Sure." He slipped his cell phone into his pocket. "Let's go to the office."

He led her down the hallway and opened the office door. The office was such an uncomfortable space, so long and narrow, with no windows at all. She wondered how he stood it.

If only it weren't the height of the Saturday lunch hour. If only the restaurant weren't so busy. They could sit in the main area and talk like civilized people, instead of being crammed into the back, in a room too small to hold all of her emotions.

He held the door for her. Ariel stepped inside and immediately went to the back. She wanted to be as far from him as possible.

"What's wrong?" he asked again.

"I'm really sorry," she said, and marveled at how her words echoed Vari's. "I'm going to have to quit, effective immediately."

"Quit? Why?" Blackstone looked concerned. "What happened between you and Sa—Mer—Andrew?"

All the nicknames the man had. She had forgotten that. It seemed strange, like so many things about him. "I just made a fool of myself one too many times."

"The dog?"

Her smile was small. "The dog. The missed lunch. The misunderstandings. I'm apparently the queen of misreading signals."

"Signals?"

She shook her head. "Long story."

"What can I do to convince you to stay?" Blackstone asked.

"Nothing," she said. "I really can't face him again."

"I don't think he'll want to hear that. He cares about you."

"Oh, I suppose he does in his own way. But not the way I want him to."

Blackstone frowned. "What do you mean?"

She held up a hand as if she were warding off his words. She didn't want to talk about this at all anymore. "It doesn't matter. He feels one way, I feel another, and that's all there is. We can't work together. Not after today."

"Did he keep the dog?" Blackstone leaned toward her as he asked the question, as if her answer meant everything. She had no idea why he cared about the dog now, when earlier the dog had annoyed him.

"Yes, of course," she said. "But promise me you'll call me if he decides he doesn't want the dog anymore."

"I promise." Blackstone sounded confused. "I think we could work out some kind of schedule where the two of you wouldn't see each other."

"Thanks," she said, "but no. I'm sorry to leave you in

the lurch like this. I know you've been having trouble with the staff lately."

"We go through phases like this," he said. "Usually around Halloween. I didn't expect it in March."

She wished she hadn't gone as deep into the room. It was time to make her exit, and she wouldn't be able to do it gracefully.

"I owe you so much for taking me on," she said. "I'm sorry it didn't end better."

"I'm not sure it's over," he said.

She sighed. "I am," she said.

Darius arrived in a dark room that smelled of chocolate, wine, and perfume. A light flickered on a far wall, and it took him a moment to realize that someone had mounted a movie screen there.

Gregory Peck stood before a pack of people, a faraway look on his face as he stared at Audrey Hepburn. The black-and-white film was crisper than any Darius had ever seen.

The three Fates were sprawled on the floor. One of them was hugging a pillow and crying. The other two leaned against her, staring at the film with rapt attention.

Darius cleared his throat.

"Shhh," one of the Fates said. He couldn't tell which one in this darkness. "It's almost over."

"He can't leave her," the crying woman said.

"He's not leaving her, stupid," said another Fate.

"She's leaving him," the third Fate said.

"Nooo." The crying Fate raised her hand. "I'm changing it."

"You don't have to," Darius said.

"Shhh." The Fates shushed him in unison.

"Really," he said. "You don't. Richard Curtis answered *Roman Holiday* with his film *Notting Hill.* Of course, by 1999 Gregory Peck was too old for the lead and Audrey

Hepburn was dead, so they had to make do with Hugh Grant and Julia Roberts—"

"*Shhhh!!!*" the Fates said again.

Darius sighed and sat cross-legged on the floor, staring at the film, which he had seen a dozen times. It was one of his favorite movies, although he'd never admitted that to anyone, and he could recite the lines with the characters.

He used to watch it to remind himself that not all romance was about happily ever after. Sometimes romance was about happily for the moment.

He should have remembered that with Ariel. He should have taken the moment, and the future be damned.

Darius shook the thought from his head. He couldn't change the past. He glanced around the room, his eyes finally getting used to the near-darkness.

Heart-shaped boxes of chocolates littered the floor. A carton of Ben and Jerry's—a large carton—was tipped on its side near a table. Pillows were piled high behind the Fates, and in front of them were several blankets all bunched together, as if they had been used.

Empty bags of popcorn littered the other side of the room. The crying Fate was wearing bunny slippers that were so big, they obscured the bottom part of the film. She was outlined against the screen—they all were, their faces in shadow. He couldn't make out who was who.

The scene was nearly over. Audrey Hepburn would say her famous last lines and the scene would end, and then the words THE END would appear. There wouldn't be a five-minute long list of credits like there were in modern movies. In the old days, the credits were a single sheet, usually up-front.

The Fates had huddled even closer. The Fate to his right reached into a box of chocolates, stuck her thumb in the bottom of a piece, and inspected it to see if it was a kind she liked before popping the chocolate in her mouth.

"This isn't right," the crying Fate said again. "How can anyone think this film is romantic?"

"Shhhh!" one of the others said to her.

"He's dreamy," said the third Fate. "Don't you think he's dreamy?"

"Dreamy" was a slang word that had gone out forty years ago, but Darius didn't tell them that. He was irritated that they were making him wait. He had something important for them to do and they were pretending to have a sleepover, complete with footie pajamas and bad food.

"It's the voice," said the crying Fate. "That part *is* romantic."

"Shhh!" said the second Fate.

And then, mercifully, the film ended. It flipped through an imaginary projector and made a whipping noise Darius hadn't heard in decades. The screen went white, sending light through the room.

Suddenly the Fates became recognizable in all their— um—glory.

Clotho wiped tears from her face. Lachesis tucked her pajama-covered feet beneath her, and Atropos grabbed a satin robe from a nearby table.

"Didn't anyone ever tell you never to visit a lady's boudoir in the middle of the night?" Atropos asked.

"It's not the middle of the night," Darius said. "It's lunchtime."

"It is?" Clotho's voice sounded watery.

Lachesis turned slightly, twisting her footie pajamas. "What day is it?"

"Saturday," he said.

"Saturday? Really?" Atropos let out a short whistle.

"We've been watching movies for a whole week?" Clotho sounded as if she were going to cry again.

"Maybe two," Lachesis said. "After all, he didn't tell us which Saturday."

"You should know," Darius said, feeling annoyed. They still had the most irritating style of conversation he'd ever participated in. "You're supposed to know everything."

"If we knew everything," Atropos said, "we wouldn't be studying Twentieth-century film."

"You're studying film?" Darius asked, feeling surprised.

"I thought it would be easier than reading all those mindless novels," Clotho said. "I never expected this to be such an emotionally wrenching experience."

"I suggested reading only the classics," Lachesis said archly, although her superior attitude was a stretch for a woman wearing footie pajamas decorated with little teddy bears.

"We need to know what happens in the modern world," Atropos said, "so I think television would have been the better choice."

Darius frowned at them, caught up even though he didn't want to be. "You're trying to learn about reality by studying fiction?"

"Is that so odd?" Clotho's face was red. She was still dabbing tears.

"Atropos wanted us to watch reality programming." Lachesis shuddered. "But it's filled with such violence."

"Violence bothers you?" Darius couldn't keep the surprise out of his voice.

"It bothers them." Atropos took out her shears and cut open the cellophane on another box of chocolates.

"I thought you three were a team," Darius said.

"Were is fast becoming the operative word," Clotho said with a sigh.

"Even Fates have fates," Lachesis said.

"Our time is running out." Atropos couldn't get the cellophane off so she stabbed the box with the scissors.

Darius had never seen the Fates like this. Although he hadn't seen them for a very long time. Everyone was supposed to change. Still, he needed their help. They couldn't be powerless when he needed them. It wasn't fair. "What do you mean, time is running out?"

"We have term limits," said Clotho.

"Who would have thought the Powers That Be—"

And with that all three Fates bowed their heads and spread out their hands in a reflexive movement, the way a Catholic might cross himself—

"Would succumb to public pressure." Lachesis's face scrunched up, as if the chocolate she had just eaten was spoiled.

"Four thousand years is simply too short. We've only just gotten used to the way power works, and now they want to take it away from us." Atropos stabbed the box again.

Clotho took the shears away from her. Atropos grabbed at them, but Clotho moved them out of her way.

"Succumb to public pressure?" Darius asked. "What do you mean? You're not Fates anymore?"

"We're still Fates," Clotho said. "We just have to reapply for the job after four thousand years."

"Our term is up in a heartbeat." Lachesis sighed and flopped back on the pillows.

"A heartbeat?" Darius held his breath. No. This couldn't be happening to him. "What happens if you're no longer the Fates?"

"Well, there will be the Interim Fates," Atropos said, reaching for her shears. Clotho held them away from her.

"Interim Fates?" Darius asked.

"Mere placeholders," Clotho said, standing so that Atropos couldn't grab the shears. "They certainly won't have the connections we do."

"Certainly." Darius felt even more uncomfortable than he had been when he arrived. "Do I have to wait to talk to them, then?"

"No!" the Fates said in unison.

"Unless you want to," Lachesis added in a tone that made it clear she had no idea why he would want to wait. "But it seems to me that something pretty drastic must have happened to bring you here."

"Yes," Darius said. "I want you to reverse Cupid's spell."

"Which one?" Atropos was still sitting down, but she was watching the shears the way a cat watched a bird.

"The one he did on Ariel."

"Ariel?" Clotho stopped in front of the lit screen. The light seemed to go through her, and she had no shadow. The flipping sound from the imaginary projector had stopped long ago. "Ariel who?"

"Ariel Summers," he said. "You had Cupid shoot her with an arrow so that she would fall in love with me."

"The idiot," Lachesis said.

Darius had had enough. He stood as tall as he could, which wasn't that tall, considering. "Ariel is not an idiot. She's a very good woman with a soul mate, and she has had no opportunity to meet him because of Cupid's spell that was supposed to make her fall in love with me. Set her free so that she can live her life. I got your point. I'll put the hundredth couple together. I'll live a better, more reformed life. Just give Ariel her life back."

All three Fates were watching him closely now.

"We need a more proper setting." Atropos waved a hand.

The dark, close, chocolate-smelling room vanished. Instead, Darius found himself in the front parlor of a farmhouse. Sunlight streamed in through the windows that overlooked the porch. He sat on a horsehair sofa pushed against a wall covered with blue-and-white-flowered wallpaper.

Clotho sat near the fireplace. She wore a demure white dress that went to her knees. Her blond hair was pulled on top of her head in a topknot. She clutched the shears in her hand as if they were a bouquet of flowers.

Lachesis stood near the matching sofa on the other side of the room. She wore a dark dress that reminded Darius of a matron's uniform in World War I. Her high-button shoes looked uncomfortable and so did her hair, which was bound so tightly on the back of her skull that it pulled the skin on her face.

Atropos sat at the upright piano in the corner. Her pink dress was covered with fringe and didn't go past her knees.

On her legs she wore no stockings, and her shoes were the flat-soled ones of a flapper. Her black hair was cut short and made Darius think of all the women he'd seen fawning over Scott Fitzgerald.

"You think this is more formal?" Darius asked. He held a bowler hat between his hands. He looked down at himself. He was wearing a blue wool suit and spats. "It's only formal if I was going to propose to someone, which I am not."

"Really?" Clotho clutched the scissors even more tightly and looked somewhat offended. He supposed if the little scene before him was any indication, the woman he would have been sparking was Clotho in her demure white dress.

The idea of dating her made him nauseous.

He said, "All I mean is—"

"Don't explain yourself, Darius," Lachesis said. "You've already said enough."

"No, I haven't." He stood and flung the bowler hat on the scratchy couch. "You're picking on an innocent woman. I want you to let her out of your clutches."

"She's not in our clutches," Atropos said, running her hands over the keys without pressing them.

"Then she's in Cupid's clutches, which is worse." Darius wanted nothing more than to get out of this cloying room.

"You know," Clotho said, "Eros is no longer on probation."

"Wonderful," Darius said. "He's a schmuck and he gets time off for good behavior. I serve my sentence, and the woman I care about loses the life she's supposed to have."

"We didn't say he got his sentence reduced," Lachesis said.

"He made an illegal deal with the faeries," Atropos said. "Inferior arrows, pretend shootings, faked affairs."

"Not to mention the loan-sharking." Clotho shook her head. "He claims they were repaying him for a slight that happened—oh, a long time ago. That horrible man you brought here, what was his name?"

"Shakespeare," Darius said reluctantly.

"The man who thought we were evil," Lachesis said.

"Boil, boil, or whatever he wrote about us," Atropos said.

"I told you we should have destroyed that play," Clotho said.

"Art is sacred," Lachesis said.

"Whose rule is that?" Atropos said.

"Guess," Clotho said.

"We were talking about Cupid," Darius said.

Lachesis shook her head. "The man has more magical IOUs than anyone in the history of our people, which is saying a lot when you consider Caligula."

Darius had had no idea that Caligula had been a mage, but that didn't surprise him. Nothing surprised him anymore.

"What are you saying?" he asked.

"We're saying that Eros has been sent up." Atropos was now holding a cigarette in a very long holder. A feather had appeared in her black hair.

"Sent up?" Darius wasn't following the conversation anymore.

"He'll be gone for a very long time," Clotho said, her lips pursed in disapproval. "Hadn't you heard?"

"Heard what?" Darius asked.

"About the attempted murder?" Lachesis sat on the couch as if this conversation tired her. "Actually, it should have been attempted genocide, but the Powers That Be—"

And again the three genuflected.

"—felt that the genocide charge should be reserved for creatures like Vlad the Impaler, and shouldn't be applied to lesser cases—"

"As if this is a lesser case," Atropos sniffed.

Cupid had just been in the restaurant. Sofia and the busboys had seen him. "What did he do?" Darius asked.

"Oh." Clotho waved her hand in dismissal. "It is too disgusting to discuss. Besides, he didn't succeed."

"Fortunately for the faeries," Lachesis said.

"For all involved, really." Atropos took a long drag off the cigarette. "It could have set a nasty precedent."

"Considering the fight was over money," Clotho said.

"Well, it couldn't have been over love." Lachesis stretched out on the couch. Her outfit changed as she did so, from the prim, matronly one she had worn a moment before to something diaphanous.

Darius had to look away so that he didn't see anything improper. "How does Psyche feel about this?"

"Psyche?" Atropos exhaled cigarette smoke through her nose. "Manipulative little schemer. We nailed her as an accessory."

Now Darius had to sit down. He sat on the bowler, crushing it, but he didn't care. "Psyche? I thought she was too smart for that."

"So did we." Clotho sighed. She set the shears down and leaned back in the chair.

"But who knew the head always followed the heart?" Lachesis said.

"We thought it was the other way around," Atropos said.

"I could have told you it wasn't," Darius said.

"Not three thousand years ago, you couldn't," Clotho said.

"I've changed," Darius said.

"Indeed." Lachesis tilted her head back. Above her, a red velvet curtain appeared. The rest of the room lost its blue wallpaper.

"I suspect," Atropos said, as if she hadn't heard that little interchange, "that we would have more clout with the Powers That Be—"

A third genuflection.

"—if the whole Eros thing wouldn't have happened."

"True enough," Clotho said. "They would have trusted our judgment more."

"After all, we were the ones who put him on probation in the first place," Lachesis said.

"For a second charge. The guidelines have changed over

the years. Three strikes and you're out. But we still saw him as that cute chubby boy—''

"He never was a cute chubby boy," Darius said.

"Sure he was," Clotho said. "We've known him since he was a baby."

"Although he had a foul temper even then," Lachesis said. "We probably made a mistake giving him a weapon so young."

"Never say we made a mistake," Atropos said. "Someone Important might hear you."

"So what does all this news about Cupid have to do with me?" Darius was trying not to let his own anger show. The Fates had defended Cupid all those years ago. If they hadn't thought Cupid was so important, Darius might not have spent the past three millennia looking like a lawn ornament.

"The assignment was a mistake on our part," Clotho said.

"We should have trusted the process," Lachesis said.

"But we're so used to meddling ..." Atropos took another puff from her cigarette.

"Trusted what?" Darius asked.

"You, my dear," Clotho said. "You've come a long way."

"Indeed." Lachesis turned her head and smiled at him. Her hair had fallen about her face. It wasn't as pretty a red as Ariel's.

"Really, if I had had to choose three thousand years ago, I would have said you were the irredeemable one." Atropos frowned. "Maybe there is a reason we have to reapply for these jobs."

"Posh," Clotho said. "We've done well enough."

"I don't know," Lachesis said. "Atropos has a point. After all, there's the whole Eros problem—"

"And then the way we treated Aethelstan when he really was doing the right thing—"

"Not to mention all those lost years Emma endured—"

"Oh, dear." Lachesis closed her eyes. "Maybe you do become complacent when you've had a job too long."

"Hello!" Darius said. "Can we get back to me?"

"Why, darling?" Clotho said. "What problems do you have? You're our only success story this year."

"I'm not a success story," Darius said.

"Of course you are, my dear," Lachesis said. "Didn't you come to us because the girl is obsessed with you?"

"Yes," Darius said. "But it's wrong. She has a soul mate. Being under a magical spell is bad for her—"

"She's not under a spell," Atropos said.

"What?" Darius asked.

"Think, darling," Clotho said. "What did we tell you about Eros?"

"Irredeemable," Lachesis said.

"Criminal," Atropos said.

"Inferior arrows," Clotho said.

"He shot her with an inferior arrow?" Darius asked, feeling panic build.

"No, silly," Lachesis said softly. "He didn't shoot her at all."

"He was supposed to," Atropos said. "Again, a mistake on our part. We really should have trusted you."

"But we haven't spoken to you in so long," Clotho said. "We thought the arrogance remained."

"And arrogance is so unattractive in a man," Lachesis said.

"Especially unfounded arrogance," Atropos said. "You were such a youngling in those days."

"Green," Clotho said.

"Untested," Lachesis said.

"Full of yourself," Atropos added.

"Wait." Dar's head was spinning. Something on the bowler was stabbing him in an uncomfortable place. He rose slightly, removed the hat from beneath him, and tossed it on the floor. "He didn't shoot her?"

"No," Clotho said. "He missed."

"But he told me he shot her."

"He also told you that he had forgiven you," Lachesis said.

"He was going to implicate you in the faerie affair," Atropos said.

"In fact, he tried," Clotho said.

"But we know all, see all," Lachesis said.

"Except you rent movies so that you can understand the real world," Darius said.

"All right," Atropos said, glaring at him. "Know some, see most."

"You can still be a royal pain, Darius," Clotho said.

"I don't understand," Darius said. "If he missed her, what about her soul mate?"

All three Fates stared at him.

"Apparently he's still somewhat clueless," Lachesis said.

"Well," Atropos said, "not everything can be corrected in three thousand years."

Darius was watching them, that dizzy feeling returning. Clotho smiled at him. "Darling, *you* are her soul mate."

"What?" Darius asked.

"She's told you she loves you, right?" Lachesis paused and stared at him.

"Yes." Darius still didn't believe it.

"Wonderful," Atropos said. "Someone has shown an interest."

"Not just any someone," Clotho said. "The right someone."

"And it happened without magic or potions or spells."

"With Darius actively trying not to let anything happen," Atropos said.

"We were the ones who tried to force the hand," Clotho said.

"After all," Lachesis said, "three thousand years is a long time. We did want your sentence to end, but we couldn't change it entirely. Not without a bit of help."

"Fat lot of good that plan did us."

They were all silent for a moment. Darius was breathing shallowly. Ariel was attracted to him? To both hims? To the tall, slender, runner, handsome him and the short, stocky, obnoxious him? She could actually fall in love with him?

She had a soul mate and it was him? How had he missed that?

"We do have one other thing to tell you before we declare your sentence fulfilled." Clotho stood. She ran a hand along her side, changing her clothing into the black robes of a judge.

Lachesis stood and did the same. So did Atropos. Suddenly they were in a courtroom. Darius stood before the bench as the three women looked down on him.

"We will tell you this," Lachesis said, "but you are not to tell your lady love this until after you are married."

"Or you don't have to tell her at all if you choose not to," Atropos said.

"But you cannot tell her before she agrees to spend her life with you," Clotho said.

"Not because she doesn't love you," Lachesis said. "She does."

"But you have to be able to trust the emotion," Atropos said. "Years from now, you don't want to have that voice of doubt, wondering if she decided to be with you for the perks."

"Perks?" Darius asked.

"We have spoken to the Powers That Be," Clotho said, and they all genuflected for the fourth time.

"We did it about two centuries ago when we thought you were getting close to completing the sentence," Lachesis said.

"We really had hopes for you in London during the Season, until we realized the Marriage Mart was all about power and money," Atropos said.

"There were a few love matches," Clotho said.

"But not as many as in the books," Lachesis said. "If you read those novels they publish these days, you'd think that everyone was wealthy, titled, and in desperate need of a special license.''

"And it really wasn't that way," Atropos said.

"I know," Darius said. "I was there."

They paused, as if they had forgotten what they were doing.

"Oh, yes," Clotho said, sounding surprised. "You were."

"Anyway," Lachesis said, "we spoke to the Powers That Be—"

Darius waited through the fifth genuflection.

"—and they gave us permission that we have only received twice before."

"He doesn't need that much information," Atropos said.

"Well, he needs to know how special this is," Clotho said.

"*And,*" Lachesis said over her companions, "we received permission to extend your Ariel's lifespan to match yours, should she desire to spend the rest of her life with you."

"They let you do that?" Darius asked.

"Yes," Atropos said. "Didn't we just say so?"

"But I thought that wasn't allowed."

"It takes a special request," Clotho said.

"Which we made before this century of debacles."

"Really," Atropos said, "it was just a decade or two of debacles. It only felt like a century."

"Still," Clotho said, "we checked. The dispensation remains."

"For Ariel," Darius said. "Who wasn't born yet."

"For your soul mate." Lachesis peered at him. "She is so well suited to you. She sees the magical edges. The familiar she found you came none too soon."

"Do you watch everything?" Darius asked.

"Goodness, no," Atropos said. "Only the good parts."

Clotho punched her on the arm. Atropos glared at her. Lachesis leaned over and separated them.

"We will share our lifespans," Darius said. It wasn't a question. He was only beginning to understand.

"You will share everything," Clotho said.

"Remember," Lachesis said, "you are our success story."

"Congratulations," Atropos said.

"You are free to go," Clotho said.

And together all three Fates clapped their hands. A bright light filled Darius's eyes, and then he found himself back in his own kitchen. The smell of spaghetti sauce threatened to overwhelm him. The noodles had congealed in the sink, and Munin was nowhere to be seen.

Darius leaned forward, putting his hands on the table. He felt dizzy and out of sorts. The world seemed like it had tilted somehow.

Ariel was his soul mate, and he had sent her away.

"Who the hell are you?" asked a voice from behind him. He jumped, then turned around.

Blackstone stood there, arms crossed, looking more ferocious than Darius had ever seen him.

Darius let out a breath. "Jeez, Aethelstan, am I glad to see you."

"Really?" Blackstone's voice was cold. "Have we met?"

"Yes, of course we have." Darius felt a shiver run through him. In exchange for ending his sentence, had the Fates taken away the last three millennia? Was he going to have to rebuild everything?

"I don't remember it," Blackstone said.

They ended his sentence. The chill Darius felt grew. He looked down at himself. No wonder the world had felt as if it tilted. It had. It had grown smaller.

His custom-designed house no longer fit him. He was too tall, too thin, too young.

"Hey!" he shouted to the Fates, hoping they could hear him. "You can't do this! It's too soon!"

But no one answered him. Blackstone was still staring at him. "You want to explain that little comment?"

Darius swallowed. Lovely. He hadn't expected this twist. "Aethelstan, it's me. Andvari."

"Sure it is," Blackstone said. "And I'm really Chauncey Blodgett, brought back from the dead."

"Who?" Darius asked.

"The greatest chef in Europe in the mid-Fourteenth—oh, never mind," Blackstone said. "What have you done with him?"

"Chauncey Blodgett?"

"No. Andvari."

"Nothing," Darius said. "I *am* him."

Blackstone took a step forward, face dark, eyes narrowed. He looked very menacing—or he would have looked very menacing if he could have towered over Dar. But he didn't. Darius looked him directly in the eye.

"Andvari," Blackstone said with great precision, "has been my best friend for a thousand years. If he looked like you, don't you think I'd know that?"

"It would be logical." Darius was amazed at how calm he sounded.

Blackstone raised his eyebrows, his mocking look. Darius had always found these movements threatening, but they weren't, not really. Not when he could look at Blackstone directly, maybe even a little down on him.

Blackstone wasn't as large a man as Darius thought he was.

"So why are you lying to me?" Blackstone asked.

Darius sighed. This was going to be hard. No wonder the Fates were in trouble. Hadn't they thought about the effect his change would have on his world?

Of course they hadn't. They were only thinking in terms of crime and punishment. When they thought in other terms, they seemed to get themselves in trouble.

"Sit down, Aethelstan," Darius said.

"I'll stand, thank you."

"No, really," Darius said. "I'll make some more pasta, and we can sit down and discuss this like real people over a meal."

"I'm not hungry." Blackstone actually sounded petulant. "I want to know what you've done with Andvari."

"Nothing," Darius said again. "I *am* Andvari."

Blackstone's lower lip jutted out slightly. "All right. In Fourteen-ninety-one, who convinced Isabella that Columbus's hare-brained schemes weren't so crazy?"

"You did." Dar's stomach was rumbling. He was going to eat, even if Blackstone wasn't. "I guarded the door while you met with her, and I even managed to convince Ferdinand that she was in the garden by making a ghost-spell for the space of that afternoon. Every time he looked out, he saw her down there, but when he went down, she was gone. He was really annoyed. We almost blew it that time. If he'd caught you with her, you might have been arrested."

"As if that were a problem," Blackstone said.

"The Chief Inquisitor was one of us."

"Andvari used to say that." Blackstone had his arms crossed. "Obviously he's told you this story."

"Obviously," Darius said sarcastically, "since I couldn't have lived through it and remembered it."

He put more water on the stove, then cursed. He didn't want to wait to eat. Instead he conjured up a plate of pasta and then ladled sauce onto it.

"Andvari never wastes his magic," Blackstone said.

"Andvari has had a rough day," Darius said, "and it's about to get rougher. You sure you don't want some?"

Blackstone shook his head as Munin walked into the room. The puppy's tail started to wag when he saw Darius. By the time Munin had crossed the room, it looked as if his tail were a propeller forcing him forward.

"Hey, boy," Darius said, crouching toward him. Munin licked his face, then shoved his snout toward the plateful of food. Darius moved the food away.

Blackstone watched it all carefully. Familiars didn't get that familiar with other magical types. They were friendly, but not that friendly.

"So he's your puppy," Blackstone said. "Now this is all making sense."

"It's not like you to make things up," Darius said. "Nothing is making sense to you. You need my explanation."

Blackstone continued to stare at him. Darius sighed and set the plate on the table. Munin stretched himself to his full length, doing a dance on his short, stubby hind legs as he tried to reach the table. He wasn't even close.

"Please sit, Aethelstan," Darius said.

Blackstone still didn't move.

Darius sat down, reached for his fork, and then pushed his plate away. "I can go through story after story after story. Let's try Nineteen-twelve, when Emma's coffin fell overboard as they were trying to load it onto the *Titanic*. You had to do a spell in front of huge crowds to prevent water from seeping inside, and then you had to make them forget we even existed, so we couldn't take the ship after all, which you always regretted, saying you could have repaired that iceberg damage."

"Everyone knows that story," Blackstone said.

"Except the Emma part," Darius said. "Or how about Ten-sixty-six? William is conquering, and I said we'd be better off in China. You'd never even heard of China, so I popped us to Beijing, which wasn't Beijing at the time, and into a restaurant—which you'd never even heard of before, because the Chinese were the people who invented restaurants—and you had rice for the very first time. I did that because I knew that the way to convince you of anything was to have you eat first and think later, which I've been trying to have you do ever since I popped back here—"

"Back from where?" Blackstone asked. His arms were still crossed, but he snuck a glance at the stove.

The sauce did smell good. Darius pulled his plate closer. "The damn Fates, who aren't helping me at all right now!"

He said that last part loudly, in case they heard him. It would be easier if they heard him. They could explain everything to Blackstone. And to Ariel.

Oh, no. How was he going to explain any of this to Ariel?

"Why would the Fates help you?" Blackstone asked.

"Do you remember what you said when I told you I knew Darius?"

Blackstone's eyes narrowed. "Are you Darius?"

"I'm Andvari," Darius said. "And I'm—"

"You look like Ariel's description of Darius."

"Whom you don't respect," Darius said. "You've told me a thousand times that you think it's silly for someone to take three thousand years to fulfill a sentence as easy as that one. You've said there must be something wrong with a man who couldn't put together people who were meant to be together."

Blackstone sank into a chair. His cheeks were turning red.

"We weren't that close in the beginning," Darius said. "You thought I was a short, obnoxious guy, just like everyone else did. You didn't find out until Thirteen-thirty-three that I was Andvari, and that was only because that elderly Scandinavian woman pointed at me and screamed that I was a dead ringer for him. So I told you that story, and you assumed that's where I started. It wasn't, Aethelstan."

Blackstone's flush had grown darker. His mouth worked, but no words emerged.

"Somewhere in there—I can't remember the exact year—I started to tell you about my past. Only I opened with, 'Have you ever heard of Darius?' and you launched into that speech of yours that has remained unchanged for over six hundred years, and I decided not to tell you. But didn't you wonder, Aethelstan, why I disappeared for ten days out of every year and never, ever let you come with me? You were surprised when you found out I had a home in Idaho. Didn't you think it odd that I knew someone you've never met, considering how long we've known each other?"

Blackstone was just staring at him. For the first time since Darius had known the man, he couldn't tell what Blackstone was thinking.

"Or do you just need proof?" Darius snapped his fingers and made himself look like the body he'd worn for years. It felt more comfortable to be small, but it also felt weird. This body wasn't the same. It felt like a construct—a suit of clothes. An ill-fitting one at that.

"See?" Darius said in his gruff, nasal Andrew Vari voice. "Now you recognize me."

Blackstone continued to stare at him. Then he looked at Munin, who was sitting on the floor, staring at the table, tail wagging. The dog looked completely unconcerned, just like a good familiar would. A good familiar would recognize his owner no matter what form the owner wore.

"Which is your normal form?" Blackstone asked.

Darius changed back. "This one."

Blackstone nodded, his mouth set in a grim line. "You'd better tell me everything, then."

So Darius did. He told Blackstone about the problems, the first meeting with the Fates, the part of the sentence no one knew. He told Blackstone how difficult it had been to be two different people at the same time, and how being small had changed him almost more than being a matchmaker had.

Then he told Blackstone about his most recent meeting with the Fates and how they had determined that his sentence was fulfilled.

Blackstone listened silently, occasionally nodding. At one point, he conjured a plate of spaghetti for himself and put sauce on it, pausing to give some tomato-covered meat to Munin, who ate it too fast to be grateful.

"And then I came back to find you here," Darius said. Then he frowned. "Why are you here?"

Blackstone shrugged. "I came to find out why Ariel quit."

"She quit?"

He nodded. "Said she couldn't stay, not after she embarrassed herself like that. Said it was one too many times with you."

"Oh, jeez," Darius said, pushing away from the table.

The tiny chair he'd been sitting on nearly tumbled over backwards. He had to bend to keep it from falling. "I have to see her."

"Not yet," Blackstone said. "We're not done with this conversation."

Darius held the chair, staring at his old friend. He knew what was coming—he'd been dreading it for centuries—but he always figured he'd have time to prepare for it, maybe even time to tell Blackstone the story before the change.

But time had just run out.

"I understand why you didn't tell me when we first met," Blackstone said. "But surely there should have been one moment in the past thousand years where you felt it was right to tell me the truth."

Darius shook his head. "I knew how you felt about me."

"You knew how I felt about you?" Blackstone's voice had grown softer, which Darius somehow found ominous.

"Yes."

"You knew how I felt about Andvari or about Darius?"

"Both," Darius said.

"If you knew how I felt about Andvari, you shouldn't have worried about my reaction to Darius."

"No?" Darius asked. "Your good opinion is very important to me, and you don't have a good opinion of Darius."

"I didn't know Darius," Blackstone said. "I knew you. And you—in one thousand years—never trusted me enough to tell me the truth."

"I told you the truth about everything else," Darius said.

"Just not the most important thing," Blackstone said. "Who you really were."

"You didn't like who I really was."

"I didn't know who you really were," Blackstone said. Then he tilted his head. "I guess I still don't."

"That's not fair."

"Really?" Blackstone leaned back. The small chair creaked beneath his weight. He had always looked out of place in this tiny kitchen, but the new position made things even worse. "I'm being unfair? Just like I'm the one at fault for the fact that you never told me the truth."

"I didn't say that," Darius said.

"Yes, you did." Blackstone brought the chair forward with a clunk. "You said you couldn't tell me because you already knew my reaction. You thought I wouldn't respect you. Well, I did respect you. I respected you until I found out you lied to me for generations."

"I didn't lie."

"Oh? Then why would you refer to Darius in the third person?"

"I've been doing that since long before you were born." Darius stood. "I wore this body for two weeks out of every year. It didn't feel like me."

"Good excuse," Blackstone said.

"It's not an excuse." Darius knew he sounded defensive, but he wasn't sure how to stop. "It didn't feel like me anymore. It still doesn't. My whole world has changed."

"Yes." Blackstone stood. "It has."

"Where are you going?" Darius asked.

"Back to the restaurant. From there, I'm calling Ariel to tell her that you've been fired. She can come back any time she wants."

"F-fired?" Darius frowned. "You can't fire me. You never officially hired me. I don't even get a salary."

"I can fire you. Volunteers get fired all the time." Blackstone tilted his head slightly. He was actually looking up at Dar. "And you deserve to be fired. You'd fire an employee for consistently lying to you."

"I didn't consistently lie."

Blackstone stared at him for a long moment. "Maybe you didn't learn as much from your time in that self-made prison as you thought. Maybe you'll relapse, just like your friend Cupid did."

"He's not my friend," Darius said.

"Neither, apparently, am I." And with that, Blackstone turned and stalked out of the kitchen.

Darius stood immobile. Munin whined. After a moment, Darius heard Blackstone's car start and then drive away.

Darius was alone, just like he had been the first time his body had changed. Only this time, he had some apologies to make. This time, he wouldn't hide.

He'd been hiding for too long.

Eighteen

Ariel hung up the phone and stared at it as if she had never seen it before. The kitchen counter cut into her back and her legs were sore from the extra effort she had put out during the race that day. She was tired, and thirsty, and now very confused.

She went to the refrigerator and pulled the door open, staring inside. Orange juice, milk, some oranges, and a grapefruit. It was pretty clear that she only ate breakfast at home.

With her left hand, she took out the orange juice, poured herself a glass, and then closed her eyes.

Blackstone had fired Vari. She still couldn't believe it. Blackstone hadn't sounded like himself on the phone.

It's okay to come back now, he said. *Andrew Vari won't bother you again.*

When she'd asked for clarification, Blackstone had told her that he'd fired Vari.

Not over me, she had said, panicked.

No, Blackstone said. *I found out he had lied to me since the moment we met. He never was the man I thought he was.*

She had tried to find out what Blackstone meant, but he had said no more. Then he had told her to report at her usual time on Monday and hung up.

Hung up, leaving her with the sound of his normally warm voice still ringing in her ear, a voice gone cold with anger and hurt. What had happened between the two men? And why today? She had a hunch her quitting had triggered something; she just wasn't sure what.

And she wasn't sure what she should do. She wasn't sure she wanted to be at Quixotic without Vari there. The job wasn't one she loved—it wasn't even how she planned to spend the rest of her life. But she needed something to support the running, and a hostess job was perfect for that. It required no thought on her part, just some of her time.

Time she now had in abundance.

She walked to the couch where the classified sections from all of the week's newspapers were spread open. She had been going through the sections line by line, job by job, to see what she was qualified for. Not a heck of a lot, as it turned out. Her job skills were simply not at the proper corporate level.

And her concentration skills were gone. She couldn't even look at the newstype before her. She wanted to call Blackstone back and find out what happened.

She wanted to call Vari to see if he was all right.

Instead she sipped her orange juice and wished this day had never happened.

A knock on the door echoed throughout the tiny cottage. She was so startled that her hand jerked upward and she spilled orange juice all over herself. No one had knocked on that door, not in the six months she'd lived there.

"Just a minute," she called, dabbing at the orange juice. It was a lost cause. The stain ran down the front of her shirt, soaking into the top of her jeans. She had a choice between cleaning up and answering the door.

She went for the door.

There was no peephole—this place hadn't initially been designed as a rental—and so she couldn't see who was there before the door opened. She hadn't even realized that was a problem until now.

She pulled the door back and gasped. Darius stood before her.

His golden curls caught the sun. His blue eyes were the color of the sky. He looked trim and fit and beautiful, more beautiful than she remembered. She had kept a snapshot of him in her mind, but it hadn't done him justice. If anything, he was more vibrant, more stunning, than he had been in her imagination.

Her heart was pounding.

"Mind if I come in?" he asked.

She shook her head, momentarily unable to speak. Instead, she stepped back and let him inside the cottage, closing the door behind him.

He surveyed the interior as if he were searching for something.

"H-how did you find me?" she asked, her voice coming out small and weak. Her hands were clammy and she wiped them against her jeans. The orange juice on her shirt stuck to her skin. She felt frumpier than she ever had in her life.

He turned, his blue eyes sad. For a moment, he reminded her of Andrew Vari—Vari was the only person she had ever seen who looked that sad—and then the expression passed.

"Do you have a thing about dogs?" he asked.

"What?" She didn't follow what he meant.

"Inside. Would you mind if a dog came inside?"

Her brain wasn't working. For a moment, she thought he was referring to himself and his behavior. And then she realized that he meant a real live dog.

"No," she said, "I don't mind."

He nodded, opened the door, and whistled. A basset hound puppy came bounding in, all wriggles and excitement.

It was Munin.

"This is Andrew Vari's dog," she said, not understanding.

Darius nodded. Then he frowned. "You spilled something."

"I know," she said. "I was just going to clean it up."

"Give it a moment," he said. "I need to talk to you."

"I've been searching for you for months," she said, not willing to tell him that she'd given up weeks ago. "I think you can wait a few minutes while I get the orange juice off my shirt."

She didn't wait for his response. Instead, she went to the bedroom and changed clothes, feeling oddly exposed with him in the next room.

She should have been excited that he was here. Three months ago, she would have thrown herself into his arms. But now she wasn't sure how she felt.

He was a complication, one she didn't want. She had been hoping it was Vari at the door, so that she could talk to him. Maybe he would apologize, take her in his arms, tell her that he cared for her.

Instead, he sent his elusive friend and his dog.

That irritated her. She wasn't sure why, but it did. Was it a slap in the face or a way to reestablish trust between them? Or was Darius the bad penny Vari had said he was, the kind of man who always took advantage of a difficult situation?

Well, he wouldn't take advantage of her. She slipped on the T-shirt she'd gotten at the race and a different pair of jeans. Her stomach was still sticky, but she'd deal with that later.

When she entered the living room again, she saw Darius standing by the couch. He was looking at the newspapers, a frown on his face, as if he didn't approve.

How much did he know? Did he know that she had fallen in love with his friend? Did he know that she had left her job so that she would never have to face Andrew Vari again? Did he know that she had searched for him first, thinking him to be someone he wasn't?

He looked up, and she felt an unexpected jolt. So there was a pull between them, even when she didn't want it. And he still looked sad. She didn't remember him being this sad.

"Ariel," he said, "do you believe in magic?"

Whatever she had expected him to say, it wasn't that. It sounded like a cheap pickup line.

"Magic?" she asked, trying not to keep the contempt out of her voice. "If you're going to try something that tired, why not ask me if I believe in love at first sight?"

His expression didn't change. "Ariel, please. This is hard enough."

"What is? Coming to see me after six months? There were no promises between us, Darius."

"Ariel—"

"I just wish things had been different. I tried to find you. Didn't Andrew Vari tell you? Or did he protect you to the last?"

"Ariel, please—"

"Am I making you uncomfortable?" She took a step toward him. All the anger and frustration from the day filled her. "Well, I was uncomfortable for a long time. That kiss threw me, and then you disappeared on me, as if I wasn't worth anything."

"Ariel, it wasn't like that—"

"I tried to get information to you, but your friend protected you, just like he was supposed to." She straightened. "He's twenty times the man you are. He's good-hearted and warm, and loyal."

Darius's mouth opened slightly. This time he didn't try to say anything.

She took another step forward. "He just got in trouble with a good friend of his because of me, and I don't really have the time to deal with you. I have to solve this other problem first."

Darius extended a hand as if he were going to try and stop her. "Ariel, you have to listen to me."

"I don't have to listen to anything, Darius. All I have to do is go to Quixotic and make Blackstone realize I don't want his silly job, and that he needs to rehire his old friend. He overreacted and —"

"No, Ariel, he didn't overreact." Darius's voice was soft.

She frowned at him. He finally had her attention.

"He was right."

She shook her head slightly. "Andrew Vari sticks up for you and you stab him in the back first thing? You really are as bad as he says. You're very pretty to look at, but that's all. There's nothing else to you, is there? No loyalty, no—"

"Ariel." This time he spoke forcefully. "Sit down."

"I'm not Munin," she said.

"Please," he said. "You have to hear me out."

"I don't have to do anything." She was resolved now. He had clarified her thoughts. She did need to go to Quixotic and talk to Blackstone, and then she had to leave Portland. The last thing Vari needed was for her to be mixed up in his life again.

"Yes," Darius said, "you do."

There was nothing she could say to that. Instead, she turned and headed toward the door. She would see if Vari was right. If she left Darius alone, he'd probably search the place, take what little she had.

Not that it mattered. There was nothing here she really cared about.

"Come on, Munin," she said as she grabbed the doorknob. "Let's take you back to your owner."

The puppy whined.

Ariel tugged on the door, but it didn't open. "What the—?"

"It stays closed, Ariel," Darius said.

"What?" She turned around. "What are you talking about?"

"The door. I'm going to hold it closed until you listen to me."

"It's stuck, Darius," she said. He had a strange sense of humor. "You have nothing to do with it."

He waved a hand, and suddenly she was sitting on the couch. She had no idea how she got there.

"What was that?" she asked, trying not to show how unsettled she was.

"Magic," he said, and sat down on the rocking chair across from her. Munin looked back and forth between both of them, as if he wasn't sure what they were going to do.

"Magic," she said, feeling unsettled. What had Darius done? How come she didn't remember crossing the room?

He nodded. "You've seen edges of it your whole life."

"Edges of what?" She wasn't really following him. Instead she was frowning at the door, trying to figure out how she'd lost some seconds of her life. He hadn't given her anything to eat or drink. Her head didn't hurt. She felt very funny, though.

"Magic," he said again.

"What about magic?" She finally focused on him. "Why are you talking about magic?"

"Because I should have told you about it a long time ago."

She blinked. "Huh?"

He looked down, then ran his hands through his hair. "Oh, God, Ariel, I don't know how to start this."

"How to start what?"

"Telling you everything."

She shook her head. Lost seconds or no, she wasn't staying here any longer. She stood. "You can tell me later. I'm going to Quixotic."

"To see Andrew Vari," he said. It wasn't a question.

"Yes. That's what I said."

He nodded. "Even though I barred the door and pulled you back here, you insist on seeing him."

She frowned at him. "I thought you were his friend."

"No," Darius said quietly. "I've never been his friend."

She snapped her fingers. "Munin, come on."

The puppy looked at Darius as if asking for permission.

"Ariel," Darius said, "no matter what I tell you, you're going to be mad at me, but this might be easier if you just listen for a minute."

She headed toward the door. Munin was not following her and she didn't feel good leaving the dog alone with this man. She walked back, scooped the puppy up in her arms, and felt him wriggle. He was as focused on Darius as he had been on Andrew Vari. What was it about Darius? Some sort of pheromone that he gave off that appealed to helpless women and puppies?

"So I'm sorry to tell you this way," Darius was saying, "but I see no other choice."

She turned away from him again and headed toward the door. If it didn't open this time, she was going through the window.

A light flashed behind her, and Munin whined, struggling hard in her arms. She gripped him tightly with her left arm while reaching for the door with her right.

"Ariel."

A shiver ran up her spine. That voice belonged to Andrew Vari. How had he gotten in? She had locked the back door. In fact, she never unlocked it.

She looked over her shoulder.

Andrew Vari was sitting where Darius had been.

Munin wriggled out of her arms and slid down to the floor. Then he ran to Vari, his tail wagging happily.

"Where's Darius?" she asked. "How did you get here?"

"You let me in," he said.

"I didn't let you in," she said.

"Yes," he said. "You did. Just a minute ago."

"You came in with Darius?"

"In a manner of speaking."

"What manner of speaking?"

"This manner." He snapped his fingers. His entire body was wrapped in white light. The light got so bright that it blinded her, and when the light cleared, Darius was sitting in the chair.

His arms were in the same position Vari's had been in. He was even wearing the same clothes—only they were larger to accommodate his frame.

"Whatever it is you two are doing to me," she said, "I don't like it. It stops now."

"Sit down, Ariel, please," he said.

"I don't take orders from you." She crossed her arms. This was getting creepy. "Where's Andrew?"

"Right here," Darius said.

She looked around the room. "Where?"

He raised his eyebrows. The look transformed his face. He was impossibly handsome. She should have been suspicious of that from the start. Men who were impossibly handsome were trouble.

"You want to hold my hand this time?" he asked.

"What do you mean?"

He held out his hand.

She shook her head. "I'm not touching you."

"It's the only way you'll believe me."

"That's a new one." She hugged herself even tighter.

"Ariel, please, I'm trying to tell you. I am Andrew Vari. Really."

"And I'm Raquel Welch." She held herself so tightly that she could feel her fingers dig into her ribs. "Get out of my house."

"Ariel—"

"Get out." She had lowered her voice even though she wanted to scream.

Munin was sitting between them, his tail thumping worriedly on the floor.

Darius studied her for a moment, then he nodded. "All right." He sounded disappointed. "All right. I'll leave."

He stood up. Munin watched him, not moving.

Darius walked toward her. Ariel decided she wasn't going

to move either. He wasn't going to intimidate her. He wasn't going to have any effect on her at all.

As he brushed past her, he reached out and swung her around. He pulled her against him. Her arms were trapped against his chest. She tried to move them, but she couldn't.

"Ariel," he said softly. "Please listen to me."

She struggled against him, slipping her right hand down until it was below her left elbow. Then she started to move her right arm away from her body.

At that moment, a bright light enveloped her, blinding her. Her arms popped free, but she still felt hands—his hands. They had slid down her back until they rested just above her buttocks. Only he hadn't loosened his grip. His hands had just . . . moved.

The light faded. She staggered and nearly fell, but he held her up. Sort of. She looked down.

Andrew Vari had his arms around her. He was looking up at her with those sad eyes. When their gazes met, he let go.

"I'm sorry," he said. "You had to know it was real."

"What's real?" She was whispering and she didn't know why.

"What you were seeing. I am Darius, Ariel. That's the name I was born with, two thousand, eight hundred and one years ago."

She could still feel his arms around her. Both sets. The tall arms that had held her against a firm, muscular chest, and the short arms that had struggled to clasp her near her hips.

She had seen it. She had felt it, and dammit, deep down she did believe it. She knew that he wasn't lying to her.

Because the eyes were the same. Both men had the same gorgeous blue eyes. The same sad blue eyes.

She walked over to her couch, amazed that her knees could hold her. When she reached it, she sat down. Munin jumped up beside her and licked her arm. She petted him absently.

"Two thousand years ago?" Somehow she believed that too. "How is that possible?"

Vari walked back to his original chair and sat down. "There are a group of us—how many I don't know—who are born with magic. We're not the same as mortals. With the magic comes an extraordinarily long life. If we use too much magic, the life gets cut shorter. But I've lived almost three thousand years, and I'm sure that unless I do something stupid, I have a thousand more."

"A thousand years." Maybe she had lapsed into a coma after her run. Maybe she was dreaming all this.

Munin licked her again and whined. Poor dog. All of this on his first day with a new owner.

"Blackstone is one of us, and Nora will be someday."

"Will be?" Ariel asked.

"Women don't come into their powers until after menopause. Something about surging hormones, I guess."

He smiled as he said that, but she could tell he wasn't really joking.

"I'm not one, though, am I?" she asked. "That's why you've been brushing me off. Because I'm just a fruitfly compared to you."

"No, Ariel, that's not it." He ran his hands through his hair. "May I change back? I'm using a lot of magic for this right now."

"So?" she asked. "You always look like that."

He shook his head. "This is part of the problem. I have so much to tell you."

Munin whined again. Ariel could feel her heart beating as if she had just finished a long run.

Vari sat still, as if he were waiting for her to say something, which, apparently, he was. He had asked for her permission, after all.

"Okay," she said. "Change back."

The white light flared again. It didn't startle Munin. For a young pup, that dog was amazingly calm. The light didn't startle her as much either. In fact, she had seen a lot of light like that, starting after her fall. In the cabin. When she'd first met Darius.

Darius, who was now sitting across from her. She could see it now. They were the same man. Their facial shape was exactly the same, long and narrow. Vari's features were Darius's, only exaggerated. On Andrew Vari, Darius's Roman nose became a broken beak. His fine thin lips were stretched to nonexistence. His high forehead became a round bald ridge.

Even their build was the same. Darius had broad shoulders, and so did Vari. The only difference was in length. Vari was a truncated version—a man, literally, cut off at the knees.

"I'm so sorry," he said. Darius's voice was musical where Vari's was made of gravel. A beautiful voice distorted through a synthesizer, or ruined by too many cigarettes. Or maybe by a larynx that had been truncated too.

"For what?" she asked.

Darius ran his hands through his hair—long fingers through golden curls this time—and shook his head. "Can you just listen to me for five minutes?"

"All right." She folded her hands on her lap like a student and braced herself against the couch.

"When I was a young man," he said, "which was a very long time ago now, I was a famous athlete. An arrogant, nasty, horrible person who had just come into his magic."

"I thought you said your people didn't come into their magic until they got older."

"I said women didn't. Men get theirs at twenty-one."

"Like men have no hormonal problems at that age," she muttered.

He smiled, but it was a distracted smile. "We have a lot of problems at that age, and I had most of them worse than others. I was an idiot, Ariel. An idiot and an asshole and the worst kind of person. Everything I told you about me—about Darius—was true."

His voice was trembling. His eyes wouldn't leave hers,

and she felt herself being drawn into them in spite of herself. She remembered that conversation in the deli vividly. He had called Darius—himself—all sorts of foul things. Did he actually feel that way about himself? No one should feel that way about himself. No one at all.

"I did something unpardonable. I—ah, hell. It's almost impossible to explain."

"Unpardonable," she repeated. "You were a serial killer?"

He smiled. It was a relieved smile. "No."

"So you murdered just one person."

He shook his head. "No, no. Nothing like that."

"Then what's unpardonable?" she asked, feeling even more confused than she had a moment ago.

"I was told that I might have made true love impossible."

"For you."

"For anyone."

She frowned. "What are you talking about? Does your magic put you in charge of us lowly—what did you call us?—mortals?"

He stood and walked around the chair. "I'm going about this all wrong. Look, Ariel, we're not better than you. We're just different. And because of our longer lifespan, we have more of an effect on history. That's all. What I did was, I interfered with something I shouldn't have because I was stupid."

"What did you do?"

He shook his head. "I'm not going to explain it. Not yet. I—ah, hell."

Munin leaped off the couch and ran to him, jumping up on his hind legs and pawing at Darius's thigh.

"He thinks I should tell you," Darius said.

"He—Munin?" She felt surprised. She wasn't sure why she felt surprised. The whole afternoon was strange enough that she shouldn't have felt surprised about anything.

"He's my familiar."

"He's your new pet. I just bought him for you. For

Andrew Vari, actually, but I guess that's you.'' She sounded bitter, and she hadn't meant to. But she didn't take it back.

"That's why you thought he should be mine. Because you see magic around the edges of things. Most people don't see white lights when spells get cast. Most people can't track magic to its source, but you did. Blackstone told me about that day in the restaurant.''

"So?'' Ariel asked, not sure which day in the restaurant he was referring to.

He let the puppy lick his face, then he moved Munin over his shoulder as if Munin were a baby and Darius was about to burp him. "Okay. In a nutshell. I broke a major law among my people, and to punish me, the Fates decided that I had to unite a hundred soul mates.''

"The . . . Fates?''

"Our governing body. Like a panel of judges with some legislative power. They're the active arm of the Powers That Be.''

"The Powers That Be?''

"You know. The ones in charge of everything. Just like it sounds. The Fates carry out a lot of their pronouncements. Mount Olympus wasn't that far off.''

"Wonderful,'' she said.

"So I had to unite a hundred soul mates,'' he said again.

"Unite? As in marry them?''

"As in make sure they were together for the rest of their lives.''

"Then what would happen?''

"They'd live happily ever after.''

"No,'' she said. "To you, once you did this.''

He closed his eyes, tilted his head back, and squeezed the dog until Munin made a small squeal of protest. "I would get to look like myself again.''

"What?'' How could she be getting more confused? Weren't explanations supposed to make a person less confused?

"For two weeks out of the year," he said, setting Munin down, "I got to look like this."

He ran his hands along his body—his lean, trim, too-handsome body.

"I could pick those two weeks. Usually I went somewhere fun, like Cannes, only the last ten years or so I got tired of all that. I went to my place in Idaho."

"To be alone," she said, remembering what he had told her all those months ago. "And reflect."

He nodded. "The rest of the time, I was being punished for thinking myself greater than everyone else because of my physical prowess, because my body worked better than other people's even before I came into my magic. So the Fates decided to teach me what it was like to be someone whose body didn't automatically open doors."

"Andrew Vari," she said.

"Andvari," he said, putting a different emphasis on the name. "Only you don't know Norse mythology."

"You're a Norse god?"

"No." He came back to his chair and sat down. "I'm the dumb dwarf who tormented a Norse god. Loki. That's where my Andrew Vari—Andvari—form first enters written history. That's how Blackstone knew me. Only he met me hundreds of years later, when everyone was calling me . . ."

He paused and looked at her sideways, as if he didn't want to say any more.

"Calling you what?" she asked, somehow knowing she wasn't going to like this.

"Merlin."

"That's it." She was off the couch before she knew it. "Where's the hidden camera? Where are your friends? You can all come out now and laugh at me to my face."

"I'm serious, Ariel."

She whirled on him. "So Blackstone calls you Sancho because you're the original Sancho Panza?"

"Yes," he said.

She sank back onto the couch. Her knees weren't working again.

"And the original Ghost of Christmas Present, if you have to know, and Shakespeare claimed that I was Falstaff to annoy me, but if you look at Puck, you see where that character came from."

Ariel bowed her head and laced her hands over the back of it, protecting herself. She didn't want to hear any more.

"But that doesn't matter, Ariel." Darius got out of the chair and came toward her. He crouched in front of her and put his finger beneath her chin, raising her head so that she would look at him. "What matters is, I was a failure."

She moved her head away from him, but she couldn't stop looking at those eyes. They seemed even sadder.

"A thousand years, two thousand, almost three went by, and I still hadn't united a hundred couples. Early on, I made terrible messes of things. I'll tell you about it sometime. Anthony and Cleopatra, Troilus and Cressida—I was so inept."

Ariel brought her arms down and rested them on her thighs, but she didn't look away from him. And Darius didn't move. He continued to crouch before her. He rested his own arms on the couch beside her, almost but not quite touching her.

"I didn't tell Blackstone any of this. I can see soul mates, Ariel. I can see in a person's eyes if they have one. Blackstone did, and I knew it. I knew one day I'd have to help him find his ideal lover."

"Nora," Ariel said.

"Nora." Darius gave her a small smile. "It took a thousand years to find her."

Ariel let out a small breath. The confusion was lessening. This incredible story was making sense. "So you help your people find their perfect love."

"Not my people," he said. "All people. You have a soul mate, Ariel. I knew it when you looked up at me that first evening, on my couch. I knew it, and it broke my heart."

He got up and moved away, as if some parts of his own story made him so restless he had to try to shake them off.

"You see, as the Fates explained it to me, my job was to unite two other people in their perfect relationship. Nora and Blackstone were number ninety-eight."

"And you never told him," Ariel said, suddenly remembering Blackstone's comment. "You never told him any of this."

Darius nodded. "He found out today. He's mad. He's real mad. He thinks I've been lying to him all along."

Darius walked to the kitchen counter and braced himself against it, then looked at his hands, as if he hadn't expected them to move that way.

"My friend Emma and her husband Michael were number ninety-nine," Darius said, no longer looking at Ariel. "Then I see you and I know, I just know, deep down, that you're part of the hundredth couple."

Her heart rose a little. She had a soul mate. She would never have thought of that. She wasn't romantic enough to believe in such things—or so she would have thought.

"The problem was," he said, still not facing her, "I fell in love with you the moment I saw you walking on that path."

Ariel raised her head. She was holding her breath, and her heart was still rising—floating, almost.

"You were so confident and so strong," he said, head bowed. "You moved with such grace. And then, when the ground dissolved beneath you, you did everything right. You didn't panic. You used all your resources to save yourself, and when it was clear that wasn't enough, you let yourself go with the moment. I'll never forget that."

Ariel swallowed. "There was no ledge, was there?"

"No." His voice was soft. "I created it. And screwed up, just like I always do."

"What do you mean?"

"You were so broken when I got down there." He turned. She could still see the traces of fear on his face, and she wondered what he had gone through that afternoon. "Internal bleeding, damage everywhere. I fixed it. I stopped the bleeding, got you breathing again, made sure everything was all right. But I missed the ankle."

His lips thinned and he moved away from the counter, walking to the window.

"I didn't know about it until you woke up, and by then it was too late. I couldn't spell it back to normal. I couldn't fix it or you'd know about the magic. And you couldn't know. It wasn't right. Those aren't the rules we live by."

I thought I went all the way down your leg, he had said when she had first told him about the broken ankle. She hadn't understood it at the time, thought it was a nonsequiter. Then he had apologized.

I didn't know you had broken your ankle.

And he had seemed so guilty. That entire day, he had acted guilty and she hadn't understood why.

She did now.

"You were an athlete," he said, "and I ruined it. I got in the way of your trip. You could have kept going, but I shortened it. Then I was afraid there was permanent damage. There was nothing I could do. I was so glad when you started to run again."

He meant it. He was saying all of this as if he meant it. "And all the time you were so strong. Taking everything with grace and humor."

She stood. Maybe, when she heard things that made her uncomfortable, she was as restless as he was.

"I looked into those eyes of yours, and I was so lost." He emphasized the word "lost" and she wondered if he knew that she had thought of Andrew Vari as lost, in a different way. Like a lost soul. "You had me from that moment."

She took a step toward him.

"Then I saw someone else in there, someone lurking. I didn't know who it was—I never do. I only know when I see you both together. The soul mate. He was in there, waiting—for how long I had no idea, and I knew. I knew I would have to pair you with another man, and I couldn't face it.'' He leaned against the window frame, still not looking at her. ''God knows, I couldn't face it. So I tried to shove you away. I only had one more couple to put together, and I figured that if I didn't see you, I might meet another pair of soul mates, someone else. Someone who wouldn't break my heart.''

Ariel took another step toward him.

He turned, slowly, and for the first time, she saw both of them at the same time in his face—Andrew Vari and Darius—tall and short, handsome and homely, warm and cynical, all wrapped in one person, and looking at her with such sadness, and such love.

''And there I was,'' he said. ''A full-time troll pretending to be Prince Charming. I thought it was a plus. I thought you'd never have to see me again. I thought you'd never recognize Andvari as Darius.''

''So you ran away,'' she said.

''I didn't run away.'' Then he shook his head slightly. ''All right, that day I stayed away. And I didn't expect you at the airport. Everywhere I turned around, there you were.''

He ran his fingers through his hair again. She had never noticed that as one of his nervous tics before. There was so much she didn't know about him.

''I fell for you so hard that I thought it had to be some kind of spell. I even went to Cupid, because he had visited me that morning, and told him to take the spell off.''

''Cupid?'' she asked. ''The real Cupid?''

''The real Cupid,'' Darius said. ''Not the cherub you're thinking of. A grubby little man who occasionally wears wings. He lied to me. He said he'd hit you with an arrow, not me.''

Her entire body froze. She had seen that man in the woods just before she met Darius. But Cupid hadn't hit her with an arrow. He had missed, then snapped the arrow in half and tossed it in his quiver.

"I don't," she started, stopped, and then tried again. "I don't understand. Who did he hit?"

"No one. He screwed up. The Fates have sent him away, permanently. Those wings and arrows were a sentence just like mine was."

"How romantic," Ariel said.

Darius smiled. "I guess, yeah. It's weird that he's become the spitting image for all that's romantic. He's the least romantic man on the planet."

"So what are you telling me?" she asked.

"I went to the Fates," he said. "I asked them to give you your life back, to take the spell off."

She slipped her own hands in the pockets of her jeans. For some reason, she was feeling very nervous.

"And they told me there was no spell, and that you were my soul mate, and that we were the hundredth couple. We were always meant to be the hundredth couple. And they congratulated me, took their spell off me, and gave me my life back."

He blinked hard, then crouched and whistled for Munin. The dog came right to him.

"Only they didn't give me my life back. They took it from me. I've been Andvari for almost three thousand years. I don't know how to be Darius. Blackstone won't speak to me. No one will recognize me. And you—they thought I was honest with you, but I wasn't. I didn't know how to be. I thought it wasn't possible, you and me, so I didn't pursue it. I sent you away at every turn. And there's just no hope. I've done horrible things to you, Ariel."

She couldn't move. She felt that if she said anything, she would stop him from speaking.

"I don't expect you to forgive me," he said. "I don't even really expect you to believe me. I've seen what happens to soul mates when things don't work out, when something gets in the way, and I have to be honest, usually it was me getting in the way. I'm not just Merlin. I'm the mythological

Lancelot, and half a dozen others because I was a fool. Just like I've been a fool with you.''

"Lancelot?" she asked.

"He got blamed, actually, for what I did. My life, my history, it's not pretty, Ariel."

"You've learned from it," she said. "Right?"

"The Fates think so."

"Do you think so?"

"I don't know," he said. "I've only looked like this for thirty-seven-thousand days out of the last twenty-seven-hundred years, in two-week intervals. And now I'm trapped in this body for the rest of my life."

"It's not a bad body," Ariel said with great understatement.

"It's not the one I'm used to. It's the one that made me an arrogant bastard the first time. I might revert."

"I doubt that," she said.

His gaze met hers. Munin wasn't even wriggling in his arms. "Thank you for that."

"I don't mean to be kind," she said.

"Sure you do," he said. "You're overwhelmed. I've just told you the moon is made of green cheese and I've shown you proof. Everything you believe is different now."

"Or maybe you just explained some parts of my life that seemed very odd to me," she said.

He walked toward her, still holding the puppy. "I'm sorry," he said again. "I'm sorry I did this wrong. I'm the one who is supposed to know all about love—that's what my life lesson was supposed to be—and I screwed it up. I hurt us both, and I didn't mean to."

Darius stopped in front of her and put a hand on her cheek. His skin was warm, his touch gentle.

"Dar—"

"Shh." He put a finger on her lips. Then he leaned in and kissed her. It was a slow kiss, a gentle kiss, so tender that it broke her heart.

Then, just as he had before, he pulled away. "I love you, Ariel. I will until the day I die."

With his thumb, he wiped his kiss off her lips and walked out the front door.

For the briefest of moments, she didn't move. He was right. He had turned her world around, but not for the reasons he thought. She had seen hints of things on the side of her vision, things that didn't seem quite normal. Believing in magic was not a stretch for her.

Believing that someone could love her was.

And he loved her enough to walk away because he thought he had hurt her beyond repair.

She ran toward the door and threw it open to see the last of a white light fading away in the driveway.

He had vanished. Literally. And she had no idea where he had gone.

Nineteen

Darius had zapped himself and his car home because he couldn't face the drive across town. He landed in the driveway, in the shade on the side of the house, and closed his eyes, no longer feeling safe here.

But he hadn't known where else to go. He knew he'd replay that disastrous conversation in his mind until the end of time. What he wanted the most was to distract himself from it.

He couldn't go back to Quixotic; Blackstone had made that clear. And Darius didn't dare see Ariel again.

He needed to leave Portland, start all over. Sell the house that no longer suited him, discover who Darius was without Andrew Vari, and figure out what he would do with his life. He no longer had a mission.

He was free.

Then why did he feel so trapped?

Darius got out of the car, then helped Munin out of the back. It felt as if he had had the puppy all his life. Munin seemed to feel that way as well. He wasn't disconcerted by the magic or the changes in Dar's appearance. He seemed to accept all of it as normal.

"Sancho?" a female voice said.

Darius turned. Nora was standing on his front porch. He'd never realized how tiny she was. She had always been taller than he was. But not any longer. She was petite and compact, her blond hair catching the sun.

She was holding her purse in front of her, looking uncertain. He hadn't seen her look uncertain in years. But she clearly didn't recognize him. There was only one way she could have known it was him.

Blackstone had told her everything.

"I'm sorry, Nora," Darius said. "I didn't mean to hurt anyone. It's just—"

"Nonsense," she said, coming down the steps toward him. "All you did was hurt Aethelstan's pride. He wasn't thinking about you. He was wondering how he could have missed all of this when the evidence was there. He was thinking about himself, forgetting that this isn't about him."

"It's about him, Nora," Darius said. "I haven't been honest with him from the start."

"Fiddle," she said, using a word he'd never heard her use before. "You were as honest as you could be. You wouldn't have been able to help us if Aethelstan had known that you were our matchmaker. He's so stubborn, he would have found a way around you. He would have chastised you or ignored you or made your life hell. You did the best you could. You always have."

"You're very kind," Darius said.

"No, I'm not," Nora said. "I'm a lawyer. We're never kind."

He smiled in spite of himself.

"I figured you need a friend right now. You were there for me. I'm here for you. I don't have magical powers yet. I can't give you your heart's desire, but I can listen." She slipped her arm through his. "Let's go inside. I'll make you some tea, we'll talk about your new puppy, and if you want to tell me what you're feeling, you can. And if you want to be the strong silent type, you can do that too."

"You don't have to do this, Nora," Darius said.

"I know," she said. "And you didn't have to stay in Portland after our wedding, but you did. You're our friend, Sancho—Andrew—what do you prefer?"

"Dar, I guess. That's me now."

"Whatever you want to be, that's you," she said. "Although I'm not sure about this height thing. I'm going to be surrounded by a male forest."

"I wasn't thinking—"

"Of staying; I know," she said. "You feel like you've let everyone down. You haven't, San—Dar. If you left, everyone would figure out just how very important you are."

He put his hand over hers. He was touched beyond measure. He didn't deserve her kindness, not after the way he'd tricked them all. "Anyone could have done the things I did, Nora."

"Anyone?" she asked. "Just anyone could have cut short his vacation to prove to me that Aethelstan loved me."

"I didn't prove anything," Darius said. "He proved that to you."

"You kept us together, just like you made sure Michael and Emma got together. And I'll bet if we go inside, I could get you to tell me about dozens of other couples whose lives you've enriched."

"Because it was my sentence, Nora. My punishment. My job."

She slipped her hand out of his arm. "It seems to me that there's a strange little man named Cupid who violated probation because he couldn't do his job properly. Every single time he tried."

"He was just—"

"What? Wrong for the job? Bad at what he did? Didn't care about others? Unable to learn?"

Darius stared down at her. She had her hands on her hips. She looked fierce.

"I'd forgotten what a good attorney you are," he said.

She smiled. "I haven't used any of my attorney skills on you yet."

"But you will."

"If you persist in thinking you're the villain of this piece, yes, I will. I will use all my argumentative powers to prove you wrong. Now," she said, slipping her hand back through his arm, "we are going inside. And you're going to drink tea and talk with me, and we're going to have a pleasant afternoon."

"Yes, ma'am," he said.

"And I'm going to learn everything there is to know about you, because I want to know," she said. "Not because I have to."

Darius let those words sink in. "Nora—"

"If you tell me I'm too kind again, I'll slap you," she said. "That'll put an end to that argument."

"Yes, ma'am."

"And don't 'Yes, ma'am' me. I'm one one-thousandth your age."

"Yes, ma'am," he said.

She laughed. "There's the man I know and love."

Nora dragged him inside his house, which was built for a man much smaller than he was. His dog followed. And the afternoon, which had seemed so dark, didn't seem quite as hopeless after all.

Ariel finished washing the orange juice off herself while she tried to figure out what to do. She was feeling disconcerted. The world had changed, just not in the way that Darius thought.

Even if she went to him now, what would happen? Why would the universe put together two people with such radically different lifespans? Had his crime been so bad that he only got fifty years out of four thousand with the person he loved? That couldn't be fair. Or was he allowed more than one soul mate in that long life of his?

She frowned. She didn't like that idea. And she didn't know how to approach him. He was so convinced that she hated him now. Maybe Blackstone had had that reaction, but she hadn't. Darius's confession put her last six months in order. She finally understood them, and she felt much better for it.

A knock sounded at her door and she ran to it. Thank heavens he had come back. She had wanted to talk with him, and she didn't even know where he had gone.

Ariel yanked the door open, started to tell Darius she was glad he'd returned, and stopped.

Blackstone was standing before her, looking as if he hadn't slept in two days. Considering that he looked fine that morning, she figured something else was wrong with him.

"May I come in?" he asked.

She let out a small puff of air. No visitors the entire time she lived here, then two men in the same day.

"Why not?" She held the door open.

He stepped inside.

"If you're here to convince me to come back to the job," she said, "you're wasting your breath. I—"

"I'm not here for that." Blackstone shoved his hands in his pockets. What was it with magical men? Did they have to control their hands when they were nervous?

"Then what do you want?" She sounded ruder than she had planned to, but she was angry with him. She hadn't realized that until now.

"I came to tell you something about Andrew Vari."

Ariel slammed the door. Blackstone jumped.

"He was just here," she said. "I know everything."

"Everything?" he asked.

She nodded. "And I think you are being colossally unfair to him. He just had his whole life screwed up and you blamed him for not being honest with you? Where's your compassion? Don't you know what it's like to go through life taking care of others and doing nothing for yourself?''

Blackstone winced. "Nora already gave me this lecture."

"Good," Ariel said. "Dar left here all upset. You should make sure he's all right."

"Why aren't you doing that?"

"Because he thinks I hate him."

"Do you?" Blackstone asked.

"No," she said. "I'm in love with him."

"Does he know that?"

"I told him this morning." She crossed her arms.

"This morning he was someone else," Blackstone said.

"No, he wasn't."

"But you thought he was." Blackstone peered at her. "You need to tell him now."

"You've been mad at him all day and suddenly you're arguing his case?" Ariel took a step away from him. She had respected Blackstone until today, but now she wasn't sure what kind of man he was. "What's going on here?"

Blackstone closed his eyes and shook his head. "Nora reminded me that I mixed up my role in this little drama."

"Role?" Ariel asked.

Blackstone nodded. "I'm not the center of this story. I'm the sidekick. And the sidekick's job is to make sure everyone lives happily ever after."

"How do you plan on doing that?" Ariel asked. "You're not the matchmaker here."

"That's right," Blackstone said. "But my best friend is a good one, and I think it's time that you and he have a little talk."

Nora had found some chocolate chip cookies in his cupboard, and then she had brewed some Awake tea—apparently on the theory that Darius's system hadn't been stimulated enough that day. She fed Munin some of his puppy chow and made up a bed for him. The little guy ate as if he'd been starving, then fell into the sleep of the pure at heart.

Darius had just started his fifth cookie and fourth apology of the hour when the air crackled. Then Ariel appeared before him, Blackstone at her side.

Ariel looked confused. She blinked, then seemed to recognize where she was. And she didn't seem at all angry that Blackstone had brought her here.

"What's this?" Darius asked Blackstone. "Yet another way to make me feel guilty? I know what I've done to you. I know what I've done to Ariel. I'm trying to convince Nora to stop being so nice to me. You can all leave me alone. I'll be fine. I've been fine for three thousand years. A few more won't hurt."

Blackstone raised that eyebrow of his in that odd way he had and then he smiled. "I'm the one who should apologize," he said. "I treated you very badly this afternoon. You've always been a good friend to me, and when you've needed someone I haven't been there. Well, I'm here now— and I'm in the way."

He held out his hand to his wife. Nora smiled and stood, slipping her fingers around his. They suited each other so well. Ariel watched them with clear envy. Darius felt that envy too.

"You couldn't tell couples they were meant for each other," Blackstone said, "or you'd screw up your stupid sentence. Well, I don't have a sentence, so I can tell you that you two are meant for each other, and if you don't get together, you'll screw up your lives."

"Aethelstan," Nora said, pulling on his arm, "that's enough."

"No, it's not." Blackstone's gaze met Darius's. "We're still friends, you're staying here, and you're not fired from the restaurant. You can come back if you want to work for an idiot boss."

"So nothing's changed then?" Darius asked, with a touch of Andrew Vari's humor.

Blackstone seemed to catch it. "Nothing's changed. Yet."

He put his hand behind Ariel and pushed her a step forward. She staggered toward Darius as if she hadn't expected the motion.

"Have fun, kids," Blackstone said, then he raised his arms. He and his wife disappeared in a clap of thunder. Ariel blinked, as if the magic had blinded her.

"I wonder what they're going to do about the car," Darius said.

"The car?" Ariel asked.

"Nora drove here."

Ariel put her hands on the back of one of his kitchen chairs. "Somehow I don't think that'll be a problem."

She stared at him for a long moment, as if she wasn't sure what to say. He stared back, feeling guarded and alone and manipulated. He'd already said his good-byes to her. What right did Blackstone have to throw them together again?

"I have some questions," Ariel said after a long moment.

"Okay." Darius picked up his sixth cookie, then realized he hadn't eaten the fifth. "Fire away."

"How come you magic people get more than one soul mate and we mere mortals get only one?"

"Huh?" he asked.

"You heard me."

"I did," he said. "I didn't understand you."

"Well, I figure it like this," she said. "You live for thousands of years, and I only live for maybe seventy-five. If I'm your soul mate, then you only get to be happy for, maybe, fifty years. And that's not fair. No matter what you've done—considering that you said it wasn't genocide or anything—you don't deserve that."

"I guess not." He was feeling a bit confused. Why was she going on about this?

"So I want to tell those Fates or is it the B Powers—?"

"The Powers That Be."

"Them," Ariel said, "that you deserve better than this.

I mean, Blackstone and Nora are both magic, so they get the rest of their lives together. I don't know about the other people you've put together, but I assume their lives are pretty similar.''

He nodded, not sure what to say.

''So I want to tell off those people in charge of your life. They haven't been nice or fair to you. And that's wrong. How come no one can see what a good person you are? Is it because you're sarcastic or because they put some other spell on you to make it seem like you don't do half the things you do and only I can see what you do because I see magic around the edges?''

He stood. Her cheeks were flushed, and she looked more beautiful than he had ever seen her. She was defending him. He had told her the truth, let her go, and she had come here, ready to defend him. What had he done to deserve her?

''If I asked you to marry me,'' he asked, ''would you do it?''

She took a deep breath, tilted her head, and looked at him sideways. Then she blinked, as if she were coming out of a deep sleep, and said, ''No.''

All the hope he'd been feeling a moment before faded. He sat back down in the chair.

She came toward him and knelt before him, taking his hand in hers. ''It's not because I don't love you. I love you more than anyone, Darius or Andrew or Andvari or whoever you are. I didn't think it was possible to love anyone like I love you. But marrying you just isn't fair. I won't live long enough to approximate anything like happily ever after with you.''

Damn the rules. The Fates were even going to screw up his chance at being with his soul mate. But the Fates were right; if he told her that she could live as long as he did so long as they were a couple, he'd always wonder if it was the lifespan that kept them together.

''What if I tell you I'd take you for five minutes, if that's all I had?" He leaned toward her. Their faces were only inches apart.

"I'd say you're a fool. You can do better."

"No," he said. "I can't. I've lived long enough to know that you're the only woman for me."

She paled, and his heart sank even farther. She didn't want him. When she finally had to choose, she didn't want him. She had tried to hide it under a rational argument, making it sound as if she didn't want to be unfair to him. And maybe she didn't. Ariel was an inherently kind person, and he was asking her—forcing her—to live in a world that she hadn't even known existed a few hours ago. Talk about unfair. He was the one who was being unfair.

"You'd take me for only five minutes?" she asked.

He nodded. "And I'd cherish every single one of those minutes for as long as I lived."

She stared at him for a long time. He couldn't read the emotion in her green eyes. She was probably thinking of a way to leave him, to let him off easily. But he wasn't giving it to her. This was his last chance, and he wasn't going to screw it up.

"Five minutes," she said again. "Out of four thousand years?"

"Yes."

She closed her eyes and he felt bereft, as if he had already lost her. "Ask me again."

He had so expected her to say something else that her words barely registered. "What?"

"Ask me again. That question you asked earlier. Ask me again." She opened her eyes, and he saw pleading in them, but he wasn't sure what it meant.

"If I asked you to marry me, would—ah, hell." He pulled her off her knees, stood, whirled them both around until she was sitting in the chair. Then he knelt in front of her. "Ariel, will you marry me?"

"It's not fair," she whispered.

"Answer the question," he said, taking her right hand in his left.

"I'd be the only one who'd benefit from this."

"No, you wouldn't, Ariel. Five minutes, fifty years. It's about living happily in the moment, not ever after. Ever after doesn't exist for anyone. We all die, eventually. Even those of us who have long lives. It's about living day to day, the best way you can, not knowing what will happen next."

He was drowning and she didn't seem to know it. He had allowed himself to hope and he knew it was wrong. The door would slam and he'd be here, alone, knowing that he had no future at all. But he had to try.

"Ariel," he said, "will you—"

"Yes!" She flung herself into his arms. "Oh, God, yes."

She was kissing him or he was kissing her, and he barely noticed that they had fallen back onto his hardwood floor. In fact, he would have lost track of everything if Munin hadn't decided to create a threesome by licking both of their faces at the same time.

Darius shoved the puppy away, but Munin wouldn't back off.

"Not now," he said to the dog.

"What?" Ariel looked mussed. She would be so beautiful after lovemaking. She'd be beautiful during lovemaking. She was beautiful all the time.

"He doesn't want any secrets between us."

She froze. "There's more?"

"There's about three thousand years of more," Darius said, giving her one last chance to back out.

"I'm not talking about history," Ariel said. "We all have that. You said secrets."

He nodded. "I had to wait until you answered my question. The Fates made me wait."

"The Fates?" She sounded as if they were the devil incarnate. "What about them?"

"They said that our lifespans will match."

Her eyes teared. "You'll die young? Dar, that's still not fair—"

"No, Ariel," he said. "Yours will match mine. You'll never have magic, but you'll have a long life like Blackstone and Nora and me. If you want it."

"If I want it," she said.

He nodded. She was so ethical that this might bother her too.

"They made you wait because they believed I'd marry you for the long lifespan." Her eyes narrowed. "Where are these Fates? I'd like to give them a piece of my mind. They don't treat you right."

"They treat me fine," he said, gathering her in his arms again. "Considering everything I've done, they treat me more than fine."

Ariel frowned. "I still don't like them."

"You don't have to."

She slipped her arms around the back of his neck. "But I'll take the gift because I can spend more time with you."

He kissed her again. Munin sighed happily and headed back to his puppy bed. Ariel slipped her hands through Dar's curls and pulled her face from his.

"And for the record," she said, "I love you. Every facet of you. And I'll take you, long life or not. You can tell that to your Fates."

"I'm sure they know," he said. "They told me they always watch the good parts."

Ariel's eyes widened. "They're spying on us?"

Darius reached a hand over his head and spelled the room into complete darkness.

"Not anymore," he said. Then he dipped his head, found her lips, and began a kiss that neither of them pulled away from.

And as he kissed her, he realized he had been the one who had fallen off a cliff, and she had been the one who had saved him. Not with magic, but by believing in him, and by caring for him, no matter how ugly he was.

"One more thing," she whispered out of the darkness, as they paused to catch a breath. "I believe in happily ever after, not just happily in the moment."

He smiled, hoping she could feel it, even though she couldn't see it. "So do I," he said as he bent down to kiss her again. "So do I."